POEMS OF SCIENCE

John Heath-Stubbs was born in 1918 and educated at the Worcester College for the Blind and Queen's College, Oxford. He has published several volumes of poetry, including *A Parliament of Birds* and *The Watchman's Flute*, a play, and several books of criticism. He has translated (with Peter Avery) the lyrics of Hafiz and *The Ruba'iyat of Omar Khayyam* (Penguin Classics), and (with Iris Origo) Leopardi's poetry and prose. He has also edited selections of Swift, Shelley, Tennyson and Pope, as well as various anthologies, including (with David Wright) *The Faber Book of Twentieth Century Verse*.

Phillips Salman was born in 1936 and educated at Harvard College, Massachusetts, where he received his BA in 1958, and Columbia University where he gained an MA in 1962 and his PhD in 1968. He has held several teaching posts and since 1974 has been Associate Professor of English at Cleveland State University, where he was previously Assistant Professor of English for six years. He is interested in and teaches both literature and science and literary theory, particularly that of the Renaissance.

POEMS OF SCIENCE

EDITED BY JOHN HEATH-STUBBS
AND PHILLIPS SALMAN

PENGUIN BOOKS

Penguin Books Ltd, Harmondsworth, Middlesex, England
Penguin Books, 40 West 23rd Street, New York, New York 10010, U.S.A.
Penguin Books Australia Ltd, Ringwood, Victoria, Australia
Penguin Books Canada Ltd, 2801 John Street, Markham, Ontario, Canada L3R 1B4
Penguin Books (N.Z.) Ltd, 182–190 Wairau Road, Auckland 10, New Zealand

First published 1984

Printed and bound in Great Britain by
Hazell Watson & Viney Limited,
Member of the BPCC Group,
Aylesbury, Bucks
Set in Bembo 9/11 (Linotron 202)

CONTENTS

CONTENTS

CONTENTS

CONTENTS

CONTENTS

CONTENTS

CONTENTS

CONTENTS

CONTENTS

CONTENTS

PREFACE

In compiling this anthology, the editors have been helped by the resources of several American and English libraries. We are indebted to the staffs of the British Library, the Cleveland State University Library, the London Library, and the Library of The Warburg Institute. Stratis Haviaris made available the collection of the Woodbury Poetry Room, Harvard University, and offered valuable advice. We cannot sufficiently thank Jonathan Barker and his assistant, Jennifer Insull, of the Arts Council of Great Britain Poetry Library, London, for their help and encouragement during the year most of our work was carried out.

We have also incurred many debts to colleagues, students, and friends, too numerous for all of them to be mentioned here. Some, however, deserve special thanks. Professor James Barthelmess, Mr Charles Causley, Professor Dorothy Emmet, Professor Stuart Friebert, Professor Barton J. Friedman, Dr Ian McPhail, Professor C. B. Schmitt, A. Benedict Schneider, MD, Mr Richard Simpson, Dr Kirsti Simonsurri, Professor Leonard Trawick, and Professor Beatrice White offered useful suggestions and criticism. Professor J. B. Trapp made it possible for one of us to offer a seminar at the Warburg Institute on the topic of the anthology. Robert Wallace made available his extensive personal collection of twentieth-century poetry and advised on the project. A Cleveland State University Development Grant supported some of the research. The errors in the anthology are, of course, the editors' responsibility.

JOHN HEATH-STUBBS

PHILLIPS SALMAN

INTRODUCTION

This is an anthology of poems in English about science or employing its concepts, themes, and images for other purposes than expressing scientific themes.* For the most part their subject is 'pure' science. Poems on applied science and technology generally do not occur here, but the editors have exercised some degree of pragmatism in determining what science is and what are to be considered poems of science. In modern times, setting aside fields like the social sciences and psychology, it is relatively easy to define pure science as research into natural phenomena carried out by experimental method, quantified, and yielding results capable of replication by others. A poem on science in these terms is represented here by one such as R. S. Thomas's 'The Gap', in which the genetic code is seen as the contemporary form of the *logos*, the Word made flesh. This test of subject matter holds reasonably well into the eighteenth century, but becomes less reliable in the seventeenth century and before when science as we know it did not exist. Thus, Blake's attack on Newton's attractive and powerful ways of imagining the universe in mathematical terms relies on our common sense of science, where Donne's comment in his *Second Anniversarie* on the changes wrought by the 'new philosophy' is based on an older concept of science as an apparent inquiry into nature, but one not capable of verified results or a continued programme of discovery. Poems that image science exploit its poetic capacities, as in Lorenzo's speech on the music of the spheres in *The Merchant of Venice*, where Shakespeare turns the medieval theory that the planets make harmonious sounds as they move in their orbits into visual and aural imagery. And Alexander Pope's *An Essay on Man* has a passage continuing the ancient cosmological image of a chain of creatures endowed with descending degrees of consciousness as one moves from God, omniscience itself, down through the angels, man, and the lower orders. The poems of

* With two exceptions, the editors have chosen to include no translations. Thomas Gray's *Luna Habitabilis* was originally in Latin and Miroslav Holub's poems in Czech. Holub's poems have been Englished by Dana Hábová, a Czech fluent in English, and Stuart Friebert, an American poet, in close consultation with Holub, who also knows English. The English form of the poems is not exactly a translation.

applied science and technology included here tend to reflect the profession of the poet or some question of the difference between pure science and technology. Many poets have been physicians, for example, and it has been natural for their medical profession to provide matter for their poetic one. Thus the picture of the human body, the investigation of its anatomy, and even its psychology have also played a central role in poems of science. A fourth group, one that could probably be sheltered in our first, is represented here. These are fields like mathematics and natural history that are ambiguously science. Mathematics, for example, was more of a science in the early days before experimental method. Now it at once aids science and even precedes it in its speculations and appears in some quarters almost to have the status of an art. Natural history was at first important for classifying natural objects – animal, vegetable, and mineral – and then became something of a polite diversion as biology, botany, and geology became true sciences. We have included poems of natural history only when the poet seems to be exercising the function of a theoretical observer rather than a purely descriptive or celebratory one.

It may be objected that science and technology are indivisible, as seems to be the view of many in the nineteenth century, and indeed that the power which science gives to man as a means of modifying and controlling his environment by mechanical inventions is the true aim and justification of science. But in most of the period covered by this anthology both the poets and the scientists themselves have viewed science as a way of explaining the world as well as, incidentally, of changing it. Technology and mechanical inventions play a part in poetry, but to have put too great a stress on them would have extended our field too widely and blurred some important concerns and distinctions of the poets themselves. The poetry of technology has, indeed, been covered before by other anthologies.

The poets' attitudes on science, as distinct from technology, become clearer if one traces certain changes in cosmologies that scientific discoveries have produced and then considers some of the results.

In all periods, in responding to the natural world, poets have employed an intellectual framework derived from the science of their day and expressed in characteristic sets of images. These images have progressively been developed and altered or they have been discarded as others have taken their place. In astronomy, for example, the Ptolemaic system dominated the thinking of the Middle Ages, our starting point. It presented a logical and intellectually satisfying picture of the universe with the earth as its centre (but also the lowest point) surrounded by the spheres of the seven planets and, beyond these, that of the fixed stars. Beyond this again was the *primum mobile*, which was set in motion by God and which imparted its motion to all the lower spheres. Towards the end of the period we know as the Renaissance, this picture was replaced by the Copernican system, with the sun at the centre around which moved the earth and the other planets. This system, which explained the motion of the heavenly bodies much more elegantly and simply in mathematical terms than did the Ptolemaic, was also congenial to the humanistic and Platonic thinking of the age. For the earth was no longer relegated to the lowest and most abject position in the scheme of things, but was seen as taking part along with the other planets in a dance about the sun, which itself was the visible image of the invisible God. The development of mechanics and the discoveries of Newton provided for the eighteenth century an equally satisfying and coherent explanation of the world. In our own day, this picture has yet again been superseded as the universe of Newton has given place to that of Einstein. These largely cosmological discoveries have complements in those of evolution and the genetic code. Darwin, Crick, and Watson have also altered both our knowledge and our sense of ourselves as humans.

With both the very large discoveries and the smaller, poets have responded to the power of science. Willingly or unwillingly, they have had to come to terms with the entity that Alfred North Whitehead saw as the major influence on Western culture since the seventeenth century. After the several significant scientific poems of the Middle English period, one finds increasing numbers of poets responding to science. In the earlier English Renaissance, poets tend to restate medieval views, even as the work of Copernicus, Galileo, Gilbert or Tycho Brahe is discarding those views. In the later Renaissance and into the eighteenth century, as the thought and research of Bacon, Locke, Hobbes, Kepler, and Descartes exert pressure, medieval views show surprising tenacity, but are finally supplanted as Newton's discoveries and solutions to ancient problems become widely known. Through the eighteenth and nineteenth centuries and into our own, science becomes a powerful entity for poets to deal with. It is not surprising that many poets have responded to science in diverse ways in an attempt to come to terms with it. Inevitably, the poets, even when appearing to remain neutral, take points of view on science, and it is useful to think about those points of view in terms of didactic poetry, poetry intended to instruct. It is forcing the word 'didactic' to apply it as broadly as we do here; however, there are some advantages to doing so in an introduction. Although there clearly are poems of science that by no stretch of the imagination can be considered didactic, science has so often forced poets into a position on it and its implications that the word 'didactic' becomes very handy to suggest the tendency of poems of science to present a stand on science to an audience. As English and American literature proceeds from the Middle Ages onwards, science as we know it is born, develops, and imposes itself on the world. Poets make their peace with it, or do not, and try to reveal and persuade us to accept their attitudes. In these senses, virtually all poetry of science is didactic. There is seldom the feeling in poems of science that the poets are finally comfortable with the subject: they usually make us aware that science is a special sort of subject for them, different from, say, love or politics.

In fact, some readers may object that poetry and science can have nothing to do with one another. They represent, it will be said, two entirely different, if perhaps complementary, ways of looking at the world. Science, it will be maintained, is based on fact and reason, poetry on emotion and imagination. More subtly, many modern critics have analysed the poetic process as primarily a means of expressing a subjective and psychological truth or as a means of regulating our thoughts and our moral feelings. But this kind of distinction is a relatively modern one. It begins essentially with the Romantic movement of the nineteenth century and has been progressively refined in the present age. In general the poets of earlier ages accepted implicitly or explicitly the Horatian view that the aim of poetry was to instruct by pleasing. And this instruction, it was thought, might just as well be about the nature of the objective universe and man's place in it, as about ethics or manners. It cannot be denied that this traditional view could often be simplistic and could even lead to a certain degree of grotesqueness, when unpoetic fact was tricked out in what was regarded as poetic diction. Failures of this kind to grasp the true nature of poetic language, especially in the later eighteenth century, led to a reaction the results of which are still with us. But perhaps it is already time to reconsider the relationship between poetic expression and objective fact. For one thing, the idea that science itself is a purely intellectual process must also be seen as simplistic. More than one scientist has paid tribute to the role played by imagination and intuition in the formation of a hypothesis. This may even take the form of an actual visual image, perceived with something of the clarity of a dream. It may be that the poet and the scientist have much in common in both creating and describing the world in which they exist.

Accordingly, this anthology contains only a few poems that are didactic in the sense that they wish to convey only information about the world. Dr John Armstrong's *The Art of Preserving Health* is one of these and even here someone could argue that Armstrong's information is intended to persuade one to remain healthy and holds out health as a good to be sought. In fact, most of the poems in this volume wish to teach us to think about science and its role. Blackmore, Pope, Wordsworth, Tennyson, Jeffers, and Frost plainly wish their poetry to determine our attitudes towards science and they make their passages on science carry various devices of argumentation or assertion to achieve this purpose. A question originating in the seventeenth century is the role of science in human affairs. Poets as diverse as Pope, Blake, and Jeffers press for the subordination of science to human purposes and reject the mentality that a purely scientific training produces.

The debate on the role of science in human life has a counterpart in the use of scientific knowledge in poetry. In asking about its use we broach two related issues about poetry of science: (1) the form of knowledge poetry represents; and (2) the way changes in scientific information over time affect what can appear in poetry. The first of these issues is a philosophical one which can best be considered in historical terms provided by a consideration of the changes occurring in the periods running from the Middle Ages to the twentieth century, periods in which scientific activity not only produced a new methodology and discovered new knowledge, but also transformed the ways man considers himself and uses language. For the poet in Western culture scientific discovery has been a cause of his transformation from a public speaker entrusted with propagating the knowledge and morality of his tribe to a relative outsider speaking for himself and largely about himself and his views.

It is certain that in the earliest times the distinctions which we make between poetry, in the widest sense of the term, science, and philosophy simply did not exist. Ancient Greek poetry, and hence the whole European tradition of poetry, begins with two names, those of Homer and Hesiod. The latter, who lived perhaps in the eighth century BC, is chiefly remembered for two poems, the *Theogony* and the *Works and Days*. The first of these summarized the traditional ideas of his time about the origin and relationship of the gods. It began with the quasi-philosophical concept of Chaos – a yawning gulf from which were born such primal powers as Night, Sea, Earth, Heaven, and also Eros. From the union of Earth and Heaven sprang the earliest dynasty of the gods, that of the Titans, which was to be replaced, in a kind of cosmic revolution, by Zeus and the Olympians, who now rule the world. This mythology, whose origins can be traced to earlier mythological systems of the Hittite and Sumero-Babylonian civilizations, already presents a quasi-revolutionary view of the cosmos. Hesiod's *Works and Days* is a poem of practical instructions for the farmer. It also incorporates the historical myth of the four ages of man – those of Gold, Silver, Bronze, and Iron – representing a progressive deterioration from an original ideal state to the world of Hesiod's own day, the Iron Age dominated by harsh necessity and violence. This myth, which later became fused with the Judaeo-Christian concept of a Fall from a pristine state of innocence, was to have a dominant place in European thinking for centuries to come.

The earliest philosophical speculations of the Greeks, represented by the so-called pre-Socratic thinkers, took the form of essentially imaginative and intuitive speculations about the nature and prime substance of the universe. At this period it was perfectly understandable that ideas of this kind should be presented in poetic form, indeed in verse. Thus Empedocles (fifth century BC) composed a long poem, of which only fragments survive, on the nature and origin of the world. It was Empedocles, likewise, who was responsible for the formulation of the four elements – Fire, Air, Water, and Earth – considered as the primary substances of the world, the concept which was to be an important part of Western thinking right down to the seventeenth century. The tradition of expounding scientific theories in verse was continued by the Roman poets. One of the greatest of these was Lucretius (*c.* 99–*c.* 55 BC). His *De Rerum Natura* ('On the Nature of Things') was to be an important model for expository and philosophical verse from the Renaissance onwards. Lucretius adopted the philosophy of Epicurus and along with it the earlier atomic speculations of Democritus (born *c.* 400 BC). Democritus had postulated the existence of atoms in empty space, from whose motions the cosmos came into being by pure chance. Epicurus (341–270 BC) had used this as the basis for his own materialist philosophy. He denied the immortality of the soul and denied that the gods played any part in the direction of human affairs and held that moderate pleasure was the supreme good. Lucretius embraced these ideas with passion and, in seeking to liberate man from the fear of death and still more from the fear of punishment after death, created one of the greatest poems of antiquity. In the succeeding age of Augustus, Virgil (70–19 BC) was a philosophical eclectic. In the sixth of his pastorals he represents the wise satyr Silenus as expounding a theory of the origin of the universe which was influenced by

Lucretius. Virgil's *Georgics* is a poem about agriculture. Its model is Hesiod, but it is a far more sophisticated poem, incorporating an almost romantic feeling for nature as well as much of the scientific speculation of Virgil's age. Virgil's contemporary, Ovid (43 BC– AD 18) in his *Metamorphoses*, a collection of mythological tales, includes an account of the creation of the world based on the philosophical ideas of Pythagoras. Among other Roman poets, Manilius (first century BC), with his *Astronomica*, and Oppian (early third century AD), whose *Halieutica*, a poem about fishes, was to be translated into English by the eighteenth-century poet William Diaper, must also be mentioned. It is mainly these Latin poems, rediscovered in the Renaissance, which, especially in the eighteenth century, provided the models for the exposition of scientific ideas in verse.

The Middle Ages are generally thought of as a period when the memory of the scientific discoveries which the Greeks and Romans had pioneered was lost. This is only partially true. Much ancient learning survived through the medium of writers like Boethius (480–524), Isidor of Seville (c. 480–575), and Martianus Capella (early fifth century). These writers wrote summaries and epitomes, sometimes using the quasi-poetical mode of allegory, and formed the basis of much medieval encyclopedic writing. The *Physiologus*, a collection of accounts of the supposed habits of animals, was probably Egyptian in origin and dated in its initial form from c. 1050–1070. It used the animals as types of moral and spiritual lessons. This work formed the basis of the so-called Anglo-Saxon bestiary poems from the Exeter manuscript, and the tradition continued well into the Middle Ages. It was used by Bartholomaeus Anglicus in his *De Proprietatibus Rerum* and in the anonymous twelfth-century bestiary translated by T. H. White. Greek scientific ideas and Greek medical knowledge, on the other hand, found their way into the Arab Moslem world, being largely transmitted in the first instance by Christian physicians of the Syrian, Jacobite, and Nestorian churches. The Arabs continued and developed the tradition they had received, making important advances in mathematics, astronomy, and chemistry. In the twelfth century this tradition re-entered the Western world when Latin translations of Aristotle and of his Arab commentators began to appear in the West. St Thomas Aquinas (c. 1225–74), in his *Summa Theologica*, strove to reconcile the philosophy of Aristotle and an essentially rational and scientific view of the world, with Biblical teaching and Christian tradition. This Aristotelian synthesis formed the basis of medieval thinking and literature from the twelfth century onwards. The world view thus presented is only unscientific in the sense that few attempts were made to check it or to extend it by actual experimental investigation. It was thus that for the thinkers of the Renaissance and for the proponents of the new scientific philosophy of the seventeenth century the authority of Aristotle became a dogmatic tyranny. Against this they were compelled to rebel in the name of experiment and direct observation.

Thirteenth-century poems of science in English are in the Aristotelian tradition and begin this anthology. The author of the 'Legend of St Michael' in the *South English Legendary* is not only quite clear about the way the moon derives its light from the sun but also shows how this can be demonstrated with the help of an apple and a candle. Later on, in *The House of Fame*, we find Chaucer giving a perfectly adequate account, as far as it goes, of the propagation of sound waves. This should surprise no one who has any real knowledge of the nature of medieval thought. The idea that the Renaissance, which reached its peak in England in the sixteenth century, was a period when man was liberated from irrational superstitions is largely a misconception. The Renaissance in fact replaced the Aristotelian philosophy of the later Middle Ages with a revived Platonism. Humanism laid stress on the ethical nature of man and the legitimacy of his activities in promoting the good life in this world rather than forsaking it for the cloister. Stress was laid on the moral lessons which history and philosophy could teach and on the discipline of rhetoric (including poetry). Abstract speculation, whether concerning the nature of God or of the universe at large, tended to be thought of as a distraction. At the same time, the dominant Neo-Platonism, with its view of the material world as a symbolic reflection of a transcendent world of ideas, encouraged the revival of magical thinking and a renewed interest in astrology and alchemy. These pseudo-sciences had played a less important part during the Middle Ages. We find Chaucer in 'The Canon's Yeoman's Tale' exposing the tricks of a fraudulent alchemist. Renaissance alchemy seems essentially to have been a technique for the attainment of an esoteric spiritual knowledge through the manipulation of material substances, seen as symbols of spiritual realities. To this the ambition of actually transmuting base metals into gold was perhaps incidental. The experiments of the alchemist accompany actual chemical discoveries, and the astrologists' investigation of the stars, actual advances in astronomy. But their basis in both cases was essentially magical.

Medieval poems like the *Cursor Mundi* and *South English Legendary* show didactic properties in diverse ways. Their material teaches science

24

and also offers their teachings as a way towards worshipping God. As in Psalm 104, their science declares the glory of God and assumes that learning about the creation directs one towards divinity. The poems follow out St Augustine's point that the significant miracles are not those of the loaves and the fishes, cures, or raisings from the dead, but rather the daily orderly workings of the universe – the rising and setting of the sun, the procession of the seasons, the growth of plants from seeds (*In Joannis Evangelium, Tractatus* XXIV). Later, in the seventeenth century and also in the eighteenth, this use of science to advance worship is revived in poems that accommodate new discoveries to the ancient Biblical form of the psalm. Chaucer, by contrast, puts medieval science at the service of revealing character: the Doctour of Phisik in the 'General Prologue' comes off much like a modern physician in private practice – accomplished and wealthy; the Eagle in *The House of Fame* and Pertelote in 'The Nun's Priest's Tale' discoursing on the movement of the elements or on dreams are the overbearing lecturer with the captive audience; the Canon's Yeoman, telling of his master's alchemical experiments and frauds, relives and intensifies the error and anxiety of one engaged in deception against his will and simultaneously reveals the desperation of his master and the gullibility of his clients before an alchemical raree show. The poem's handling of science teaches us about these characters' natures.

In Renaissance England, medieval scientific learning continues strong even as the work of men like Copernicus is engineering its demise. His proof that the earth rotates around the sun does not figure in literary texts until the seventeenth century and even then there is some hesitation about replacing the Ptolemaic system with his heliocentric construct. Christopher Marlowe's Dr Faustus has been represented as a symbol of the Renaissance quest for unlimited knowledge. In Marlowe's play, the first questions Faustus puts to Mephistopheles concern the nature of the universe, but the answers which he gets are based on the old Scholastic–Ptolemaic doctrine which the Elizabethans had inherited from the Middle Ages. This is the same universe he sees when the chorus of the play represents him as exploring the universe to observe it at first hand in a magic chariot (we might almost say, 'in a spaceship'). At least one poet, Edmund Spenser, lets on that he knows something about the astronomical observations of his day. The 'Proem' of Book V of the *Faerie Queene* refers to the shifts known to have occurred in the constellations and in the sun,

> since the term of fourteene hundred yeres,
> That learned Ptolomaee his height did take; (5 Proem 7, 5–6)

however, he is mainly concerned to retain and elaborate medieval science for his philosophical purpose of fashioning a courtier in poetry. His 'Cantos of Mutabilitie' develop the theme of change in all things beneath God's throne. For his theory of mutability he draws on the Pythagorean theory of change in the fifteenth book of Ovid's *Metamorphoses*, a theory and text that fascinated Isaac Newton.

Shakespeare at once relies on earlier scientific notions and verges on turning them into images that represent his characters. Edmund ridiculing astrology and Menenius' account of digestion and the circulation of the blood are stock science that serve characterization and dramaturgy. Lorenzo's description of the stars and the music of the spheres, although it might have had reality for Shakespeare's audiences, is couched far less philosophically than the speeches of Edmund and Menenius. Their visual and aural effect seems to undermine their importance as science, and yet they reveal another aspect of scientific material as it is used by some poets. To be scientific is to find out the divine order and is also to find it beautiful because it offers certitude and because it reaches the sense in a proportion that is pleasing. Nevertheless, in the later Shakespeare of the great tragedies, we seem to be in a universe where such traditional images are under threat. *King Lear*, in particular, can be interpreted as a debate on the ambiguities of the word 'Nature'. For Lear, Kent, and Cordelia, Nature underpins a traditional moral framework of feudal and family loyalties and duties. But for the sceptical Edmund and for Lear's other daughters, Nature is something which sanctifies only their unbridled appetites and ambitions.

Since Renaissance science still largely operates at the level of the senses, it can pass readily into the imagery of poems. In the seventeenth century, however, the situation begins to change as science develops a mathematical experimental method capable of finding out facts not available to the unaided senses. This move away from immediate sensual reality necessarily alters what poetry can draw on for imagery from science and what poetry can talk about in science. It necessarily also begins to participate in changing the role of the poet. John Donne encapsulated these issues in lines on the effect of the new science that are always quoted:

> And New Philosophy calls all in doubt,
> The element of fire is quite put out:
> The sun is lost, and the earth, and no man's wit
> Can well direct him where to look for it.

It must be said that Donne knew less about the new science than has sometimes been supposed. The roots of his metaphysical poetry are in the scholasticism of the Middle Ages and in such studies as alchemy. Nevertheless, it is true that the seventeenth century saw the emergence of a new world picture and that its implications were sometimes disturbing. At the same time, many intelligent men embraced with enthusiasm the ideas which Francis Bacon had put forward in his *Novum Organum* and *New Atlantis*. The knowledge that was to be gained from the direct observation of nature under careful experimental method and without premature generalization could, it was seen, lead to great improvements in such arts as agriculture, navigation, and fortification.

Donne's observation is merely the most effective of others on the same subject. We have seen Spenser's probable awareness of bits of the 'New Philosophy'. Spenser's near contemporary, Sir John Davies, in *Nosce Teipsum*, had raised the question of the role of forms of knowledge in human life and had placed all lower forms, including the scientific, at the service of self-knowledge, the Socratic 'Know thyself'. The question had also been considered by Francis Bacon's friend and biographer, Fulke Greville, in *A Treatie of Humane Learning*. This is a directly didactic poem of some interest, not so much for the quality of its poetry as for the influence of Bacon upon it. There is good evidence for believing that Greville wrote the poem after having read Bacon's *Advancement of Learning*. And, although the *Treatie* is not simply versified Bacon, Greville is impatient with work that passes for rigorous study, but is essentially useless and illusionary, 'idols', as Bacon would term it. Greville makes a shift from the ideal of self-knowledge to a view that we are first at the service of what we learn and then may become its manager.

Donne's reference to the extinguished 'element of fire' stands for the rejection of the four 'elements' of Earth, Air, Fire, and Water. Donne has also been seen as referring to an end to a unity in the Ptolemaic cosmos, a unity seen in terms of the perfect form of the circle and its three-dimensional form, the sphere. The effect of the 'New Philosophy', particularly the astronomical, was, in Marjorie Nicolson's phrase, 'the breaking of the circle'. The 'New Philosophy' supplanted this finite nest with an infinity of space and possibility. An early example of this is a nova that appeared in the constellation Cassiopeia in 1572. Given that God had finished the creation and had rested, the nova implied that God had begun again. And beyond that were the observations that could now be made with the telescope and the microscope.

These began to show the old cosmology to be a fiction on other issues, as well as that of the geocentric or heliocentric cosmology, and they put a challenge to the poets. The case of Milton, who, it may be said, was much more modern and forward-looking than Donne, is especially interesting. We know that he was aware of both the Ptolemaic and Copernican systems and that he chose the Ptolemaic for its images, correspondences, associations, and appeal to the wide readership his epic aimed at. He also seems to have recognized that it worked better for a theological poetry because it had been used that way so often before. It revealed God's order even if, by the time *Paradise Lost* was published in 1667, it did so metaphorically rather than factually. Milton's sonnet to Cyriack Skinner shows what kind of reading one might expect to find going on in his circle of friends. The seventeenth century is indeed an age of puzzling contradictions and cross-currents. Astrology and alchemical studies continued and perhaps increased in popularity but were intertwined with the studies of astronomy and chemistry.

Henry More and Richard Blackmore, both poets inferior to Milton but nonetheless interesting for their attempts, tried to accommodate the new science to their religious beliefs. In several poems, More happily confronts the Copernican system. It appears just and proper to More that the sun should now be at the centre of the universe. Similarly, the physician Richard Blackmore, although he seems ignorant of Newton on gravity, displays a fine knowledge of scientific discoveries, as well as an ability to summarize them concisely in poetry, and shows how no claim that these discoveries answer ultimate questions is valid. His poem *The Creation*, which Samuel Johnson admired, argues that only religious belief answers questions of the origin and purpose of the world.

More and Blackmore illustrate two possible responses to scientific discoveries, but it would be wrong to say that there is a polarity between them. Neither questions scientific discovery; both use it for religious argument, and Blackmore tries to scotch any arrogant atheistic use of the discoveries. These positions are generally typical of responses to the new science. The celebration implicit in More's poems is replicated in Cowley's praise of the Royal Society and of William Harvey or in Pope's 'Epitaph: Intended for Sir Isaac Newton', which concludes, 'God said, *Let Newton be!* and All was light.' The ideals of Bacon were in some respects realized by the foundation of the Philosophical Society in 1645. This developed into the Royal Society, which received its charter in 1662. Abraham Cowley's ode on this subject is full of an uncritical enthusiasm. Cowley was equally enthusiastic about the medical discoveries of his friend Harvey and about the revival of the materialistic atomic philosophy of Democritus by Thomas Hobbes. John Dryden, the greatest poet of his age after Milton, was, for a time, a member of the Royal Society. His wide-ranging poetry can make use of traditional ideas, such as that of the music of the spheres, and equally Platonism or Cartesianism, as poetic fancy dictates. Pope was capable of following Blackmore's lead also, as in *An Essay on Man*, where he encompasses science within a sphere of providence, or in the *Dunciad* with its ridicule of mindless and trivial collecting instead of deep analytical thought about natural phenomena.

In the discoveries of Isaac Newton all this reached a climax. Newton was himself a complex character. In spite of the clarity and logic of his mathematical and scientific thinking, he was also involved in numerological and apocalyptic interpretations of Biblical prophecy. But to his contemporaries and to the whole of the eighteenth century he seemed to have produced a synthesis which gave a simple and logical explanation to all natural phenomena such as had scarcely been available to the imagination since the breakdown of the medieval world picture. The Newtonian view of the universe seemed an argument for the existence of a deity who ruled the cosmos by mathematical laws – whether the god of orthodox Christianity or of Deism. Thus, in Addison's hymn 'The spacious firmament on high . . .' the circling planets give testimony to the divine hand that made them, though the music of the spheres is gone. The eighteenth century proliferated with poems that attempted to instruct by straightforwardly expounding moral and natural philosophy or which combined description with scientific theory. These poems parallel the incredible scientific activity of the period, some of it professional, some of it amateur and subject to ridicule, as in the case of those randomly collecting objects from the natural world.

Yet even that collecting relates to honest science and to poems of science. To be sure, Pope and, later, Samuel Johnson in prose were correct to ridicule those who gathered material and performed experiments without any concept of how they might relate or any method of relating them. Johnson sadly describes Sober, the would-be scientist:

But his daily amusement is Chemistry. He has a small furnace, which he employs in distillation and which has long been the solace of his life. He draws oils and waters, and essences and spirits, which he knows to be of no use; sits and counts the drops as they come from his retort, and forgets that, whilst a drop is falling, a moment flies away.

(*Idler*, 31, Saturday 18 November 1758)

This is someone not only out of touch with reality and drawn into himself, but also someone of no use to his fellows. But founding members of the Royal Society, for example, were also ridiculed for their experiments, for scientific method was still innovatory and uncertain at the time. Fumbling was inevitable, especially in taxonomic fields like botany or zoology. It has been pointed out that the earlier detailed filling in of species in the framework of the tenacious Great Chain of Being prepared the way for Charles Darwin's inferences on evolution, and much responsible work was done in this field by collectors.

In the eighteenth and nineteenth centuries we have the poetry of natural history, which has its origin and greatest influence in James Thomson's *The Seasons*. There, Thomson presents many forms of natural description that accord with each of the four seasons. Numerous later poets, probably even among the Romantics, follow Thomson's method, among them Gilbert White of Selborne, whose 'The Naturalist's Summer-Evening Walk' represents perfectly the poem that relies on observation of nature. The Romantics were to react against the over-simplified concept of poetry which this kind of writing implies, but if one is prepared to make allowances for its conventions, the writings of the eighteenth century contain much that is curious, interesting, and entertaining. In Erasmus Darwin's *The Loves of the Plants*, a poem that was enormously popular in his time, this tendency was carried almost to the point of absurdity. The great Swedish botanist Linnaeus had devised a classification of plants according to the arrangement and number of their sexual organs, the stamens and pistils. Erasmus Darwin translates this system into polished eighteenth-century heroic couplets, the female organs or pistils becoming nymphs and the stamens, swains. The results are often hilarious and were to be parodied by James and Horace Smith in the *Antijacobin* as *The Loves of the Triangles*, in which the propositions of Euclid are given a similar treatment. But Darwin's tone was rarely mock-heroic. He was a very considerable thinker as well as a polished versifier, and anticipated many of the ideas of his grandson, Charles Darwin, as well as influencing such poets as Coleridge and Shelley. His later poem, *The Temple of Nature*, is more ambitious than *The Botanic Garden* and contains many striking items.

The issue that 'collectors' raise is not a trivial one, for the eighteenth or any of the centuries in which quantitative science is a central influence. Very early, as science became quantified and, as we have said, went beneath the sensually perceptible surface of things, it deprived poetry of a major source of images and themes. The genre of natural-history poems is part of what was left. Clearly, the scientist now had the greater authority. As science began to make major demonstrations about the natural world and as those demonstrations led to important practical application, the poet grew less important as a purveyor of knowledge. The increase in scientific power partly shifted the kind of knowledge the poet could include in his work. As others have shown, and for additional reasons, the poet was in general caused to write about subjective inner reality so that what the poem presented was not so much objective truth as truth seen by a particular writer.

In addition, the so-called Romantic movement in English poetry both grew out of and reacted against the tendencies of the eighteenth century. One of its characteristics was a rejection of mechanistic philosophy and the feeling that man's spiritual health could be restored only by re-establishing an organic union with nature. Blake and Wordsworth clearly recognize the effects of mechanistic science on poetry and they make criticisms in terms of the faculty of imagination. Their major point, which was shared by other Romantic poets, was that scientific thinking was attractive as well as powerful, but was only a partial mode of thought, for it ignored other human realities, notably those of the imagination and emotions. The reaction against the mechanism of the age is seen in its most extreme form in William Blake, for whom a false philosophy is typified by the three figures of Newton, Locke, and Bacon. Blake clearly saw that Newton's theories and procedures make a great claim on the mind. He knew Newton's work and grasped that it was possible to adopt the scientific mentality and to perceive reality through it and it alone. Science could replace what, for Blake, was the inclusive, more fruitful mentality of the religious and visionary imagination. Wordsworth, who read mathematics at Cambridge, gives us in *The Prelude* the great dream of the Arab who is saving the stone of mathematics and the shell of poetry from a threatened cataclysm. For Wordsworth, the stone and the shell – science and poetry, reason and feeling – were ultimately one. Wordsworth writes in admiration of Newton, but, principally in *The Excursion*, also uses Blake's arguments and takes them a step further. Where Blake writes in a prophetic or visionary mode about science, Wordsworth finally adopts the earlier philosophical approach, demonstrating that science must continue powerful, but must not have independent life; it must exist as an assistant to humans. Blake does not take the step of subordination and might be happy abolishing science; Wordsworth seems more a respecter of mind and perhaps, although angry with the industries of his day, is influenced by the possibility of a beneficial technology deriving from science, where Blake saw only 'dark, satanic mills'.

Among the other Romantics, Coleridge, in his prose writings and lectures, was aiming equally at a synthesis of religion, philosophy, science, and poetry. The actual references to science in his verse are, however, comparatively few. Coleridge may be seen as the heir of a long tradition of Cambridge Platonism represented by More in the seventeenth century and by Christopher Smart in the eighteenth century, and stretching back before More through Milton and the brothers Giles and Phineas Fletcher to Spenser. As we have seen, this tradition, whose lost heirs may perhaps be found in the New England Transcendentalists, was always hospitable to scientific ideas and, in its interest in revealing permanent elements beneath the surface of things, indicates a natural compatibility between poetry and science. Against the long tradition of poetry, emotionally introspective writing appears almost a modern aberration from the main line.

The later nineteenth century, represented in England by the Victorian Age, was one of immense scientific and technological advances. The poets, although they had inherited much of the legacy of Romanticism, lacked, on the whole, the Romantic capacity of vision. In this period, poetry was striving to come to terms with an age whose ideals seemed to conflict with it. The one strand of the conflict is represented in Victorian poems of science as technology. In an interesting sonnet, Charles Tennyson Turner, Alfred's brother, identifies science with technology, as does George Meredith only slightly later. Turner sees no danger from science–technology, but only progress. Like Blake, however, Meredith understands that an abuse of technology can destroy and calls on science to be an 'olive branch' and bring peace. Meredith's 'The Olive Branch' is so diffuse and general that it is hard to know whether he is directly concerned with military inventions or whether he is rejecting some forms of industrial machinery, plants, or technological aspirations. His ambiguity is at least of historical interest, given the specific rejection by some twentieth-century poets of modern military uses of science – conventional, nuclear, and biochemical.

The evolutionary theory of Charles Darwin and the discoveries which the geologist Lyell made concerning the antiquity of the earth showed man to be, perhaps, only a latecomer among many species doomed to extinction. All this seemed to call into question not only the accuracy of Scripture and the literal interpretation of its account of Creation, but the very existence of a God and of a Divine Providence.

As in so much else, Tennyson is representative of his age in his persistent grappling with these problems. Browning, a more intellectual poet, was, surprisingly, not very directly concerned with scientific ideas. But his 'Epistle of Karshish' dramatizes the debate between science and revelation in terms of an imaginary Arab physician of the first century AD brought face to face with the miraculous. In 'Caliban upon Setebos' he represents Shakespeare's monster as a primitive man of the kind that contemporary anthropology was postulating and traces the way that religious ideas might be apprehended in such a mind.

By the closing decades of the century, Darwinian ideas of evolution seemed to many to have won the day. In Swinburne's 'Hertha' the poet imagines a kind of vitalistic force in nature in relation to which man himself is only a transient phenomenon. Similar ideas were seen as underpinning the optimistic humanism of George Meredith and the pessimistic humanism of Thomas Hardy. Hardy was able to represent those who grasped the theory of evolution, accepted it, and made some accommodation with it. Hardy's 'Epitaph for G. K. Chesterton' shows both Hardy's adaptation and his contempt for those who cannot face unpalatable truths. Both he and Tennyson indicate a new phase in the history of poetry's response to science. It is an interesting phase because Darwin's work, although rigorous, is not couched in symbols inaccessible to poetry. Quite the reverse, in fact, since it deals with the various classes of animals, including man, and is presented in prose that can lend itself to imagery. Darwin's wording, in fact, can be thought of as replacing that of the Great Chain of Being. We have, as in Swinburne's 'Hertha', accepted instead the metaphor of the tree. The Chain itself had faded as a controlling metaphorical concept, but its element of primacy for man and connection of man to God remained and surely determined how the animal world was perceived. In terms accessible to poetry and avoidable by few, Darwin destroyed the verbal opportunities of the Chain and one's sense of man's importance in the order of nature. Darwin had an undesirable social effect as well when so-called 'social Darwinism' justified man's 'redness' to other men presumed lower and supported a myth of progress which Eliot characterized as 'a partial fallacy/ encouraged by superficial notions of evolution' ('The Dry Salvages', II, 11, 39–40). On the other hand, Socialists also accepted Darwinism, which they saw supporting their position in terms of competing societies rather than individuals – Socialist societies being predestined to outbid capitalism because of their greater efficiency.

It will be seen, from this brief survey of the subject, that practically all of the major poets, from Chaucer onwards, have, in some way, been concerned with the science of their day. When we come to the twentieth century, the picture is rather different. W. B. Yeats, perhaps the greatest poet of the first half of the century, attempted to escape both from historical and scientific ideas into an esoteric system of symbols. Although in their prose writings both T. S. Eliot and Ezra Pound evince considerable respect for science and scientific method, neither of them have much in their verse that can be said to relate to science. In 'The Dry Salvages', Eliot wrote

To communicate with Mars, converse with spirits,
To report the behaviour of the sea monster,
Describe the horoscope, haruspicate or scry,
Observe disease in signatures, evoke
Biography from the wrinkles of the palm
And tragedy from fingers; release omens
By sortilege, or tea leaves, riddle the inevitable
With playing cards, fiddle with pentagrams
Or barbituric acids, or dissect
The recurrent image into pre-conscious terrors –
To explore the womb, or tomb, or dreams; all these are usual
Pastimes and drugs, and features of the press:
And always will be, some of them especially
When there is distress of nations and perplexity
Whether on the shores of Asia, or in the Edgware Road.   (V, ll, 1–15)

Eliot here condescends to science and almost seems to place scientific research on the same level as fortune-telling and table-turning. Some poets of a lesser, though considerable stature, such as W. H. Auden and William Empson, have a much greater grasp of science, have filled their poems with imagery drawn from science, and have handled scientific themes. Other poets experience admiration and wonder over science and scientists. Hugh MacDiarmid, Marianne Moore, and A. M. Sullivan express their delight with science in poems that draw on its theories or its instruments. Eva Royston and Miroslav Holub celebrate the rigorous pleasures of working in a laboratory, one as a technician, the other as a research chemist. Louis MacNeice and David Ignatow construct pictures of scientists that stress the devotion to difficult symbolic work.

Until recently, strong objections have been urged against science. Robinson Jeffers and Robert Frost, for example, are, in their turn, angry or sarcastic about the claims and power of science. Jeffers several times reviles science for arrogance and carelessness in the face of what it produces. In the selection here from *Roan Stallion*, he puts the premises of his criticism in terms Wordsworth and Blake anticipated and would understand. His speaker thinks that science, in prosecuting its hunt for knowledge, forgets humanity, indulges its own mentality, and disowns responsibility for what it has discovered. The issues his poems raise continue in contemporary debates about the role of science. It is possible to argue that Jeffers and those like him confuse pure science with applied science and that it is the applications of scientific discoveries that need criticism and control. One can also argue, as some do, that because pure science takes place in a social context and because there is a scientific culture and mentality, science cannot consider itself 'pure' or 'neutral'. In this view, the consequences of discoveries must always be considered.

These and other poets of our century draw on the imagery and themes of science for poetic and philosophical purposes. Peter Straub's 'Wolf on the Plains' sees the movements of a wolf from inside the animal's brain and as an instance of the genetic code determining behaviour. At the same time, Straub suggests the nature of the wolf's small degree of consciousness and volition. William Bronk works out implications of Werner Heisenberg's uncertainty principle in a directly philosophical poem, 'How Indeterminacy Determines Us', that shows how observers and observed are functions of one another. Peter Redgrove foreshortens his life in 'Relative' with the simple device of seeing his periods of physical growth and change in terms of Einstein's relativity principle.

This survey suggests the range of modern and contemporary responses. It also indicates a feature of poems of science written since about 1945: the poets are living entirely within a scientific age. This might appear too obvious to mention; however, if we consider the poems we have already described, we see that many of them, in fact the most important of them, are responses to the growing power of science and yet that current critical theory tends to delimit poetry and to discourage attempts at any extended expositions in verse of scientific theory. In practice, poets are considerably more concerned with science and its opportunities for their poetry than has been recognized. As yet, no poet we have seen perceives science as some modern critics do, operating within a social context of virtually inevitable destructive application and therefore not exactly 'pure'. A sign of their acceptance is the attempts poets have made to understand scientific discoveries and the mentality of the scientist. Another is the fact that some poets have been able to wrest imagery from the quantitative discoveries of science or from its procedures. Perhaps it is time to alter critical theory to admit more scientific poetry, particularly because some scientists help the poet's efforts, even if indirectly. In particle physics, for example, one phenomenon has been named a 'quark' after the word in James Joyce's 'A quark for Mr Mark' in *Finnegan's Wake* and has been invested with the quality of 'charm'. Also in theoretical physics, some have found identities between new discoveries and the insights of Buddhism and Taoism. The main identity is found very deep in the atom where cause and effect are said not to exist and where phenomena are labelled 'events' that emanate from no one knows where. These findings are compared to the Taoist and Buddhist notion that the world of cause and effect is illusion and that the highest reality is beyond causality. Nor is oriental religion alone in question when we consider Teilhard de Chardin's attempts to reconcile an evolutionary view of the universe with Christian teachings. Then, too, some scientists rely on the poets for words when they go outside their own sciences, as does Freeman Dyson, who, in writing his autobiography, finds the language of science or sociology inadequate for his needs and explains that he will use the language of poetry for human questions. And some scientists make their own metaphors. In *The Lives of a Cell*, Lewis Thomas constructs a new cosmology. He compares the universe to an hierarchy of cells, starting with that which we normally consider to be a cell and then moving up to name bodies, families, societies, and finally the terrestrial globe itself as a cell, with the ozone layer as its membrane. Literary historians will be forgiven for thinking that Thomas has invented a series of correspondences much like those in the Great Chain of Being; however, his unitary metaphor comes very close to doing just that. The scientists themselves give rise, therefore, to possibilities for poets. This fact and the poets' acceptance of science suggest a further interesting possibility. It is as if we had returned to the mentality of an earlier time when science was not antithetical to the poets but rather formed part of their world view and helped them write. An analogy can be drawn between the poets' celebration of the cosmos in scientific terms in, say, the *South English Legendary* and Marianne Moore's admiration for scientific discovery in 'Four Quartz Crystal Clocks'. Perhaps we are witnessing another age in which science and poetry are not antithetical but are mutually necessary knowledge.

The possibility bears on a further difficult question: what kind of knowledge is poetry? Moderns have perhaps been trained to believe that the only certain knowledge is quantitative knowledge. We have been raised on the notion that reality is defined by science. The nature of poetic truth comes home to us when we see what poems of science try to do. Generally, poetry cannot accommodate scientific truths in quantitative form. One or two poets have tried to do so, but have failed. The poems are opaque to one who is not a specialist, and it is more difficult to grasp the system of notation for the poems than it is for one to acquire the information necessary to understand other kinds of obscure poem. The best judge of the success of one of these poems has to be the literate scientist. The poem of science that directly incorporates quantitative or formulaic scientific material has to remain an aloof sub-genre within the larger genre we represent here until and unless scientific material becomes more like 'common knowledge'.

We do not claim that all the verse included in this anthology is great poetry, though many great poets as well as many interesting minor poets are represented here. But we hope that all of it is of some interest – often curious or entertaining and not seldom beautiful. That it may stimulate those educated in scientific discipline to explore what poets have said and those schooled in the humanities to an interest in science and its history is part of our ambition. It may appear after all that poetry and science are not so far apart as has often been thought. The poet has something of the scientist about him, many now think, and the scientist something of the poet. The starting point for both of their activities is the imagination.

ANONYMOUS

(late 13th century)

Cursor Mundi

lines 271–404, 481–510, 517–50

SPACE AND ELEMENTS

Alle men aue that lauerd drede,
That mirthes settis man to mede,
That ever was and ay sal be,
Widuten ende in trinite.
He that lauerd, bath godd and man,
Anekines thing of him bigan,
Thou he bigan all other thing,
Himself had never biginyng;
Of him can all, in him is al,
All haldis he up fra dunefall;
He haldis heven and erde stedfast;
Widuten him may na thing last.
This lauerd that es sua mekil of might
Purvaid all in his aun sight,
And that he ordained wid his witt
He multepliis and gouernis itt,
Thar for es he cald the trinite,
For he es an-fold god in thre;
And if thu wenis it may noght be,
Bihald the sune, than may thu se,
In the sune that schines clere
Es a thing and thre thinges sere,
A bodi round, hote, and light,
Thir thre we find all at a sight;

aue: owe	*dunefall*: downfall	*an-fold*: single
lauerd: lord	*erde*: earth	*thu*: thou, you
drede: dread	*na*: no	*wenis*: think
mirthes: mirths	*sua*: so	*sune*: sun
settis: puts	*mekil*: great	*than*: then
mede: reward	*Purvaid*: provided	*se*: see
Widuten: without	*aun*: own	*sere*: several (i.e. three
Anekines: all kinds of	*Thar for*: therefore	several things)
Thou: although	*es*: is	*Thir*: these
haldis: holds		

Thir thinges thre wid nankin arte
Ne may noght be fra other part,
For if thu take the light away
The erd it has na sune parfay;
And if the hete away be tan
Sune forsoth ne has thu nan,
On ilk a maner ilk man wate,
It es the kind of sune be hate.
The sunes bodi that i neven
Bi-takins the fader self of heven,
And bi the light that es lastand
It es the sone thu understand,
And bi the hete thu understand so,
The hali gast comes of thaim to.
And fader es he calde forthi,
For he es welle that never is drey;
And ovyr that him selven wroght
All thinges quen that thai war noght.
His sun is wisdam that all thing wate,
For all the werld he haldis in state;
He haldis all thinges fra misfare,
That thai noght turne to soru and care.
The hali gast es that goddhed,
He gives the liif and mas onede.
Minning es the fadir cald,
The sune es understanden tald,
The hali gast es that wille,
The fadir and sune bath fulfille.
This lauerd that I bi-fore of said,
First in his wit he all purvaid,

nankin: no kind of	Bi-takins: betokens	quen: when
Ne … noght: not	fader: father	noght: nothing
fra other part: separated	lastand: lasting	wate: knows
parfay: indeed	hali gast: Holy Ghost	misfare: misfortune
tan: taken	thaim: them	soru: sorrow
nan: none	to: two	liif: life
ilk: each	forthi: therefore	mas: makes
wate: knows	drey: dry	onede: unity
kind: nature	ovyr: over	Minning: memory
hate: hot	him selven: himself	cald: called
neven: name	wroght: worked	tald: accounted

His werk us dos a sotil wright,
And sithen he raises it in sight.
For-thi is Gode as seis scripture
Non elder than his creature,
Eldir of time ne is noght he,
Bot ellis more in dignite.
This writh that I speke of here,
Over all other he is prinse widuten pere,
For other writhes bos other tymber take,
Bot this him self can tymber make;
For of him self he toke his even,
That he made bath of erde and heven.
Bot thu sal noght understand
Tha he wrog[t] al his werke wid hand,
Bot said wid word, and als sone
All his comandment was done,
Smartlier than eie may winck,
Or ani manes hert may thinck.
And als clerkes seis that er wise,
He wrogt noght first with partis,
Bot he that made all of noght,
All this werld to-gider he wroght,
To be sett in lenth and brede.
The mater first thar-of I rede,
That es the elementis to say,
That first schaples all samen lay;
He delt thaim fin in sex dais
In partis als the scripture sais;
The elementis first in dais thrin,
Thre thinges thaim es widin;
Thir elementis that all thing bindes,
Foure thar er as clerkes findes,

dos: does	*writh*: workman	*brede*: breadth
us: as	*pere*: peer	*mater*: matter
sotil: subtle	*bos*: must	*thar-of*: thereof
wright: workman	*even*: image	*rede*: tell of
sithen: afterwards	*sal*: shall	*samen*: together
Gode: God	*als*: as	*fin*: finally
seis: says	*manes*: man's	*thrin*: three
Non: not	*seis*: say	*widin*: within
Bot: but	*er*: are	*Thir*: their
ellis: else	*partis*: parts	

The lauest than es water and erde,
The thrid es ayr, and fyre the ferde.
Ayder say we that he thus bigan,
As Austin sais, that hali man,
Als we in his bokis find.
First than wroght he angel kind,
The world, and tyme, this thinges thre
Bifore all other thing wroght he.
The worlde I calle wid min ententis
The mater of foure elementis,
That yeit was than of forme unschapin,
Quare-of was sithen serenes schapin;
All schaples was it noght for-thi,
For it of schap had sum parti,
Bot thar-for schaples was it hou,
For it had nogh[t] as it has nou.
He wroght apon the tother day
The firmament, that es to say,
The sky wid sterris gret and small,
Wid watir schinand als cristall,
That es on hey, that es under,
In this he soundid al to wonder.
The thrid day godd did thoru his grace
The watris draue intill a place,
And bad a dri place suld be:
The watris all he calid the se.
The drey he calid erd, that lauerd king,
And bad it griss and fruit forth bring.
All thinges waxand thare
That in thaim selff thair sedis bare.
The feird he bad and was done,
Bath war mad sune and mone,

lauest: lowest	*parti*: part	*suld*: should
ferde: fourth	*hou*: how	*se*: sea
Ayder: either	*tother*: other	*drey*: dry
Austin: St Augustine	*sterris*: stars	*erd*: earth
min: my	*schinand*: shining	*griss*: increase
ententis: intention	*That*: that which	*waxand*: growing
yeit: yet	*hey*: high	*sedis*: seeds
Quare-of: whereof	*soundid*: sundered	*bare*: bore
serenes: difference, variety	*intill*: into	*feird*: furth

Aither wid [his] sere light,
To part the dai fra the night,
In takinyng of tydis to stand,
Dais and yeris bath duelland,
And the sternis grett and smale,
That we may se widuten tale.
In the heiest element of all,
Thar in the fire has his stall.
The fiifte day that faylis noght,
Of water foul and fiss he wroght,
The fiss to water als we finde,
The foul he bitok to the wind.
All gangand bestis the sexte day,
And Adam als he made of clay,
He was last made als lauerthing,
To be maistir overall thing.

★

Fra ful hey he fell ful lawe,
That of his lauerd wild stand non awe,
Widuten coveryng of his care,
For merci getis he neuer mare;
For God au noght give him mercy,
That thar eftir wild noght cri.
And thus he tint that grete honour,
Thar badd he noght fulli on our,
For alsua suith as he was made,
He fel, was thar no langer bade.
The tother angelis that fell him wid,
The quilk forsok Goddes grid,
Efter the will thai to him bare,
Fell thai to hell, lesse and mare,

sere: different
takinyng: token
tydis: tides
Dais: days
yeris: years
duelland: dwelling
sternis: stars
tale: count
faylis: fails
foul: fowl
fiss: fish

gangand: walking
als: also
lauerthing: lord
hey: high
ful lawe: full low
wild: will
neuer mare: nevermore
au noght: ought not
tint: lost
Thar: there

badd: abided
fulli: fully
on our: an hour
alsua: also
suith as: as soon as
bade: abiding
quilk: which
forsok: forsook
grid: grace
bare: bore

Sum in the aire and sum in the lift,
Thar thai drey ful hard drift.
Thair [p]ine thai bere apon thaim ay,
And sua thai sal to domesday.
Bot thos that left widuten wite,
Thai were confermed thare als tite,
Thai may nevermar hald to ill,
Na mare than wic may to gode will.
The numbre that ute of heven fell
No tunge in erd noght can tell,
Ne fra that throne of that bliss,
Hou fer in to hell pitt es,
Bot Bede sais fra erd to heven
Is vii thousand yere and hundredis vii;
Bi jornayis qua that gang it may,
Fourti mile everilk a day.

*

Of erd alsua ne was he noght,
Bot of foure elementis wroght.
Of water his bodi, is fless of laire,
His here of fir, his ond of aire,
His hede wid-ine bath eien tuin,
The skey bath sune and mone wid-in,
Right als men eien er sett to sight,
So servis sune and mone of light.
Seven mayster sternis er sett in heven,
And manys hede has thirlis seven,
The quilk if thu wil the umthinck
Thu may thaim find wid littel suink.
This wind that men draus oft

lift: sky
drey: endure
pine: torment
ay: forever
sua: so
wite: guilt
tite: quickly
hald to: assent to
wic: the wicked
to gode will: may will good
ute: out
Hou: how

Bede: the Venerable Bede
Is ... vii: 7,700 years
jornayis: journeys
qua ... may: whoever
   might go on it
everilk a: every
fless: flesh
laire: the air
here: bodily warmth
ond: hand
bath: both
eien: eyes

tuin: two
skey: sky
mone: moon
als: as
men: men's
thirlis: holes
quilk: which
the: thou, you
umthinck: consider
suink: labour
draus: draws

Bitakins wind that blauis on loft,
Of quilk es thoner and leve[n]ing ledd
Als onde wid host in brest is bred.
Into the see all watir sinkis,
And manes wambe all licur drinkis,
His fete him beris up fra fal,
Alsua the erde uphaldis all.
The ovyr fir ges manes sight,
The ovyr air of hering might,
This underth wind him gives his ond,
The erd tast to fele and fond,
The hardnes that men has in bonis.
It is mad of the kind of stonis,
On erd it grouis tres and gris,
And nayle and her [of] manes fless.
Wid bestes dumb man hath his fele
Of thing men likis, evil or wele.
Of thir thinges I have here said
Was Adam cors togider graid.

on loft: aloft	*Alsua*: just as	*fond*: endeavours
thoner: thunder	*ovyr*: heavenly	*bonis*: bones
levening: lightning	*ges*: gives	*gris*: grass
onde: wind	*hering might*: power of	*nayle*: nails
host: cough	hearing	*her*: hair
wambe: womb	*underth*: lower	*likis*: like
licur: liquor, liquids	*ond*: breath	*cors*: body
fete: feet	*tast*: touch	*graid*: composed
beris: bear	*fele*: feeling	

ANONYMOUS

(late 13th or early 14th century)

The South English Legendary

St Michael, Part III, ii, lines 391–416

THE STRUCTURE OF THE COSMOS

De Inferno

The righte put of helle is · amidde eorthe withinne
Oure Louerd there al made iwis · queintise of gynne
Hevene and eorthe he made verst · and suththe al thing that is
Eorthe is a lite hurst · agen hevene iwis
Hevene geth aboute eorthe · evene it mot weie
Eorthe is amidde evene · as the stre amidde an eiye
Much is ther on more than the other · for the leste sterre iwis
In hevene as the boc us seith · more thanne the eorthe is
For [ho] so were anhei bi a sterre · yif it so mighte be [o]
So lite wolde the eorthe thenche · that he nessolde hure noght ise [o]
  Enes geth hevene aboute thoru the day · and thoru the night
And the mone and the sterren with him bereth · and the sonne so
  bright
For that is evene above thin heved · aboute nones stonde
Under thi vet hevene it is · at midnight under gronde
And cometh up wanne the sonne arist · and over the is at none
Hevene maketh thus hure cours · and aboute cometh sone
  As appel the eorthe is round · so that evere mo
Half the eorthe the sonne bissint · hou so it evere go
And non it is here bynethe us · wanne it is here midnight

righte: well ordered	*amidde*: within	*hure*: it
put: pit	*evene*: heaven	*iseo*: see
eorthe: earth	*stre*: yolk	*Enes*: once
withinne: within	*eiye*: egg	*thoru*: through
Louerd: Lord	*on*: of one	*bereth*: carries
iwis: indeed	*sterre*: star	*thin*: thine
queintise: ingenuity	*boc*: book	*heved*: head
gynne: device	*seith*: tells	*nones stonde*: noon time
verst: first	*thanne*: then	*vet*: feet
suththe: afterward	*ho so*: whoever	*arist*: rises
hurst: hillock	*anhei*: on high	*sone*: soon
agen: next to	*yif*: if	*bissint*: shines on
geth: goes	*lite*: little	*hou so*: how so
mot: must	*thenche*: seem	*non*: noon
weie: move	*nessolde*: should not	*wanne*: when

As me mai to sothe iseo · wo so hath god insight
And yif thou helde a cler candel · biside an appel right
Evene halvondel then appel · he wolde give here light
   There beoth atte firmamens · such as we iseoth
The ovemoste is the righte hevene · in wan the sterren beoth
For there above is Godes riche · that last withoute ende
That we beoth therto imaked

GEOFFREY CHAUCER

(1340?–1400)

The House of Fame

lines 725–864

SOUND WAVES

Now herkene wel, for-why I wille★
Tellen the a propre skille★
And a worthy demonstracion
In myn ymagynacion.
   'Geffrey, thou wost ryght wel this,
That every kyndely thyng that is
Hath a kyndely stede ther he
May best in hyt conserved be;
Unto which place every thyng,
Thorgh his kyndely enclynyng,
Moveth for to come to,
Whan that hyt is awey therfro;
As thus: loo, thou maist alday se
That any thing that hevy be,
As stoon, or led, or thyng of wighte,

me mai to sothe iseo: may truly appear to me	*candel*: candle	*stede*: place
wo so: whoso	*halvondel*: half	*ther*: where
god: good	*riche*: kingdom	*Whan that hyt*: when it
helde: held	*imaked*: made	*loo*: lo
cler: bright	*for-why*: because	*alday*: continually
	kyndely: natural	*wighte*: weight

★ An asterisk indicates that there is an explanatory note at the end of the book (pp. 316 ff).

And bere hyt never so hye on highte,
Lat goo thyn hand, hit falleth doun.
Ryght so seye I be fyr or soun,
Or smoke, or other thynges lyghte;
Alwey they seke upward on highte.
While ech of hem is at his large,
Lyght thing upward, and downward charge.
And for this cause mayst thou see
That every ryver to the see
Enclyned ys to goo by kynde,
And by these skilles, as I fynde,
Hath fyssh duellynge in flood and see,
And treës eke in erthe bee.
Thus every thing, by thys reson,
Hath his propre mansyon,
To which hit seketh to repaire,
Ther-as hit shulde not apaire.
Loo, this sentence ys knowen kouth
Of every philosophres mouth,
As Aristotle and daun Platon,
And other clerkys many oon;
And to confirme my resoun,
Thou wost wel this, that spech is soun,
Or elles no man myghte hyt here;
Now herke what y wol the lere.
  'Soun ys noght but eyr ybroken,
And every speche that ys spoken,
Lowd or pryvee, foul or fair,
In his substaunce ys but air;
For as flaumbe ys but lyghted smoke,
Ryght soo soun ys air ybroke.
But this may be in many wyse,
Of which I wil the twoo devyse,
As soun that cometh of pipe or harpe.
For whan a pipe is blowen sharpe,
The air ys twyst with violence

---

bere hyt: no matter how
  high you take it
his large: its own inclination
mansyon: abiding-place

Ther-as ... apaire: so that it
  shouldn't perish
kouth: familiarly
wost: know

lere: teach
pryvee: softly
devyse: explain

And rent; loo, thys ys my sentence;
Eke, whan men harpe-strynges smyte,
Whether hyt be moche or lyte,
Loo, with the strok the ayr tobreketh;
And ryght so breketh it when men speketh.
Thus wost thou wel what thing is speche.
　'Now hennesforth y wol the teche
How every speche, or noyse, or soun,
Thurgh hys multiplicacioun,
Thogh hyt were piped of a mous,
Mot nede come to Fames Hous.
I preve hyt thus – take hede now –
Be experience; for yf that thow
Throwe on water now a stoon,
Wel wost thou, hyt wol make anoon
A litel roundell as a sercle,
Paraunter brod as a covercle;
And ryght anoon thow shalt see wel,
That whel wol cause another whel,
And that the thridde, and so forth, brother,
Every sercle causynge other
Wydder than hymselve was;
And thus fro roundel to compas,
Ech aboute other goynge
Causeth of othres sterynge
And multiplyinge ever moo,
Til that hyt be so fer ygoo,
That hyt at bothe brynkes bee.
Although thou mowe hyt not ysee
Above, hyt gooth yet alway under,
Although thou thenke hyt a gret wonder.
And whoso seyth of trouthe I varye,
Bid hym proven the contrarye.
And ryght thus every word, ywys,
That lowd or pryvee spoken ys,
Moveth first an ayr aboute,

sentence: meaning	*y*: I	*Wydder*: wider
Eke: also	*Paraunter*: perhaps	*ygoo*: gone
lyte: gently	*covercle*: pot-lid	*mowe*: might
hennesforth: henceforth	*whel*: wheel	*ywys*: indeed

And of thys movynge, out of doute,
Another ayr anoon ys meved,
As I have of the watir preved,
That every cercle causeth other.
Ryght so of ayr, my leve brother;
Everych ayr another stereth
More and more, and speche up bereth,
Or voys, or noyse, or word, or soun,
Ay through multiplicacioun,
Til hyt be atte Hous of Fame, –
Take yt in ernest or in game.
    'Now have I told, yf thou have mynde,
How speche or soun, of pure kynde,
Enclyned ys upward to meve;
This, mayst thou fele, wel I preve.
And that same place, ywys,
That every thyng enclyned to ys,
Hath his kyndelyche stede:
That sheweth hyt, withouten drede,
That kyndely the mansioun
Of every speche, of every soun,
Be hyt eyther foul or fair,
Hath hys kynde place in ayr.
And syn that every thyng that is
Out of hys kynde place, ywys,
Moveth thidder for to goo,
Yif hyt aweye be therfroo,
As I have before preved the,
Hyt seweth, every soun, parde,
Moveth kyndely to pace
Al up into his kyndely place.
And this place of which I telle,
Ther as Fame lyst to duelle,
Ys set amyddys of these three,
Heven, erthe, and eke the see,
As most conservatyf the soun.
Than ys this the conclusyoun,
That every speche of every man,

---

leve: dear
syn: since

therfroo: from there
seweth: follows

amyddys: amidst
conservatyf: preserving of

As y the telle first began,
Moveth up on high to pace
Kyndely to Fames place.
  'Telle me this now feythfully,
Have y not preved thus symply,
Withoute any subtilite
Of speche, or gret prolixite
Of termes of philosophie,
Of figures of poetrie,
Or colours of rethorike?
Pardee, hit oughte the to lyke!
For hard langage and hard matere
Ys encombrous for to here
Attones; wost thou not wel this?'
And y answered and seyde, 'Yis.'

The Canterbury Tales

General Prologue, lines 411–44

'THE DOCTOUR OF PHISIK'

With us ther was a DOCTOUR OF PHISIK;
In al this world ne was ther noon hym lik,
To speke of phisik and of surgerye,
For he was grounded in astronomye.
He kepte his pacient a ful greet deel
In houres by his magyk natureel.*
Wel koude he fortunen the ascendent
Of his ymages for his pacient.
He knew the cause of everich maladye,
Were it of hoot, or coold, or moyste, or drye,
And where they engendred, and of what humour.
He was a verray, parfit praktisour:
The cause yknowe, and of his harm the roote,
Anon he yaf the sike man his boote.
Ful redy hadde he his apothecaries

Pardee: certainly   *encombrous*: cumbersome   *To speke of*: in regard to
lyke: please   *Attones*: at the same time   *astronomye*: astrology

To sende hym drogges and his letuaries,
For ech of hem made oother for to wynne –
Hir frendshipe nas nat newe to bigynne.
Wel knew he the olde Esculapius,★
And Deyscorides, and eek Rufus,
Olde Ypocras, Haly, and Galyen,
Serapion, Razis, and Avycen,
Averrois, Damascien, and Constantyn,
Bernard, and Gatesden, and Gilbertyn.
Of his diete mesurable was he,
For it was of no superfluitee,
But of greet norissyng and digestible.
His studie was but litel on the Bible.
In sangwyn and in pers he clad was al,
Lyned with taffata and with sendal;
And yet he was but esy of dispence;
He kepte that he wan in pestilence.
For gold in phisik is a cordial,
Therefore he lovede gold in special.

The Canterbury Tales

The Nun's Priest's Tale, lines 62–149

THE NATURE OF DREAMS

And so bifel that in a dawenynge,
As Chauntecleer among his wyves alle
Sat on his perche, that was in the halle,
And next hym sat this faire Pertelote,
This Chauntecleer gan gronen in his throte,
As man that in his dreem is drecched soore.
And whan that Pertelote thus herde hym roore,
She was agast, and seyde, 'Herte deere,
What eyleth yow, to grone in this manere?
Ye been a verray sleper; fy, for shame!'

letuaries: remedies
sangwyn: red cloth
pers: Persian blue cloth
sendal: thin silk

esy of dispence: slow to
  spend money
bifel: it happened

drecched: annoyed
eyleth: ails
verray: deep

And he answerde, and seyde thus: 'Madame,
I pray yow that ye take it nat agrief.
By God, me mette I was in swich meschief
Right now, that yet myn herte is soore afright.
Now God,' quod he, 'my swevene recche aright,
And kepe my body out of foul prisoun!
Me mette how that I romed up and doun
Withinne our yeerd, wheer as I saugh a beest
Was lyk an hound, and wolde han maad areest
Upon my body, and wolde han had me deed.
His colour was bitwixe yelow and reed,
And tipped was his tayl and bothe his eeris
With blak, unlyk the remenant of his heeris;
His snowte smal, with glowynge eyen tweye.
Yet of his look for feere almoost I deye;
This caused me my gronyng, doutelees.'

    'Avoy!' quod she, 'fy on yow, hertelees!
Allas!' quod she, 'for, by that God above,
Now han ye lost myn herte and al my love.
I kan nat love a coward, by my feith!
For certes, what so any womman seith,
We alle desiren, if it myghte bee,
To han housbondes hardy, wise, and free,
And secree, and no nygard, ne no fool,
Ne hym that is agast of every tool,
Ne noon avauntour, by that God above!
How dorste ye seyn, for shame, unto youre love
That any thyng myghte make yow aferd?
Have ye no mannes herte, and han a berd?
Allas! and konne ye been agast of swevenys?
Nothyng, God woot, but vanitee in sweven is.
Swevenes engendren of replecciouns,
And ofte of fume and of complecciouns,*
Whan humours* been to habundant in a wight.

---

mette: dreamed
swevene: dream
recche: interpret
wolde . . . areest: would
   have seized
deed: dead
heeris: hairs

snowte: snout
eyen tweye: two eyes
Avoy: Fie!
hertelees: heartless
secree: secret
nygard: miserly person
ne: nor

tool: weapon
avauntour: boaster
dorste ye seyn: dare you say
engendren of replecciouns: are
   born of repletion
   (over-eating)
fume: vapour

Certes this dreem, which ye han met to-nyght,
Cometh of the greete superfluytee
Of youre rede colera,* pardee,
Which causeth folk to dreden in hir dremes
Of arwes, and of fyr with rede lemes,
Of rede beestes, that they wol hem byte,
Of contek, and of whelpes, grete and lyte;
Right as the humour of malencolie
Causeth ful many a man in sleep to crie
For feere of blake beres, or boles blake,
Or elles blake develes wole hem take.
Of othere humours koude I telle also
That werken many a man sleep ful wo;
But I wol passe as lightly as I kan.
    Lo Catoun,* which that was so wys a man,
Seyde he nat thus, "Ne do no fors of dremes?"
    Now sire,' quod she, 'whan we flee fro the bemes,
For Goddes love, as taak som laxatyf.
Up peril of my soule and of my lyf,
I conseille yow the beste, I wol nat lye,
That bothe of colere and of malencolye
Ye purge yow; and for ye shal nat tarie,
Though in this toun is noon apothecarie,
I shal myself to herbes techen yow
That shul been for youre hele and for youre prow;
And in oure yeerd tho herbes shal I fynde
The whiche han of hire propretee by kynde
To purge yow bynethe and eek above.
Foryet nat this, for Goddes owene love!
Ye been ful coleryk of compleccioun;
Ware the sonne in his ascencioun
Ne fynde yow nat repleet of humours hoote.
And if it do, I dar wel leye a grote,
That ye shul have a fevere terciane,
Or an agu, that may be youre bane.

---

lemes: flames
contek: conflict
whelpes: cubs
lyte: small
boles: bulls

Ne do no fors: pay no
    attention
bemes: beams, i.e. be
    frightened off your perch
as taak: take (imperative)
prow: benefit

Ware: beware
leye a grote: bet
fevere terciane: a fever that
    returns every third day
agu: ague

A day or two ye shul have digestyves
Of wormes, er ye take youre laxatyves
Of lawriol, centaure, and fumetere,
Or elles of ellebor, that groweth there,
Of katapuce, or of gaitrys beryis,
Of herbe yve, growyng in oure yeerd, ther mery is;
Pekke hem up right as they growe and ete hem yn.
Be myrie, housbonde, for youre fader kyn!
Dredeth no dreem, I kan sey yow namoore.'

The Canterbury Tales
The Canon's Yeoman's Tale, lines 535–622

A FRAUDULENT ALCHEMIST

This chanon was my lord, ye wolden weene?
Sire hoost, in feith, and by the hevenes queene,
It was another chanoun, and nat hee,
That kan an hundred foold moore subtiltee.
He hath bitrayed folkes many tyme;
Of his falsnesse it dulleth me to ryme.
Evere whan that I speke of his falshede,
For shame of hym my chekes wexen rede.
Algates they bigynnen for to glowe,
For reednesse have I noon, right wel I knowe,
In my visage; for fumes diverse
Of metals, whiche ye han herd me reherce,
Consumed and wasted han my reednesse.
Now taak heede of this chanons cursednesse!
    'Sire,' quod he to the preest, 'lat youre man gon
For quyksilver, that we it hadde anon;
And lat hym bryngen ounces two or three;
And whan he comth, as faste shal ye see
A wonder thyng, which ye saugh nevere er this.'

er: before	*ellebor*: hellebore	*ye . . . weene*: you would
lawriol: spurge-laurel	*katapuce*: lesser spurge	think
centaure: centaury	*gaitrys beryis*: dogwood	*kan*: knew
fumetere: fumitory	berries	*Algates*: in every way

'Sire,' quod the preest, 'it shal be doon, ywis.'
He bad his servant fecchen hym this thyng,
And he al redy was at his biddyng,
And wente hym forth, and cam anon agayn
With this quyksilver, shortly for to sayn,
And took thise ounces thre to the chanoun;
And he hem leyde faire and wel adoun,
And bad the servant coles for to brynge,
That he anon myghte go to his werkynge.

   The coles right anon weren yfet,
And this chanoun took out a crosselet
Of his bosom, and shewed it to the preest.
'This instrument,' quod he, 'which that thou seest,
Taak in thyn hand, and put thyself therinne
Of this quyksilver an ounce, and heer bigynne,
In name of Crist, to wexe a philosofre.
Ther been ful fewe to whiche I wolde profre
To shewen hem thus muche of my science.
For ye shul seen heer, by experience,
That this quyksilver I wol mortifye
Right in youre sighte anon, withouten lye,
And make it as good silver and as fyn
As ther is any in youre purs or myn,
Or elleswhere, and make it malliable;
And elles holdeth me fals and unable
Amonges folk for evere to appeere.
I have a poudre heer, that coste me deere,
Shal make al good, for it is cause of al
My konnyng, which that I yow shewen shal.
Voyde youre man, and lat hym be theroute,
And shette the dore, whils we been aboute
Oure pryvetee, that no man us espie,
Whils that we werke in this philosophie.'

   Al as he bad fulfilled was in dede.
This ilke servant anonright out yede

---

fecchen: fetch
thre: three
hem: them
coles: coals
myghte: might
crosselet: crucible

profre: proffer
mortifye: change into silver
withouten lye: in truth
konnyng: knowledge
Voyde: dismiss

theroute: outside
pryvetee: secret activity
philosophie: science
anonright out yede:
   immediately left

And his maister shette the dore anon,
And to hire labour spedily they gon.
   This preest, at this cursed chanons biddyng,
Upon the fir anon sette this thyng,
And blew the fir, and bisyed hym ful faste.
And this chanoun into the crosselet caste
A poudre, noot I wherof that it was
Ymaad, outher of chalk, outher of glas,
Or somwhat elles, was nat worth a flye,
To blynde with this preest; and bad hym hye
The coles for to couchen al above
The crosselet. 'For in tokenyng I thee love,'
Quod this chanoun, 'thyne owene handes two
Shul werche al thyng which that shal heer be do.'
   'Graunt mercy,' quod the preest, and was ful glad,
And couched coles as that the chanoun bad.
And while he bisy was, this feendly wrecche,
This false chanoun – the foule feend hym fecche! –
Out of his bosom took a bechen cole,
In which ful subtilly was maad an hole,
And therinne put was of silver lemaille
An ounce, and stopped was, withouten faille,
This hole with wex, to kepe the lemaille in.
And understondeth that this false gyn
Was nat maad ther, but it was maad bifore;
And othere thynges I shal tellen moore
Herafterward, whiche that he with hym broghte.
Er he cam there, hym to bigile he thoghte,
And so he dide, er that they wente at wynne;
Til he had terved hym, koude he nat blynne.
It dulleth me whan that I of hym speke.
On his falshede fayn wolde I me wreke,
If I wiste how, but he is heere and there;
He is so variaunt, he abit nowhere.

Ymaad: made
To blynde with: with which to blind
hye: quickly

for to couchen: to place
bechen: made of beech
lemaille: filings
wynne: getting profit

terved: stripped
blynne: leave off, cease
wreke: avenge
abit: abides

ANONYMOUS

(late 15th century)

Pearce the Black Monke upon the Elixir

lines 1–56, 125–42

Take Erth of Erth, Erths Moder,
And Watur of Erth yt ys no oder,
And Fier of Erth that beryth the pryse,
But of that Erth louke thow be wyse,
The trew *Elixer* yf thow wylt make,
Erth owte of Erth looke that thow take,
Pewer sutel faire and good,
And than take the Water of the Wood:
Cleere as Chrystall schynyng bryght:
And do hem togeder anon ryght,
Thre dayes than let hem lye,
And than depart hem pryvyly and slye,
Than schale be browght Watur schynyng,
And in that Watur ys a soule reynynge,
Invisible and hyd and unseene,
A marvelous matter yt ys to weene.
Than departe hem by dystillynge,
And you schalle see an Erth apperinge,
Hevie as metale schalle yt be;
In the wych is hyd grete prevety,
Destil that Erth in grene hewe,
Three dayes during well and trew;
And do hem in a body of glass,
In the wych never no warke was.
In a Furnas he must be sett,
And on hys hede a good lymbeck;
And draw fro hym a Watur clere
The wych Watur hath no peere,
And aftur macke your Fyer stronger,
And there on thy Glasse continew longer,
So schal yow se come a Fyer;
Red as blode and of grete yre,
And aftur that an Erth leue there schale,
The wych is cleped the Moder of alle;
Then into Purgatory sche must be doe,

And have the paynes that longs thereto,
Tyl sche be bryghter than the Sune,
For than thow hast the Maystrey wone;
And that schalbe wythin howres three,
The wych forsooth ys grete ferly:
Than do her in a clene Glass,
Wyth some of the Watur that hers was.
And in a Furnas do her againe,
Tyl sche have drunke her Watur certaine,
And aftur that Watur give her Blood,
That was her owne pewre and good,
And whan sche hath dranke alle her Fyer,
Sche wyll wex strong and of grete yre.
Than take yow mete and mylcke thereto,
And fede the Chylde as you schowlde do,
Tyl he be growne to hys full age,
Than schal he be of strong courage;
And tourne alle Bodies that leyfull be,
To hys owne powre and dignitye,
And this ys the makyng of owre *Stone*,
The trewth here ys towlde yow evereech one.

★

I am *Mercury* the myghty Flower,
I am most worthy of Honour;
I am sours of *Sol*, *Luna*, and *Mars*,
I am genderer of *Iovis*, many be my snares:
I am setler of *Saturne*, and sours of *Venus*,
I am Empresse, Pryncesse and Regall of Queenes,
I am Mother of Myrrour, and maker of lyght,
I am head and hyghest and fayrest in syght:
I am both *Sun*, and *Moone*,
I am sche that alle thynges must doone.
I have a Daughter hight *Saturne* that ys my darlyng,
The wych ys Mother of all werkyng,
For in my Daughter there byne hydd,
Fowre thyngs Commonly I kydd:
A Golden seede, and a spearme rych,
And a Silver seede none hym lich;
And a *Mercury* seede full bryght,
And a *Sulphur* seede that ys ryght.

EDMUND SPENSER

(1552?–99)

The Faerie Queene
Book II, Canto IX, stanzas 44–60

THE STRUCTURE OF THE MIND

Up to a stately Turret she them brought,
Ascending by ten steps of Alablaster wrought.

That Turrets frame most admirable was,
  Like highest heaven compassed around,
  And lifted high above this earthly masse,
  Which it survew'd, as hils doen lower ground;
  But not on ground mote like to this be found,
  Not that, which antique *Cadmus* whylome built
  In *Thebes*, which *Alexander* did confound;
  Nor that proud towre of *Troy*, though richly guilt,
From which young *Hectors* bloud by cruell *Greekes* was spilt.

The roofe hereof was arched over head,
  And deckt with flowers and herbars daintily;
  Two goodly Beacons, set in watches stead,
  Therein gave light, and flam'd continually:
  For they of living fire most subtilly
  Were made, and set in silver sockets bright,
  Cover'd with lids deviz'd of substance sly,
  That readily they shut and open might.
O who can tell the prayses of that makers might!

Ne can I tell, ne can I stay to tell
  This parts great workmanship, and wondrous powre,
  That all this other worlds worke doth excell,
  And likest is unto that heavenly towre,
  That God hath built for his owne blessed bowre.
  Therein were diverse roomes, and diverse stages,
  But three the chiefest, and of greatest powre,
  In which there dwelt three honorable sages,
The wisest men, I weene, that lived in their ages.

Not he, whom *Greece*, the Nourse of all good arts,
  By *Phoebus* doome, the wisest thought alive,

Might be compar'd to these by many parts:
  Nor that sage *Pylian* syre, which did survive
  Three ages, such as mortall men contrive,
  By whose advise old *Priams* cittie fell,
  With these in praise of pollicies mote strive.
    These three in these three roomes did sundry dwell,
And counselled faire *Alma*, how to governe well.

The first of them could things to come foresee:
  The next could of things present best advize;
  The third things past could keepe in memoree,
  So that no time, nor reason could arize,
  But that the same could one of these comprize.
    For thy the first did in the forepart sit,
  That nought mote hinder his quicke prejudize:
  He had a sharpe foresight, and working wit,
That never idle was, ne once could rest a whit.

His chamber was dispainted all within,
  With sundry colours, in the which were writ
  Infinite shapes of things dispersed thin;
  Some such as in the world were never yit,
  Ne can devized be of mortall wit;
    Some daily seene, and knowen by their names,
  Such as in idle fantasies doe flit:
  Infernall Hags, *Centaurs*, feendes, *Hippodames*,
Apes, Lions, Aegles, Owles, fooles, lovers, children, Dames.

And all the chamber filled was with flyes,
  Which buzzed all about, and made such sound,
  That they encombred all mens eares and eyes,
  Like many swarmes of Bees assembled round,
  After their hives with honny do abound:
    All those were idle thoughts and fantasies,
  Devices, dreames, opinions unsound,
  Shewes, visions, sooth-sayes, and prophesies;
And all that fained is, as leasings, tales, and lies.

Emongst them all sate he, which wonned there,
  That hight *Phantastes* by his nature trew;
  A man of yeares yet fresh, as mote appere,
  Of swarth complexion, and of crabbed hew,
  That him full of melancholy did shew;

Bent hollow beetle browes, sharpe staring eyes,
That mad or foolish seemd: one by his vew
Mote deeme him borne with ill disposed skyes,
When oblique *Saturne* sate in the house of agonyes.

Whom *Alma* having shewed to her guestes,
Thence brought them to the second roome, whose wals
Were painted faire with memorable gestes,
Of famous Wisards, and with picturals
Of Magistrates, of courts, of tribunals,
Of commen wealthes, of states, of pollicy,
Of lawes, of judgements, and of decretals;
All artes, all science, all Philosophy,
And all that in the world was aye thought wittily.

Of those that roome was full, and them among
There sate a man of ripe and perfect age,
Who did them meditate all his life long,
That through continuall practise and usage,
He now was growne right wise, and wondrous sage.
Great pleasure had those stranger knights, to see
His goodly reason, and grave personage,
That his disciples both desir'd to bee;
But *Alma* thence them led to th'hindmost roome of three.

That chamber seemed ruinous and old,
And therefore was removed farre behind,
Yet were the wals, that did the same uphold,
Right firme and strong, though somewhat they declind;
And therein sate an old oldman, halfe blind,
And all decrepit in his feeble corse,
Yet lively vigour rested in his mind,
And recompenst him with a better scorse;
Weake body well is chang'd for minds redoubled forse.

This man of infinite remembrance was,
And things foregone through many ages held,
Which he recorded still, as they did pas,
Ne suffred them to perish through long eld,
As all things else, the which this world doth weld,
But laid them up in his immortall scrine;
Where they for ever incorrupted dweld:

The warres he well remembred of king *Nine*,
Of old *Assaracus*, and *Inachus* divine.

The years of *Nestor* nothing were to his,
  Ne yet *Mathusalem*, though longest liv'd;
  For he remembred both their infancies:
  Ne wonder then, if that he were depriv'd
  Of native strength now, that he them surviv'd.
  His chamber all was hangd about with rolles,
  And old records from auncient times deriv'd,
  Some made in books, some in long parchment scrolles,
That were all worme-eaten, and full of canker holes.

Amidst them all he in a chaire was set,
  Tossing and turning them withouten end;
  But for he was unhable them to fet,
  A litle boy did on him still attend,
  To reach, when ever he for ought did send;
  And oft when things were lost, or laid amis,
  That boy them sought, and unto him did lend.
  Therefore he *Anamnestes* cleped is,
And that old man *Eumnestes*, by their propertis.

The knights there entring, did him reverence dew
  And wondred at his endlesse exercise,
  Then as they gan his Librarie to vew,
  And antique Registers for to avise,
  There chaunced to the Princes hand to rize,
  An auncient booke, hight *Briton moniments*,
  That of this lands first conquest did devize,
  And old division into Regiments,
Till it reduced was to one mans governments.

Sir *Guyon* chaunst eke on another booke,
  That hight *Antiquitie* of *Faerie* lond,
  In which when as he greedily did looke,
  Th'off-spring of Elves and Faries there he fond,
  As it delivered was from hond to hond:
  Whereat they burning both with fervent fire,
  Their countries auncestry to understond,
  Crav'd leave of *Alma*, and that aged sire,
To read those bookes; who gladly graunted their desire.

The Faerie Queene

Book V, Proem, stanzas 5–8

STAR SHIFTS

For who so list into the heavens looke,
  And search the courses of the rowling spheares,
  Shall find that from the point, where they first tooke
  Their setting forth, in these few thousand yeares
  They all are wandred much; that plaine appeares.
  For that same golden fleecy Ram, which bore
  Phrixus and *Helle* from their stepdames feares,
  Hath now forgot, where he was plast of yore,
And shouldred hath the Bull, which fayre *Europa* bore.

And eke the Bull hath with his bow-bent horne
  So hardly butted those two twinnes of *Jove*,
  That they have crusht the Crab, and quite him borne
  Into the great *Nemaean* lions grove.
  So now all range, and doe at randon rove
  Out of their proper places farre away,
  And all this world with them amisse doe move,
  And all his creatures from their course astray.
Till they arrive at their last ruinous decay.

Ne is that same great glorious lampe of light,
  That doth enlumine all these lesser fyres,
  In better case, ne keepes his course more right,
  But is miscaried with the other Spheres.
  For since the terme of fourteene hundred yeres,
  That learned *Ptolomaee* his hight did take,
  He is declyned from that marke of theirs,
  Nigh thirtie minutes to the Southerne lake;
That makes me feare in time he will us quite forsake.

And if to those Aegyptian wisards old,
  Which in Star-read were wont have best insight,
  Faith may be given, it is by them told,
  That since the time they first tooke the Sunnes hight,
  Foure times his place he shifted hath in sight,
  And twice hath risen, where he now doth West,
  And wested twice, where he ought rise aright.
  But most is *Mars* amisse of all the rest,
And next to him old *Saturne*, that was wont be best.

The Faerie Queene

Two Cantos of Mutabilitie, Canto VII, stanzas 16–26

Then weigh, O soveraigne goddesse, by what right
  These gods do claime the worlds whole soveraity;
  And that is onely dew unto thy might
  Arrogate to themselves ambitiously:
  As for the gods owne principality,
  Which *Jove* usurpes unjustly; that to be
  My heritage, *Jove's* self cannot deny,
  From my great Grandsire *Titan*, unto mee,
Deriv'd by dew descent; as is well knowen to thee.

Yet mauger *Jove*, and all his gods beside,
  I doe possesse the worlds most regiment;
  As, if ye please it into parts divide,
  And every parts inholders to convent,
  Shall to your eyes appeare incontinent.
  And first, the Earth (great mother of us all)
  That only seems unmov'd and permanent,
  And unto *Mutability* not thrall;
Yet is she chang'd in part, and eeke in generall.

For, all that from her springs, and is ybredde,
  How-ever fayre it flourish for a time,
  Yet see we soone decay; and, being dead,
  To turne again unto their earthly slime:
  Yet, out of their decay and mortall crime,
  We daily see new creatures to arize;
  And of their Winter spring another Prime,
  Unlike in forme, and chang'd by strange disguise:
So turne they still about, and change in restlesse wise.

As for her tenants; that is, man and beasts,
  The beasts we daily see massacred dy,
  As thralls and vassals unto mens beheasts:
  And men themselves doe change continually,
  From youth to eld, from wealth to poverty,
  From good to bad, from bad to worst of all.
  Ne doe their bodies only flit and fly:
  But eeke their minds (which they immortall call)
Still change and vary thoughts, as new occasions fall.

Ne is the water in more constant case;
   Whether those same on high, or these belowe.
   For, th'Ocean moveth stil, from place to place;
   And every River still doth ebbe and flowe:
   Ne any Lake, that seems most still and slowe,
   Ne Poole so small, that can his smoothnesse holde,
   When any winde doth under heaven blowe;
    With which, the clouds are also tost and roll'd;
Now like great Hills; and, streight, like sluces, them unfold.

So likewise are all watry living wights
   Still tost, and turned, with continuall change,
   Never abyding in their stedfast plights.
   The fish, still floting, doe at randon range,
   And never rest; but evermore exchange
   Their dwelling places, as the streames them carrie:
   Ne have the watry foules a certaine grange,
    Wherein to rest, ne in one stead do tarry;
But flitting still doe flie, and still their places vary.

Next is the Ayre: which who feeles not by sense
   (For, of all sense it is the middle meane)
   To flit still? and, with subtill influence
   Of his thin spirit, all creatures to maintaine,
   In state of life? O weake life! that does leane
   On thing so tickle as th'unsteady ayre;
   Which every howre is chang'd, and altred cleane
    With every blast that bloweth fowle or faire:
The faire doth it prolong; the fowle doth it impaire.

Therein the changes infinite beholde,
   Which to her creatures every minute chaunce;
   Now, boyling hot: streight, friezing deadly cold:
   Now, faire sun-shine, that makes all skip and daunce:
   Streight, bitter storms and balefull countenance,
   That makes them all to shiver and to shake:
   Rayne, hayle, and snowe do pay them sad penance,
    And dreadfull thunder-claps (that make them quake)
With flames and flashing lights that thousand changes make.

Last is the fire: which, though it live for ever,
   Ne can be quenched quite; yet, every day,
   Wee see his parts, so soone as they do sever,

To lose their heat, and shortly to decay;
So, makes himself his owne consuming pray.
Ne any living creatures doth he breed:
But all, that are of others bredd, doth slay;
And, with their death, his cruell life dooth feed;
Nought leaving, but their barren ashes, without seede.

Thus, all these fower (the which the ground-work bee
   Of all the world, and of all living wights)
   To thousand sorts of *Change* we subject see:
   Yet are they chang'd (by other wondrous slights)
   Into themselves, and lose their native mights;
   The Fire to Aire, and th'Ayre to Water sheere,
   And Water into Earth: yet Water fights
With Fire, and Aire with Earth approaching neere:
Yet all are in one body, and as one appeare.

So, in them all raignes *Mutabilitie*;
   How-ever these, that Gods themselves do call,
   Of them doe claime the rule and soveranty:
   As, *Vesta*, of the fire aethereall;
   Vulcan, of this, with us so usuall;
   Ops, of the earth; and *Juno* of the Ayre;
   Neptune, of Seas; and Nymphes, of Rivers all.
   For, all those Rivers to me subject are:
And all the rest, which they usurp, be all my share.

FULKE GREVILLE, LORD BROOKE
(1554–1628)

A Treatie of Humane Learning
stanzas 73–5, 116–19

Let her that gather'd rules Emperiall,
Out of particular experiments,
And made meere contemplation of them all,
Apply them now to speciall intents;
   That she, and mutuall Action, may maintaine
   Themselves, by taking, what they give againe.

And where the progresse was to finde the cause,
First by effects out, now her regresse should
Forme Art directly under Natures Lawes;
And all effects so in their causes mould:
    As fraile Man lively, without Schoole of smart,
    Might see Successes comming in an Art.

For *Sciences* from *Nature* should be drawne,
As *Arts* from *practise*, never out of Bookes;
Whose rules are onely left with time in pawne,
To shew how in them Use, and Nature lookes:
    Out of which light, they that Arts first began,
    Pierc'd further, than succeeding ages can.

*

The grace, and disgrace of this following traine,
Arithmetike, Geometrie, Astronomy,
Rests in the *Artisans* industrie, or veine,
Not in the Whole, the Parts, or Symmetrie:
    Which being onely Number, Measure, Time,
    All following Nature, helpe her to refine.

And of these Arts it may be said againe,
That since their Theoricke is infinite;
Of infinite there can no Arts remaine.
Besides, they stand by curtesie, not right;
    Who must their principles as granted crave,
    Or else acknowledge they no being have.

Their Theoricke then must not waine their use,
But, by a practise in materiall things,
Rather awake that dreaming vaine abuse
Of *Lines*, without *breadth*; without feathers, wings:
    So that their boundlesnesse may bounded be,
    In Workes, and Arts of our Humanity.

But for the most part those *Professors* are
So melted, and transported into these;
And with the Abstract swallowed up so farre
As they lose trafficke, comfort, use, and ease:
    And are, like treasures with strange spirits guarded,
    Neither to be enjoy'd, nor yet discarded.

SIR PHILIP SIDNEY

(1554–86)

The 7 Wonders of England

Neere *Wilton* sweete, huge heapes of stones★ are found,
   But so confusde, that neither any eye
   Can count them just, nor reason reason trye,
   What force brought them to so unlikely ground.

To stranger weights my minde's waste soile is bound,
   Of passyon's hilles reaching to reason's skie,
   From fancie's earth passing all numbers' bound,
   Passing all ghesse, whence into me should fly
      So mazde a masse, or if in me it growes,
      A simple soule should breed so mixed woes.

The *Bruertons*★ have a Lake, which when the Sunne
   Approching warmes (not else) dead logges up sends,
   From hidnest depth, which tribute when it ends,
   Sore signe it is, the Lord's last thred is spun.

My lake is sense, whose still streames never runne,
   But when my Sunne her shining twinnes there bends,
   Then from his depth with force in her begunne,
   Long drowned hopes to watrie eyes it lends:
      But when that failes, my dead hopes up to take,
      Their master is faire warn'd his will to make.

We have a fish,★ by strangers much admirde,
   Which caught, to cruell search yeelds his chiefe part:
   (With gall cut out) closde up againe by art,
   Yet lives untill his life be new requirde.

A stranger fish, my selfe not yet expirde,
   Though rapt with beautie's hooke, I did impart
   My selfe unto th' Anatomy desirde,
   In steade of gall, leaving to her my hart:
      Yet live with thoughts closde up, till that she will
      By conquest's right in steade of searching kill.

Peake hath a Cave,★ whose narrow entries finde
   Large roomes within, where droppes distill amaine:
   Till knit with cold, though there unknowne remaine,
   Decke that poore place with Alablaster linde.

Mine eyes the streight, the roomie cave, my minde,
  Whose clowdie thoughts let fall an inward raine
  Of sorrowe's droppes, till colder reason binde
  Their running fall into a constant vaine
     Of trueth, farre more then Alablaster pure,
     Which though despisde, yet still doth truth endure.

A field* there is where, if a stake be prest
  Deepe in the earth, what hath in earth receipt
  Is chang'd to stone, in hardnesse, cold, and weight,
  The wood, above doth soone consuming rest.

The earth, her eares: the stake is my request:
  Of which, how much may pierce to that sweet seate,
  To honor turnd, doth dwell in honor's nest,
  Keeping that forme, though void of wonted heate:
     But all the rest, which feare durst not applie,
     Failing themselves, with withered conscience dye.

Of ships, by shipwrack cast on *Albion* coast,
  Which rotting on the rockes, their death do dye:
  From wooden bones, and bloud of pitch doth flie
  A bird* which gets more life then ship had lost.

My ship, desire, with winde of lust long tost,
  Brake on faire cleeves of constant chastitie:
  Where plagu'd for rash attempt, gives up his ghost,
  So deepe in seas of vertue beauties ly.
     But of his death flies up a purest love,
     Which seeming lesse, yet nobler life doth move.

These wonders England breedes, the last remaines,
  A Ladie in despite of nature chaste,
  On whome all love, in whom no love is plaste,
  Where fairenesse yeelds to wisdome's shortest raines.

An humble pride, a skorne that favour staines:
A woman's mould, but like an Angell graste,
An Angell's mind, but in a woman caste:
A heaven on earth, or earth that heaven containes:
     Now thus this wonder to my selfe I frame,
     She is the cause that all the rest I am.

SIR FRANCIS BACON
(1561–1626)

From *The Translation of the 104. Psalme*★

Father and King of Powers, both high and low
Whose sounding Fame all creatures serve to blow;
My Soule shall with the rest strike up thy praise,
And Caroll of thy workes and wondrous waies.
But who can blaze thy Beauties, Lord, aright?
They turne the brittle Beames of mortall sight.
Upon thy head thou wear'st a glorious Crowne,
All set with vertues, polisht with renowne:
Thence round about a Silver Vaile doth fall
Of Chrystall Light, Mother of Colours all.
The Compasse heaven, smooth without grain, or fold,
All set with Spangs of glitt'ring Stars untold,
And strip't with golden Beames of power unpent,
Is raisèd up for a removing Tent.
Vaulted and archèd are his Chamber Beames,
Upon the Seas, the Waters, and the streames:
The Clouds as Chariots swift doe scoure the sky;
The stormy Winds upon their wings doe fly.
His Angels Spirits are that wait his Will,
As flames of Fire his anger they fulfill.
In the Beginning with a mighty Hand,
He made the Earth by Counterpoyse to stand;
Never to move, but to be fixèd still;
Yet hath no Pillars but his Sacred Will.
This Earth as with a vaile, once covered was,
The Waters overflowèd all the Masse:
But upon his rebuke away they fled,
And then the Hills began to shew their Head;
The Vales their hollow Bosomes opened plaine,
The Streames ran trembling down the vales again:
And that the Earth no more might drownèd be
He set the Sea his Bounds of Liberty;
And though his Waves resound, and beat the shore,
Yet is it brideled by his holy lore.
Then did the Rivers seek their proper places
And found their Heads, their Issues, and their Races:
The Springs doe feed the Rivers all the way

And so the Tribute to the Sea repay:
Running along through many a pleasant field,
Much fruitfulnesse unto the Earth they yeeld:
That know the Beasts and Cattell feeding by,
Which for to slake their Thirst doe thither hie.
Nay Desert Grounds the Streames doe not forsake,
But through the unknown waies their journey take:
The Asses wilde that bide in Wildernesse,
Doe thither come, their Thirst for to refresh.
The shady Trees along their Bankes doe spring
In which the Birds doe build, and sit, and sing;
Stroking the gentle Ayre with pleasant notes,
Plaining or Chirping through their warbling throtes.
The higher Grounds where Waters cannot rise,
By raine and Deawes are watred from the Skies;
Causing the Earth put forth the Grasse for Beasts,
And garden Herbs, serv'd at the greatest Feasts;
And Bread that is all Viands Firmament,
And gives a firme and solid Nourishment;
And Wine Mans Spirits for to recreate;
And Oyle his Face for to exhilarate.
The sappy Cedars tall like stately Towers,
High flying Birds doe harbour in their Bowers:
The holy Storkes that are the Travellers,
Choose for to dwell and build among the Firs:
The climing Goats hang on steep Mountaines side;
The digging Conies in the Rocks doe bide.
The Moone, so constant in Inconstancy,
Doth rule the Monethly seasons orderly:
The Sunne, Eye of the World, doth know his race,
And when to shew, and when to hide his face.

CHRISTOPHER MARLOWE

(1564–93)

From *Doctor Faustus*

FAUSTUS: Come, Mephistophilis, let us dispute again,
And argue of divine astrology.
Tell me, are there many heavens above the moon?
Are all celestial bodies but one globe,
As is the substance of this centric earth?

MEPHISTOPHILIS: As are the elements, such are the spheres,
Mutually folded in each other's orb,
And, Faustus,
All jointly move upon one axletree,
Whose terminus is term'd the world's wide pole;
Nor are the names of Saturn, Mars, or Jupiter
Feign'd, but are erring stars.

FAUSTUS: But, tell me, have they all one motion, both *situ et tempore*?

MEPHISTOPHILIS: All jointly move from east to west in twenty-four
hours upon the poles of the world; but differ in their motion upon
the poles of the zodiac.

FAUSTUS: Tush,
These slender trifles Wagner can decide:
Hath Mephistophilis no greater skill?
Who knows not the double motion of the planets?
The first is finish'd in a natural day;
The second thus; as Saturn in thirty years; Jupiter in twelve; Mars in
four; the Sun, Venus, and Mercury in a year; the Moon in twenty-
eight days. Tush, these are freshmen's suppositions. But, tell me,
hath every sphere a dominion or *intelligentia*?

MEPHISTOPHILIS: Ay.

FAUSTUS: How many heavens or spheres are there?

MEPHISTOPHILIS: Nine; the seven planets, the firmament, and the
empyreal heaven.

FAUSTUS: Well resolve me in this question; why have we not conjunc-
tions, oppositions, aspects, eclipses, all at one time but in some
years we have more, in some less?

MEPHISTOPHILIS: *Per inaequalem motum respectu totius.*

FAUSTUS: Well, I am answered. Tell me who made the world?

MEPHISTOPHILIS: I will not.

FAUSTUS: Sweet Mephistophilis, tell me.

MEPHISTOPHILIS: Move me not, for I will not tell thee.
FAUSTUS: Villain, have I not bound thee to tell me anything?
MEPHISTOPHILIS: Ay, that is not against our kingdom; but this is.
  Think thou on hell, Faustus, for thou art damned.
FAUSTUS: Think, Faustus, upon God that made the world.

★

CHORUS: Learned Faustus,
  To know the secrets of astronomy
  Graven in the book of Jove's high firmament,
  Did mount himself to scale Olympus' top,
  Being seated in a chariot burning bright,
  Drawn by the strength of yoky dragons' necks
  He now is gone to prove cosmography,
  And, as I guess, will first arrive in Rome,
  To see the Pope and manner of his court,
  And take some part of holy Peter's feast,
  That to this day is highly solemnis'd.

WILLIAM SHAKESPEARE
(1564–1616)

From *The Merchant of Venice*,
Act V, scene 1

THE MUSIC OF THE SPHERES

How sweet the moonlight sleeps upon this bank!
Here will we sit, and let the sounds of music
Creep in our ears: soft stillness and the night
Become the touches of sweet harmony.
Sit, Jessica. Look, how the floor of heaven
Is thick inlaid with patines of bright gold:
There's not the smallest orb which thou behold'st
But in his motion like an angel sings,
Still quiring to the young-eyed cherubins, –
Such harmony is in immortal souls;
But whilst this muddy vesture of decay
Doth grossly close it in, we cannot hear it.

From *Troilus and Cressida*,
Act I, scene 3

ULYSSES ON DEGREE

The heavens themselves, the planets, and this centre,
Observe degree, priority, and place,
Insisture, course, proportion, season, form,
Office, and custom, in all line of order:
And therefore is the glorious planet Sol
In noble eminence enthroned and sphered
Amidst the other; whose med'cinable eye
Corrects the ill aspects of planets evil,
And posts, like the commandment of a king,
Sans check, to good and bad: but when the planets,
In evil mixture, to disorder wander,
What plagues, and what portents, what mutiny,
What raging of the sea, shaking of earth,
Commotion in the winds, frights, changes, horrors,
Divert and crack, rend and deracinate
The unity and married calm of states
Quite from their fixure! O, when degree is shaked,
Which is the ladder to all high designs,
The enterprise is sick! How could communities,
Degrees in schools, and brotherhoods in cities,
Peaceful commerce from dividable shores,
The primogenity and due of birth,
Prerogative of age, crowns, sceptres, laurels,
But by degree, stand in authentic place?
Take but degree away, untune that string,
And, hark, what discord follows! each thing meets
In mere oppugnancy: the bounded waters
Should lift their bosoms higher than the shores,
And make a sop of all this solid globe:
Strength should be lord of imbecility,
And the rude son should strike his father dead:
Force should be right; or rather, right and wrong –
Between whose endless jar justice resides –
Should lose their names, and so should justice too.
Then every thing includes itself in power,
Power into will, will into appetite;

And appetite, an universal wolf,
So doubly seconded with will and power,
Must make perforce an universal prey,
And last eat up himself.

From *King Lear*,

Act I, scene 2

EDMUND ON ASTROLOGY

This is the excellent foppery of the world, that, when we are sick in fortune, – often the surfeit of our own behaviour, – we make guilty of our disasters the sun, the moon, and the stars: as if we were villains by necessity; fools by heavenly compulsion; knaves, thieves, and treachers, by spherical predominance; drunkards, liars, and adulterers, by an enforced obedience of planetary influence; and all that we are evil in, by a divine thrusting on: an admirable evasion of whoremaster man, to lay his goatish disposition to the charge of a star! My father compounded with my mother under the dragon's tail; and my nativity was under *ursa major*; so that it follows, I am rough and lecherous. – Fut, I should have been that I am, had the maidenliest star in the firmament twinkled on my bastardizing.

From *Coriolanus*,

Act I, scene 1

THE BELLY AND THE LIMBS*

Note me this, good friend;
Your most grave belly was deliberate,
Not rash like his accusers, and thus answer'd:
'True is it, my incorporate friends,' quoth he,
'That I receive the general food at first,
Which you do live upon; and fit it is,
Because I am the store-house and the shop
Of the whole body: but, if you do remember,
I send it through the rivers of your blood,
Even to the court, the heart, – to the seat o'the brain;

And, through the cranks and offices of man,
The strongest nerves and small inferior veins
From me receive that natural competency
Whereby they live ...

SIR JOHN DAVIES

(1569–1626)

Orchestra: A Poem of Dancing

stanzas 34–7

THE COSMIC DANCE*

Behold the *World*, how it is *whirled round*,
And for it is so *whirl'd*, is namèd so;
In whose large volume many rules are found
Of this new Art, which it doth fairely show;
For your quicke eyes in wandring too and fro
  From East to West, on no one thing can glaunce,
  But if you marke it well, it seemes to daunce.

First you see fixt in this huge mirrour blew,
Of trembling lights, a number numberlesse:
Fixt they are nam'd, but with a name untrue,
For they all moove and in a Daunce expresse
That *great long yeare*,* that doth containe no lesse
  Then threescore hundreds of those yeares in all,
  Which the sunne makes with his course naturall.

What if to you these sparks disordered seeme
As if by chaunce they had beene scattered there?
The gods a solemne measure doe it deeme,
And see a just proportion every where,
And know the points whence first their movings were;
  To which first points when all returne againe,
  The axel-tree of Heav'n shall breake in twaine.

Under that spangled skye, five wandring flames
Besides the King of Day, and Queene of Night,
Are wheel'd around, all in their sundry frames,

And all in sundry measures doe delight,
   Yet altogether keepe no measure right;
      For by it selfe each doth it selfe advance,
      And by it selfe each doth a galliard daunce.

From *Nosce Teipsum*

All things without, which round about we see,
   We seeke to know, and how therewith to do;
   But that whereby we *reason, live and be*,
   Within our selves, we strangers are thereto.

We seeke to know the moving of each spheare,
   And the strange cause of th' ebs and flouds of *Nile*;
   But of that clocke within our breasts we beare,
   The subtill motions we forget the while.

We that acquaint our selves with every *Zoane*
   And pass both *Tropikes* and behold the *Poles*,
   When we come home, are to our selves unknown,
   And unacquainted still with our owne *Soules*.

The Physition

I study to uphold the slippery state of man,
Who dies, when we have done the best and all we can.
From practise and from bookes, I draw my learnèd skill,
Not from the knowne receipt of 'Pothecaries bill.
The earth my faults doth hide, the world my cures doth see,
What youth, and time effects, is oft ascribde to me.

JOHN DONNE
(1571/2–1631)

An Anatomy of the World, The First Anniversarie
lines 203–14, 247–304

THE NEW PHILOSOPHY

And now the springs and summers which we see,
Like sons of women after fifty be.
And new philosophy calls all in doubt;
The element of fire is quite put out;
The sun is lost, and th' earth, and no man's wit
Can well direct him where to look for it.
And freely men confess that this world's spent,
When in the planets, and the firmament
They seek so many new; they see that this
Is crumbled out again to his atomies,
'Tis all in pieces, all coherence gone,
All just supply, and all relation.

★

For the world's subtlest immaterial parts
Feel this consuming wound and age's darts;
For the world's beauty is decay'd, or gone
– Beauty; that's colour and proportion.
We think the heavens enjoy their spherical,
Their round proportion, embracing all;
But yet their various and perplexed course,
Observed in divers ages, doth enforce
Men to find out so many eccentric parts,
Such diverse downright lines, such overthwarts,
As disproportion that pure form; it tears
The firmament in eight-and-forty shares,
And in these constellations then arise
New stars, and old do vanish from our eyes;
As though heaven suffered earthquakes, peace or war,
When new towers rise, and old demolish'd are.
They have impaled within a zodiac
The free-born sun, and keep twelve signs awake
To watch his steps; the Goat and Crab control,

And fright him back, who else to either pole,
Did not these tropics fetter him, might run.
For his course is not round, nor can the sun
Perfect a circle, or maintain his way
One inch direct; but where he rose to-day
He comes no more, but with a cozening line,
Steals by that point, and so is serpentine;
And seeming weary with his reeling thus,
He means to sleep, being now fallen nearer us.
So of the stars which boast that they do run
In circle still, none ends where he begun.
All their proportion's lame, it sinks, it swells;
For of meridians and parallels
Man hath weaved out a net, and this net thrown
Upon the heavens, and now they are his own.
Loth to go up the hill, or labour thus
To go to heaven, we make heaven come to us.
We spur, we rein the stars, and in their race
They're diversely content to obey our pace.
But keeps the earth her round proportion still?
Doth not a Teneriffe or higher hill
Rise so high like a rock, that one might think
The floating moon would shipwreck there and sink?
Seas are so deep that whales, being struck to-day,
Perchance to-morrow scarce at middle way
Of their wish'd journey's end, the bottom, die.
And men, to sound depths, so much line untie
As one might justly think that there would rise
At end thereof one of th' antipodes.
If under all a vault infernal be
– Which sure is spacious, except that we
Invent another torment, that there must
Millions into a straight hot room be thrust –
Then solidness and roundness have no place.
Are these but warts and pockholes in the face
Of th' earth? Think so; but yet confess, in this
The world's proportion disfigured is;
That those two legs whereon it doth rely,
Reward and punishment, are bent awry.

An Anatomy of the World,
The Second Anniversarie

lines 261–80

Thou art too narrow, wretch, to comprehend
Even thyself, yea though thou wouldst but bend
To know thy body. Have not all souls thought
For many ages, that our bodies wrought
Of air, and fire, and other elements?
And now they think of new ingredients;
And one soul thinks one, and another way
Another thinks, and 'tis an even lay.
Know'st thou but how the stone doth enter in
The bladder's cave, and never break the skin?
Know'st thou how blood, which to the heart doth flow,
Doth from one ventricle to th' other go?
And for the putrid stuff which thou dost spit,
Know'st thou how thy lungs have attracted it?
There are no passages, so that there is
– For aught thou know'st – piercing of substances.
And of those many opinions which men raise
Of nails and hairs, dost thou know which to praise?
What hope have we to know ourselves, when we
Know not the least things which for our use be?

BEN JONSON

(1572–1637)

From *The Alchemist*,

Act II, scene 3

MAMMON: This gentleman you must bear withal:
  I told you he had no faith.
SURLY: And little hope, sir;
  But much less charity, should I gull myself.
SUBTLE: Why, what have you observ'd, sir, in our art,
  Seems so impossible?

SURLY: But your whole work, no more.
  That you should hatch gold in a furnace, sir,
  As they do eggs in Egypt!
SUBTLE: Sir, do you
  Believe that eggs are hatch'd so?
SURLY: If I should?
SUBTLE: Why, I think that the greater miracle.
  No egg but differs from a chicken more
  Than metals in themselves.
SURLY: That cannot be.
  The egg's ordain'd by nature to that end,
  And is a chicken *in potentia*.
SUBTLE: The same we say of lead and other metals,
  Which would be gold, if they had time.
MAMMON: And that
  Our art doth further.
SUBTLE: Ay, for 'twere absurd
  To think that nature in the earth bred gold
  Perfect in the instant: something went before.
  There must be remote matter.
SURLY: Ay, what is that?
SUBTLE: Marry, we say –
MAMMON: Ay, now it heats: stand, father,
  Pound him to dust.
SUBTLE: It is, of the one part,
  A humid exhalation, which we call
  Materia liquida, or the unctuous water;
  On the other part, a certain crass and vicious
  Portion of earth; both which, concorporate,
  Do make the elementary matter of gold;
  Which is not yet *propria materia*,
  But common to all metals and all stones;
  For, where it is forsaken of that moisture,
  And hath more driness, it becomes a stone:
  Where it retains more of the humid fatness,
  It turns to sulphur, or to quicksilver,
  Who are the parents of all other metals.
  Nor can this remote matter suddenly
  Progress so from extreme unto extreme,
  As to grow gold, and leap o'er all the means.
  Nature doth first beget the imperfect, then

Proceeds she to the perfect. Of that airy
And oily water, mercury is engender'd;
Sulphur of the fat and earthy part; the one,
Which is the last, supplying the place of male,
The other of the female, in all metals.
Some do believe hermaphrodeity,
That both do act and suffer. But these two
Make the rest ductile, malleable, extensive.
And even in gold they are; for we do find
Seeds of them, by our fire, and gold in them;
And can produce the species of each metal
More perfect thence, than nature doth in earth.
Beside, who doth not see in daily practice
Art can beget bees, hornets, beetles, wasps,
Out of the carcasses and dung of creatures;
Yea, scorpions of an herb, being rightly placed?
And these are living creatures, far more perfect
And excellent than metals.

MAMMON: Well said, father!
Nay, if he take you in hand, sir, with an argument,
He'll bray you in a mortar.

SURLY: Pray you, sir, stay.
Rather than I'll be bray'd, sir, I'll believe
That Alchemy is a pretty kind of game,
Somewhat like tricks o' the cards, to cheat a man
With charming.

SUBTLE: Sir?

SURLY: What else are all your terms,
Whereon no one of your writers 'grees with other?
Of your elixir, your *lac virginis*,
Your stone, your med'cine, and your chrysosperme,
Your sal, your sulphur, and your mercury,
Your oil of height, your tree of life, your blood,
Your marchesite, your tutie, your magnesia,
Your toad, your crow, your dragon, and your panther;
Your sun, your moon, your firmament, your adrop,
Your lato, azoch, zernich, chibrit, heautarit,
And then your red man, and your white woman,
With all your broths, your menstrues, and materials,
Of piss and egg-shells, women's terms, man's blood,
Hair o' the head, burnt clouts, chalk, merds, and clay,

Powder of bones, scalings of iron, glass,
And worlds of other strange ingredients,
Would burst a man to name?
SUBTLE: And all these named,
Intending but one thing: which art our writers
Used to obscure their art.
MAMMON: Sir, so I told him –
Because the simple idiot should not learn it,
And make it vulgar.
SUBTLE: Was not all the knowledge
Of the Aegyptians writ in mystic symbols?
Speak not the scriptures oft in parables?
Are not the choicest fables of the poets,
That were the fountains and first springs of wisdom,
Wrapp'd in perplexed allegories?
MAMMON: I urg'd that,
And clear'd to him, that Sysiphus was damn'd
To roll the ceaseless stone, only because
He would have made Ours common.

PHINEAS FLETCHER

(1582–1650)

The Purple Island*

Canto IV, stanzas 15–16, 22–4

THE THORACIC CAVITY

In middle of this middle Regiment
*Kerdia** seated lies, the centre deem'd
Of this whole Isle, and of this government:
If not the chiefest this, yet needfull'st seem'd,
    Therfore obtain'd an equall distant seat,
    More fitly hence to shed his life and heat,
And with his yellow streams the fruitfull Island wet.

[1]Flankt with two severall walls (for more defence)
Betwixt them ever flows a wheyish moat;
In whose soft waves, and circling profluence
This Citie, like an Isle, might safely float:

In motion still (a motion fixt, not roving)
  Most like to heav'n in his most constant moving:
Hence most here plant the seat of sure and active loving.

*

[2]In this Heart-citie foure main streams appeare;
One from the *Hepar*,★ where the tribute landeth,
Largely poures out his purple river here;
At whose wide mouth a band of *Tritons* standeth,
  (Three *Tritons* stand) who with their three-forkt mace
  Drive on, and speed the rivers flowing race,
But strongly stop the wave, if once it back repace.

[3]The second is that doubtfull chanel, lending
Some of this tribute to the *Pneumon* nigh;
Whose springs by carefull guards are watcht, that sending
From thence the waters, all regresse denie:
  [4]The third unlike to this, from *Pneumon* flowing,
  And his due ayer-tribute here bestowing,
Is kept by gates and barres, which stop all backward going.

[5]The last full spring out of this left side rises;
Where three fair Nymphs, like *Cynthia's* self appearing,
Draw down the stream which all the Isle suffices;
But stop back-waies, some ill revolture fearing.
  This river still it self to lesse dividing,
  At length with thousand little brooks runnes sliding,
His fellow course along with *Hepar* chanels guiding.

1. The Heart is immured partly by a membrane going round about it, (and thence receiving his name) and a peculiar tunicle; partly with an humour like whey or urine, as well to cool the heart, as to lighten the body. [This and the following footnotes are Fletcher's.]

2. In the heart are foure great vessels: the first is the hollow vein bringing in the bloud from the liver; at whose mouth stand three little folding doores, with three forks giving passage, but no return to the bloud.

3. The second vessel is called the arterie-vein, which rising from the right side of the heart, carries down the bloud here prepared to the lungs for their nourishment. Here also is the like three-folding doore, made like half-circles; giving passage from the heart, but not backward.

4. The third is called the Veiny arterie, rising from the left side, which hath two folds three-forked.

5. The fourth is the great arterie. This hath also a floudgate made of three semi-circular membranes, to give out load to the vitall spirits, and stop their regresse.

ANONYMOUS
(1600)

'Thule, the Period of Cosmography ...'

Thule, the period of Cosmography,
  Doth vaunt of Hecla, whose sulphurious fire
Doth melt the frozen clime and thaw the sky;
  Trinacrian Aetna's flames ascend not higher.
These things seem wondrous, yet more wondrous I,
Whose heart with fear doth freeze, with love doth fry.

The Andalusian merchant, that returns
  Laden with cochineal and China dishes,
Reports in Spain how strangely Fogo burns
  Amidst an ocean full of flying fishes.
These things seem wondrous, yet more wondrous I,
Whose heart with fear doth freeze, with love doth fry.

SIR WILLIAM D'AVENANT
(1606–68)

Gondibert★

stanzas 15–20

THE OPTICK TUBES

He shews them now Tow'rs of prodigious height,
  Where Natures Friends, Philosophers, remain,
To censure Meteors in their cause and flight;
  And watch the Wind's authority on Rain.

Others with Optick Tubes the Moons scant face
  (Vaste Tubes, which like long Cedars mounted lie)
Attract through Glasses to so neer a space,
  As if they came not to survey, but prie.

Nine hasty Centuries are now fulfill'd,
  Since Opticks first were known to *Astragon*;
By whom the Moderns are become so skill'd,
  They dream of seeing to the Maker's Throne.

And wisely *Astragon*, thus busy grew,
   To seek the Stars remote societies;
And judge the walks of th' old, by finding new;
   For Nature's law, in correspondence lies.

Man's pride (grown to Religion) he abates,
   By moving our lov'd Earth; which we think fix'd;
Think all to it, and it to none relates;
   With others motion scorn to have it mix'd:

As if 'twere great and stately to stand still
   Whilst other Orbes dance on; or else think all
Those vaste bright Globes (to shew God's needless skill)
   Were made but to attend our little Ball.

Gondibert

stanzas 31–5

THE CABINET OF DEATH

From hence (fresh Nature's flourishing Estate!)
   They to her wither'd Receptacle come;
Where she appears the loathsome Slave of Fate;
   For here her various Dead possess the Room.

This dismall Gall'ry, lofty, long, and wide;
   Was hung with *Skelitons* of ev'ry kinde;
Humane, and all that learned humane pride
   Thinks made t' obey Man's high immortal Minde.

Yet on that Wall hangs he too, who so thought;
   And she dry'd by him, whom that He obay'd;
By her an *El'phant* that with Heards had fought,
   Of which the smallest Beast made her afraid.

Next it, a Whale is high in Cables ty'd,
   Whole strength might Herds of Elephants controul;
Then all, (in payres of ev'ry kinde) they spy'd
   Which Death's wrack leaves, of Fishes, Beasts, and Fowl.

These *Astragon* (to watch with curious Eie
   The diff'rent Tenements of living breath)
Collects, with what far Travailers supplie;
   And this was call'd, THE CABINET OF DEATH.

JOHN MILTON

(1608–74)

Paradise Lost

Book I, lines 283–91

GALILEO

He scarce had ceas't when the superiour Fiend
Was moving toward the shore; his ponderous shield★
Ethereal temper, massy, large and round,
Behind him cast; the broad circumference
Hung on his shoulders like the Moon, whose Orb
Through Optic Glass the *Tuscan* Artist★ views
At Ev'ning from the top of *Fesole*,
Or in *Valdarno*, to descry new Lands,
Rivers or Mountains in her spotty Globe.

Paradise Lost

Book II, lines 890–938

CHAOS

Before thir eyes in sudden view appear
The secrets of the hoarie Deep, a dark
Illimitable Ocean without bound,
Without dimension, where length, bredth, and highth,
And time and place are lost; where eldest *Night*
And *Chaos*, Ancestors of Nature, hold
Eternal Anarchie, amidst the noise
Of endless warrs, and by confusion stand.
For hot, cold, moist, and dry, four Champions fierce
Strive here for Maistrie, and to Battel bring
Thir embryon Atoms; they around the flag
Of each his Faction, in thir several Clanns,
Light-armd or heavy, sharp, smooth, swift or slow,
Swarm populous, unnumberd as the Sands
Of *Barca* or *Cyrene's* torrid soil,
Levied to side with warring Winds, and poise
Thir lighter wings. To whom these most adhere,

Hee rules a moment; *Chaos* Umpire sits,
And by decision more imbroiles the fray
By which he Reigns: next him high Arbiter
Chance governs all. Into this wilde Abyss,
The Womb of Nature and perhaps her Grave,
Of neither Sea, nor Shore, nor Air, nor Fire,
But all these in thir pregnant causes mixt
Confus'dly, and which thus must ever fight,
Unless th' Almighty Maker them ordain
His dark materials to create more Worlds,
Into this wilde Abyss the warie Fiend
Stood on the brink of Hell and lookd a while,
Pondering his Voyage; for no narrow frith
He had to cross. Nor was his eare less peald
With noises loud and ruinous (to compare
Great things with small) then when *Bellona* storms,
With all her battering Engins bent to rase
Som Capital City; or less then if this frame
Of Heav'n were falling, and these Elements
In mutinie had from her Axle torn
The stedfast Earth. At last his Sail-broad Vannes
He spreads for flight, and in the surging smoak
Uplifted spurns the ground, thence many a League
As in a cloudy Chair ascending rides
Audacious, but that seat soon failing, meets
A vast vacuitie: all unawares
Fluttring his pennons vain plumb down he drops
Ten thousand fadom deep, and to this hour
Down had been falling, had not by ill chance
The strong rebuff of som tumultuous cloud
Instinct with Fire and Nitre hurried him
As many miles aloft . . .

Paradise Lost

Book VIII, lines 15–38, 66–178

'WHAT IF THE SUN BE CENTER TO THE WORLD ...?'

When I behold this goodly Frame, this World
Of Heav'n and Earth consisting, and compute
Thir magnitudes, this Earth a spot, a graine,
An Atom, with the Firmament compar'd
And all her numbered Starrs, that seem to rowle
Spaces incomprehensible (for such
Thir distance argues and thir swift return
Diurnal) meerly to officiat light
Round this opacous Earth, this punctual spot,
One day and night; in all thir vast survey
Useless besides; reasoning I oft admire,
How Nature wise and frugal could commit
Such disproportions with superfluous hand
So many nobler Bodies to create,
Greater so manifold, to this one use,
For aught appeers, and on thir Orbs impose
Such restless revolution day by day
Repeated, while the sedentarie Earth,
That better might with farr less compass move,
Serv'd by more noble then her self, attaines
Her end without least motion, and receaves
As Tribute such a sumless journey brought
Of incorporeal speed, her warmth and light;
Speed, to describe whose swiftness Number failes.

★

To ask or search I blame thee not, for Heav'n
Is as the Book of God before thee set,
Wherein to read his wondrous Works, and learne
His Seasons, Hours, or Days, or Months, or Yeares:
This to attain, whether Heav'n move or Earth,
Imports not, if thou reck'n right; the rest
From Man or Angel the great Architect
Did wisely to conceal, and not divulge
His secrets to be scannd by them who ought
Rather admire; or if they list to try

Conjecture, he his Fabric of the Heav'ns
Hath left to thir disputes, perhaps to move
His laughter at thir quaint Opinions wide
Hereafter, when they come to model Heav'n
And calculate the Starrs, how they will weild
The mightie frame, how build, unbuild, contrive
To save appeerances, how gird the Sphear
With Centric and Eccentric scribl'd ore,
Cycle and Epicycle, Orb in Orb:
Alreadie by thy reasoning this I guess,
Who art to lead thy offspring, and supposest
That Bodies bright and greater should not serve
The less not bright, nor Heav'n such journies run,
Earth sitting still, when she alone receaves
The benefit: consider first, that Great
Or Bright inferrs not Excellence: the Earth
Though, in comparison of Heav'n, so small,
Nor glistering, may of solid good containe
More plenty then the Sun that barren shines,
Whose vertue on it self works no effect,
But in the fruitful Earth; there first receavd
His beams, unactive else, thir vigor find.
Yet not to Earth are those bright Luminaries
Officious, but to thee Earths habitant.
And for the Heav'ns wide Circuit, let it speak
The Makers high magnificence, who built
So spacious, and his Line stretchd out so farr;
That Man may know he dwells not in his own;
An Edifice too large for him to fill,
Lodg'd in a small partition, and the rest
Ordaind for uses to his Lord best known.
The swiftness of those Circles attribute,
Though numberless, to his Omnipotence,
That to corporeal substances could adde
Speed almost Spiritual; mee thou thinkst not slow,
Who since the Morning hour set out from Heav'n
Where God resides, and ere mid-day arriv'd
In *Eden*, distance inexpressible
By Numbers that have name. But this I urge,
Admitting Motion in the Heav'ns to shew
Invalid that which thee to doubt it mov'd;

Not that I so affirm, though so it seem
To thee who hast thy dwelling here on Earth.
God to remove his wayes from human sense,
Plac'd Heav'n from Earth so farr, that earthly sight,
If it presume, might erre in things too high,
And no advantage gaine. What if the Sun
Be Center to the World, and other Starrs
By his attractive vertue and thir own
Incited, dance about him various rounds?
Thir wandring course now high, now low, then hid,
Progressive, retrograde, or standing still,
In six thou seest, and what if sev'nth to these
The Planet Earth, so stedfast though she seem,
Insensibly three different Motions move?
Which else to several Sphears thou must ascribe,
Mov'd contrarie with thwart obliquities,
Or save the Sun his labour, and that swift
Nocturnal and Diurnal rhomb suppos'd,
Invisible else above all Starrs, the Wheele
Of Day and Night; which needs not thy beleefe,
If Earth industrious of her self fetch Day
Travelling East, and with her part averse
From the Suns beam meet Night, her other part
Still luminous by his ray. What if that light
Sent from her through the wide transpicuous aire,
To the terrestrial Moon be as a Starr
Enlightning her by Day, as shee by Night
This Earth? reciprocal, if Land be there,
Feilds and Inhabitants: Her spots thou seest
As Clouds, and Clouds may rain, and Rain produce
Fruits in her soft'nd Soile, for some to eat
Allotted there, and other Suns perhaps
With thir attendant Moons thou wilt descrie
Communicating Male and Female Light,
Which two great Sexes animate the World,
Stor'd in each Orb perhaps with some that live.
For such vast room in Nature unpossest
By living Soule, desert and desolate,
Onely to shine, yet scarce to contribute
Each Orb a glimps of Light, conveyd so farr
Down to this habitable, which returnes

Light back to them, is obvious to dispute.
But whether thus these things, or whether not,
Whether the Sun predominant in Heav'n
Rise on the Earth, or Earth rise on the Sun,
Hee from the East his flaming rode begin,
Or Shee from West her silent course advance
With inoffensive pace that spinning sleeps
On her soft Axle, while she paces Eev'n,
And bears thee soft with the smooth Air along,
Sollicit not thy thoughts with matters hid,
Leave them to God above, him serve and feare;
Of other Creatures, as him pleases best,
Wherever plac't, let him dispose: joy thou
In what he gives to thee, this Paradise
And thy faire *Eve*; Heav'n is for thee too high
To know what passes there; be lowlie wise:
Think onely what concernes thee and thy being;
Dream not of other Worlds, what Creatures there
Live, in what state, condition or degree,
Contented that thus farr hath been reveald
Not of Earth onely but of highest Heav'n.

Sonnet XXI

TO CYRIACK SKINNER

Cyriack, whose Grandsire on the Royal Bench
  Of Brittish *Themis*, with no mean applause
  Pronounc't and in his volumes taught our Lawes,
  Which others at their Barr so often wrench:
To day deep thoughts resolve with me to drench
  In mirth, that after no repenting drawes;
  Let *Euclid* rest and *Archimedes* pause,
  And what the *Swede* intends, and what the *French*.*
To measure life, learn thou betimes, and know
  Toward solid good what leads the nearest way;
  For other things mild Heav'n a time ordains,
And disapproves that care, though wise in show,
  That with superfluous burden loads the day,
  And when God sends a cheerful hour, refrains.

SAMUEL BUTLER

(1612–80)

From *The Elephant in the Moon*

A learned society of late,
The glory of a foreign state,
Agreed, upon a summer's night,
To search the Moon by her own light;
To make an inventory of all
Her real estate, and personal;
And make an accurate survey
Of all her lands, and how they lay,
As true as that of Ireland, where
The sly surveyors stole a shire:
T' observe her country, how 'twas planted,
With what sh' abounded most, or wanted;
And make the proper'st observations
For settling of new plantations,
If the society should incline
T' attempt so glorious a design.
  This was the purpose of their meeting,
For which they chose a time as fitting;
When at the full her radiant light
And influence too were at their height.
And now the lofty tube, the scale
With which they heaven itself assail,
Was mounted full against the Moon;
And all stood ready to fall on,
Impatient who should have the honour
To plant an ensign first upon her.
When one,* who for his deep belief
Was virtuoso* then in chief,
Approved the most profound, and wise,
To solve impossibilities,
Advancing gravely, to apply
To th' optic glass his judging eye,
Cried, 'Strange!' – then reinforced his sight
Against the Moon with all his might,
And bent his penetrating brow,
As if he meant to gaze her through;

When all the rest began t' admire,
And, like a train, from him took fire,
Surprised with wonder, beforehand,
At what they did not understand,
Cried out, impatient to know what
The matter was they wondered at.
　　Quoth he, 'Th' inhabitants o' th' Moon,
Who, when the Sun shines hot at noon,
Do live in cellars underground,
Of eight miles deep, and eighty round,
In which at once they fortify
Against the sun and th' enemy,
Which they count towns and cities there,
Because their people's civiller
Than those rude peasants, that are found
To live upon the upper ground,
Called Privolvans,* with whom they are
Perpetually in open war;
And now both armies, highly enraged,
Are in a bloody fight engaged,
And many fall on both sides slain,
As by the glass 'tis clear, and plain.
Look quickly then, that every one
May see the fight before 'tis done.'
　　With that a great philosopher,*
Admired, and famous far and near,
As one of singular invention,
But universal comprehension,
Applied one eye, and half a nose
Unto the optic engine close.

*

Quoth he, 'A stranger sight appears
Than e'er was seen in all the spheres,
A wonder more unparalleled,
Than ever mortal tube beheld;
An elephant from one of those
Two mighty armies is broke loose,
And with the horror of the fight
Appears amazed, and in a fright;
Look quickly, lest the sight of us

Should cause the startled beast t' imboss.
It is a large one, far more great
Than e'er was bred in Afric yet;
From which we boldly may infer,
The Moon is much the fruitfuller.

★

'Most excellent and virtuous friends,
This great discovery makes amends
For all our unsuccessful pains,
And lost expense of time and brains.
For, by this sole phenomenon,
We 'ave gotten ground upon the Moon;
And gained a pass, to hold dispute
With all the planets that stand out;
To carry this most virtuous war
Home to the door of every star,
And plant th' artillery of our tubes
Against their proudest magnitudes . . .'

★

This said, they all with one consent,
Agreed to draw up th' instrument,
And, for the general satisfaction,
To print it in the next 'Transaction.'
   But, whilst the chiefs were drawing up
This strange memoir o' th' telescope,
One, peeping in the tube by chance,
Beheld the elephant advance.
And, from the west side of the Moon
To th' east was in a moment gone.
This being related, gave a stop
To what the rest were drawing up;
And every man, amazed anew
How it could possibly be true,
That any beast should run a race
So monstrous, in so short a space,
Resolved, howe'er, to make it good,
At least, as possible as he could;
And rather his own eyes condemn,
Than question what h' had seen with them.

★

SAMUEL BUTLER

But, while they were diverted all
With wording the memorial,
The footboys, for diversion too,
As having nothing else to do,
Seeing the telescope at leisure,
Turned virtuosos for their pleasure;
Began to gaze upon the Moon,
As those they waited on, had done,
With monkeys' ingenuity,
That love to practise what they see;
When one, whose turn it was to peep,
Saw something in the engine creep;
And, viewing well, discovered more
Than all the learned had done before.
Quoth he,* 'A little thing is slunk
Into the long star-gazing trunk;
And now is gotten down so nigh,
I have him just against mine eye.'

   This being overheard by one,
Who was not so far overgrown
In any virtuous speculation,
To judge with mere imagination,
Immediately he made a guess
At solving all appearances,
A way far more significant,
Than all their hints of th' elephant,
And found, upon a second view,
His own hypothesis most true;
For he had scarce applied his eye
To th' engine, but immediately
He found a mouse was gotten in
The hollow tube, and, shut between
The two glass windows in restraint
Was swelled into an elephant;
And proved the virtuous occasion
Of all this learnèd dissertation;
And, as a mountain* heretofore
Was great with child, they say, and bore
A silly mouse; this mouse, as strange,
Brought forth a mountain, in exchange.

*

97

But when they had unscrewed the glass,
To find out where th' impostor was,
And saw the mouse, that by mishap
Had made the telescope a trap,
Amazed, confounded, and afflicted,
To be so openly convicted,
Immediately they get them gone,
With this discovery alone;
That those who greedily pursue
Things wonderful, instead of true;
That in their speculations choose
To make discoveries strange news;
And natural history a gazette
Of tales stupendous, and far-fet;
Hold no truth worthy to be known,
That is not huge and overgrown,
And explicate appearances,
Not as they are, but as they please,
In vain strive nature to suborn,
And, for their pains, are paid with scorn.

From *Hudibras*
Canto III

SIDROPHEL

This said, he turned about his steed,
And eftsoons on th' adventure rid;
Where leave we him and Ralph a while,
And to the Conjurer turn our style,
To let our reader understand
What's useful of him before-hand.
He had been long t'wards mathematics,
Optics, philosophy, and statics,
Magic, horoscopy, astrology,
And was old dog at physiology;
But as a dog that turns the spit
Bestirs himself, and plies his feet
To climb the wheel, but all in vain,
His own weight brings him down again,

And still he's in the self-same place
Where at his setting out he was;
So in the circle of the arts
Did he advance his natural parts,
Till falling back still, for retreat,
He fell to juggle, cant, and cheat:
For as those fowls that live in water
Are never wet, he did but smatter;
Whate'er he laboured to appear,
His understanding still was clear;
Yet none a deeper knowledge boasted,
Since old Hodge Bacon, and Bob Grosted.
Th' intelligible world he knew,
And all men dream on't to be true,
That in this world there's not a wart
That has not there a counterpart;
Nor can there, on the face of ground
An individual beard be found
That has not, in that foreign nation,
A fellow of the self-same fashion;
So cut, so coloured, and so curled,
As those are in th' inferior world.
He 'ad read Dee's prefaces★ before
The devil, and Euclid, o'er and o'er;
And all th' intrigues 'twixt him and Kelly,★
Lescus★ and th' emperor, wou'd tell ye:
But with the moon was more familiar
Than e'er was almanack well-willer;
Her secrets understood so clear,
That some believed he had been there;
Knew when she was in fittest mood
For cutting corns, or letting blood;
When for anointing scabs and itches,
Or to the bum applying leeches;
When sows and bitches may be spay'd,
And in what sign best cyder's made;
Whether the wane be, or increase,
Best to set garlic, or sow peas;
Who first found out the man i' th' moon,
That to the ancients was unknown;
How many dukes, and earls, and peers,

Are in the planetary spheres,
Their airy empire, and command,
Their several strengths by sea and land . . .

HENRY MORE
(1614–87)

Psychathanasia or The Immortality of the Soul
Book III, Canto III, stanzas 59–60

THE SUN AS LOGOS

The Argument,

That th'earth doth move, proofs Physicall
    Unto us do descrie;
Add reasons Theosophicall,
    Als add Astronomie.

The Eternall Son of God, who *Logos* hight,
Made all things in a fit proportion;
Wherefore, I wote, no man that judgeth right
In Heaven will make such a confusion,
That courses of unlike extension,
Vastly unlike, in like time shall be run
By the flight stars. Such huge distension
Of place, shews that their time is not all one;
Saturn his ring no'te finish as quick as the moon.

Yet if the earth stand stupid and unmov'd,
This needs must come to passe. For they go round
In every twice twelve hours, as is prov'd
By dayly experience. But it would confound
The worlds right order, if't were surely found
A reall motion. Wherefore let it be
In them but seeming, but a reall round
In th' Earth it self. The world so's setten free
From that untoward disproportionalitie.

The Infinity of Worlds

stanzas 20–22, 77–9

THE COPERNICAN COSMOLOGY; NOVAS

And to speak out; though I detest the sect
Of *Epicurus* for their manners vile,
Yet what is true I may not well reject.
Truth's incorruptible, ne can the style
Of vitious pen her sacred worth defile.
If we no more of truth should deign t' embrace
Then what unworthy mouths did never soyle,
No truths at all 'mongst men would finden place,
But make them speedy wings and back to Heaven apace.

I will not say our world is infinite,
But that infinity of worlds there be;
The Centre of our world's the lively light
Of the warm sunne, the visible Deity
Of this externall Temple. *Mercurie*
Next plac'd and warm'd more throughly by his rayes,
Right nimbly 'bout his golden head doth fly:
Then *Venus* nothing slow about him strayes,
And next our *Earth* though seeming sad full sprightly playes.

And after her *Mars* rangeth in a round
With fiery locks and angry flaming eye,
And next to him mild *Jupiter* is found,
But *Saturn* cold wons in our outmost sky.
The skirts of his large Kingdome surely ly
Near to the confines of some other worlds
Whose Centres are the fixèd starres on high,
'Bout which as their own proper Suns are hurld
Joves, *Earths*, and *Saturns*: round on their own axes twurld.

*

Witnesse ye Heavens if what I say's not true,
Ye flaming Comets wandering on high,
And new fixt starres found in that Circle blue,
The one espide in glittering *Cassiopie*,*
The other near to *Ophiucbus** thigh.
Both bigger then the biggest starres that are,

And yet as farre remov'd from mortall eye
As are the furthest, so those Arts declare
Unto whose reaching sight Heavens mysteries lie bare.

Wherefore these new-seen lights were greater once
By many thousand times then this our sphear
Wherein we live, 'twixt good and evil chance.
Which to my musing mind doth strange appear
If those large bodies then first shapèd were.
For should so goodly things so soon decay?
Neither did last the full space of two year.
Wherefore I cannot deem that their first day
Of being, when to us they sent out shining ray.

But that they were created both of old,
And each in his due time did fair display
Themselves in radiant locks more bright then gold,
Or silver sheen purg'd from all drossie clay,
But how they could themselves in this array
Expose to humane sight who did before
Lie hid, is that which well amazen may
The wisest man and puzzle evermore:
Yet my unwearied thoughts this search could not give o're.

From *Insomnium Philosophicum**

Behold a mighty Orb right well compil'd
And kned together of opacous mould.
That neither curse of God nor man defil'd,
Though wicked wights as shall anon be told
　　Did curse the ill condition of the place,
　　And with foul speech this goodly work disgrace.

But vain complaints may weary the ill tongue
And evil speeches the blasphemer stain,
But words Gods sacred works can never wrong,
Nor wrongful deeming work dame Natures bane.
　　Who misconceives, conceives but his own ill,
　　Brings forth a falshood, shows his want of skill.

This globe in all things punctually did seem
Like to our earth saving in magnitude:

For it of so great vastnesse was, I ween,
That if that all the Planets were transmewd
 Into one Ball, they'd not exceed this Round
 Nor yet fall short though close together bound.

At a farre distance from this sphear was pight
(More then the journey of ten thousand year
An hundred times told over, that swiftest flight
Of bird should mete, that distance did appear)
 There was there pight a massie Orb of light
 Aequall with this dark Orb in bignesse right.

Half therefore just of this dark Orb was dight
With goodly glistre and fair golden rayes,
And ever half was hid in horrid Night.
A duskish Cylindre through infinite space
 It did project, which still unmovèd staid,
 Strange sight it was to see so endlesse shade.

Th' Diametre of that Nocturnall Roll
Was the right Axis of this opake sphear.
On which eternally it round did roll.
In Aequinoctiall posture 't did appear,
 So as when Libra weighs out in just weight
 An equall share to men of Day and Night.

ABRAHAM COWLEY
(1618–67)

Ode upon Dr Harvey

Coy Nature, (which remain'd, though aged grown,
A Beauteous virgin still, injoy'd by none,
 Nor seen unveil'd by any one)
When *Harveys* violent passion she did see,
Began to tremble, and to flee,
Took Sanctuary like *Daphne* in a tree:
There *Daphnes* lover stop't, and thought it much
 The very Leaves of her to touch,
But *Harvey* our *Apollo*, stopt not so,
Into the Bark, and root he after her did goe:

No smallest Fibres of a Plant,
For which the eiebeams Point doth sharpness want,
His passage after her withstood.
What should she do? through all the moving wood
Of Lives indow'd with sense she took her flight,
Harvey persues, and keeps her still in sight.
But as the Deer long-hunted takes a flood,
She leap't at last into the winding streams of blood;
Of mans *Meander* all the Purple reaches made,
Till at the heart she stay'd,
Where turning head, and at a Bay,
Thus, by well-purged ears, was she o're-heard to say.

Here sure shall I be safe (said she)
None will be able sure to see
This my retreat, but only He
Who made both it and me.
The heart of Man, what Art can e're reveal?
A wall impervious between
Divides the very Parts within,
And doth the Heart of man ev'n from its self conceal.
She spoke, but e're she was aware,
Harvey was with her there,
And held this slippery *Proteus* in a chain,
Till all her mighty Mysteries she descry'd,
Which from his wit the attempt before to hide
Was the first Thing that Nature did in vain.

He the young Practise of New life did see,
Whil'st to conceal its toilsome Poverty,
It for a living wrought, both hard, and privately.
Before the Liver understood
The noble Scarlet Dye of Blood,
Before one drop was by it made,
Or brought into it, to set up the Trade;
Before the untaught Heart began to beat
The tuneful March to vital Heat,
From all the Souls that living Buildings rear,
Whether imply'd for Earth, or Sea, or Air,
Whether it in the Womb or Egg be wrought,
A strict account to him is hourly brought,
How the Great Fabrick does proceed,

What time and what materials it does need.
He so exactly does the work survey,
As if he hir'd the workers by the day.

Thus *Harvey* sought for Truth in Truth's own Book
    The Creatures, which by God himself was writ;
        And wisely thought 'twas fit,
Not to read Comments only upon it,
But on th'original it self to look.
Methinks in Arts great Circle others stand
    Lock't up together, Hand in Hand,
    Every one leads as he is led,
    The same bare path they tread,
A Dance like Fairies a Fantastick round,
But neither change their motion, nor their ground:
Had *Harvey* to this Road confin'd his wit,
His noble Circle of the Blood, had been untroden yet.
Great Doctor! Th' Art of Curing's cur'd by thee,
    We now thy patient Physick see,
From all inveterate diseases free,
    Purg'd of old errors by thy care,
New dieted, put forth to clearer air,
    It now will strong and healthful prove,
It self before Lethargick lay, and could not move.

These useful secrets to his Pen we owe,
And thousands more 'twas ready to bestow;
Of which a barb'rous Wars unlearned Rage
    Has robb'd the ruin'd age;
O cruel loss! as if the Golden Fleece,
    With so much cost, and labour bought,
And from a far by a Great *Heroe* brought
    Had sunk ev'n in the Ports of *Greece*.
O cursed Warr! who can forgive thee this?
    Houses and Towns may rise again,
    And ten times easier it is
To rebuild *Pauls*, than any work of his.
That mighty Task none but himself can do,
    Nay, scarce himself too now,
For though his Wit the force of Age withstand,
His Body alas! and Time it must command,
And Nature now, so long by him surpass't,
Will sure have her revenge on him at last.

Ode to the Royal Society

Philosophy the great and only Heir
  Of all that Human Knowledge which has bin
Unforfeited by Mans rebellious Sin,
  Though full of years He do appear,
(Philosophy, I say, and call it, He,
For whatso'ere the Painters Fancy be,
  It a Male-virtue seemes to me)
Has still been kept in Nonage till of late,
Nor manag'd or enjoy'd his vast Estate:
Three or four thousand years one would have thought,
To ripeness and perfection might have brought
  A Science so well bred and nurst,
And of such hopeful parts too at the first.
But, oh, the Guardians and the Tutors then,
(Some negligent, and some ambitious men)
  Would ne're consent to set him Free,
Or his own Natural Powers to let him see,
Lest that should put an end to their Autoritie.

That his own business he might quite forget,
They' amus'd him with the sports of wanton Wit,
With the Desserts of Poetry they fed him,
In stead of solid meats t' encrease his force;
In stead of vigorous exercise they led him
Into the pleasant Labyrinths of ever-fresh Discourse:
  In stead of carrying him to see
The Riches which doe hoorded for him lie
  In Natures endless Treasurie,
  They chose his Eye to entertain
  (His curious but not covetous Eye)
With painted Scenes, and Pageants of the Brain.
Some few exalted Spirits this latter Age has shown,
That labour'd to assert the Liberty
(From Guardians, who were now Usurpers grown)
Of this old *Minor* still, Captiv'd Philosophy;
  But 'twas Rebellion call'd to fight
  For such a long-oppressed Right.
Bacon at last, a mighty Man, arose
  Whom a wise King and Nature chose
  Lord Chancellour of both their Lawes,
And boldly undertook the injur'd Pupils cause.

Autority, which did a Body boast,
Though 'twas but Air condens'd, and stalk'd about,
Like some old Giants more Gigantic Ghost,
   To terrifie the Learned Rout
With the plain Magick of true Reasons Light,
   He chac'd out of our sight,
Nor suffer'd Living *Men* to be misled
   By the vain shadows of the Dead:
To Graves, from whence it rose, the conquer'd Phantome fled;
   He broke that Monstrous God which stood
In midst of th' Orchard, and the whole did claim,
   Which with a useless Sith of Wood,
   And something else not worth a name,
   (Both vast for shew, yet neither fit
   Or to Defend, or to Beget;
   Ridiculous and senceless Terrors!) made
Children and superstitious Men afraid.
   The Orchard's open now, and free;
Bacon has broke that Scar-crow Deitie;
   Come, enter, all that will,
Behold the rip'ned Fruit, come gather now your Fill.
   Yet still, methinks, we fain would be
   Catching at the Forbidden Tree,
   We would be like the Deitie,
When Truth and Falshood, Good and Evil, we
Without the Sences aid within our selves would see;
   For 'tis God only who can find
   All Nature in his Mind.

From Words, which are but Pictures of the Thought,
   (Though we our Thoughts from them perversly drew)
To things, the Minds right Object, he it brought,
Like foolish Birds to painted Grapes we flew;
He sought and gather'd for our use the True;
And when on heaps the chosen Bunches lay,
He prest them wisely the Mechanick way,
Till all their juyce did in one Vessel joyn,
Ferment into a Nourishment Divine,
   The thirsty Souls refreshing Wine.
Who to the life an exact Piece would make,
Must not from others Work a Copy take;
   No, not from *Rubens* or *Vandike*;

Much less content himself to make it like
Th' Idaeas and the Images which lie
In his own Fancy, or his Memory.
 No, he before his sight must place
 The Natural and Living Face;
 The real object must command
Each Judgment of his Eye, and Motion of his Hand.

From these and all long Errors of the way,
In which our wandring Praedecessors went,
And like th' old *Hebrews* many years did stray
 In Desarts but of small extent,
Bacon, like *Moses*, led us forth at last,
 The barren Wilderness he past,
 Did on the very Border stand
 Of the blest promis'd Land,
And from the Mountains Top of his Exalted Wit,
 Saw it himself, and shew'd us it.
But Life did never to one Man allow
Time to Discover Worlds, and Conquer too;
Nor can so short a Line sufficient be
To fadome the vast depths of Natures Sea:
 The work he did we ought t' admire,
And were unjust if we should more require
From his few years, divided 'twixt th' Excess
Of low Affliction, and high Happiness.
For who on things remote can fix his sight,
That's alwayes in a Triumph, or a Fight?

From you, great Champions, we expect to get
These spacious Countries but discover'd yet;
Countries where yet in stead of Nature, we
Her Images and Idols worship'd see:
These large and wealthy Regions to subdue,
Though Learning has whole Armies at command,
 Quarter'd about in every Land,
A better Troop she ne're together drew.
 Methinks, like *Gideon*'s little Band,
 God with Design has pickt out you,
To do these noble Wonders by a Few:
When the whole Host he saw, They are (said he)
 Too many to O'rcome for Me;

And now he chuses out his Men,
Much in the way that he did then:
Not those many whom he found
Idely extended on the ground,
To drink with their dejected head
The Stream just so as by their Mouths it fled:
No, but those Few who took the waters up,
And made of their laborious Hands the Cup.

Thus you prepar'd; and in the glorious Fight
Their wondrous pattern too you take:
Their old and empty Pitchers first they brake,
And with their Hands then lifted up the Light.
Io! Sound too the Trumpets here!
Already your victorious Lights appear;
New Scenes of Heaven already we espy,
And Crowds of golden Worlds on high;
Which from the spacious Plains of Earth and Sea;
Could never yet discover'd be
By Sailers or *Chaldaeans* watchful Eye.
Natures great Workes no distance can obscure,
No smalness her near Objects can secure
Y' have taught the curious Sight to press
Into the privatest recess
Of her imperceptible Littleness.
Y' have learn'd to Read her smallest Hand,
And well begun her deepest Sense to Understand.

Mischief and true Dishonour fall on those
Who would to laughter or to scorn expose
So Virtuous and so Noble a Design,
So Human for its Use, for Knowledge so Divine.
The things which these proud men despise, and call
Impertinent, and vain, and small,
Those smallest things of Nature let me know,
Rather than all their greatest Actions Doe.
Whoever would Deposed Truth advance
Into the Throne usurp'd from it,
Must feel at first the Blows of Ignorance,
And the sharp Points of Envious Wit.
So when by various turns of the Celestial Dance,
In many thousand years

A Star, so long unknown, appears,
Though Heaven it self more beauteous by it grow,
It troubles and alarms the World below,
Does to the Wise a Star, to Fools a Meteor show.

With Courage and Success you the bold work begin;
   Your Cradle has not Idle bin:
None e're but *Hercules* and you could be
At five years Age worthy a History.
   And ne're did Fortune better yet
   Th' Historian to the Story fit:
   As you from all Old Errors free
And purge the Body of Philosophy;
   So from all Modern Folies He
Has vindicated Eloquence and Wit.
His candid Stile like a clean Stream does slide,
   And his bright Fancy all the way
   Does like the Sun-shine in it play;
It does like *Thames*, the best of Rivers, glide,
Where the God does not rudely overturn,
   But gently pour the Crystal Urn,
And with judicious hand does the whole Current Guide.
T' has all the Beauties Nature can impart,
And all the comely Dress without the paint of Art.

ANDREW MARVELL
(1621–78)

The Definition of Love

My Love is of a birth as rare
   As 'tis for object strange and high;
It was begotten by Despair,
   Upon Impossibility.

Magnanimous Despair alone
   Could show me so divine a thing,
Where feeble hope could ne'er have flown,
   But vainly flapped its tinsel wing.

And yet I quickly might arrive
  Where my extended soul is fixed;
But Fate does iron wedges drive,
  And always crowds itself betwixt.

For Fate with jealous eye does see
  Two perfect loves, nor lets them close;
Their union would her ruin be,
  And her tyrannic power depose

And therefore her decrees of steel
  Us as the distant poles have placed,
(Though Love's whole world on us doth wheel),
  Not by themselves to be embraced,

Unless the giddy heaven fall,
  And earth some new convulsion tear,
And, us to join, the world should all
  Be cramped into a planisphere.

As lines, so love's oblique, may well
  Themselves in every angle greet:
But ours, so truly parallel,
  Though infinite, can never meet.

Therefore the love which us doth bind,
  But Fate so enviously debars,
Is the conjunction of the mind,
  And opposition of the stars.

JOHN DRYDEN
(1631–1700)

Upon the Death of the Lord Hastings

Must Noble *Hastings* Immaturely die,
(The Honour of his ancient Family?)
Beauty and Learning thus together meet,
To bring a *Winding* for a *Wedding-sheet*?
Must *Vertue* prove *Death*'s Harbinger? Must She,

With him expiring, feel Mortality?
Is *Death* (Sin's wages) Grace's now? shall Art
Make us more Learned, onely to depart?
If Merit be Disease, if Vertue Death;
To be Good, Not to be; who'd then bequeath
Himself to Discipline? Who'd not esteem
Labour a Crime, Study Self-murther deem?
Our *Noble Youth* now have pretence to be
Dunces securely, Ign'rant healthfully.
Rare Linguist! whose Worth speaks it self, whose Praise,
Though not his Own, all Tongues Besides do raise:
Then Whom, Great *Alexander* may seem Less;
Who conquer'd Men, but not their Languages.
In his mouth Nations speak; his Tongue might be
Interpreter to *Greece, France, Italy.*
His native Soyl was the Four parts o' th' Earth;
All *Europe* was too narrow for his Birth.
A young Apostle; and (with rev'rence may
I speak'it) inspir'd with gift of Tongues, as They.
Nature gave him, a Childe, what Men in vain
Oft strive, by Art though further'd, to obtain.
His Body was an Orb, his sublime Soul
Did move on Vertue's and on Learning's Pole:
Whose Reg'lar Motions better to our view,
Then *Archimedes* Sphere, the Heavens did shew.
Graces and Vertues, Languages and Arts,
Beauty and Learning, fill'd up all the parts.
Heav'ns Gifts, which do, like falling Stars, appear
Scatter'd in Others; all, as in their Sphear,
Were fix'd and conglobate in 's Soul; and thence
Shone th'row his Body, with sweet Influence;
Letting their Glories so on each Limb fall,
The whole Frame render'd was Celestial.
Come, learned *Ptolomy*, and trial make,
If thou this Hero's Altitude canst take;
But that transcends thy skill; thrice happie all,
Could we but prove thus Astronomical.
Liv'd *Tycho* now, struck with this Ray, (which shone
More bright i' th' Morn, then others beam at Noon)
He'd take his *Astrolabe,*★ and seek out here
What new Star 't was did gild our Hemisphere.

Replenish'd then with such rare Gifts as these,
Where was room left for such a Foul Disease?*
The Nations sin hath drawn that Veil, which shrouds
Our Day-spring in so sad benighting Clouds.
Heaven would no longer trust its Pledge; but thus
Recall'd it; rapt its *Ganymede* from us.
Was there no milder way but the Small Pox,
The very Filth'ness of *Pandora*'s Box?
So many Spots, like *naeves*,* our *Venus* soil?
One Jewel set off with so many a Foil?
Blisters with pride swell'd; which th'row 's flesh did sprout
Like Rose-buds, stuck i' th' Lily-skin about.
Each little Pimple had a Tear in it,
To wail the fault its rising did commit:
Who, Rebel-like, with their own Lord at strife,
Thus made an Insurrection 'gainst his Life.
Or were these Gems sent to adorn his Skin,
The Cab'net of a richer Soul within?
No Comet need foretel his Change drew on,
Whose Corps might seem a *Constellation*.
O had he di'd of old, how great a strife
Had been, who from his Death should draw their Life?
Who should, by one rich draught, become what ere
Seneca, Cato, Numa, Cesar, were:
Learn'd, Vertuous, Pious, Great; and have by this
An universal *Metempsucbosis*.
Must all these ag'd Sires in one Funeral
Expire? All die in one so young, so small?
Who, had he liv'd his life out, his great Fame
Had swoln 'bove any *Greek* or *Romane* Name.
But hasty Winter, with one blast, hath brought
The hopes of Autumn, Summer, Spring, to nought.
Thus fades the Oak i' th' sprig, i' th' blade the Corn;
Thus, without Young, this *Phoenix* dies, new born.
Must then old three-legg'd gray-beards with their Gout,
Catarrhs, Rheums, Aches, live three Ages out?
Times Offal, onely fit for th' Hospital,
Or t' hang an Antiquaries room withal;
Must Drunkards, Lechers, spent with Sinning, live
With such helps as Broths, Possits, Physick give?
None live, but such as should die? Shall we meet

With none but Ghostly Fathers in the Street?
Grief makes me rail; Sorrow will force its way;
And, Show'rs of Tears, Tempestuous Sighs best lay.
The Tongue may fail; but over-flowing Eyes
Will weep out lasting streams of *Elegies*.

But thou, O *Virgin-Widow*, left alone,
Now thy belov'd, heaven-ravisht *Spouse* is gone,
(Whose skilful Sire in vain strove to apply
Med'cines, when thy Balm was no Remedy)
With greater then *Platonick* love, O wed
His Soul, though not his Body, to thy Bed:
Let that make thee a Mother; bring thou forth
Th' *Idea's* of his Vertue, Knowledge, Worth;
Transcribe th' Original in new Copies; give
Hastings o' th' better part: so shall he live
In 's Nobler Half; and the great Grandsire be
Of an Heroick Divine Progenie:
An Issue, which t' Eternity shall last,
Yet but th' Irradiations which he cast.
Erect no *Mausolaeums*: for his best
Monument is his Spouses Marble brest.

To my Honour'd Friend, Dr Charleton, on his Learned and Useful Works; and More Particularly This of Stone-heng, by Him Restored to the True Founders

The longest Tyranny that ever sway'd,
Was that wherein our Ancestors betray'd
Their free-born *Reason* to the *Stagirite*,
And made his Torch their universal Light.
So *Truth*, while onely one suppli'd the State,
Grew scarce, and dear, and yet sophisticate,
Until 'twas bought, like Emp'rique Wares, or Charms,
Hard words seal'd up with *Aristotle's* Armes.
Columbus was the first that shook his Throne;
And found a *Temp'rate* in a *Torrid* Zone:
The fevrish aire fann'd by a cooling breez,
The fruitful Vales set round with shady Trees;
And guiltless *Men*, who danc'd away their time,

Fresh as their *Groves*, and *Happy* as their *Clime*.
Had we still paid that homage to a *Name*,
Which onely *God* and *Nature* justly claim;
The *Western* Seas had been our utmost bound,
Where *Poets* still might dream the *Sun* was drown'd:
And all the *Starrs*, that shine in *Southern* Skies,
Had been admir'd by none but *Salvage* Eyes.
  Among th' *Assertors* of free Reason's claim,
Th' *English* are not the least in Worth, or Fame.
The World to *Bacon* does not onely owe
Its *present* Knowledge, but its *future* too.
Gilbert shall live, till *Load-stones* cease to draw,
Or *British* Fleets the boundless Ocean awe.
And noble *Boyle*, not less in *Nature* seen,
Than his great *Brother* read in *States* and *Men*.
The *Circling* streams, once thought but pools, of blood
(Whether Life's fewel, or the Bodie's food)
From dark Oblivion *Harvey*'s name shall save;
While *Ent*★ keeps all the honour that he gave.
Nor are *You*, Learned Friend, the least renown'd;
Whose Fame, not circumscrib'd with *English* ground,
Flies like the nimble journeys of the Light;
And is, like that, unspent too in its flight.
What ever *Truths* have been, by *Art*, or *Chance*,
Redeem'd from *Error*, or from *Ignorance*,
Thin in their *Authors*, (like rich veins of Ore)
Your Works unite, and still discover more.
Such is the healing virtue of Your Pen,
To perfect Cures on *Books*, as well as *Men*.
Nor is This Work the least: You well may give
To *Men* new vigour, who make *Stones* to live.
Through You, the *DANES* (their short Dominion lost)
A longer Conquest than the *Saxons* boast.
STONE-HENG, once thought a *Temple*, You have found
A *Throne*, where Kings, our Earthly Gods, were Crown'd,
Where by their wondring Subjects They were seen,
Joy'd with their Stature, and their Princely meen.
Our *Soveraign* here above the rest might stand;
And here be chose again to rule the Land.
  These Ruines sheltred once *His* Sacred Head,★
Then when from *Wor'sters* fatal Field *He* fled;

Watch'd by the Genius of this Royal place,
And mighty Visions of the *Danish* Race.
His *Refuge* then was for a *Temple* shown:
But, *He* Restor'd, 'tis now become a *Throne*.

Annus Mirabilis

stanzas 155–66

THE PROGRESS OF NAVIGATION

By viewing Nature, Natures Hand-maid, Art,
  Makes mighty things from small beginnings grow:
Thus fishes first to shipping did impart
  Their tail the Rudder, and their head the Prow.

Digression concerning Shipping and Navigation

Some Log, perhaps, upon the waters swam
  An useless drift, which, rudely cut within,
And hollow'd, first a floating trough became,
  And cross some Riv'let passage did begin.

In shipping such as this the *Irish Kern*,
  And untaught *Indian*, on the stream did glide:
Ere sharp-keel'd Boats to stem the floud did learn,
  Or fin-like Oars did spread from either side.

Adde but a Sail, and *Saturn* so appear'd,
  When, from lost Empire, he to Exile went,
And with the Golden age to *Tyber* steer'd,
  Where Coin and first Commerce he did invent.

Rude as their Ships was Navigation, then;
  No useful Compass or Meridian known:
Coasting, they kept the Land within their ken,
  And knew no North but when the Pole-star shone.

Of all who since have us'd the open Sea,
  Then the bold *English* none more fame have won:
Beyond the Year, and out of Heav'ns high-way,
  They make discoveries where they see no Sun.

But what so long in vain, and yet unknown,
　By poor man-kinds benighted wit is sought,
Shall in this Age to *Britain* first be shown,
　And hence be to admiring Nations taught.

The Ebbs of Tydes, and their mysterious flow,
　We, as Arts Elements shall understand:
And as by Line upon the Ocean go,
　Whose paths shall be familiar as the Land.

Instructed ships shall sail to quick Commerce;
　By which remotest Regions are alli'd:
Which makes one City of the Universe,
　Where some may gain, and all may be suppli'd.

Then, we upon our Globes last verge shall go,
　And view the Ocean leaning on the sky:
From thence our rolling Neighbours we shall know,
　And on the Lunar world securely pry.

This I fore-tel, from your auspicious care,
　Who great in search of God and Nature grow:
Who best your wise Creator's praise declare,
　Since best to praise his works is best to know.

Apostrophe to the Royal Society

O truly Royal! who behold the Law,
　And rule of beings in your Makers mind,
And thence, like Limbecks, rich Idea's draw,
　To fit the levell'd use of humane kind.

From *The State of Innocence and Fall of Man: An Opera*

ADAM REASONS

Act II, scene 1

ADAM: What am I? or from whence? For that I am
  I know, because I think; but whence I came,
  Or how this Frame of mine began to be,
  What other being can disclose to me?
  I move, I see; I speak, discourse, and know,
  Though now I am, I was not always so.
  Then that from which I was must be before:
  Whom, as my Spring of Being, I adore.
  How full of Ornament is all I view
  In all its parts! and seems as beautiful as new:
  O goodly order'd Work! O Pow'r Divine.
  Of thee I am; and what I am is thine!

Act III, scene 1. A night-piece of a pleasant Bower:
Adam and Eve alseep in it.

[*Enter* LUCIFER.]

LUCIFER: So, now they lye, secure in love and steep
  Their sated senses in full draughts of sleep.
  By what sure means can I their bliss invade?
  By violence? No, for they're immortal made.
  Their Reason sleeps; but Mimic fancy wakes.
  Supply's her parts, and wild Idea's takes
  From words and things, ill sorted and misjoyn'd;
  The Anarchie of thought and Chaos of the mind:
  Hence dreams confus'd and various may arise;
  These will I set before the Woman's eyes;
  The weaker she, and made my easier prey;
  Vain shows, and Pomp, the softer sex betray.

The Hind and the Panther★

lines 150–61, 182–96

THE DEVELOPMENT OF WOLVES AND FOXES

But heav'n and heav'n-born faith are far from Thee
Thou first Apostate to Divinity.
Unkennel'd range in thy *Polonian* Plains;
A fiercer foe th' insatiate *Wolfe*★ remains.
   Too boastfull *Britain* please thy self no more,
That beasts of prey are banish'd from thy shoar:
The *Bear*, the *Boar*, and every salvage name,
Wild in effect, though in appearance tame,
Lay waste thy woods, destroy thy blissful bow'r,
And muzl'd though they seem, the mutes devour.
More haughty than the rest the *wolfish* race,
Appear with belly Gaunt, and famish'd face . . .

★

In *Israel* some believe him whelp'd long since
When the proud *Sanhedrim* oppress'd the Prince.
Or, since he will be *Jew*, derive him high'r
When *Corah*★ with his brethren did conspire,
From *Moyses* hand the Sov'reign sway to wrest,
And *Aaron* of his Ephod to devest:
Till opening Earth made way for all to pass,
And cou'd not bear the burd'n of a *class*.
The *Fox*★ and he came shuffl'd in the dark,
If ever they were stow'd in *Noah*'s ark:
Perhaps not made; for all their barking train
The Dog (a common species) will contain.
And some wild currs, who from their masters ran
Abhorring the supremacy of man,
In woods and caves the rebel-race began.

SIR RICHARD BLACKMORE

(1650?–1729)

The Creation

Book II, lines 295–350, 430–53

COPERNICUS, TYCHO BRAHE, AND KEPLER

You, who so much are vers'd in causes, tell,
What from the tropicks can the sun repel?
What vigorous arm, what repercussive blow,
Bandies the mighty globe still to and fro,
Yet with such conduct, such unerring art,
He never did the trackless road desert?
Why does he never in his spiral race
The tropicks or the polar circles pass?
What gulphs, what mounds, what terrours, can control
The rushing orb, and make him backward roll?
Why should he halt at either station? why
Not forward run in unobstructive sky?
Can he not pass an astronomic line?
Or does he dread th'imaginary sign;
That he should ne'er advance to either pole,
Nor farther yet in liquid aether roll,
Till he has gain'd some unfrequented place,
Lost to the world in vast unmeasur'd space?
    If to the old you the new schools prefer,
And to the fam'd Copernicus adhere;
If you esteem that supposition best,
Which moves the earth, and leaves the sun at rest;
With a new veil your ignorance you hide,
Still is the knot as hard to be unty'd;
You change your scheme, but the old doubts remain,
And still you leave th'enquiring mind in pain.
    This problem, as philosophers, resolve:
What makes the globe from West to East revolve?
What is the strong impulsive cause declare,
Which rolls the ponderous orb so swift in air?
To your vain answer will you have recourse,
And tell us 'tis ingenite, active force,
Mobility, or native power to move,

Words which mean nothing, and can nothing prove?
That moving power, that force innate explain,
Or your grave answers are absurd and vain:
We no solution of our question find,
Your words bewilder, not direct the mind.
  If you, this rapid motion to procure,
For the hard task employ magnetic power,
Whether that power you at the centre place,
Or in the middle regions of the mass,
Or else, as some philosophers assert,
You give an equal share to every part,
Have you by this the cause of motion shown?
After explaining, is it not unknown?
Since you pretend, by reason's strictest laws,
Of an effect to manifest the cause;
Nature, of wonders so immense a field,
Can none more strange, none more mysterious yield,
None that eludes sagacious reason more
Than this obscure, inexplicable power.
Since you the the spring of motion cannot show,
Be just, and faultless ignorance allow;
Say, 'tis obedience to th'Almighty nod,
That 'tis the will, the power, the hand of God.

★

Copernicus, who rightly did condemn
This eldest system, form'd a wiser scheme;
In which he leaves the sun at rest, and rolls
The orb terrestial on its proper poles;
Which makes the night and day by this career,
And by its flow and crooked course the year.
The famous Dane,★ who oft' the modern guides,
To earth and sun their provinces divides:
The earth's rotation makes the night and day;
The sun revolving through th' ecliptic way
Effects the various seasons of the year,
Which in their turn for happy ends appear.
This scheme or that, which pleases best, embrace,
Still we the Fountain of their motion trace.
  Kepler asserts these wonders may be done
By the magnetic virtue of the sun,

Which he, to gain his end, thinks fit to place
Full in the centre of that mighty space,
Which does the spheres, where planets roll, include,
And leaves him with attractive force endued.
The sun, thus seated, by mechanic law,
The earth and every distant planet draws;
By which attraction all the planets, found
Within his reach, are turn'd in aether round.

The Creation
Book VI, lines 280–329

DEVELOPMENT OF THE EMBRYO

When the crude embryo careful Nature breeds,
See how she works, and how her work proceeds;
While through the mass her energy she darts,
To free and swell the complicated parts,
Which only does unravel and untwist
Th' invelop'd limbs, that previous there exist.
And as each vital speck, in which remains
Th' entire, but rumpled animal, contains
Organs perplext, and clues of twining veins;
So every foetus bears a secret hoard,
With sleeping, unexpanded issue stor'd;
Which numerous, but unquicken'd progeny,
Clasp'd and inwrap'd within each other lie:
Engendering heats these one by one unbind,
Stretch their small tubes, and hamper'd nerves unwind.
And thus, when time shall drain each magazine
Crowded with men unborn, unripe, unseen,
Nor yet of parts unfolded; no increase
Can follow, all prolific power must cease.

*

Th'elastic spirits,* which remain at rest
In the strait lodgings of the brain comprest,
While by the ambient womb's enlivening heat
Cheer'd and awaken'd, first themselves dilate;

Then quicken'd and expanded every way
The genial labourers all their force display:
They now begin to work the wondrous frame,
To shape the parts, and raise the vital flame;
For when th' extended fibres of the brain
Their active guests no longer can restrain,
They backward spring, which due effort compels
The labouring spirits to forsake their cells;
The spirits, thus exploded from their seat,
Swift from the head to the next parts retreat, }
Force their admission, and their passage beat; }
Their tours around th'unopen'd mass they take,
And by a thousand ways their inroads make,
Till there resisted they their race inflect,
And backward to their source their way direct,
Thus with a steady and alternate toil
They issue from, and to the head recoil;
By which their plastic function they discharge,
Extend their channels, and their tracks enlarge;
For, by the swift excursions which they make,
Still sallying from the brain, and leaping back,
They pierce the nervous fibre, bore the vein,
And stretch th' arterial channels, which contain
The various streams of life, that to and fro
Through dark meanders undirected flow;
Th'inspected egg this gradual change betrays,
To which the brooding hen expanding heat conveys.

The Creation
Book VII, lines 228–56

ASSOCIATION OF IDEAS

When man with reason dignify'd is born,
No images his naked mind adorn;
No sciences or arts enrich his brain,
Nor Fancy yet displays her pictur'd train:
He no innate ideas can discern,
Of knowledge destitute, though apt to learn.

Our intellectual, like the body's, eye,
Whilst in the womb, no object can descry;
Yet is dispos'd to entertain the light,
And judge of things when offer'd to the sight.
When objects through the senses passage gain,
And fill with various imagery the brain,
Th' ideas, which the mind does thence perceive,
To think and know the first occasion give.
Did she not use the senses' ministry,
Nor ever taste, or smell, or hear, or see, }
Could she possest of power perceptive be? }
Wretches, who sightless into being came,
Of light or colour no idea frame.
Then grant a man his being did commence,
Deny'd by Nature each external sense,
These ports unopen'd, diffident we guess,
Th' unconscious soul no image could possess;
Though what in such a state the restless train
Of spirits would produce, we ask in vain.
The mind proceeds, and to reflection goes,
Perceives she does perceive, and knows she knows;
Reviews her acts, and does from thence conclude
She is with reason and with choice endued.

SIR SAMUEL GARTH

(1661–1719)

From *The Dispensary**

Canto VI

THE CAVE OF DISEASE

And now the delegate prepares to go
And view the wonders of the realms below; }
Then takes Amomum* for the golden bough. }
Thrice did the goddess with her sacred wand
The pavement strike; and straight at her command
The willing surface opens, and descries
A deep descent that leads to nether skies.

Hygeia to the silent region tends;
And with his heav'nly guide the charge descends.
Thus Numa, when to hallow'd caves retir'd,
Was by Aegeria guarded and inspir'd.
Within the chambers of the globe they spy
The beds where sleeping vegetables lie,
Till the glad summons of a genial ray
Unbinds the glebe, and calls them out to day.
Hence Pancies trick themselves in various hew,
And hence Jonquils derive their fragant dew;
Hence the Carnation and the bashful Rose
Their virgin blushes to the morn disclose;
Hence the chaste Lilly rises to the light,
Unveils her snowy breasts, and charms the sight;
Hence arbours are with twining greens array'd,
T' oblige complaining lovers with their shade;
And hence on Daphne's laurel'd forehead grow
Immortal wreaths for Phaebus and Nassau.*

    The insects here their lingring trance survive:
Benumb'd they seem, and doubtful if alive.
From winter's fury hither they repair,
And stay for milder skies and softer air.
Down to these cells obscener reptiles creep,
Where hateful Nutes and painted Lizards sleep.
Where shiv'ring snakes the summer solstice wait;
Unfurl their painted folds, and slide in state.
Here their new form the numb'd Erucae* hide,
Their num'rous feet in slender bandage ty'd:
Soon as the kindling year begins to rise,
This upstart race their native clod despise,
And proud of painted wings attempt the skies.

    Now those profounder regions they explore,
Where metals ripen in vast cakes of ore.
Here, sullen to the sight, at large is spread
The dull unwieldy mass of lumpish lead,
There, glimm'ring in their dawning beds, are seen
The light aspiring seeds of sprightly tin.
The copper sparkles next in ruddy streaks;
And in the gloom betrays its glowing cheeks.
The silver then with bright and burnish'd grace,

Youth and a blooming lustre in its face,
To th' arms of those more yielding metals flies,
And in the folds of their embraces lies.
So close they cling, so stubbornly retire;
Their love's more violent than the chymist's fire.

Near these the delegate with wonder spies
Where floods of living silver serpentise:
Where richest metals their bright looks put on,
And golden streams through amber channels run.
Where light's gay god* descends to ripen gems,
And lend a lustre brighter than his beams.

Here he observes the subterranean cells,
Where wanton nature sports in idle shells.*
Some helicoeids, some conical appear:
These, miters emulate, those turbans are.
Here marcasites in various figure wait,
To ripen to a true metallic state:
Till drops that from impending rocks descend
Their substance petrify, and progress end.
Nigh, livid seas of kindled sulphur flow,
And, whilst enrag'd, their fiery surges glow,
Convulsions in the lab'ring mountains rise,
And hurl their melted vitals to the skies.

He views with horror next the noisy cave,*
Where with hoarse dins imprison'd tempests rave;
Where clam'rous hurricanes attempt their flight,
Or, whirling in tumultuous eddies, fight.
The warring winds unmov'd Hygeia heard,
Brav'd their loud jars, but much for Celsus fear'd.
Andromeda, so whilst her hero fought,
Shook for his danger, but her own forgot.

And now the goddess with her charge descends,
Where scarce one chearful glimpse their steps befriends.
Here his forsaken seat old Chaos keeps;
And undisturb'd by form, in silence sleeps.
A grisly wight, and hideous to the eye,
An aukward lump of shapeless anarchy.
With sordid age his features are defac'd;
His lands unpeopled, and his countries waste.

*

Nigh this recess, with terror they survey
Where Death maintains his dread tyrannic sway;
In the close covert of a cypress grove,
Where goblins frisk, and airy spectres rove,
Yawns a dark cave, with awful horror wide,
And there the monarch's triumphs are descry'd.
Confus'd, and wildly huddled to the eye,
The beggar's pouch, and prince's purple lie.
Dim lamps with sickly rays scarce seem to glow;
Sighs heave in mournful moans, and tears o'erflow.
Restless Anxiety, forlorn Despair,
And all the faded family of Care.
Old mouldring urns, racks, daggers and distress
Make up the frightful horror of the place.

Within its dreadful jaws those furies wait,
Which execute the harsh decrees of fate.
Febris* is first: the hag relentless hears
The virgin's sighs, and sees the infant's tears.
In her parch'd eye-balls fiery meteors reign;
And restless ferments revel in each vein.

Then Hydrops* next appears amongst the throng;
Bloated, and big, she slowly sails along.
But like a miser, in excess she's poor,
And pines for thirst amidst her watry store.

Now loathsome Lepra,* that offensive spright,
With foul eruptions stain'd, offends the sight;
Still deaf to beauty's soft persuading pow'r;
Nor can bright Hebe's charms her bloom secure.

Whilst meagre Pthisis* gives a silent blow,
Her strokes are sure, but her advances slow.
No loud alarms, nor fierce assaults are shown:
She starves the fortress first, then takes the town.
Behind stood crowds of much inferior name,
Too num'rous to repeat, too foul to name,
The vassals of their monarch's tyranny,
Who, at his nod, on fatal errands fly.

JONATHAN SWIFT
(1667–1745)

On Poetry
lines 319–44

GREAT FLEAS AND LESSER FLEAS

Hobbes clearly proves that ev'ry Creature
Lives in a State of War by Nature.
The Greater for the Smallest watch,
But meddle seldom with their Match.
A Whale of moderate Size will draw
A Shole of Herrings down his Maw.
A Fox with Geese his Belly crams;
A Wolf destroys a thousand Lambs.
But search among the rhiming Race,
The Brave are worried by the Base.
If, on *Parnassus'* Top you sit,
You rarely bite, are always bit:
Each Poet of inferior Size
On you shall rail and criticize;
And strive to tear you Limb from Limb,
While others do as much for him.

   The Vermin only teaze and pinch
Their Foes superior by an Inch.
So, Nat'ralists observe, a Flea
Hath smaller Fleas that on him prey,
And these have smaller Fleas to bite 'em,
And so proceed *ad infinitum:*
Thus ev'ry Poet in his Kind,
Is bit by him that comes behind;
Who, tho' too little to be seen,
Can teaze, and gall, and give the Spleen ...

JOSEPH ADDISON
(1672–1719)

An Ode

THE SPACIOUS FIRMAMENT ON HIGH

The spacious firmament on high,
With all the blue ethereal sky,
And spangled Heavens, a shining frame,
Their great Original proclaim.
Th' unwearied Sun from day to day
Does his Creator's pow'r display;
And publishes, to every land,
The work of an almighty hand.

Soon as the evening shades prevail,
The Moon takes up the wond'rous tale;
And nightly, to the listening Earth,
Repeats the story of her birth:
Whilst all the stars that round her burn,
And all the planets, in their turn,
Confirm the tidings as they roll,
And spread the truth from pole to pole.

What though, in solemn silence, all
Move round the dark terrestrial ball;
What though no real voice, nor sound
Amidst their radiant orbs be found:
In reason's ear they all rejoice,
And utter forth a glorious voice;
For ever singing as they shine:
'The hand that made us is divine.'

WILLIAM DIAPER

(1686–1717)

Nereides: or Sea-Eclogues★

Eclogue VIII, Proteus

Proteus had sent his scaly Herd to feed,
And slumber'd on a Bed of slimy Weed;
Ino and *Cete* thither chanc'd to stray,
They saw, and seiz'd him as he sleeping lay:
Anxious for Flight, now flashing Flame he seems,
Now softly glides away in melting Streams.
But they fast held him, till he smiling said;
'With Songs, nay more than Songs you shall be paid.'
He then began —
To sing of Truths unknown, unheard before,
While all the Sea was still, and Winds were heard no more.
He sung the World's first Birth, and wondrous Frame,
How Bodies all from one great Fluid came.
Of different Parts compos'd, a liquid Mass
Incessant mov'd in the unbounded Space:
(The Essence of a Fluid is confest
To move, and to be solid is to rest)
And as they flow, all Fluids ever bend
To fly around, and to a Circle tend;
Thus a true Chaos did at first arise
From moving Globules of a different Size;
But finer Atoms were more free to move,
And with the sluggish Parts too active strove }
Till they had prest them down from those above:
'Twas then th' unsullied Light did first appear,
And the bright Aether shone unmixt with grosser Air.
At length by tedious time, and slow Degrees
Was form'd the Center of unfathom'd Seas,
Made of large Globules, which th'aerial Sphere
By Motion thrust from it, and settled here;
Then first the Ocean knew his constant place,
And th'azure Deep unvail'd his smiling Face.
'Tis Motion makes (when different Bodies meet)
What Gravity we call, and pressing Weight,
While restless Fluids ever drive below

Bodies more solid, or – that move too slow.
Long rowl'd the Sea, before the Earth appear'd,
No Pastures yet were seen, no bleating Flocks were heard,
'Till th' Ocean's constant Motion closer prest
An earthy Scum, which gathering still encreast;
But here th' intrinsick Fluids still remain,
And hardest Mettle will its Flux regain.
Whene'er dissolv'd the Parts their Freedom know,
And with new Joy again they love to flow.
  He sung, how Heav'n displeas'd with earthy Man,
Disturb'd the Seas; how all the Mass began
To move enrag'd; The Motion thus encreast,
The sinking Earth down to the Center prest;
Such was the antient Deluge, when the Flood
Pour'd o'er the Plains, and on the Mountains stood;
While Earth-born Mortals too absurdly teach
That solid Bodies to the Center reach.
E'er Land was seen, the Ocean had its Birth,
And now th' Abyss supports the shallow Crust of Earth.
  Thus *Proteus* sung, and sung – yet more divine,
How Souls unbody'd act, and how incline;
That Knowledge now is at the best no more,
But a Research of what we knew before.
The Soul as yet to no dull Body joyn'd,
Sees all Idea's in th' eternal Mind;
The native Beams are sullied and obscur'd,
And quench'd at once, in grosser Clay immur'd,
'Till rouz'd at length by Thought, and studious Care,
Like latent Sparks with sudden Light they glare.
Gladly the conscious Mind the Hint pursues,
And rising Images with Wonder views;
Now finds she long before Existence had,
And that those Truths were rather found than made.
Thus Science grafted do's on Ignorance grow;
Men lose to find, and turn unwise to know.
Folly their fancy'd Knowledge do's create;
The greatest Hardship this of Human Fate, ⎫
With Pain they learn, what they with Ease forgat. ⎭
  The God thus ended his mysterious Lay,
When ruddy to the Waves, sunk the declining Day.

ALEXANDER POPE
(1688–1744)

The Rape of the Lock
Canto IV, lines 11–78

THE CAVE OF SPLEEN

For, that sad moment, when the *Sylphs* withdrew,
And *Ariel* weeping from *Belinda* flew,
Umbriel, a dusky melancholy Spright,
As ever sully'd the fair face of Light,
Down to the Central Earth, his proper Scene,
Repair'd to search the gloomy Cave of *Spleen*. ★
  Swift on his sooty Pinions flitts the *Gnome*,
And in a Vapour reach'd the dismal Dome.
No cheerful Breeze this sullen Region knows,
The dreaded *East* is all the Wind that blows.
Here, in a Grotto, sheltred close from Air,
And screen'd in Shades from Day's detested Glare,
She sighs for ever on her pensive Bed,
Pain at her Side, and *Megrim* at her Head.
  Two Handmaids wait the Throne: Alike in Place,
But diff'ring far in Figure and in Face.
Here stood *Ill-nature* like an *ancient Maid*,
Her wrinkled Form in *Black* and *White* array'd;
With store of Pray'rs, for Mornings, Nights, and Noons,
Her Hand is fill'd; her Bosom with Lampoons.
  There *Affectation* with a sickly Mien
Shows in her Cheek the Roses of Eighteen,
Practis'd to Lisp, and hang the Head aside,
Faints into Airs, and languishes with Pride;
On the rich Quilt sinks with becoming Woe,
Wrapt in a Gown, for Sickness, and for Show.
The Fair-ones feel such Maladies as these,
When each new Night-Dress gives a new Disease.
  A constant *Vapour*★ o'er the Palace flies;
Strange Phantoms rising as the Mists arise;
Dreadful, as Hermit's Dreams in haunted Shades,
Or bright as Visions of expiring Maids.
Now glaring Fiends, and Snakes on rolling Spires,

Pale Spectres, gaping Tombs, and Purple Fires:
Now Lakes of liquid Gold, *Elysian* Scenes,
And Crystal Domes, and Angels in Machines.
    Unnumber'd Throngs on ev'ry side are seen
Of Bodies chang'd to various Forms by *Spleen*.
Here living *Teapots* stand, one Arm held out,
One bent; the Handle this, and that the Spout:
A Pipkin there like *Homer*'s *Tripod* walks;
Here sighs a Jar, and there a Goose-pye talks;
Men prove with Child, as pow'rful Fancy works,
And Maids turn'd Bottels, call aloud for Corks.
    Safe past the *Gnome* thro' this fantastick Band,
A Branch of healing *Spleenwort* in his hand.
Then thus addrest the Pow'r – Hail wayward Queen!
Who rule the Sex to Fifty from Fifteen,
Parent of Vapours and of Female Wit,
Who give th' *Hysteric* or *Poetic* Fit,
On various Tempers act by various ways,
Make some take Physick, others scribble Plays;
Who cause the Proud their Visits to delay,
And send the Godly in a Pett, to pray.
A Nymph there is, that all thy Pow'r disdains,
And thousands more in equal Mirth maintains.
But oh! if e'er thy *Gnome* could spoil a Grace,
Or raise a Pimple on a beauteous Face,
Like Citron-Waters Matrons' Cheeks inflame,
Or change Complexions at a losing Game;
If e'er with airy Horns I planted Heads,
Or rumpled Petticoats, or tumbled Beds,
Or caus'd Suspicion when no Soul was rude,
Or discompos'd the Head-dress of a Prude,
Or e'er to costive Lap-Dog gave Disease,
Which not the Tears of brightest Eyes could ease:
Hear me, and touch *Belinda* with Chagrin;
That single Act gives half the World the Spleen.

From *An Essay on Man*

THE GREAT CHAIN OF BEING

Epistle I, lines 17–34

1. Say first, of God above, or Man below,
What can we reason, but from what we know?
Of Man what see we, but his station here,
From which to reason, or to which refer?
Thro' worlds unnumber'd tho' the God be known,
'Tis ours to trace him only in our own.
He, who thro' vast immensity can pierce,
See worlds on worlds compose one universe,
Observe how system into system runs,
What other planets circle other suns,
What vary'd being peoples ev'ry star,
May tell why Heav'n has made us as we are.
But of this frame the bearings, and the ties,
The strong connections, nice dependencies,
Gradations just, has thy pervading soul
Look'd thro'? or can a part contain the whole?
   Is the great chain,* that draws all to agree,
And drawn supports, upheld by God, or thee?

Epistle II, lines 1–52

Know then thyself, presume not God to scan;
The proper study of Mankind is Man.
Plac'd on this isthmus of a middle state,
A being darkly wise, and rudely great:
With too much knowledge for the Sceptic side,
With too much weakness for the Stoic's pride,
He hangs between; in doubt to act, or rest,
In doubt to deem himself a God, or Beast;
In doubt his Mind or Body to prefer,
Born but to die, and reas'ning but to err;
Alike in ignorance, his reason such,
Whether he thinks too little, or too much:
Chaos of Thought and Passion, all confus'd;
Still by himself abus'd, or disabus'd;
Created half to rise, and half to fall;
Great lord of all things, yet a prey to all;

Sole judge of Truth, in endless Error hurl'd:
The glory, jest, and riddle of the world!
  Go, wond'rous creature! mount where Science guides,
Go, measure earth, weigh air, and state the tides;
Instruct the planets in what orbs to run,
Correct old Time, and regulate the Sun;
Go, soar with Plato to th' empyreal sphere,
To the first good, first perfect, and first fair;
Or tread the mazy round his follow'rs trod,
And quitting sense call imitating God;
As Eastern priests in giddy circles run,
And turn their heads to imitate the Sun.
Go, teach Eternal Wisdom how to rule –
Then drop into thyself, and be a fool!
  Superior beings, when of late they saw
A mortal Man unfold all Nature's law,
Admir'd such wisdom in an earthly shape,
And shew'd a NEWTON as we shew an Ape.
  Could he, whose rules the rapid Comet bind,
Describe or fix one movement of his Mind?
Who saw its fires here rise, and there descend,
Explain his own beginning, or his end?
Alas what wonder! Man's superior part
Uncheck'd may rise, and climb from art to art:
But when his own great work is but begun,
What Reason weaves, by Passion is undone.
  Trace Science then, with Modesty thy guide;
First strip off all her equipage of Pride,
Deduct what is but Vanity, or Dress,
Or Learning's Luxury, or Idleness;
Or tricks to shew the stretch of human brain,
Mere curious pleasure, or ingenious pain:
Expunge the whole, or lop th' excrescent parts
Of all, our Vices have created Arts:
Then see how little the remaining sum,
Which serv'd the past, and must the times to come!

Epistle III, lines 7–26

Look round our World; behold the chain of Love
Combining all below and all above.
See plastic Nature working to this end,

The single atoms each to other tend,
Attract, attracted to, the next in place
Form'd and impell'd its neighbour to embrace.
See Matter next, with various life endu'd,
Press to one centre still, the gen'ral Good.
See dying vegetables life sustain,
See life dissolving vegetate again:
All forms that perish other forms supply,
(By turns we catch the vital breath, and die)
Like bubbles on the sea of Matter born,
They rise, they break, and to that sea return.
Nothing is foreign: Parts relate to whole;
One all-extending all-preserving Soul
Connects each being, greatest with the least;
Made Beast in aid of Man, and Man of Beast;
All serv'd, all serving! nothing stands alone;
The chain holds on, and where it ends, unknown.

The Dunciad
Book IV, lines 397–458

VIRTUOSI AND COLLECTORS

Then thick as Locusts black'ning all the ground,
A tribe, with weeds and shells fantastic crown'd,
Each with some wond'rous gift approach'd the Pow'r,
A Nest, a Toad, a Fungus, or a Flow'r.
But far the foremost, two, with earnest zeal,
And aspect ardent to the Throne appeal.
  The first thus open'd: 'Hear thy suppliant's call,
Great Queen, and common Mother of us all!
Fair from its humble bed I rear'd this Flow'r,
Suckled, and chear'd, with air, and sun, and show'r,
Soft on the paper ruff its leaves I spread,
Bright with the gilded button tipt its head,
Then thron'd in glass, and nam'd it CAROLINE:
Each Maid cry'd, charming! and each Youth, divine!
Did Nature's pencil ever blend such rays,
Such vary'd light in one promiscuous blaze?
Now prostrate! dead! behold that Caroline:

No Maid cries, charming! and no Youth, divine!
And lo the wretch! whose vile, whose insect lust
Lay'd this gay daughter of the Spring in dust.
Oh punish him, or to th' Elysian shades
Dismiss my soul, where no Carnation fades.'
   He ceas'd, and wept. With innocence of mien,
Th' Accus'd stood forth, and thus address'd the Queen.
   'Of all th' enamel'd race, whose silv'ry wing
Waves to the tepid Zephyrs of the spring,
Or swims along the fluid atmosphere,
Once brightest shin'd this child of Heat and Air.
I saw, and started from its vernal bow'r
The rising game, and chac'd from flow'r to flow'r.
It fled, I follow'd; now in hope, now pain;
It stopt, I stopt; it mov'd, I mov'd again.
At last it fix'd, 'twas on what plant it pleas'd,
And where it fix'd, the beauteous bird I seiz'd:
Rose or Carnation was below by care;
I meddle, Goddess! only in my sphere.
I tell the naked fact without disguise,
And, to excuse it, need but shew the prize;
Whose spoils this paper offers to your eye,
Fair ev'n in death! this peerless *Butterfly*.'
   'My sons! (she answer'd) both have done your parts:
Live happy both, and long promote our arts.
But hear a Mother, when she recommends
To your fraternal care, our sleeping friends.
The common Soul, of Heav'n's more frugal make,
Serves but to keep fools pert, and knaves awake:
A drowzy Watchman, that just gives a knock,
And breaks our rest, to tell us what's a clock.
Yet by some object ev'ry brain is stirr'd;
The dull may waken to a Humming-bird;
The most recluse, discreetly open'd find
Congenial matter in the Cockle-kind;
The mind, in Metaphysics at a loss,
May wander in a wilderness of Moss;
The head that turns at super-lunar things,
Poiz'd with a tail, may steer on Wilkins'* wings.
   'O! would the Sons of Men once think their Eyes
And Reason giv'n them but to study *Flies*?

See Nature in some partial narrow shape,
And let the Author of the Whole escape:
Learn but to trifle; or, who most observe,
To wonder at their Maker, not to serve.'

Epitaph: Intended for Sir Isaac Newton in Westminster Abbey

Nature, and Nature's Laws lay hid in Night.
God said, *Let Newton be!* and All was *Light*.

JAMES THOMSON
(1700–48)

To the Memory of Sir Isaac Newton
lines 68–136

O unprofuse magnificence divine!
O wisdom truly perfect! thus to call
From a few causes such a scheme of things,
Effects so various, beautiful, and great,
An universe complete! And O beloved
Of Heaven! whose well purged penetrating eye
The mystic veil transpiercing, inly scanned
The rising, moving, wide-established frame.

  He, first of men, with awful wing pursued
The comet through the long elliptic curve,
As round innumerous worlds he wound his way,
Till, to the forehead of our evening sky
Returned, the blazing wonder glares anew,
And o'er the trembling nations shakes dismay.

  The heavens are all his own, from the wide rule
Of whirling vortices and circling spheres
To their first great simplicity restored.
The schools astonished stood; but found it vain
To combat still with demonstration strong,
And, unawakened, dream beneath the blaze
Of truth. At once their pleasing visions fled,
With the gay shadows of the morning mixed,
When Newton rose, our philosophic sun!

The aerial flow of sound was known to him,
From whence it first in wavy circles breaks,
Till the touched organ takes the message in.
Nor could the darting beam of speed immense
Escape his swift pursuit and measuring eye.
Even Light itself, which every thing displays,
Shone undiscovered, till his brighter mind
Untwisted all the shining robe of day;
And, from the whitening undistinguished blaze,
Collecting every ray into his kind,
To the charmed eye educed the gorgeous train
Of parent colours. First the flaming red
Sprung vivid forth; the tawny orange next;
And next delicious yellow; by whose side
Fell the kind beams of all-refreshing green.
Then the pure blue, that swells autumnal skies,
Ethereal played; and then, of sadder hue,
Emerged the deepened indigo, as when
The heavy-skirted evening droops with frost;
While the last gleamings of refracted light
Died in the fainting violet away.
These, when the clouds distil the rosy shower,
Shine out distinct adown the watery bow;
While o'er our heads the dewy vision bends
Delightful, melting on the fields beneath.
Myriads of mingling dyes from these result,
And myriads still remain – infinite source
Of beauty, ever flushing, ever new.

   Did ever poet image aught so fair,
Dreaming in whispering groves by the hoarse brook?
Or prophet, to whose rapture heaven descends?
Even now the setting sun and shifting clouds,
Seen, Greenwich, from thy lovely heights, declare
How just, how beauteous the refractive law.

   The noiseless tide of time, all bearing down
To vast eternity's unbounded sea,
Where the green islands of the happy shine,
He stemmed alone; and, to the source (involved
Deep in primeval gloom) ascending, raised
His lights at equal distances, to guide
Historian wildered on his darksome way.

But who can number up his labours? who
His high discoveries sing? When but a few
Of the deep-studying race can stretch their minds
To what he knew – in fancy's lighter thought
How shall the muse then grasp the mighty theme?

The Seasons

Summer, lines 1531–63

BACON, BOYLE, NEWTON, AND LOCKE

                              Fair thy renown
In awful sages and in noble bards;
Soon as the light of dawning Science spread
Her orient ray, and waked the Muses' song.
Thine is a Bacon, hapless in his choice,
Unfit to stand the civil storm of state,
And, through the smooth barbarity of courts,
With firm but pliant virtue forward still
To urge his course: him for the studious shade
Kind Nature formed, deep, comprehensive, clear,
Exact, and elegant; in one rich soul,
Plato, the Stagyrite, and Tully joined.
The great deliverer he, who, from the gloom
Of cloistered monks and jargon-teaching schools,
Led forth the true philosophy, there long
Held in the magic chain of words and forms
And definitions void: he led her forth,
Daughter of Heaven! that, slow-ascending still,
Investigating sure the chain of things,
With radiant finger points to Heaven again.
The generous Ashley* thine, the friend of man,
Who scanned his nature with a brother's eye,
His weakness prompt to shade, to raise his aim,
To touch the finer movements of the mind,
And with the moral beauty charm the heart.
Why need I name thy Boyle, whose pious search,
Amid the dark recesses of his works,
The great Creator sought? And why thy Locke,
Who made the whole internal world his own?

Let Newton, pure intelligence, whom God
To mortals lent to trace his boundless works
From laws sublimely simple, speak thy fame
In all philosophy.

The Seasons

Summer, lines 81–159

MINERALS

But yonder comes the powerful king of day
Rejoicing in the east. The lessening cloud,
The kindling azure, and the mountain's brow
Illumed with fluid gold, his near approach
Betoken glad. Lo! now, apparent all,
Aslant the dew-bright earth and coloured air,
He looks in boundless majesty abroad,
And sheds the shining day, that burnished plays
On rocks, and hills, and towers, and wandering streams
High-gleaming from afar. Prime cheerer, Light!
Of all material beings first and best!
Efflux divine! Nature's resplendent robe,
Without whose vesting beauty all were wrapt
In unessential gloom; and thou, O Sun!
Soul of surrounding worlds! in whom best seen
Shines out thy Maker! may I sing of thee?
    'Tis by thy secret, strong, attractive force,
As with a chain indissoluble bound,
Thy system rolls entire – from the far bourne
Of utmost Saturn, wheeling wide his round
Of thirty years, to Mercury, whose disk
Can scarce be caught by philosophic eye,
Lost in the near effulgence of thy blaze.
    Informer of the planetary train!
Without whose quickening glance their cumbrous orbs
Were brute unlovely mass, inert and dead,
And not, as now, the green abodes of life!
How many forms of being wait on thee,
Inhaling spirit, from the unfettered mind,
By thee sublimed, down to the daily race,
The mixing myriads of thy setting beam!

The vegetable world is also thine,
Parent of Seasons! who the pomp precede
That waits thy throne, as through thy vast domain,
Annual, along the bright ecliptic road
In world-rejoicing state it moves sublime.
Meantime the expecting nations, circled gay
With all the various tribes of foodful earth,
Implore thy bounty, or send grateful up
A common hymn: while, round thy beaming car,
High-seen, the Seasons lead, in sprightly dance
Harmonious knit, the rosy-fingered hours,
The zephyrs floating loose, the timely rains,
Of bloom ethereal the light-footed dews,
And, softened into joy, the surly storms.
These, in successive turn, with lavish hand
Shower every beauty, every fragrance shower,
Herbs, flowers, and fruits; till, kindling at thy touch,
From land to land is flushed the vernal year.

    Nor to the surface of enlivened earth,
Graceful with hills and dales, and leafy woods,
Her liberal tresses, is thy force confined;
But, to the bowelled cavern darting deep,
The mineral kinds confess thy mighty power.
Effulgent hence the veiny marble shines;
Hence labour draws his tools; hence burnished war
Gleams on the day; the nobler works of peace
Hence bless mankind; and generous commerce binds
The round of nations in a golden chain.

    The unfruitful rock itself, impregned by thee,*
In dark retirement forms the lucid stone.
The lively diamond drinks thy purest rays,
Collected light compact; that, polished bright,
And all its native lustre let abroad,
Dares, as it sparkles on the fair one's breast,
With vain ambition emulate her eyes.
At thee the ruby lights its deepening glow,
And with a waving radiance inward flames.
From thee the sapphire, solid ether, takes
Its hue cerulean; and, of evening tinct,
The purple-streaming amethyst is thine
With thy own smile the yellow topaz burns;

Nor deeper verdure dyes the robe of Spring,
When first she gives it to the southern gale,
Than the green emerald shows. But, all combined,
Thick through the whitening opal play thy beams;
Or, flying several from its surface, form
A trembling variance of revolving hues
As the site varies in the gazer's hand.

DR JOHN ARMSTRONG
(1709–79)

The Art of Preserving Health
Book I, lines 134–63

MENS SANA

Oft from the body, by long ails mistuned,
These evils sprung, the most important health,
That of the mind, destroy: and when the mind
They first invade, the conscious body soon
In sympathetic languishment declines.
These chronic passions, while from real woes
They rise, and yet without the body's fault
Infest the soul, admit one only cure;
Diversion, hurry, and a restless life.
Vain are the consolations of the wise;
In vain your friends would reason down your pain.
O ye, whose souls relentless love has tamed
To soft distress, or friends untimely fallen!
Court not the luxury of tender thought;
Nor deem it impious to forget those pains
That hurt the living, nought avail the dead.
Go, soft enthusiast! quit the cypress groves,
Nor to the rivulet's lonely moanings tune
Your sad complaint. Go, seek the cheerful haunts
Of men, and mingle with the bustling crowd;
Lay schemes for wealth, or power, or fame, the wish
Of nobler minds, and push them night and day.
Or join the caravan in quest of scenes

New to your eyes, and shifting every hour,
Beyond the Alps, beyond the Apennines.
Or more adventurous, rush into the field
Where war grows hot; and, raging through the sky,
The lofty trumpet swells the maddening soul:
And in the hardy camp and toilsome march
Forget all softer and less manly cares.

The Art of Preserving Health

Book I, lines 494–534

THE COURSE OF LIFE

Perhaps no sickly qualms bedim their days,
No morning admonitions shock the head.
But ah! what woes remain! Life rolls apace!
And that incurable disease old age,
In youthful bodies more severely felt,
More sternly active, shakes their blasted prime:
Except kind Nature by some hasty blow
Prevent the lingering fates. For know, whate'er
Beyond its natural fervour hurries on
The sanguine tide; whether the frequent bowl,
High-season'd fare, or exercise to toil
Protracted; spurs to its last stage tired life,
And sows the temples with untimely snow.
When life is new, the ductile fibres feel
The heart's increasing force; and, day by day,
The growth advances: till the larger tubes,
Acquiring (from their elemental veins,
Condensed to solid chords) a firmer tone,
Sustain, and just sustain, the impetuous blood.
Here stops the growth. With overbearing pulse
And pressure, still the great destroy the small;
Still with the ruins of the small grow strong.
Life glows meantime, amid the grinding force
Of viscous fluids and elastic tubes;
Its various functions vigorously are plied
By strong machinery; and in solid health

The man confirmed long triumphs o'er disease.
But the full ocean ebbs: there is a point,
By nature fixed, whence life must downward tend.
For still the beating tide consolidates
The stubborn vessels, more reluctant still
To the weak throbs of the ill-supported heart.
This languishing, these strength'ning by degrees
To hard unyielding unelastic bone,
Through tedious channels the congealing flood
Crawls lazily, and hardly wanders on;
It loiters still: and now it stirs no more.
This is the period few attain; the death
Of nature; thus (so Heaven ordain'd it) life
Destroys itself; and could these laws have changed,
Nestor might now the fates of Troy relate;
And Homer live immortal as his song.

The Art of Preserving Health
Book II, lines 12–36

THE BLOOD

The blood, the fountain whence the spirits flow,
The generous stream that waters every part,
And motion, vigour, and warm life conveys
To every particle that moves or lives;
This vital fluid, through unnumbered tubes
Poured by the heart, and to the heart again
Refunded; scourged for ever round and round;
Enraged with heat and toil, at last forgets
Its balmy nature; virulent and thin
It grows; and now, but that a thousand gates
Are open to its flight, it would destroy
The parts it cherished and repaired before.
Besides, the flexible and tender tubes
Melt in the mildest, most nectareous tide
That ripening Nature rolls; as in the stream
Its crumbling banks; but what the vital force
Of plastic fluids hourly batters down,

That very force, those plastic particles
Rebuild: so mutable the state of man.
For this the watchful appetite was given,
Daily with fresh materials to repair
This unavoidable expense of life,
This necessary waste of flesh and blood.
Hence the concoctive powers, with various art,
Subdue the cruder aliments to chyle;*
The chyle to blood; the foamy purple tide
To liquors,* which through finer arteries
To different parts their winding course pursue;
To try new changes, and new forms put on,
Or for the public, or some private use.

THOMAS GRAY
(1716–71)

Luna Habitabilis

LIFE IN THE MOON

Translated from the Latin by Sally Purcell

While Night with her company drives through the dewfall,
Leading the stars in their silent round,
Come to me, youngest, yet not least, of the Muses,
For the doors of high heaven stand open to you,
You know the stars by number and by name.
Come, lady, let us enjoy the pure spring sky
And wander in quiet fields; hear my prayer,
Walk with me in shadows' coolness.
Surely these worlds, these jewels of high heaven,
Do not shine for us alone, a decorated ceiling,
Giant stage-flats or theatrical curtains?
Who will give me wings to rise in wonder,
To see the firmament more near,
Like you, who shed a softer light, that flows
To uncover fields and calm sad darkness?

Smiling she replied, We need no wings
To seek these heights together; you can learn

146

THOMAS GRAY

To draw the moon down from heaven, without black spells;
Like Endymion again you may see her descend;
Of her own accord she will come to you,
Greater than you have ever seen her image.
Put your eye to the telescope, stand on a little hill,
See at once the palaces of heaven,
Dare to gaze upon Luna's kingdoms, walk
On earth with your head in the clouds.
Phoebe now appears in the circle of glass,
Her Ocean, and her thickly-scattered islands.
Ocean shows clear, although he hides his face
In mist, and shrinks from prying eyes;
His surface greedily absorbs all sunlight,
Drinks in the long fiery rays.
                              In the straits arise
Islands that stud the blue with gold,
High-ridged and rock-surrounded; they by nature
Absorb the clear light less, refracting
Day's arrow-shafts, and making the flames recoil.
You will see from here long shining plains,
Mountains to rival Ossa and Rhodope,
Caverns of darkness under tree-covered crags.

This world has clouds and dewfall of its own,
And icy cold, and showers for the grass;
Here too Iris' rainbow shines, rosy dawn, and twilight.
Can you believe such a world lacks men
To till the fields, and build their cities high,
To go to war, and celebrate
Triumphs for victory? Here too great deeds win honour;
Fear, love, and human passions touch their hearts.
And as it pleases us to let our eyes
Travel their shining plains and sound their sea,
They feel the same thrill when our earth appears,
Vaster than theirs, and golden, in clear skies.
They surely study every sea and land,
Even the dwellers underneath our poles,
And stay up tireless through a summer night
To search the heaven and study its fires.
See, France appears, broad Germany behind,
And further rise the snowy Apennines;
Northward lies Britain, like a beauty patch,

Tiny, although far brighter than the rest.
At once their princes rush to see that light,
That speck of brilliance, gazing long and late,
And vying each to call it by his name.
Perhaps some lordly monarch on the moon
Calls himself master and swaggers in our place.
I could tell of lands warmed by the nearer sun
And others that more sparingly use his rays,
Whole clusters of moons that Phoebus hardly knows
– But my sister* plans a poem on this theme
And is tuning her lyre already to begin.

Still I shall sing out my praises, oracles
Of England's fame, and prophecies Fate long ago wrote down.
A time will come that sees great hastening crowds
Of colonists leaving for the moon, exchanging
Known for unknown homes, as old inhabitants
Watch in amazement flying fleets and novel 'birds' on high.
As when Columbus crossed the broad unknown
Sailing to seek new kingdoms, and the shores
And waters all around saw wondering
His mounted troops in armour clad, his ships
Like Trojan horses, and their man-made lightning –
Soon treaties are drawn up, and trade begins
Between the worlds, through now-familiar space.
Our England, that already rules the waves
And keeps the winds in awe, shall now extend
Her ancient triumphs over conquered air.

GILBERT WHITE

(1720–93)

The Naturalist's Summer-Evening Walk

To Thomas Pennant, Esquire

... equidem credo, quia sit divinitus illis
Ingenium.   Virg., *Georg.*

When day declining sheds a milder gleam,
What time the may-fly haunts the pool or stream;
When the still owl skims round the grassy mead,

What time the timorous hare limps forth to feed;
Then be the time to steal adown the vale,
And listen to the vagrant cuckoo's tale;
To hear the clamorous curlew* call his mate,
Or the soft quail his tender pain relate;
To see the swallow sweep the dark'ning plain
Belated, to support her infant train;
To mark the swift in rapid giddy ring
Dash round the steeple, unsubdu'd of wing:
Amusive birds! – say where your hid retreat
When the frost rages and the tempests beat;
Whence your return, by such nice instinct led,
When spring, soft season, lifts her bloomy head?
Such baffled searches mock man's prying pride,
The GOD of NATURE is your secret guide!
   While deep'ning shades obscure the face of day
To yonder bench, leaf-shelter'd, let us stray,
Till blended objects fail the swimming sight,
And all the fading landscape sinks in night;
To hear the drowsy dor* come brushing by
With buzzing wing, or the shrill cricket cry;
To see the feeding bat glance through the wood;
To catch the distant falling of the flood;
While o'er the cliff th' awakened churn-owl hung
Through the still gloom protracts his chattering song;
While high in air, and pois'd upon his wings,
Unseen, the soft enamour'd woodlark sings:
These, NATURE's works, the curious mind employ,
Inspire a soothing melancholy joy:
As fancy warms, a pleasing kind of pain
Steals o'er the cheek, and thrills the creeping vein!
   Each rural sight, each sound, each smell combine;
The tinkling sheep-bell, or the breath of kine;
The new-mown hay that scents the swelling breeze,
Or cottage-chimney smoking through the trees.
   The chilling night-dews fall: away, retire;
For see, the glow-worm lights her amorous fire!
Thus, ere night's veil had half obscured the sky,
Th' impatient damsel hung her lamp on high:
True to the signal, by love's meteor led,
Leander hasten'd to his Hero's bed.

                    I am, etc.

MARK AKENSIDE

(1721–70)

Hymn to Science

O vitae Philosophia dux! O virtutis indagatrix, expultrixque vitiorum. Tu urbes peperisti; tu inventrix legum, tu magistra morum et disciplinae fuisti: ad te confugimus, a te opem petimus.

Cic., Tusc. Quaest.

Science! thou fair effusive ray
From the great source of mental day,
   Free, generous, and refined!
Descend with all thy treasures fraught,
Illumine each bewilder'd thought,
   And bless my labouring mind.

But first with thy resistless light,
Disperse those phantoms from my sight,
   Those mimic shades of thee:
The scholiast's learning, sophist's cant,
The visionary bigot's rant,
   The monk's philosophy.

Oh! let thy powerful charms impart
The patient head, the candid heart,
   Devoted to thy sway;
Which no weak passions e'er mislead,
Which still with dauntless steps proceed
   Where reason points the way.

Give me to learn each secret cause;
Let Number's, Figure's, Motion's laws
   Reveal'd before me stand;
These to great Nature's scenes apply,
And round the globe, and through the sky,
   Disclose her working hand.

Next, to thy nobler search resign'd,
The busy, restless, Human Mind
   Through every maze pursue;
Detect Perception where it lies,
Catch the Ideas as they rise,
   And all their changes view.

Say from what simple springs began
The vast ambitious thoughts of man,
   Which range beyond control,
Which seek eternity to trace,
Dive through the infinity of space,
   And strain to grasp the whole.

Her secret stores let Memory tell,
Bid Fancy quit her fairy cell,
   In all her colours dress'd;
While prompt her sallies to control,
Reason, the judge, recalls the soul
   To Truth's severest test.

Then launch through Being's wide extent;
Let the fair scale with just ascent
   And cautious steps be trod;
And from the dead, corporeal mass,
Through each progressive order pass
   To Instinct, Reason, God.

There, Science! veil thy daring eye;
Nor dive too deep, nor soar too high,
   In that divine abyss;
To Faith content thy beams to lend,
Her hopes to assure, her steps befriend
   And light her way to bliss.

Then downwards take thy flight again,
Mix with the policies of men,
   And social Nature's ties;
The plan, the genius of each state,
Its interest and its powers relate,
   Its fortunes and its rise.

Through private life pursue thy course,
Trace every action to its source,
   And means and motives weigh:
Put tempers, passions, in the scale;
Mark what degrees in each prevail,
   And fix the doubtful sway.

That last best effort of thy skill,
To form the life, and rule the will,
   Propitious power! impart:
Teach me to cool my passion's fires,
Make me the judge of my desires,
   The master of my heart.

Raise me above the vulgar's breath,
Pursuit of fortune, fear of death,
   And all in life that's mean:
Still true to reason be my plan,
Still let my actions speak the man,
   Through every various scene.

Hail! queen of manners, light of truth;
Hail! charm of age, and guide of youth;
   Sweet refuge of distress:
In business, thou! exact, polite;
Thou giv'st retirement its delight,
   Prosperity its grace.

Of wealth, power, freedom, thou the cause;
Foundress of order, cities, laws,
   Of arts inventress thou!
Without thee, what were human-kind?
How vast their wants, their thoughts how blind!
   Their joys how mean, how few!

Sun of the soul! thy beams unveil:
Let others spread the daring sail
   On Fortune's faithless sea:
While, undeluded, happier I
From the vain tumult timely fly,
   And sit in peace with thee.

CHRISTOPHER SMART

(1722–71)

From *On the Omniscience of the Supreme Being*

BIRD MIGRATION

When Philomela, e'er the cold domain
Of cripled winter 'gins t'advance, prepares
Her annual flight, and in some poplar shade
Takes her melodious leave, who then's her pilot?
Who points her passage thro' the pathless void
To realms from us remote, to us unknown?
Her science is the science of her God.
Not the magnetic index* to the North
E'er ascertains her course, nor buoy, nor beacon.
She heav'n-taught voyager, that sails in air,
Courts nor coy West nor East, but instant knows
What Newton, or not sought, or sought in vain.[1]

   Illustrious name, irrefragable proof
Of man's vast genius, and the soaring soul!
Yet what wert thou to him, who knew his works,
Before creation form'd them, long before
He measur'd in the hollow of his hand
Th' exulting ocean, and the highest Heav'ns
He comprehended with a span, and weigh'd
The mighty mountains in his golden Scales:
Who shone supreme, who was himself the light,
E'er yet Refraction learn'd her skill to paint,
And bend athwart the clouds her beauteous bow.

1. The Longitude. [Smart's note.]

ERASMUS DARWIN

(1731–1802)

The Botanic Garden,
Part II, *The Loves of the Plants*

Canto I, lines 279–98 and
401–14 and Canto III, lines 131–78

E'en round the pole the flames of Love aspire,
And icy bosoms feel the *secret* fire! –
Cradled in snow and fann'd by arctic air
Shines, gentle BAROMETZ![1] thy golden hair;
Rooted in earth each cloven hoof descends,
And round and round her flexile neck she bends;
Crops the gray coral moss, and hoary thyme,
Or laps with rosy tongue the melting rime.
Eyes with mute tenderness her distant dam,
Or seems to bleat, a *Vegetable Lamb.*
– So, warm and buoyant in his oily mail,
Gambols on seas of ice the unwieldy Whale;
Wide waving fins round floating islands urge
His bulk gigantic through the troubled surge;
With hideous yawn the flying shoals he seeks,
Or clasps with fringe of horn his massy cheeks;
Lifts o'er the tossing wave his nostrils bare,
And spouts pellucid columns into air;
The silvery arches catch the setting beams,
And transient rainbows tremble o'er the streams.

*

As dash the waves on India's breezy strand,
Her flush'd cheek press'd upon her lily hand,

---

1. Polypodium Barometz. Tartarian Lamb. Clandestine Marriage. This species of Fern is a native of China, with a decumbent root, thick, and everywhere covered with the most soft and dense wool, intensely yellow.

This curious stem is sometimes pushed out of the ground in its horizontal situation by some of the inferior branches of the root, so as to give it some resemblance to a Lamb standing on four legs; and has been said to destroy all other plants in its vicinity. Sir Hans Sloane describes it under the name of Tartarian Lamb, and has given a print of it ... but thinks some art had been used to give it an animal appearance. Dr Hunter, in his edition of the *Terra* of Evelyn, has given a more curious print of it, much resembling a sheep. The down is used in India externally for stopping hemorrhages, and is called golden moss. [Darwin's note.]

VALLISNER[2]★ sits, up-turns her tearful eyes,
Calls her lost lover, and upbraids the skies;
For him she breathes the silent sigh, forlorn,
Each setting day; for him each rising morn. –
'Bright orbs, that light yon high ethereal plain,
Or bathe your radiant tresses in the main;
Pale moon, that silver'st o'er night's sable brow; –
For ye were witness to his parting vow!
Ye shelving rocks, dark waves, and sounding shore, –
Ye echoed sweet the tender words he swore! –
Can stars or seas the sails of love retain?
O guide my wanderer to my arms again!'

★

With fierce distracted eye IMPATIENS[3] stands,
Swells her pale cheeks, and brandishes her hands,
With rage and hate the astonish'd groves alarms,
And hurls her infants from her frantic arms.
– So when Medea left her native soil,
Unaw'd by danger, unsubdued by toil;
Her weeping sire and beckoning friends withstood,
And launch'd enamour'd on the boiling flood;
One ruddy boy her gentle lips caress'd,
And one fair girl was pillow'd on her breast;
While high in air the golden treasure burns,
And Love and Glory guide the prow by turns.
But, when Thessalia's inauspicious plain
Received the matron-heroine from the main;
While horns of triumph sound, and altars burn,
And shouting nations hail their Chief's return;
Aghast, she saw new-deck'd the nuptial bed,
And proud Creusa to the temple led;

2. This extraordinary plant is found in the East Indies, in Norway, and various parts of Italy. They have their roots at the bottom of the Rhone; the flowers of the female plant float on the surface of the water, and are furnished with an elastic spiral stalk, which extends or contracts as the water rises and falls; this rise or fall, from the rapid descent of the river, and the mountain torrents which flow into it, often amounts to many feet in a few hours. The flowers of the male plant are produced under water, and as soon as their farina, or dust, is mature, they detach themselves from the plant, and rise to the surface, continue to flourish, and are wafted by the air or borne by the currents to the female flowers. [Darwin's note.]

3. Touch me not. The seed vessel consists of one cell with five divisions; each of these, when the seed is ripe, on being touched, suddenly folds itself into a spiral form, leaps from the stalk, and disperses the seeds to a great distance by its elasticity. [Darwin's note.]

Saw her in Jason's mercenary arms
Deride her virtues, and insult her charms;
Saw her dear babes from fame and empire torn,
In foreign realms deserted and forlorn;
Her love rejected, and her vengeance braved,
By him her beauties won, her virtues saved. –
With stern regard she eyed the traitor-king,
And felt, Ingratitude! thy keenest sting;
'Nor Heaven,' she cried, 'nor Earth, nor Hell can hold
A heart abandon'd to the thirst of gold!'
Stamp'd with wild foot, and shook her horrent brow,
And call'd the furies from their dens below.
– Slow out of earth, before the festive crowds,
On wheels of fire, amid a night of clouds,
Drawn by fierce fiends arose a magic car,
Received the Queen, and hovering flamed in air. –
As with raised hands the suppliant traitors kneel,
And fear the vengeance they deserve to feel,
Thrice with parch'd lips her guiltless babes she press'd,
And thrice she clasp'd them to her tortured breast;
Awhile with white uplifted eyes she stood,
Then plunged her trembling poniard in their blood.
'Go, kiss your sire! go, share the bridal mirth!'
She cried, and hurl'd their quivering limbs on earth.
Rebellowing thunders rock the marble towers,
And red-tongued lightnings shoot their arrowy showers;
Earth yawns! – the crashing ruin sinks! – o'er all
Death with black hands extends his mighty pall;
Their mingling gore the fiends of Vengeance quaff,
And Hell receives them with convulsive laugh.

The Temple of Nature

Canto I, lines 1–32, 223–50

PRODUCTION OF LIFE

By firm immutable immortal laws
Impress'd on Nature by the GREAT FIRST CAUSE,
Say, MUSE! how rose from elemental strife
Organic forms, and kindled into life;

How Love and Sympathy with potent charm
Warm the cold heart, the lifted hand disarm;
Allure with pleasures, and alarm with pains,
And bind Society in golden chains.

    Four past eventful Ages then recite,
And give the fifth, new-born of Time, to light;
The silken tissue of their joys disclose,
Swell with deep chords the murmur of their woes;
Their laws, their labours, and their loves proclaim,
And chant their virtues to the trump of Fame.

    IMMORTAL LOVE! who ere the morn of Time,
On wings outstretch'd, o'er Chaos hung sublime;
Warm'd into life the bursting egg of Night,
And gave young Nature to admiring Light! –
YOU! whose wide arms, in soft embraces hurl'd
Round the vast frame, connect the whirling world!
Whether immers'd in day, the Sun your throne,
You gird the planets in your silver zone;
Or warm, descending on ethereal wing,
The Earth's cold bosom with the beams of spring;
Press drop to drop, to atom atom bind,
Link sex to sex, or rivet mind to mind;
Attend my song! – With rosy lips rehearse,
And with your polish'd arrows write my verse! –
So shall my lines soft-rolling eyes engage,
And snow-white fingers turn the volant page;
The smiles of Beauty all my toils repay,
And youths and virgins chant the living lay.

*

'GOD THE FIRST CAUSE!'[1] – in this terrene abode
Young Nature lisps,[2] she is the child of GOD.
From embryon births her changeful forms improve,
Grow, as they live, and strengthen as they move.

---

1. *A Jove principium, musae! Jovis omnia plena.* (Virgil) In him we live, and move, and have our being. (St Paul) [This and the following footnotes are Darwin's.]

2. The perpetual production and increase of the strata of limestone from the shells of aquatic animals; and of all those incumbent on them from the recrements of vegetables and of terrestial animals, are now well understood from our improved knowledge of geology; and show, that the solid parts of the globe are gradually enlarging, and consequently that it

'Ere Time began, from flaming Chaos hurl'd
Rose the bright spheres, which form the circling world;
Earths from each sun with quick explosions burst,
And second planets issued from the first.
Then, whilst the sea at their coeval birth,
Surge over surge, involv'd the shoreless earth;
Nurs'd by warm sun-beams in primeval caves
Organic Life began beneath the waves.

'First HEAT[3] from chemic dissolution springs,
And gives to matter its eccentric wings;
With strong REPULSION parts the exploding mass,
Melts into lymph, or kindles into gas.
ATTRACTION[4] next, as earth or air subsides,

---

is young; as the fluid parts are not yet all converted into solid ones. Add to this, that some parts of the earth and its inhabitants appear younger than others; thus the greater height of the mountains of America seems to show that continent to be less ancient than Europe, Asia, and Africa; as their summits have been less washed away, and the wild animals of America, as the tigers and crocodiles, are said to be less perfect in respect to their size and strength; which would show them to be still in a state of infancy, or of progressive improvement. Lastly, the progress of mankind in arts and sciences, which continues slowly to extend, and to increase, seems to evince the youth of human society; whilst the unchanging state of the societies of some insects, as of the bee, wasp, and ant, which is usually ascribed to instinct, seems to evince the longer existence, and greater maturity of those societies. The Juvenility of the earth shows that it has had a beginning or birth, and is a strong natural argument evincing the existence of a cause of its production, that is of the Deity.

3. The matter of heat is an ethereal fluid, in which all things are immersed, and which constitutes the general power of repulsion; as appears in explosions which are produced by the sudden evolution of combined heat, and by the expansion of all bodies by the slower diffusion of it in its uncombined state. Without heat all the matter of the world would be condensed into a point by the power of attraction; and neither fluidity nor life could exist. There are also particular powers of repulsion, as those of magnetism and electricity, and of chemistry, such as oil and water; which last may be as numerous as the particular attractions which constitute chemical affinities; and may both of them exist as atmospheres round the individual particles of matter.

4. The power of attraction may be divided into general attraction, which is called gravity; and into particular attraction, which is termed chemical affinity. As nothing can act where it does not exist, the power of gravity must be conceived as extending from the sun to the planets, occupying that immense space; and may therefore be considered as an ethereal fluid, though not cognizable by our senses like heat, light, and electricity.

Particular attraction, or chemical affinity, must likewise occupy the spaces between the particles of matter which they cause to approach each other. The power of gravity may therefore be called the general attractive ether, and the matter of heat may be called the general repulsive ether; which constitute the two great agents in the changes of inanimate matter.

The ponderous atoms from the light divides,
Approaching parts with quick embrace combines,
Swells into spheres, and lengthens into lines.
Last, as fine goads the gluten-threads excite,
Cords grapple cords, and webs with webs unite;
And quick CONTRACTION[5] with ethereal flame
Lights into life the fibre-woven frame. –
Hence without parent by spontaneous birth
Rise the first specks of animated earth;
From Nature's womb the plant or insect swims,
And buds or breathes, with microscopic limbs . . .'

The Temple of Nature

Canto III, IV, lines 335–64

LANGUAGE

'When strong desires or soft sensations move
The astonish'd Intellect to rage or love;
Associate tribes of fibrous motions rise,
Flush the red cheek, or light the laughing eyes.
Whence ever-active Imitation finds
The ideal trains, that pass in kindred minds;
Her mimic arts associate thoughts excite
And the first LANGUAGE[6] enters at the sight.

5. The power of contraction which exists in organized bodies, and distinguishes life from inanimation, appears to consist of an ethereal fluid which resides in the brain and nerves of living bodies, and is expended in the act of shortening their fibres. The attractive and repulsive ethers require only the vicinity of bodies for the exertion of their activity, but the contractive ether requires at first the contact of a goad or stimulus, which appears to draw it off from the contracting fibre, and to excite the sensorial power of irritation. These contractions of animal fibres are afterwards excited or repeated by the sensorial powers of sensation, volition, or association.

6. There are two ways by which we become acquainted with the passions of others: first, by having observed the effects of them, as of fear or anger, on our own bodies, we know at sight when others are under the influence of these affections . . .

Secondly, when we put ourselves into the attitude that any passion naturally occasions, we soon in some degree acquire that passion . . .

These are natural signs by which we understand each other, and on this slender basis is built all human language. For without some natural signs no artificial ones could have been invented or understood.

'Thus jealous quails or village-cocks inspect
Each other's necks with stiffen'd plumes erect;
Smit with the wordless eloquence, they know
The rival passion of the threatning foe.
So when the famish'd wolves at midnight howl,
Fell serpents hiss, or fierce hyenas growl;
Indignant Lions rear their bristling mail,
And lash their sides with undulating tail.
Or when the Savage-Man with clenched fist
Parades, the scowling champion of the list;
With brandish'd arms, and eyes that roll to know
Where first to fix the meditated blow;
Association's* mystic power combines
Internal passions with external signs.

'From these dumb gestures first the exchange began
Of viewless thought in bird, and beast, and man;
And still the stage by mimic art displays
Historic pantomime in modern days;
And hence the enthusiast orator affords
Force to the feebler eloquence of words.

'Thus the first LANGUAGE, when we frown'd or smiled,
Rose from the cradle, Imitation's child ...'

PETER PINDAR/JOHN WOLCOT
(1738–1819)

From *Peter's Prophecy*

BANKS AND HERSCHEL

SIR JOSEPH*

By heav'ns! I've merit, say whate'er you please!
Can name the vegetable tribes with ease –
What monkey walks the woods or climbs a tree
Whose genealogy's unknown to *me*?

PETER

I grant you, sir, in monkey knowledge great;
Yet say, should monkeys give you Newton's seat?
Such merit scarcely is enough to dub
A man a member of a country club.

With novel specks on eggs to feast the eye,
Or gaudy colours of a butterfly,
Or new-found fibre of some grassy blade,
Well suits the idle hours of some old maid
(Whose sighs each lover's vanish'd sighs deplore),
To murder time when Cupids kill no more;
Not men, who, lab'ring with a Titan mind,
Should scale the skies to benefit mankind,
I grant you full of anecdote, my friend –
Bon mots, and wondrous stories without end;
Yet if a tale can claim, or jest so rare,
Ten thousand gossips might demand the chair.
To shoot at boobies, noddies, with such luck,
And pepper a poor Indian like a duck;
To hunt for days a lizard or a gnat,
And run a dozen miles to catch a bat;
To plunge in marshes, and to scale the rocks,
Sublime, for scurvygrass and lady-smocks,
Are matters of proud triumph, to be sure,
And such as *Fame's* fair volume should secure:
Yet to my mind, it is not such a feat,
As gives a man a claim to Newton's seat.

SIR JOSEPH

Yet are there men of genius who support me!
Proud of my friendship, see Sir William court me!

PETER

Great in the eating knowledge all allow;
Who sent you once the *sumen*[1] of a sow;

---

1. Sir W. Hamilton, who sent Sir Joseph from Italy this precious present – The mode of making it properly is, by tying the teats of a sow, soon after she hath littered, continuing the ligature till the poor creature is nearly exhausted with torture, and then cutting her throat. The effects of the milk diffused through this belly part are so delicious, as to be thought to make ample atonement for the barbarity. [Pindar's note.]

Far richer food than pigs that lose their breath,
Whipp'd like poor soldiers on parades, to death.
Sir William, hand and glove with *Naples' king!*
Who made with rare antiques the nation ring;
Who when *Vesuvius* foam'd with melted matter,
March'd up and clapp'd his nose into the *crater*,
Just with the same *sang froid* that Joan the cook
Casts on her dumplings in the crock a look.

But more the world reports (I hope untrue)
That half Sir William's mugs and gods are *new*;
Himself the baker of th' Etrurian ware,
That made our British antiquarians stare;
Nay, that he means ere long to cross the main,
And at his Naples oven sweat again;
And by his late successes render'd bolder,
To bake *new* mugs, and gods some ages *older!*

SIR JOSEPH

God bless us! what to Herschel* dare you say?
The astronomic genius of the day,
Who soon will find more wonders in the skies,
And with more *Georgium Siduses* surprise?

PETER

More Aetnas in the moon – *more* cinder loads!
Perhaps mail coaches on her turnpike roads,
By some great Lunar Palmer taught to fly,
To gain the gracious glances of the eye
Of some penurious prince of high degree,
And charm the monarch with a *postage free*;
Such as to *Chelt'nam* waters urg'd their way,
Where Cloacina holds her *easy* sway;
Where paper mills shall load with wealth the town,
And ev'ry shop shall deal in *whitish brown;*
Where for the coach the *king* was wont to watch,
Loaded with fish, fowl, bacon, and dispatch;[2]

2. Mr Palmer very *generously* offered his *sovereign* a mail coach to carry letters and dispatches to and from Cheltenham – the offer was *too great* to be refused – a splendid carriage was built for the occasion: his most oeconomic majesty, however, wisely knowing that something more than a few letters might be contained in Mr Palmer's vehicle, converted it, as the poet hath observed, into a cart, and saved many a sixpence. [Pindar's note.]

Eggs and small beer, potatoes, too, a store,
That cost in *Chelt'nam* market twopence more;
Converting thus a coach of matchless art,
With two rare geldings, to a *sutler's cart* –
But, voluble Sir Joseph – not so fast –
The fame of Herschel is a dying blast:
When on the moon he first began to peep,
The wond'ring world pronounc'd the gazer deep:
But wiser now th' *un*-wond'ring world, alas!
Gives all poor Herschel's glory to his *glass;*
Convinc'd his boasted astronomic strength,
Lies in his *tube's*, not *head's* prodigious length.

WILLIAM BLAKE

(1757–1827)

From *Vala or the Four Zoas*

Night the Sixth, lines 180–228

VORTICES AND CHAOS

Oft would he sit in a dark rift & regulate his books,
Or sleep such sleep as spirits eternal, wearied in his dark
Tearful & sorrowful state; then rise, look out & ponder
His dismal voyage, eyeing the next sphere tho' far remote;
Then darting into the Abyss of night his venturous limbs
Thro' lightnings, thunders, earthquakes & concussions, fires & floods
Stemming his downward fall, labouring up against futurity,
Creating many a Vortex,* fixing many a Science in the deep,
And thence throwing his venturous limbs into the vast unknown,
Swift, swift from Chaos to chaos, from void to void, a road immense.
For when he came to where a Vortex ceas'd to operate,
Nor down nor up remain'd, then if he turn'd & look'd back
From whence he came, 'twas upward all; & if he turn'd and view'd
The unpass'd void, upward was still his mighty wand'ring,
The midst between, an Equilibrium grey of air serene
Where he might live in peace & where his life might meet repose.

But Urizen said: 'Can I not leave this world of Cumbrous wheels,
'Circle o'er Circle, nor on high attain a void

'Where self sustaining I may view all things beneath my feet?
'Or sinking thro' these Elemental wonders, swift to fall,
'I thought perhaps to find an End, a world beneath of voidness
'Whence I might travel round the outside of this dark confusion.
'When I bend downward, bending my head downward into the deep,
''Tis upward all which way soever I my course begin;
'But when A Vortex, form'd on high by labour & sorrow & care
'And weariness, begins on all my limbs, then sleep revives
'My wearied spirits; waking then 'tis downward all which way
'Soever I my spirits turn, no end I find of all
'O what a world is here, unlike those climes of bliss
'Where my sons gather'd round my knees! O, thou poor ruin'd world!
'Thou horrible ruin! once like me thou wast all glorious,
'And now like me partaking desolate thy master's lot.
'Art thou, O ruin, the once glorious heaven? are these thy rocks
'Where joy sang in the trees & pleasure sported on the rivers,
'And laughter sat beneath the Oaks, & innocence sported round
'Upon the green plains, & sweet friendship met in palaces,
'And books & instruments of song & pictures of delight?
'Where are they, whelmed beneath these ruins in horrible destruction?
'And if, Eternal falling, I repose on the dark bosom
'Of winds & waters, or thence fall into a Void where air
'Is not, down falling thro' immensity ever & ever,
'I lose my powers, weaken'd every revolution, till a death
'Shuts up my powers; then a seed in the vast womb of darkness
'I dwell in dim oblivion; brooding over me, the Enormous worlds
'Reorganize me, shooting forth in bones & flesh & blood,
'I am regenerated, to fall or rise at will, or to remain
'A labourer of ages, a dire discontent, a living woe
'Wandering in vain. Here will I fix my foot & here rebuild.
'Here Mountains of Brass promise much riches in their dreadful
    bosoms.'

WILLIAM BLAKE

From *Jerusalem*
Chapter I, lines 6–20

BACON, NEWTON, AND LOCKE

I see the Four-fold Man,* The Humanity in deadly sleep
And its fallen Emanation, The Spectre & its cruel Shadow.
I see the Past, Present & Future existing all at once
Before me. O Divine Spirit, sustain me on thy wings,
That I may awake Albion from his long & cold repose;
For Bacon & Newton, sheath'd in dismal steel, their terrors hang
Like iron scourges over Albion: Reasonings like vast Serpents
Infold around my limbs, bruising my minute articulations.

I turn my eyes to the Schools & Universities of Europe
And there behold the Loom of Locke, whose Woof rages dire,
Wash'd by the Water-wheels of Newton: black the cloth
In heavy wreathes folds over every Nation: cruel Works
Of many Wheels I view, wheel without wheel, with cogs tyrannic
Moving by compulsion each other, not as those in Eden, which,
Wheel within Wheel, in freedom revolve in harmony & peace.

'Mock on, Mock on Voltaire, Rousseau'

Mock on, Mock on Voltaire, Rousseau:
Mock on, Mock on: 'tis all in vain!
You throw the sand against the wind,
And the wind blows it back again.

And every sand becomes a Gem
Reflected in the beams divine;
Blown back they blind the mocking Eye,
But still in Israel's paths they shine.

The Atoms of Democritus
And Newton's Particles of light
Are sands upon the Red sea shore,
Where Israel's tents do shine so bright.

WILLIAM WORDSWORTH
(1770–1850)

The Tables Turned
An Evening Scene

Up! up! my friend, and clear your looks,
Why all this toil and trouble?
Up! up! my friend, and quit your books,
Or surely you'll grow double.

The sun above the mountain's head,
A freshening lustre mellow,
Through all the long green fields has spread,
His first sweet evening yellow.

Books! 'tis a dull and endless strife,
Come, hear the woodland linnet,
How sweet his music; on my life
There's more of wisdom in it.

And hark! how blithe the throstle sings!
And he is no mean preacher;
Come forth into the light of things,
Let Nature be your teacher.

She has a world of ready wealth,
Our minds and hearts to bless –
Spontaneous wisdom breathed by health,
Truth breathed by chearfulness.

One impulse from a vernal wood
May teach you more of man;
Of moral evil and of good,
Than all the sages can.

Sweet is the lore which nature brings;
Our meddling intellect
Misshapes the beauteous forms of things;
– We murder to dissect.

Enough of science and of art;
Close up these barren leaves;
Come forth, and bring with you a heart
That watches and receives.

Lucy Poem VI
'A Slumber Did My Spirit Seal ...'

A slumber did my spirit seal;
    I had no human fears:
She seemed a thing that could not feel
    The touch of earthly years.

No motion has she now, no force;
    She neither hears nor sees;
Rolled round* in earth's diurnal course,
    With rocks, and stones, and trees.

The Prelude
Book III, lines 46–63

NEWTON'S STATUE

The Evangelist St John my patron was:
Three Gothic courts are his, and in the first
Was my abiding-place, a nook obscure;
Right underneath, the College kitchens made
A humming sound, less tuneable than bees,
But hardly less industrious; with shrill notes
Of sharp command and scolding intermixed.
Near me hung Trinity's loquacious clock,
Who never let the quarters, night or day,
Slip by him unproclaimed, and told the hours
Twice over with a male and female voice.
Her pealing organ was my neighbour too;
And from my pillow, looking forth by light
Of moon or favouring stars, I could behold
The antechapel where the statue stood
Of Newton with his prism and silent face,
The marble index of a mind for ever
Voyaging through strange seas of Thought, alone.

The Prelude
Book VI, lines 115–41

GEOMETRIC SCIENCE

Yet may we not entirely overlook
The pleasure gathered from the rudiments
Of geometric science. Though advanced
In these enquiries, with regret I speak,
No farther than the threshold, there I found
Both elevation and composed delight:
With Indian awe and wonder, ignorance pleased
With its own struggles, did I meditate
On the relation those abstractions bear
To Nature's laws, and by what process led,
Those immaterial agents bowed their heads
Duly to serve the mind of earth-born man;
From star to star, from kindred sphere to sphere,
From system on to system without end.

` More frequently from the same source I drew
A pleasure quiet and profound, a sense
Of permanent and universal sway,
And paramount belief; there, recognised
A type, for finite natures, of the one
Supreme Existence, the surpassing life
Which – to the boundaries of space and time,
Of melancholy space and doleful time,
Superior and incapable of change,
Nor touched by welterings of passion – is,
And hath the name of, God. Transcendent peace
And silence did await upon these thoughts
That were a frequent comfort to my youth.

The Excursion

Book IV, lines 1230–75, Book VIII, lines 196–230,
and Book IX, lines 1–20

THE PROPER PLACE OF SCIENCE

And further; by contemplating these Forms
In the relations which they bear to man,
He shall discern, how, through the various means
Which silently they yield, are multiplied
The spiritual presences of absent things.
Trust me, that for the instructed, time will come
When they shall meet no object but may teach
Some acceptable lesson to their minds
Of human suffering, or of human joy.
So shall they learn, while all things speak of man,
Their duties from all forms; and general laws,
And local accidents, shall tend alike
To rouse, to urge; and, with the will, confer
The ability to spread the blessings wide
Of true philanthropy. The light of love
Not failing, perseverance from their steps
Departing not, for them shall be confirmed
The glorious habit by which sense is made
Subservient still to moral purposes,
Auxiliar to divine. That change shall clothe
The naked spirit, ceasing to deplore
The burthen of existence. Science then
Shall be a precious visitant; and then,
And only then, be worthy of her name:
For then her heart shall kindle; her dull eye,
Dull and inanimate, no more shall hang
Chained to its object in brute slavery;
But taught with patient interest to watch
The processes of things, and serve the cause
Of order and distinctness, not for this
Shall it forget that its most noble use,
Its most illustrious province, must be found
In furnishing clear guidance, a support
Not treacherous, to the mind's *excursive* power.
– So build we up the Being that we are;

Thus deeply drinking-in the soul of things
We shall be wise perforce; and, while inspired
By choice, and conscious that the Will is free,
Shall move unswerving, even as if impelled
By strict necessity, along the path
Of order and of good. Whate'er we see,
Or feel, shall tend to quicken and refine;
Shall fix, in calmer seats of moral strength,
Earthly desires; and raise, to loftier heights
Of divine love, our intellectual soul.

*

Triumph who will in these profaner rites
Which we, a generation self-extolled,
As zealously perform! I cannot share
His proud complacency: – yet do I exult,
Casting reserve away, exult to see
An intellectual mastery exercised
O'er the blind elements; a purpose given,
A perseverance fed; almost a soul
Imparted – to brute matter. I rejoice,
Measuring the force of those gigantic powers
That, by the thinking mind, have been compelled
To serve the will of feeble-bodied Man.
For with the sense of admiration blends
The animating hope that time may come
When, strengthened, yet not dazzled, by the might
Of this dominion over nature gained,
Men of all lands shall exercise the same
In due proportion to their country's need,
Learning, though late, that all true glory rests,
All praise, all safety, and all happiness,
Upon the moral law. Egyptian Thebes,
Tyre, by the margin of the sounding waves,
Palmyra, central in the desert, fell;
And the Arts died by which they had been raised.
– Call Archimedes from his buried tomb
Upon the grave of vanished Syracuse,
And feelingly the Sage shall make report
How insecure, how baseless in itself,
Is the Philosophy whose sway depends

On mere material instruments; – how weak
Those arts, and high inventions, if unpropped
By virtue. – He, sighing with pensive grief,
Amid his calm abstractions, would admit
That not the slender privilege is theirs
To save themselves from blank forgetfulness!

*

'To every Form of being is assigned,'
Thus calmly spake the venerable Sage,
'An *active* Principle: – howe'er removed
From sense and observation, it subsists
In all things, in all natures; in the stars
Of azure heaven, the unenduring clouds,
In flower and tree, in every pebbly stone
That paves the brooks, the stationary rocks,
The moving waters, and the invisible air.
Whate'er exists hath properties that spread
Beyond itself, communicating good,
A simple blessing, or with evil mixed;
Spirit that knows no insulated spot,
No chasm, no solitude; from link to link
It circulates, the Soul of all the worlds.
This is the freedom of the universe;
Unfolded still the more, more visible,
The more we know; and yet is reverenced least,
And least respected in the human Mind,
Its most apparent home. . .'

To the Planet Venus[1]

What strong allurement draws, what spirit guides
Thee, Vesper! brightening still, as if the nearer
Thou com'st to man's abode the spot grew dearer
Night after night? True is it Nature hides
Her treasures less and less. – Man now presides
In power, where once he trembled in his weakness;
Science advances with gigantic strides;

1. Upon its approximation (as an Evening Star) to the Earth, Jan. 1838. [Wordsworth's note.]

But are we aught enriched in love and meekness?
Aught dost thou see, bright Star! of pure and wise
More than in humbler times graced human story;
That makes our hearts more apt to sympathise
With heaven, our souls more fit for future glory,
When earth shall vanish from our closing eyes,
Ere we lie down in our last dormitory?

SAMUEL TAYLOR COLERIDGE
(1772–1850)

Religious Musings
lines 224–59

THE ORIGINS OF SCIENCE

From Avarice thus, from Luxury and War
Sprang heavenly Science; and from Science Freedom.
O'er waken'd realms Philosophers and Bards
Spread in concentric circles: they whose souls,
Conscious of their high dignities from God,
Brook not Wealth's rivalry! and they, who long
Enamoured with the charms of order, hate
The unseemly disproportion: and whoe'er
Turn with mild sorrow from the Victor's car
And the low puppetry of thrones, to muse
On that blest triumph, when the Patriot Sage
Called the red lightnings from the o'er-rushing cloud
And dashed the beauteous terrors on the earth
Smiling majestic. Such a phalanx ne'er
Measured firm paces to the calming sound
Of Spartan flute! These on the fated day,
When, stung to rage by Pity, eloquent men
Have roused with pealing voice the unnumbered tribes
That toil and groan and bleed, hungry and blind –
These, hush'd awhile with patient eye serene,
Shall watch the mad careering of the storm;
Then o'er the wild and wavy chaos rush
And tame the outrageous mass, with plastic might

Moulding Confusion to such perfect forms,
As erst were wont, – bright visions of the day! –
To float before them, when, the summer noon,
Beneath some arched romantic rock reclined
They felt the sea-breeze lift their youthful locks;
Or in the month of blossoms, at mild eve,
Wandering with desultory feet inhaled
The wafted perfumes, and the flocks and woods
And many-tinted streams and setting sun
With all his gorgeous company of clouds
Ecstatic gazed! then homeward as they strayed
Cast the sad eye to earth, and inly mused
Why there was misery in a world so fair.

Religious Musings

lines 322–76

NEWTON ON PERCEPTION; PRIESTLEY

O return!
Pure Faith! meek Piety! The abhorrèd Form
Whose scarlet robe was stiff with earthly pomp,
Who drank iniquity in cups of gold,
Whose names were many and all blasphemous,
Hath met the horrible judgment! Whence that cry?
The mighty army of foul Spirits shrieked
Disherited of earth! For she hath fallen
On whose black front was written Mystery;
She that reeled heavily, whose wine was blood;
She that worked whoredom with the Daemon Power,
And from the dark embrace all evil things
Brought forth and nurtured: mitred Atheism!
And patient Folly who on bended knee
Gives back the steel that stabbed him; and pale Fear
Haunted by ghastlier shapings than surround
Moon-blasted Madness when he yells at midnight!
Return pure Faith! return meek Piety!
The kingdoms of the world are yours: each heart
Self-governed, the vast family of Love

Raised from the common earth by common toil
Enjoy the equal produce. Such delights
As float to earth, permitted visitants!
When in some hour of solemn jubilee
The massy gates of Paradise are thrown
Wide open, and forth come in fragments wild
Sweet echoes of unearthly melodies,
And odours snatched from beds of Amaranth,
And they, that from the crystal river of life
Spring up on freshened wing, ambrosial gales!
The favoured good man in his lonely walk
Perceives them, and his silent spirit drinks
Strange bliss which he shall recognise in heaven.
And such delights, such strange beatitudes
Seize on my young anticipating heart
When that blest future rushes on my view!
For in his own and in his Father's might
The Saviour comes! While as the Thousand Years
Lead up their mystic dance, the Desert shouts!
Old Ocean claps his hands! The mighty Dead
Rise to new life, whoe'er from earliest time
With conscious zeal had urged Love's wondrous plan,
Coadjutors of God. To Milton's trump
The high groves of the renovated Earth
Unbosom their glad echoes: inly hushed,
Adoring Newton his serener eye
Raises to heaven: and he of mortal kind
Wisest, he first who marked the ideal tribes
Up the fine fibres through the sentient brain.
Lo! Priestley there, patriot, and saint, and sage,
Him, full of years, from his loved native land
Statesmen blood-stained and priests idolatrous
By dark lies maddening the blind multitude
Drove with vain hate. Calm, pitying he retired,
And mused expectant on these promised years.

SARAH HOARE

(1777–1856)

Poems on Conchology and Botany

Conchology, 12–13, 57–8, 64

Deem not thyself from harm secur'd
Pholas!★ in rock or oak immur'd
    Or more tenacious clay;
Howe'er thy wish to live retir'd,
Unseen, unsought, and unadmir'd,
Yet, by thy tempting beauty fir'd,
    We bring thee forth today.

Gracefully striate is thy shell,
Transverse and longitudinal,
    And delicately fair;
But why that magic luster bright?
For sure thou are no erudite,
Studious to trim the lamp by night,
    Or breathe the vesper prayer.

★

Nerita![1] I have gaz'd on thee,
'Till thought of suff'ring infancy,
    Impell'd the lengthen'd sigh;
And though the spirit fain would soar,
Yet suff'ring nature could deplore,
That 'to be born seem'd little more
    Than to begin to die.'

Not Artists' skill, nor Poet's lyre,
Though genius' self the chords inspire,
    And matchless taste impart;
Suffice with all their powers to shew,
Thy irridescent splendid glow,
Bright as the tints in Iris' bow,
    Or paint thee as thou art.

★

1. Linnaeus describes it as having the lip toothed, and the pillar impressed with a saffron spot. [Hoare's note.]

I would not doubt with impious mind,
Toredo![2] good in thee to find,
    Though navigators dread
Thy piercing power – and with dismay
Cast thee as direful foe away,
And, ah! for thee – profusely pray
    For curses on thy head.

Poems on Conchology and Botany
Botany, 1–10

Science, illuminating ray!
Fair mental beam, extend thy sway,
    And shine from pole to pole!
From thy accumulated store,
O'er every mind thy riches pour,
Excite from low desires to soar,
    And dignify the soul.

Science! thy charms will ne'er deceive,
But still increasing pleasure give,
    And varied joys combine;
Nor ever leave on memory's page
A pang repentance would assuage;
But purest, happiest, thoughts engage
    To sweeten life's decline.

To thee, oh Botany! I owe
Of pure delight, the ardent glow,
    Since childhood's playful day;
E'en then I sought the sweet perfume,
Exhal'd along the banks of Froome;*
Admir'd the rose's opening bloom,
    And nature's rich array.

The exhilarating mountain gale,
The velvet slope, the shady vale,
    Have given their sweets to me;

---

2. *Toredo Navalis*, or ship worm, readily enters the stoutest timber, and ascends the sides of stately vessels, which it insidiously destroys. [Hoare's note.]

Eager to seize the fav'rite flower,
I heeded not the tempest's lower,
Nor mid-day sun's exhausting power,
    Impell'd by love of thee.

The search repays by health improv'd,
Amply supplies the mind with food
        Of rich variety;
Awakens hope of brighter joy,
Presents with sweets that never cloy,
And prompts the happiest employ,
        Of praise to Deity.

But not alone for pleasure's sake,
We search the thicket, copse, and brake,
        Or rove from clime to clime;
Nor yet for the abundant store
Of plants, that fragrant balsams pour,
Whether they deck the valleys o'er,
        Or mountain's brow sublime.

'Tis that with scientific eye
We explore the vast variety,
        To find the hidden charm:
'Tis to allay the fever's rage,
The pang arthritic to assuage,
To aid the visual nerve of age,
        And fell disease disarm.

Linné,* by thy experience taught,
And ample page so richly fraught
        With scientific lore:
I scann'd thy curious system clear,
Of plants that court the mountain air,
That bloom o'er hills, o'er meadows fair,
        The forest and the moor.

And plants that court the mountain air,
That bloom o'er hills, o'er meadows fair,
        The forest and the moor, –
That flourish on the rocky steep,
Or in the wood's recesses deep,
By lucid streams, where willows weep,
        The silvery surface o'er, –

I sought, and still delight to view
Whate'er of beautiful or new,
   Around me daily shine,
Beaming from nature's ample page –
And, ah! may ne'er the chill of age,
My love of loveliness assuage,
   Its source and end divine.

From *Poems of Conchology and Botany*

Pleasures of Botanical Pursuits

And DIGITALIS wisely given,
Another proof of favouring Heaven
   Will happily display,
The rapid pulse it can abate,
The hectic flush can moderate,
And blest by him, whose will is fate,
   May give a happier day.

SIR HUMPHREY DAVY
(1778–1829)

From *The Sons of Genius*

SCIENTIFIC STUDY

The sons of nature, – they alike delight
  In the rough precipice's broken steep;
In the bleak terrors of the stormy night;
  And in the thunders of the threatening deep.

When the red lightnings through the ether fly,
  And the white foaming billows lash the shores;
When to the rattling thunders of the sky
  The angry demon of the waters roars;

And when, untouch'd by Nature's living fires,
  No native rapture fills the drowsy soul;
Then former ages, with their tuneful lyres,
  Can bid the fury of the passions fall.

By the blue taper's melancholy light,
　　Whilst all around the midnight torrents pour,
And awful glooms beset the face of night,
　　They wear the silent, solitary hour.

Ah! then how sweet to pass the night away
　　In silent converse with the Grecian page,
Whilst Homer tunes his ever-living lay,
　　Or reason listens to the Athenian sage.

To scan the laws of Nature, to explore
　　The tranquil reign of mild Philosophy;
Or on Newtonian wings sublime to soar
　　Through the bright regions of the starry sky.

Ah! who can paint what raptures fill the soul
　　When Attic freedom rises to the war,
Bids the loud thunders of the battle roll,
　　And drives the tyrant trembling from her shore?

From these pursuits the sons of genius scan
　　The end of their creation, – hence they know
The fair, sublime, immortal hopes of man,
　　From whence alone undying pleasures flow.

By science calmed, over the peaceful soul,
　　Bright with eternal Wisdom's lucid ray,
Peace, meek of eye, extends her soft control,
　　And drives the puny Passions far away.

The Sybil's Temple

Thy faith, O Roman! was a natural faith,
Well suited to an age in which the light
Ineffable gleam'd thro' obscuring clouds
Of objects sensible, – not yet revealed
In noontide brightness on the Syrian mount.
For thee, the Eternal Majesty of heaven
In all things lived and moved, – and to its power
And attributes poetic fancy gave
The forms of human beauty, strength, and grace.
The Naiad murmur'd in the silver stream,

The Dryad whisper'd in the nodding wood,
(Her voice the music of the Zephyr's breath);
On the blue wave the sportive Nereid moved,
Or blew her conch amidst the echoing rocks.
I wonder not, that, moved by such a faith,
Thou raisedst the Sybil's temple in this vale,
For such a scene was suited well to raise
The mind to high devotion, – to create
Those thoughts indefinite which seem above
Our sense and reason, and the hallowed dream
Prophetic. – In the sympathy sublime,
With natural forms and sounds, the mind forgets
Its present being, – images arise
Which seem not earthly, – 'midst the awful rocks
And caverns bursting with the living stream, –
In force descending from the precipice, –
Sparkling in sunshine, nurturing with dews
A thousand odorous plants and fragrant flowers.
In the sweet music of the vernal woods,
From winged minstrels, and the louder sounds
Of mountain storms, and thundering cataracts,
The voice of inspiration well might come!

'The Massy Pillars of the Earth . . .'

The massy pillars of the earth,
  The inert rocks, the solid stones,
Which give no power, no motion birth,
  Which are to Nature lifeless bones,

Change slowly; but their dust remains,
  And every atom, measured, weigh'd,
Is whirl'd by blasts along the plains,
  Or in the fertile furrow laid.

The drops that from the transient shower
  Fall in the noon-day bright and clear,
Or kindle beauty in the flower,
  Or waken freshness in the air.

Nothing is lost; the etherial fire,
    Which from the farthest star descends,
Through the immensity of space
    Its course by worlds attracted bends,

To reach the earth; the eternal laws
    Preserve one glorious wise design;
Order amidst confusion flows,
    And all the system is divine.

If *matter* cannot be destroy'd,
    The *living mind* can *never* die;
If e'en creative when alloy'd,
    How sure its immortality!

Then think that intellectual light
    Thou loved'st on earth is burning still,
Its lustre purer and more bright,
    Obscured no more by mortal will.

All things most glorious on the earth,
    Though transient and short-lived they seem,
Have yet a source of heavenly birth
    Immortal, – not a fleeting dream.

The lovely changeful light of even,
    The fading gleams of morning skies,
The evanescent tints of heaven,
    From the eternal sun arise.

LORD BYRON

(1788–1824)

From *Cain*

NOTE ON CUVIER

The reader will perceive that the author has partly adopted in this poem the notion of Cuvier, that the world had been destroyed several times before the creation of man. This speculation, derived from the different strata and the bones of enormous and unknown animals found in them, is not contrary to the Mosaic account, but rather confirms it; as no human bones have yet been discovered in those strata, although those of many known animals are found near the remains of the unknown. The assertion of Lucifer, that the pre-Adamite world was also peopled by rational beings much more intelligent than man, and proportionably powerful to the mammoth, etc. etc., is, of course, a poetical fiction to help him to make out his case.

From *Cain*

PREHISTORIC REPTILES

Cain. What are these mighty phantoms which I see
    Floating around me? – They wear not the form
    Of the intelligences I have seen
    Round our regretted and unenter'd Eden,
    Nor wear the form of man as I have view'd it
    In Adam's and in Abel's, and in mine,
    Nor in my sister-bride's, nor in my children's:
    And yet they have an aspect, which, though not
    Of men nor angels, looks like something, which
    If not the last, rose higher than the first,
    Haughty, and high, and beautiful, and full
    Of seeming strength, but of inexplicable
    Shape; for I never saw such. They bear not
    The wing of seraph, nor the face of man,
    Nor form of mightiest brute, nor aught that is
    Now breathing; mighty yet and beautiful
    As the most beautiful and mighty which
    Live, and yet so unlike them, that I scarce
    Can call them living.

★

Cain.   And those enormous creatures,
   Phantoms inferior in intelligence
   (At least so seeming) to the things we have pass'd,
   Resembling somewhat the wild habitants
   Of the deep woods of earth, the hugest which
   Roar nightly in the forest, but ten-fold
   In magnitude and terror; taller than
   The cherub-guarded walls of Eden, with
   Eyes flashing like the fiery swords which fence them,
   And tusks projecting like the trees stripp'd of
   Their bark and branches – what were they?
Lucifer.   That which
   The Mammoth is in thy world; – but these lie
   By myriads underneath its surface.

★

Cain.   And yon immeasurable liquid space
   Of glorious azure which floats on beyond us,
   Which looks like water, and which I should deem
   The river which flows out of Paradise
   Past my own dwelling, but that it is bankless
   And boundless, and of an ethereal hue –
   What is it?
Lucifer.   There is still some such on earth,
   Although inferior, and thy children shall
   Dwell near it – 'tis the phantasm of an ocean.
Cain.   'Tis like another world, a liquid sun –
   And those inordinate creatures sporting o'er
   Its shining surface?
Lucifer.   Are its habitants,
   The past leviathans.
Cain.   And yon immense
   Serpent, which rears his dripping mane and vasty
   Head ten times higher than the haughtiest cedar
   Forth from the abyss, looking as he could coil
   Himself around the orbs we lately look'd on –
   Is he not of the kind which bask'd beneath
   The tree in Eden?
Lucifer.   Eve, thy mother, best
   Can tell what shape of serpent tempted her.

Don Juan
Canto IX, stanzas 36–40

CATACLYSMS

Oh, ye great authors! – 'Apropos des bottes,' –
   I have forgotten what I meant to say,
As sometimes have been greater sages' lots; –
   'Twas something calculated to allay
All wrath in barracks, palaces, or cots;
   Certes it would have been but thrown away,
And that's one comfort for my lost advice,
Although no doubt it was beyond all price.

But let it go: – it will one day be found
   With other relics of 'a former world,'
When this world shall be *former*, underground,
   Thrown topsy-turvy, twisted, crisp'd, and curl'd,
Baked, fried, or burnt, turn'd inside-out, or drown'd,
   Like all the worlds before, which have been hurl'd
First out of, and then back again to chaos,
The superstratum which will overlay us.

So Cuvier says; – and then shall come again
   Unto the new creation, rising out
From our old crash, some mystic, ancient strain
   Of things destroy'd and left in airy doubt:
Like to the notions we now entertain
   Of Titans, giants, fellows of about
Some hundred feet in height, *not* to say *miles*,
And mammoths, and your winged crocodiles.

Think if then George the Fourth should be dug up!
   How the new worldlings of the then new East
Will wonder where such animals could sup!
   (For they themselves will be but of the least:
Even worlds miscarry, when too oft they pup,
   And every new creation hath decreased
In size, from overworking the material –
Men are but maggots of some huge Earth's burial.)

How will – to these young people, just thrust out
   From some fresh Paradise, and set to plough,

And dig, and sweat, and turn themselves about,
    And plant, and reap, and spin, and grind, and sow,
Till all the arts at length are brought about,
    Especially of war and taxing, – how,
I say, will these great relics, when they see 'em,
Look like the monsters of a new museum!

PERCY BYSSHE SHELLEY

(1792–1822)

Queen Mab★

lines 68–96

A VISION OF THE UNIVERSE

The Fairy and the Spirit
Approached the overhanging battlement. –
    Below lay stretched the universe!
    There, far as the remotest line
    That bounds imagination's flight,
        Countless and unending orbs
    In mazy motion intermingled,
    Yet still fulfilled immutably
        Eternal Nature's law.
        Above, below, around,
        The circling systems formed
    A wilderness of harmony;
    Each with undeviating aim,
In eloquent silence, through the depths of space
    Pursued its wondrous way.

    There was a little light
That twinkled in the misty distance:
    None but a spirit's eye
    Might ken that rolling orb;
    None but a spirit's eye,
    And in no other place
But that celestial dwelling, might behold
Each action of this earth's inhabitants.

But matter, space and time
In those aëreal mansions cease to act;
And all-prevailing wisdom, when it reaps
The harvest of its excellence, o'erbounds
Those obstacles, of which an earthly soul
    Fears to attempt the conquest.

Queen Mab

lines 38–46

POLAR SHIFTS AND FOSSILS

'How sweet a scene will earth become!
Of purest spirits a pure dwelling-place,
Symphonious with the planetary spheres;
When man, with changeless Nature coalescing,
Will undertake regeneration's work,
When its ungenial poles no longer point
    To the red and baleful sun
    That faintly twinkles there . . .'[1]

1. The north polar star, to which the axis of the earth, in its present state of obliquity, points. It is exceedingly probable, from many considerations, that this obliquity will gradually diminish, until the equator coincides with the ecliptic: the nights and days will then become equal on the earth throughout the year, and probably the seasons also. There is no great extravagance in presuming that the progress of the perpendicularity of the poles may be as rapid as the progress of intellect; or that there should be a perfect identity between the moral and physical improvement of the human species ... Astronomy teaches us that the earth is now in its progress, and that the poles are every year becoming more and more perpendicular to the ecliptic. The strong evidence afforded by the history of mythology, and geological researches, that some event of this nature has taken place already, affords a strong presumption that this progress is not merely an oscillation, as has been surmised by some late astronomers. Bones of animals peculiar to the torrid zone have been found in the north of Siberia, and on the banks of the river Ohio. Plants have been found in the fossil state in the interior of Germany, which demand the present climate of Hindostan for their production. The researches of M. Bailly establish the existence of a people who inhabited a tract in Tartary 49° north latitude, of greater antiquity than either the Indians, the Chinese, or the Chaldeans, from whom these nations derived their sciences and theology. We find, from the testimony of ancient writers, that Britain, Germany, and France were much colder than at present, and that their great rivers were annually frozen over. Astronomy teaches us also that since this period the obliquity of the earth's position has been considerably diminished. [Shelley's note.]

Queen Mab

lines 146–73

'A SPIRIT OF ACTIVITY AND LIFE'

'Throughout these infinite orbs of mingling light,
Of which yon earth is one, is wide diffused
A Spirit of activity and life,
That knows no term, cessation, or decay;
That fades not when the lamp of earthly life,
Extinguished in the dampness of the grave,
Awhile there slumbers, more than when the babe
In the dim newness of its being feels
The impulses of sublunary things,
And all is wonder to unpractised sense:
But, active, steadfast, and eternal, still
Guides the fierce whirlwind, in the tempest roars,
Cheers in the day, breathes in the balmy groves,
Strengthens in health, and poisons in disease;
And in the storm of change, that ceaselessly
Rolls round the eternal universe, and shakes
Its undecaying battlement, presides,
Apportioning with irresistible law
The place each spring of its machine shall fill;
So that when waves on waves tumultuous heap
Confusion to the clouds, and fiercely driven
Heaven's lightnings scorch the uprooted ocean-fords,
Whilst, to the eye of shipwrecked mariner,
Lone sitting on the bare and shuddering rock,
All seems unlinked contingency and chance:
No atom of this turbulence fulfils
A vague and unnecessitated task,
Or acts but as it must and ought to act. . .'

Prometheus Unbound

Act IV, lines 325–492

THE MOON AND THE EARTH

The Moon

> Brother mine, calm wanderer,
> Happy globe of land and air,
> Some Spirit is darted like a beam from thee,
> Which penetrates my frozen frame,
> And passes with the warmth of flame,
> With love, and odour, and deep melody
> Through me, through me!

The Earth

> Ha! ha! the caverns of my hollow mountains,
> My cloven fire-crags, sound-exulting fountains
> Laugh with a vast and inextinguishable laughter.
> The oceans, and the deserts, and the abysses,
> And the deep air's unmeasured wildernesses,
> Answer from all their clouds and billows, echoing after.
>
> They cry aloud as I do. Sceptred curse,
> Who all our green and azure universe
> Threatenedst to muffle round with black destruction, sending
> A solid cloud to rain hot thunderstones,
> And splinter and knead down my children's bones,
> All I bring forth, to one void mass battering and blending, –
>
> Until each crag-like tower, and storied column,
> Palace, and obelisk, and temple solemn,
> My imperial mountains crowned with cloud, and snow, and fire,
> My sea-like forests, every blade and blossom
> Which finds a grave or cradle in my bosom,
> Were stamped by thy strong hate into a lifeless mire:
>
> How art thou sunk, withdrawn, covered, drunk up
> By thirsty nothing, as the brackish cup
> Drained by a desert-troop, a little drop for all;
> And from beneath, around, within, above,
> Filling thy void annihilation, love
> Burst in like light on caves cloven by the thunder-ball.

The Moon

The snow upon my lifeless mountains
Is loosened into living fountains,
My solid oceans flow, and sing, and shine:
A spirit from my heart bursts forth,
It clothes with unexpected birth*
My cold bare bosom: Oh! it must be thine
    On mine, on mine!

Gazing on thee I feel, I know
Green stalks burst forth, and bright flowers grow,
And living shapes upon my bosom move:
Music is in the sea and air,
Wingèd clouds soar here and there,
Dark with the rain new buds are dreaming of:
    'Tis love, all love!

The Earth

It interpenetrates my granite mass,
Through tangled roots and trodden clay doth pass
Into the utmost leaves and delicatest flowers;
Upon the winds, among the clouds 'tis spread,
It wakes a life in the forgotten dead,
They breathe a spirit up from their obscurest bowers.

And like a storm bursting its cloudy prison
With thunder, and with whirlwind, has arisen
Out of the lampless caves of unimagined being:
With earthquake shock and swiftness making shiver
Thought's stagnant chaos, unremoved for ever,
Till hate, and fear, and pain, light-vanquished shadows, fleeing,

Leave Man, who was a many-sided mirror,
Which could distort to many a shape of error,
This true fair world of things, a sea reflecting love;
Which over all his kind, as the sun's heaven
Gliding o'er ocean, smooth, serene, and even,
Darting from starry depths radiance and life, doth move:

Leave Man, even as a leprous child is left,
Who follows a sick beast to some warm cleft
Of rocks, through which the might of healing springs is poured;

Then when it wanders home with rosy smile,
   Unconscious, and its mother fears awhile
It is a spirit, then, weeps on her child restored.

Man, oh, not men! a chain of linkèd thought,
   Of love and might to be divided not,
Compelling the elements with adamantine stress;
   As the sun rules, even with a tyrant's gaze,
   The unquiet republic of the maze
Of planets, struggling fierce towards heaven's free wilderness.

Man, one harmonious soul of many a soul,
   Whose nature is its own divine control,
Where all things flow to all, as rivers to the sea;
   Familiar acts are beautiful through love;
   Labour, and pain, and grief, in life's green grove
Sport like tame beasts, none knew how gentle they could be!

His will, with all mean passions, bad delights,
   And selfish cares, its trembling satellites,
A spirit ill to guide, but mighty to obey,
   Is as a tempest-wingèd ship, whose helm
   Love rules, through waves which dare not overwhelm,
Forcing life's wildest shores to own its sovereign sway.

All things confess his strength. Through the cold mass
   Of marble and of colour his dreams pass;
Bright threads whence mothers weave the robes their children wear;
   Language is a perpetual Orphic song,
   Which rules with Daedal harmony a throng
Of thoughts and forms, which else senseless and shapeless were.

The lightning is his slave; heaven's utmost deep
   Gives up her stars, and like a flock of sheep
They pass before his eye, are numbered, and roll on!
   The tempest is his steed, he strides the air;
   And the abyss shouts from her depth laid bare,
Heaven, hast thou secrets? Man unveils me; I have none.

The Moon

The shadow of white death has passed
From my path in heaven at last,
A clinging shroud of solid frost and sleep;

And through my newly-woven bowers,
  Wander happy paramours,
Less mighty, but as mild as those who keep
    Thy vales more deep.

The Earth

As the dissolving warmth of dawn may fold
A half unfrozen dew-globe, green, and gold,
And crystalline, till it becomes a wingèd mist,
  And wanders up the vault of the blue day,
  Outlives the noon, and on the sun's last ray
Hangs o'er the sea, a fleece of fire and amethyst.

The Moon

  Thou art folded, thou art lying
  In the light which is undying
Of thine own joy, and heaven's smile divine;
  All suns and constellations shower
  On thee a light, a life, a power
Which doth array thy sphere; thou pourest thine
    On mine, on mine!

The Earth

I spin beneath my pyramid of night,
  Which points into the heavens dreaming delight,
Murmuring victorious joy in my enchanted sleep;
  As a youth lulled in love-dreams faintly sighing,
  Under the shadow of his beauty lying,
Which round his rest a watch of light and warmth doth keep.

The Moon

  As in the soft and sweet eclipse,
  When soul meets soul on lovers' lips,
High hearts are calm, and brightest eyes are dull;
  So when thy shadow falls on me,
  Then am I mute and still, by thee
Covered; of thy love, Orb most beautiful,
    Full, oh, too full!

  Thou art speeding round the sun
  Brightest world of many a one;
  Green and azure sphere which shinest

With a light which is divinest
Among all the lamps of Heaven
To whom life and light is given;
I, thy crystal paramour
Borne beside thee by a power
Like the polar Paradise,
Magnet-like of lovers' eyes;
I, a most enamoured maiden
Whose weak brain is overladen
With the pleasure of her love,
Maniac-like around thee move
Gazing, an insatiate bride,
On thy form from every side
Like a Maenad, round the cup
Which Agave lifted up
In the weird Cadmaean forest.
Brother, wheresoe'er thou soarest
I must hurry, whirl and follow
Through the heavens wide and hollow,
Sheltered by the warm embrace
Of thy soul from hungry space,
Drinking from thy sense and sight
Beauty, majesty, and might,
As a lover or a chameleon
Grows like what it looks upon,
As a violet's gentle eye
Gazes on the azure sky
Until its hue grows like what it beholds,
As a gray and watery mist
Glows like solid amethyst
Athwart the western mountain it enfolds,
When the sunset sleeps
Upon its snow —

The Earth

And the weak day weeps
That it should be so.

PERCY BYSSHE SHELLEY

Letter to Maria Gisborne
lines 15–105

SHELLEY'S SCIENTIFIC EXPERIMENTS

Whoever should behold me now, I wist,
Would think I were a mighty mechanist,
Bent with sublime Archimedean art
To breathe a soul into the iron heart
Of some machine portentous, or strange gin,
Which by the force of figured spells might win
Its way over the sea, and sport therein;
For round the walls are hung dread engines, such
As Vulcan never wrought for Jove to clutch
Ixion or the Titan: – or the quick
Wit of that man of God, St Dominic,
To convince Atheist, Turk, or Heretic,
Or those in philanthropic council met,
Who thought to pay some interest for the debt
They owed to Jesus Christ for their salvation,
By giving a faint foretaste of damnation
To Shakespeare, Sidney, Spenser, and the rest
Who made our land an island of the blest.
When lamp-like Spain, who now relumes her fire
On Freedom's hearth, grew dim with Empire: –
With thumbscrews, wheels, with tooth and spike and jag,
Which fishers found under the utmost crag
Of Cornwall and the storm-encompassed isles,
Where to the sky the rude sea rarely smiles
Unless in treacherous wrath, as on the morn
When the exulting elements in scorn,
Satiated with destroyed destruction, lay
Sleeping in beauty on their mangled prey,
As panthers sleep; – and other strange and dread
Magical forms the brick floor overspread, –
Proteus transformed to metal did not make
More figures, or more strange; nor did he take
Such shapes of unintelligible brass,
Or heap himself in such a horrid mass
Of tin and iron not to be understood;
And forms of unimaginable wood,

193

To puzzle Tubal Cain and all his brood:
Great screws, and cones, and wheels, and groovèd blocks,
The elements of what will stand the shocks
Of wave and wind and time. – Upon the table
More knacks and quips there be than I am able
To catalogize in this verse of mine: –
A pretty bowl of wood – not full of wine,
But quicksilver; that dew which the gnomes drink
When at their subterranean toil they swink,
Pledging the demons of the earthquake, who
Reply to them in lava – cry halloo!
And call out to the cities o'er their head, –
Roofs, towers, and shrines, the dying and the dead,
Crash through the chinks of earth – and then all quaff
Another rouse, and hold their sides and laugh.
This quicksilver no gnome has drunk – within
The walnut bowl it lies, veinèd and thin,
In colour like the wake of light that stains
The Tuscan deep, when from the moist moon rains
The inmost shower of its white fire – the breeze
Is still – blue Heaven smiles over the pale seas.
And in this bowl of quicksilver – for I
Yield to the impulse of an infancy
Outlasting manhood – I have made to float
A rude idealism of a paper boat: –
A hollow screw with cogs – Henry will know
The thing I mean and laugh at me, – if so
He fears not I should do more mischief. – Next
Lie bills and calculations much perplexed,
With steam-boats, frigates, and machinery quaint
Traced over them in blue and yellow paint.
Then comes a range of mathematical
Instruments, for plans nautical and statical;
A heap of rosin, a queer broken glass
With ink in it; – a china cup that was
What it will never be again, I think, –
A thing from which sweet lips were wont to drink
The liquor doctors rail at – and which I
Will quaff in spite of them – and when we die
We'll toss up who died first of drinking tea,
And cry out, – 'Heads or tails?' where'er we be.

Near that a dusty paint-box, some odd hooks,
A half-burnt match, an ivory block, three books,
Where conic sections, spherics, logarithms,
To great Laplace, from Saunderson and Sims,
Lie heaped in their harmonious disarray
Of figures, – disentangle them who may.
Baron de Tott's Memoirs beside them lie,
And some odd volumes of old chemistry.
Near those a most inexplicable thing,
With lead in the middle – I'm conjecturing
How to make Henry understand; but no –
I'll leave, as Spenser says, with many mo,
This secret in the pregnant womb of time,
Too vast a matter for so weak a rhyme.

The Cloud★

I bring fresh showers for the thirsting flowers,
    From the seas and the streams;
I bear light shade for the leaves when laid
    In their noonday dreams.
From my wings are shaken the dews that waken
    The sweet buds every one,
When rocked to rest on their mother's breast,
    As she dances about the sun.
I wield the flail of the lashing hail,
    And whiten the green plains under,
And then again I dissolve it in rain,
    And laugh as I pass in thunder.

I sift the snow on the mountains below,
    And their great pines groan aghast;
And all the night 'tis my pillow white,
    While I sleep in the arms of the blast.
Sublime on the towers of my skiey bowers,
    Lightning my pilot sits;
In a cavern under is fettered the thunder,
    It struggles and howls at fits;
Over earth and ocean, with gentle motion,
    This pilot is guiding me,

Lured by the love of the genii that move
    In the depths of the purple sea;
Over the rills, and the crags, and the hills,
    Over the lakes and the plains,
Wherever he dream, under mountain or stream,
    The Spirit he loves remains;
And I all the while bask in Heaven's blue smile,
    Whilst he is dissolving in rains.

The sanguine Sunrise, with his meteor eyes,
    And his burning plumes outspread,
Leaps on the back of my sailing rack,
    When the morning star shines dead;
As on the jag of a mountain crag,
    Which an earthquake rocks and swings,
An eagle alit one moment may sit
    In the light of its golden wings.
And when Sunset may breathe, from the lit sea beneath,
    Its ardours of rest and of love,
And the crimson pall of eve may fall
    From the depth of Heaven above,
With wings folded I rest, on mine aëry nest,
    As still as a brooding dove.

That orbèd maiden with white fire laden,
    Whom mortals call the Moon,
Glides glimmering o'er my fleece-like floor,
    By the midnight breezes strewn;
And wherever the beat of her unseen feet,
    Which only the angels hear,
May have broken the woof of my tent's thin roof,
    The stars peep behind her and peer;
And I laugh to see them whirl and flee,
    Like a swarm of golden bees,
When I widen the rent in my wind-built tent.
    Till the calm rivers, lakes, and seas,
Like strips of the sky fallen through me on high,
    Are each paved with the moon and these.

I bind the Sun's throne with a burning zone,
    And the Moon's with a girdle of pearl;
The volcanoes are dim, and the stars reel and swim,
    When the whirlwinds my banner unfurl.

From cape to cape, with a bridge-like shape,
    Over a torrent sea,
Sunbeam-proof, I hang like a roof, –
    The mountains its columns be.
The triumphal arch through which I march
    With hurricane, fire, and snow,
When the Powers of the air are chained to my chair,
    Is the million-coloured bow;
The sphere-fire above its soft colours wove,
    While the moist Earth was laughing below.

I am the daughter of Earth and Water,
    And the nursling of the Sky;
I pass through the pores of the ocean and shores;
    I change, but I cannot die.
For after the rain when with never a stain
    The pavilion of Heaven is bare,
And the winds and sunbeams with their convex gleams
    Build up the blue dome of air,
I silently laugh at my own cenotaph,
    And out of the caverns of rain,
Like a child from the womb, like a ghost from the tomb,
    I arise and unbuild it again.

JOHN KEATS

(1795–1821)

Lamia

lines 185–99, 221–38

'THERE WAS AN AWFUL RAINBOW ONCE IN HEAVEN...'

    Ah, happy Lycius! – for she was a maid
    More beautiful than ever twisted braid,
    Or sigh'd, or blush'd, or on spring-flowered lea
    Spread a green kirtle to the minstrelsy:
    A virgin purest lipp'd, yet in the lore
    Of love deep learned to the red heart's core:
    Not one hour old, yet of sciential brain
    To unperplex bliss from its neighbour pain;

Define their pettish limits, and estrange
Their points of contact, and swift counterchange;
Intrigue with the specious chaos, and dispart
Its most ambiguous atoms with sure art;
As though in Cupid's college she had spent
Sweet days a lovely graduate, still unshent,
And kept his rosy terms in idle languishment.

*

What wreath for Lamia? What for Lycius?
What for the sage, old Apollonius?
Upon her aching forehead be there hung
The leaves of willow and of adder's tongue;
And for the youth, quick, let us strip for him
The thyrsus, that his watching eyes may swim
Into forgetfulness; and, for the sage,
Let spear-grass and the spiteful thistle wage
War on his temples. Do not all charms fly
At the mere touch of cold philosophy?
There was an awful rainbow* once in heaven:
We know her woof, her texture; she is given
In the dull catalogue of common things.
Philosophy will clip an Angel's wings,
Conquer all mysteries by rule and line,
Empty the haunted air, and gnomed mine –
Unweave a rainbow, as it erewhile made
The tender-person'd Lamia melt into a shade.

THOMAS LOVELL BEDDOES

(1803–49)

A Subterranean City

I followed once a fleet and mighty serpent
Into a cavern in a mountain's side;
And, wading many lakes, descending gulphs,
At last I reached the ruins of a city,
Built not like ours but of another world,
As if the aged earth had loved in youth
The mightiest city of a perished planet,

And kept the image of it in her heart,
So dream-like, shadowy, and spectral was it.
Nought seemed alive there, and the very dead
Were of another world the skeletons.
The mammoth, ribbed like to an arched cathedral,
Lay there, and ruins of great creatures else
More like a shipwrecked fleet, too great they seemed
For all the life that is to animate:
And vegetable rocks, tall sculptured palms,
Pine grown, not hewn, in stone; and giant ferns
Whose earthquake-shaken leaves bore graves for nests.

RALPH WALDO EMERSON

(1803–82)

Monadnoc

lines 244–81

'THE ATOMS MARCH IN TUNE...'

'If thou trowest
How the chemic eddies* play,
Pole to pole, and what they say;
And that these grey crags
Not on crags are hung,
But beads are of a rosary
On prayer and music strung;
And, credulous, through the granite seeming,
Seest the smile of Reason beaming; –
Can thy style-discerning eye
The hidden-working Builder spy,
Who builds, yet makes no chips, no din,
With hammer soft as snow-flake's flight; –
Knowest thou this?
O pilgrim, wandering not amiss!
Already my rocks lie light,
And soon my cone will spin.

'For the world was built in order,
And the atoms march in tune;

Rhyme the pipe, and Time the warder,
Cannot forget the sun, the moon.
Orb and atom forth they prance,
When they hear from far the rune;
None so backward in the troop,
When the music and the dance
Reach his place and circumstance,
But knows the sun-creating sound,
And, though a pyramid, will bound.

'Monadnoc is a mountain strong,
Tall and good my kind among;
But well I know, no mountain can
Measure with a perfect man.
For it is on zodiacs writ,
Adamant is soft to wit:
And when the greater comes again
With my secret in his brain,
I shall pass, as glides my shadow,
Daily over hill and meadow ...'

CHARLES TENNYSON TURNER

(1808–79)

Old Ruralities: A Regret

With joy all relics of the past I hail;
The heath-bell, lingering in our cultured moor,
Or the dull sound of the slip-shoulder'd flail,
Still busy on the poor man's threshing-floor:
I love this unshorn hedgerow, which survives
Its stunted neighbours, in this farming age:
The thatch and house-leek, where old Alice lives
With her old herbal, trusting every page;
I love the spinning-wheel, which hums far down
In yon lone valley, though, from day to day,
The boom of Science shakes it from the town.
Ah! sweet old world! thou speedest fast away!
My boyhood's world! but all last looks are dear;
More touching is the death-bed than the bier!

OLIVER WENDELL HOLMES

(1809–94)

From *Extracts from a Medical Poem*

THE STABILITY OF SCIENCE

The feeble sea-birds, blinded in the storms
On some tall lighthouse dash their little forms,
And the rude granite scatters for their pains
Those small deposits that were meant for brains.
Yet the proud fabric in the morning's sun
Stands all unconscious of the mischief done;
Still the red beacon pours its evening rays
For the lost pilot with as full a blaze,
Nay, shines, all radiance, o'er the scattered fleet
Of gulls and boobies brainless at its feet.

I tell their fate, though courtesy disclaims
To call our kind by such ungentle names;
Yet, if your rashness bid you vainly dare,
Think of their doom, ye simple, and beware!

See where aloft its hoary forehead rears
The towering pride of twice a thousand years!
Far, far below the vast incumbent pile
Sleeps the gray rock from art's Aegean isle;
Its massive courses, circling as they rise,
Swell from the waves to mingle with the skies;
There every quarry lends its marble spoil,
And clustering ages blend their common toil;
The Greek, the Roman, reared its ancient walls,
The silent Arab arched its mystic halls;
In that fair niche, by countless billows laved,
Trace the deep lines that Sydenham engraved;
On yon broad front that breasts the changing swell,
Mark where the ponderous sledge of Hunter fell;
By that square buttress look where Louis stands,
The stone yet warm from his uplifted hands;
And say, O Science, shall thy life-blood freeze,
When fluttering folly flaps on walls like these?

EDGAR ALLAN POE

(1809–49)

To Science

Science! true daughter of Old Time thou art!
  Who alterest all things with thy peering eyes.
Why preyest thou thus upon the poet's heart,
  Vulture, whose wings are dull realities?
How should he love thee? or how deem thee wise,
  Who wouldst not leave him in his wandering
To seek for treasure in the jewelled skies,
  Albeit he soared with an undaunted wing?
Hast thou not dragged Diana from her car?
  And driven the Hamadryad from the wood
To seek a shelter in some happier star?
  Hast thou not torn the Naiad from her flood,
The Elfin from the green grass, and from me
The summer dream beneath the tamarind tree?

ALFRED, LORD TENNYSON

(1809–92)

From *Locksley Hall*

'I DIPT INTO THE FUTURE ...'

For I dipt into the future, far as human eye could see,
Saw the Vision of the world, and all the wonder that would be;

Saw the heavens fill with commerce, argosies of magic sails,
Pilots of the purple twilight, dropping down with costly bales;

Heard the heavens fill with shouting, and there rain'd a ghastly dew
From the nations' airy navies grappling in the central blue;

Far along the world-wide whisper of the south-wind rushing warm,
With the standards of the peoples plunging thro' the thunder-storm;

Till the war-drum throbb'd no longer, and the battle-flags were furl'd
In the Parliament of man, the Federation of the world.

There the common sense of most shall hold a fretful realm in awe,
And the kindly earth shall slumber, lapt in universal law.

So I triumph'd ere my passion sweeping thro' me left me dry,
Left me with the palsied heart, and left me with the jaundiced eye;

Eye, to which all order festers, all things here are out of joint:
Science moves, but slowly slowly, creeping on from point to point:

Slowly comes a hungry people, as a lion, creeping nigher,
Glares at one that nods and winks behind a slowly-dying fire.

Yet I doubt not thro' the ages one increasing purpose runs,
And the thoughts of men are widen'd with the process of the suns.

What is that to him that reaps not harvest of his youthful joys,
Tho' the deep heart of existence beat for ever like a boy's?

Knowledge comes, but wisdom lingers, and I linger on the shore,
And the individual withers, and the world is more and more.

Knowledge comes, but wisdom lingers, and he bears a laden breast,
Full of sad experience, moving toward the stillness of his rest.

In Memoriam A. H. H.
Sections LVI and CXXIII

GOD AND NATURE AT STRIFE?

'So careful of the type?' but no.
  From scarpèd cliff and quarried stone
  She cries, 'A thousand types* are gone:
I care for nothing, all shall go.

'Thou makest thine appeal to me:
  I bring to life, I bring to death:
  The spirit does but mean the breath:
I know no more.' And he, shall he,

Man, her last work, who seemed so fair,
  Such splendid purpose in his eyes,
  Who rolled the psalm to wintry skies,
Who built him fanes of fruitless prayer,

Who trusted God was love indeed
  And love Creation's final law –
  Though Nature, red in tooth and claw
With ravine, shrieked against his creed –

Who loved, who suffered countless ills,
  Who battled for the True, the Just,
  Be blown about the desert dust,
Or sealed within the iron hills?

No more? A monster then, a dream,
  A discord. Dragons of the prime,
  That tare each other in their slime,
Were mellow music matched with him.

O life as futile, then, as frail!
  O for thy voice to soothe and bless!
  What hope of answer, or redress?
Behind the veil, behind the veil.

*

There rolls the deep where grew the tree.
  O earth, what changes hast thou seen!
  There where the long street roars, hath been
The stillness of the central sea.

The hills are shadows, and they flow
  From form to form, and nothing stands;
  They melt like mist, the solid lands,
Like clouds they shape themselves and go.

But in my spirit will I dwell,
  And dream my dream, and hold it true;
  For though my lips may breathe adieu,
I cannot think the thing farewell.

From *Lucretius*★

Lucilia, wedded to Lucretius, found
  Her master cold; for when the morning flush
  Of passion and the first embrace had died
  Between them, tho' he loved her none the less,

Yet often when the woman heard his foot
Return from pacings in the field, and ran
To greet him with a kiss, the master took
Small notice, or austerely, for – his mind
Half buried in some weightier argument,
Or fancy-borne perhaps upon the rise
And long roll of the Hexameter – he past
To turn and ponder those three hundred scrolls
Left by the Teacher whom he held divine.
She brook'd it not; but wrathful, petulant,
Dreaming some rival, sought and found a witch
Who brew'd the philtre which had power, they said,
To lead an errant passion home again.
And this, at times, she mingled with his drink,
And this destroy'd him; for the wicked broth
Confused the chemic labour of the blood,
And tickling the brute brain within the man's
Made havock among those tender cells, and check'd
His power to shape: he loath'd himself; and once
After a tempest woke upon a morn
That mock'd him with returning calm, and cried ...

*

'Storm, and what dreams, ye holy Gods, what dreams!
For thrice I waken'd after dreams. Perchance
We do but recollect the dreams that come
Just ere the waking: terrible! for it seem'd
A void was made in Nature; all her bonds
Crack'd; and I saw the flaring atom-streams
And torrents of her myriad universe,
Ruining along the illimitable inane,
Fly on to clash together again, and make
Another and another frame of things
For ever: that was mine, my dream, I knew it –
Of and belonging to me, as the dog
With inward yelp and restless forefoot plies
His function of the woodland: but the next!
I thought that all the blood by Sylla shed
Came driving rainlike down again on earth,
And where it dash'd the reddening meadow, sprang
No dragon warriors from Cadmean teeth,

For these I thought my dream would show to me,
But girls, Hetairai, curious in their art,
Hired animalisms, vile as those that made
The mulberry-faced Dictator's orgies worse
Than aught they fable of the quiet Gods.
And hands they mixt, and yell'd and round me drove
In narrowing circles till I yell'd again
Half-suffocated, and sprang up, and saw –
Was it the first beam of my latest day? . . .

*

'The Gods! and if I go *my* work is left
Unfinish'd – *if* I go. The Gods, who haunt
The lucid interspace of world and world,
Where never creeps a cloud, or moves a wind,
Nor ever falls the least white star of snow,
Nor ever lowest roll of thunder moans,
Nor sound of human sorrow mounts to mar
Their sacred everlasting calm! and such,
Not all so fine, nor so divine a calm,
Not such, nor all unlike it, man may gain
Letting his own life go. The Gods, the Gods!
If all be atoms, how then should the Gods
Being atomic not be dissoluble,
Not follow the great law? My master* held
That Gods there are, for all men so believe.
I prest my footsteps into his, and meant
Surely to lead my Memmius in a train
Of flowery clauses onward to the proof
That Gods there are, and deathless. Meant? I meant?
I have forgotten what I meant: my mind
Stumbles, and all my faculties are lamed. . . .

*

                    'And therefore now
Let her, that is the womb and tomb of all,
Great Nature, take, and forcing far apart
Those blind beginnings that have made me man,
Dash them anew together at her will
Through all her cycles – into man once more,
Or beast or bird or fish, or opulent flower –

But till this cosmic order everywhere
Shatter'd into one earthquake in one day
Cracks all to pieces, – and that hour perhaps
Is not so far when momentary man
Shall seem no more a something to himself,
But he, his hopes and hates, his homes and fanes,
And even his bones long laid within the grave,
The very sides of the grave itself shall pass,
Vanishing, atom and void, atom and void,
Into the unseen for ever, – till that hour,
My golden work in which I told a truth
That stays the rolling Ixionian wheel,
And numbs the Fury's ringlet-snake, and plucks
The mortal soul from out immortal hell,
Shall stand: aye, surely: then it fails at last
And perishes as I must; for O Thou,
Passionless bride, divine Tranquillity,
Yearn'd after by the wisest of the wise,
Who fail to find thee, being as thou art
Without one pleasure and without one pain,
Howbeit I know thou surely must be mine
Or soon or late, yet out of season, thus
I woo thee roughly, for thou carest not
How roughly men may woo thee so they win –
Thus – thus: the soul flies out and dies in the air.'
  With that he drove the knife into his side:
She heard him raging, heard him fall; ran in,
Beat breast, tore hair, cried out upon herself
As having fail'd in duty to him, shriek'd
That she but meant to win him back, fell on him,
Clasp'd, kiss'd him, wail'd: he answer'd, 'Care not thou!
What matters? All is over: Fare thee well!'

ROBERT BROWNING

(1812–89)

Caliban upon Setebos; or Natural Theology* in the Island

lines 1–56, 241–end

'Thou thoughtest that I was altogether such a one as thyself.'*

['Will sprawl, now that the heat of day is best,
Flat on his belly in the pit's much mire,
With elbows wide, fists clenched to prop his chin.
And, while he kicks both feet in the cool slush,
And feels about his spine small eft-things course,
Run in and out each arm, and make him laugh:
And while above his head a pompion-plant,
Coating the cave-top as a brow its eye,
Creeps down to touch and tickle hair and beard,
And now a flower drops with a bee inside,
And now a fruit to snap at, catch and crunch, –
He looks out o'er yon sea which sunbeams cross
And recross till they weave a spider-web
(Meshes of fire, some great fish breaks at times)
And talks to his own self, howe'er he please,
Touching that other, whom his dam* called God.
Because to talk about Him,* vexes – ha,
Could He but know! and time to vex is now,
When talk is safer than in winter-time.
Moreover Prosper and Miranda sleep
In confidence he drudges at their task,
And it is good to cheat the pair, and gibe,
Letting the rank tongue blossom into speech.]

Setebos, Setebos, and Setebos!
'Thinketh, He dwelleth in the cold o' the moon.

'Thinketh, He made it, with the sun to match,
But not the stars; the stars came otherwise;
Only made clouds, winds, meteors, such as that:
Also this isle, what lives and grows thereon,
And snaky sea which rounds and ends the same.

'Thinketh, it came of being ill at ease:
He hated that He cannot change His cold,

Nor cure its ache. 'Hath spied an icy fish
That longed to 'scape the rock-stream where she lived,
And thaw herself within the lukewarm brine
O' the lazy sea her stream thrusts far amid,
A crystal spike 'twixt two warm walls of wave;
Only, she ever sickened, found repulse
At the other kind of water, not her life,
(Green-dense and dim-delicious, bred o' the sun)
Flounced back from bliss she was not born to breathe,
And in her old bounds buried her despair,
Hating and loving warmth alike: so He.

'Thinketh, He made thereat the sun, this isle,
Trees and the fowls here, beast and creeping thing.
Yon otter, sleek-wet, black, lithe as a leech;
Yon auk, one fire-eye in a ball of foam,
That floats and feeds; a certain badger brown
He hath watched hunt with that slant white-wedge eye
By moonlight; and the pie with the long tongue
That pricks deep into oakwarts for a worm,
And says a plain word when she finds her prize,
But will not eat the ants; the ants themselves
That build a wall of seeds and settled stalks
About their hole – He made all these and more,
Made all we see, and us, in spite: how else?

*

'Conceiveth all things will continue thus,
And we shall have to live in fear of Him
So long as He lives, keeps His strength: no change,
If He have done His best, make no new world
To please Him more, so leave off watching this, –
If He surprise not even the Quiet's self
Some strange day, – or, suppose, grow into it
As grubs grow butterflies: else, here are we,
And there is He, and nowhere help at all.
'Believeth with the life, the pain shall stop.
His dam held different, that after death
He both plagued enemies and feasted friends:
Idly! He doth His worst in this our life,
Giving just respite lest we die through pain,
Saving last pain for worst, – with which, an end.

Meanwhile, the best way to escape His ire
Is, not to seem too happy. 'Sees, himself,
Yonder two flies, with purple films and pink,
Bask on the pompion-bell above: kills both.
'Sees two black painful beetles roll their ball
On head and tail as if to save their lives:
Moves them the stick away they strive to clear.

Even so, 'would have Him misconceive, suppose
This Caliban strives hard and ails no less,
And always, above all else, envies Him;
Wherefore he mainly dances on dark nights,
Moans in the sun, gets under holes to laugh,
And never speaks his mind save housed as now:
Outside, 'groans, curses. If He caught me here,
O'erheard this speech, and asked 'What chucklest at?'
'Would, to appease Him, cut a finger off,
Or of my three kid yearlings burn the best,
Or let the toothsome apples rot on tree,
Or push my tame beast for the orc to taste:
While myself lit a fire, and made a song
And sung it, *'What I hate, be consecrate*
To celebrate Thee and Thy state, no mate
For Thee; what see for envy in poor me?'
Hoping the while, since evils sometimes mend,
Warts rub away and sores are cured with slime,
That some strange day, will either the Quiet catch
And conquer Setebos, or likelier He
Decrepit may doze, doze, as good as die.

[What, what? A curtain o'er the world at once!
Crickets stop hissing; not a bird – or, yes,
There scuds His raven that has told Him all!
It was fool's play, this prattling! Ha! The wind
Shoulders the pillared dust, death's house o' the move,
And fast invading fires begin! White blaze –
A tree's head snaps – and there, there, there, there, there,
His thunder follows! Fool to gibe at Him!
Lo! 'Lieth flat and loveth Setebos!
'Maketh his teeth meet through his upper lip,
Will let those quails fly, will not eat this month
One little mess of whelks, so he may 'scape!]

An Epistle Containing the Strange Medical Experience of Karshish, the Arab Physician

lines 1–61, 79–117, 243–303

Karshish, the picker-up of learning's crumbs,
The not-incurious in God's handiwork
(This man's-flesh he hath admirably made,
Blown like a bubble, kneaded like a paste,
To coop up and keep down on earth a space
That puff of vapour from his mouth, man's soul)
– To Abib, all-sagacious in our art,
Breeder in me of what poor skill I boast,
Like me inquisitive how pricks and cracks
Befall the flesh through too much stress and strain,
Whereby the wily vapour fain would slip
Back and rejoin its source before the term, –
And aptest in contrivance (under God)
To baffle it by deftly stopping such: –
The vagrant Scholar to his Sage at home
Sends greeting (health and knowledge, fame with peace)
Three samples of true snakestone – rarer still,
One of the other sort, the melon-shaped,
(But fitter, pounded fine, for charms than drugs)
And writeth now the twenty-second time.

My journeyings were brought to Jericho:
Thus I resume. Who studious in our art
Shall count a little labour unrepaid?
I have shed sweat enough, left flesh and bone
On many a flinty furlong of this land.
Also, the country-side is all on fire
With rumours of a marching hitherward:
Some say Vespasian cometh, some, his son.
A black lynx snarled and pricked a tufted ear;
Lust of my blood inflamed his yellow balls:
I cried and threw my staff and he was gone.
Twice have the robbers stripped and beaten me,
And once a town declared me for a spy;
But at the end, I reach Jerusalem,
Since this poor covert where I pass the night,
This Bethany, lies scarce the distance thence
A man with plague-sores at the third degree

Runs till he drops down dead. Thou laughest here!
'Sooth, it elates me, thus reposed and safe,
To void the stuffing of my travel-scrip
And share with thee whatever Jewry yields.
A viscid choler is observable
In tertians, I was nearly bold to say;
And falling-sickness hath a happier cure
Than our school wots of: there's a spider here
Weaves no web, watches on the ledge of tombs,
Sprinkled with mottles on an ash-grey back;
Take five and drop them ... but who knows his mind,
The Syrian runagate I trust this to?
His service payeth me a sublimate
Blown up his nose to help the ailing eye.
Best wait: I reach Jerusalem at morn,
There set in order my experiences,
Gather what most deserves, and give thee all –
Or I might add, Judea's gum-tragacanth
Scales off in purer flakes, shines clearer-grained,
Cracks 'twixt the pestle and the porphyry,
In fine exceeds our produce. Scalp-disease
Confounds me, crossing so with leprosy –
Thou hadst admired one sort I gained at Zoar –
But zeal outruns discretion. Here I end.

*

'Tis but a case of mania – subinduced
By epilepsy, at the turning-point
Of trance prolonged unduly some three days:
When, by the exhibition of some drug
Or spell, exorcization, stroke of art
Unknown to me and which 'twere well to know,
The evil thing out-breaking all at once
Left the man whole and sound of body indeed, –
But, flinging (so to speak) life's gates too wide,
Making a clear house of it too suddenly,
The first conceit that entered might inscribe
Whatever it was minded on the wall
So plainly at that vantage, as it were,
(First come, first served) that nothing subsequent
Attaineth to erase those fancy-scrawls

The just-returned and new-established soul
Hath gotten now so thoroughly by heart
That henceforth she will read or these or none.
And first – the man's own firm conviction rests
That he was dead (in fact they buried him)
– That he was dead and then restored to life
By a Nazarene physician of his tribe:
– 'Sayeth, the same bade 'Rise,' and he did rise.
'Such cases are diurnal,' thou wilt cry.
Not so this figment! – not, that such a fume,
Instead of giving way to time and health,
Should eat itself into the life of life,
As saffron tingeth flesh, blood, bones and all!
For see, how he takes up the after-life.
The man – it is one Lazarus a Jew,
Sanguine, proportioned, fifty years of age,
The body's habit wholly laudable,
As much, indeed, beyond the common health
As he were made and put aside to show.
Think, could we penetrate by any drug
And bathe the wearied soul and worried flesh,
And bring it clear and fair, by three days' sleep!
Whence has the man the balm that brightens all?
This grown man eyes the world now like a child.

*

Thou wilt object – Why have I not ere this
Sought out the sage himself, the Nazarene
Who wrought this cure, inquiring at the source,
Conferring with the frankness that befits?
Alas! it grieveth me, the learned leech
Perished in a tumult many years ago,
Accused, – our learning's fate, – of wizardry,
Rebellion, to the setting up a rule
And creed prodigious as described to me.
His death, which happened when the earthquake fell
(Prefiguring, as soon appeared, the loss
To occult learning in our lord the sage
Who lived there in the pyramid alone)
Was wrought by the mad people – that's their wont!
On vain recourse, as I conjecture it,

To his tried virtue, for miraculous help –
How could he stop the earthquake? That's their way!
The other imputations must be lies:
But take one, though I loathe to give it thee,
In mere respect for any good man's fame.
(And after all, our patient Lazarus
Is stark mad; should we count on what he says?
Perhaps not: though in writing to a leech
'Tis well to keep back nothing of a case.)
This man so cured regards the curer, then,
As – God forgive me! who but God himself,
Creator and sustainer of the world,
That came and dwelt in flesh on it awhile!
– 'Sayeth that such an one was born and lived,
Taught, healed the sick, broke bread at his own house,
Then died, with Lazarus by, for aught I know,
And yet was ... what I said nor choose repeat,
And must have so avouched himself, in fact,
In hearing of this very Lazarus
Who saith – but why all this of what he saith?
Why write of trivial matters, things of price
Calling at every moment for remark?
I noticed on the margin of a pool
Blue-flowering borage, the Aleppo sort,
Aboundeth, very nitrous. It is strange!

    Thy pardon for this long and tedious case,
Which, now that I review it, needs must seem
Unduly dwelt on, prolixly set forth!
Nor I myself discern in what is writ
Good cause for the peculiar interest
And awe indeed this man has touched me with.
Perhaps the journey's end, the weariness
Had wrought upon me first. I met him thus:
I crossed a ridge of short sharp broken hills
Like an old lion's cheek teeth. Out there came
A moon made like a face with certain spots
Multiform, manifold and menacing:
Then a wind rose behind me. So we met
In this old sleepy town at unaware,
The man and I. I send thee what is writ.

Regard it as a chance, a matter risked
To this ambiguous Syrian – he may lose,
Or steal, or give it thee with equal good.
Jerusalem's repose shall make amends
For time this letter wastes, thy time and mine;
Till when, once more thy pardon and farewell!

ARTHUR HUGH CLOUGH
(1819–61)

When Israel Came out of Egypt
lines 47–82

SCIENCE DENIES GOD

God spake it out, I, God, am One;
   The unheeding ages ran,
And baby-thoughts again, again,
   Have dogged the growing man:
And as of old from Sinai's top
   God said that God is One,
By Science strict so speaks He now
   To tell us, There is None!
Earth goes by chemic forces;* Heaven's
   A Mécanique Céleste!*
And heart and mind of human kind
   A watch-work as the rest!

Is this a Voice, as was the Voice
   Whose speaking told abroad,
When thunder pealed, and mountain reeled,
   The ancient Truth of God?
Ah, not the Voice; 'tis but the cloud,
   Of outer darkness dense,
Where image none, nor e'er was seen
   Similitude of sense.
'Tis but the cloudy darkness dense
   That wrapt the Mount around;
While in amaze the people stays,
   To hear the Coming Sound.

Is there no chosen prophet-soul
   To dare, sublimely meek,
Within the shroud of blackest cloud
   The Deity to seek?
'Midst atheistic systems dark,
   And darker hearts' despair,
His very word it may have heard,
   And on the dusky air
His skirts, as passed He by, to see
   Have strained on their behalf,
Who on the plain, with dance amain,
   Adore the Golden Calf.

Uranus

When on the primal peaceful blank profound,
Which in its still unknowing silence holds
All knowledge, ever by withholding holds –
When on that void (like footfalls in far rooms),
In faint pulsations from the whitening East
Articulate voices first were felt to stir,
And the great child, in dreaming grown to man,
Losing his dream to piece it up began;
Then Plato in me said,
''Tis but the figured ceiling overhead,
With cunning diagrams bestarred, that shine
In all the three dimensions, are endowed
With motion too by skill mechanical,
That thou in height, and depth, and breadth, and power,
Schooled unto pure Mathesis, might proceed
To higher entities, whereof in us
Copies are seen, existent they themselves
In the sole Kingdom of the Mind and God.
Mind not the stars, mind thou thy Mind and God.'
By that supremer Word
O'ermastered, deafly heard
Were hauntings dim of old astrologies;
Chaldean mumblings vast, with gossip light
From modern ologistic fancyings mixed,
Of suns and stars, by hypothetic men

Of other frame than ours inhabited,
Of lunar seas and lunar craters huge.
And was there atmosphere, or was there not?
And without oxygen could life subsist?
And was the world originally mist? –
Talk they as talk they list,
I, in that ampler voice,
Unheeding, did rejoice.

HERMAN MELVILLE
(1819–91)

The New Zealot to the Sun

Persian, you rise
Aflame from climes of sacrifice
　　Where adulators sue,
And prostrate man, with brow abased,
Adheres to rites whose tenor traced
　　All worship hitherto.

Arch type of sway,
Meetly your over-ruling ray
　　You fling from Asia's plain,
Whence flashed the javelins abroad
Of many a wild incursive horde
　　Led by some shepherd Cain.

Mid terrors dinned
Gods too came conquerors from your Ind,
　　The brood of Bramha throve;
They came like to the scythed car,
Westward they rolled their empire far,
　　Of night their purple wove.

Chemist, you breed
In orient climes each sorcerous weed
　　That energizes dream –
Transmitted, spread in myths and creeds,
Houris and hells, delirious screeds
　　And Calvin's last extreme.

What though your light
In time's first dawn compelled the flight
  Of Chaos' startled clan,
Shall never all your darted spears
Disperse worse Anarchs, frauds and fears,
  Sprung from these weeds to man?

  But Science yet
An effluence ampler shall beget,
  And power beyond your play –
Shall quell the shades you fail to rout,
Yea, searching every secret out
  Elucidate your ray.

WALT WHITMAN
(1819–92)

From *Leaves of Grass*
EIDÓLONS
lines 49–64

All space, all time,
(The stars, the terrible perturbations of the suns,
Swelling, collapsing, ending, serving their longer, shorter use,)
  Fill'd with eidólons only.

  The noiseless myriads,
The infinite oceans where the rivers empty,
The separate countless free identities, like eyesight,
  The true realities, eidólons.

  Not this the world,
Nor these the universes, they the universes,
Purport and end, ever the permanent life of life,
  Eidólons, eidólons.

  Beyond thy lectures learn'd professor,
Beyond thy telescope or spectroscope observer keen, beyond all
  mathematics,
Beyond the doctor's surgery, anatomy, beyond the chemist with his
  chemistry,
  The entities of entities, eidólons.

Song of Myself
lines 1159–69

CYCLES

Cycles ferried my cradle, rowing and rowing like cheerful boatmen,
For room to me stars kept aside in their own rings,
They sent influences to look after what was to hold me.

Before I was born out of my mother generations guided me,
My embryo has never been torpid, nothing could overlay it.

For it the nebula cohered to an orb,
The long slow strata piled to rest it on,
Vast vegetables gave it sustenance,
Monstrous sauroids transported it in their mouths and deposited it
    with care.

All forces have been steadily employ'd to complete and delight me,
Now on this spot I stand with my robust soul.

When I Heard the Learn'd Astronomer

When I heard the learn'd astronomer,
When the proofs, the figures, were ranged in columns before me,
When I was shown the charts and diagrams, to add, divide, and
    measure them,
When I sitting heard the astronomer where he lectured with much
    applause in the lecture-room,
How soon unaccountable I became tired and sick,
Till rising and gliding out I wander'd off by myself,
In the mystical moist night-air, and from time to time,
Look'd up in perfect silence at the stars.

MATTHEW ARNOLD

(1822–88)

From *Empedocles on Aetna*

All things the world that fill
Of but one stuff are spun,
That we who rail are still
With what we rail at one:
One with the o'er-labour'd Power that through the breadth and length

Of Earth, and Air, and Sea,
In men, and plants, and stones,
Has toil perpetually,
And struggles, pants, and moans;
Fain would do all things well, but sometimes fails in strength.

And, punctually exact,
This universal God
Alike to any act
Proceeds at any nod,
And patiently declaims the cursings of himself.

This is not what Man hates,
Yet he can curse but this.
Harsh Gods and hostile Fates
Are dreams: this only *is:*
Is everywhere: sustains the wise, the foolish elf.

Nor only, in the intent
To attach blame elsewhere,
Do we at will invent
Stern Powers who make their care,
To embitter human life, malignant Deities;

But, next, we would reverse
The scheme ourselves have spun,
And what we made to curse
We now would lean upon,
And feign kind Gods who perfect what man vainly tries.

Look, the world tempts our eye,
And we would know it all.
We map the starry sky,
We mind this earthen ball,
We measure the sea-tides, we number the sea-sands:

We scrutinise the dates
Of long-past human things,
The bounds of effaced states,
The lines of deceas'd kings:
We search out dead men's words, and works of dead men's hands:

We shut our eyes, and muse
How our own minds are made;
What springs of thought they use,
How righten'd, how betray'd;
And spend our wit to name what most employ unnamed:

But still, as we proceed,
The mass swells more and more
Of volumes yet to read,
Of secrets yet to explore.
Our hair grows grey, our eyes are dimmed, our heat is tamed –

We rest our faculties,
And thus address the Gods: –
'True Science if there is,
It stays in your abodes.
Man's measures cannot span the illimitable All:

'You only can take in
The world's immense design.
Our desperate search was sin,
Which henceforth we resign:
Sure only that *your* mind sees all things which befall.'

COVENTRY PATMORE

(1823–96)

The Two Deserts

Not greatly moved with awe am I
To learn that we may spy
Five thousand firmaments beyond our own.
The best that's known
Of the heavenly bodies does them credit small.
View'd close, the Moon's fair ball
Is of ill objects worst,
A corpse in Night's highway, naked, fire-scarr'd, accurst;
And now they tell
That the Sun is plainly seen to boil and burst
Too horribly for hell.
So, judging from these two,
As we must do,
The Universe, outside our living Earth,
Was all conceiv'd in the Creator's mirth,
Forecasting at the time Man's spirit deep,
To make dirt cheap.
Put by the Telescope!
Better without it man may see,
Stretch'd awful in the hush'd midnight,
The ghost of his eternity.
Give me the nobler glass that swells to the eye
The things which near us lie,
Till Science rapturously hails,
In the minutest water-drop,
A torment of innumerable tails.
These at the least do live.
But rather give
A mind not much to pry
Beyond our royal-fair estate
Betwixt these deserts blank of small and great.
Wonder and beauty our own courtiers are,
Pressing to catch our gaze,
And out of obvious ways
Ne'er wandering far.

Legem Tuam Dilexi*

The 'Infinite.' Word horrible! at feud
With life, and the braced mood
Of power and joy and love;
Forbidden, by wise heathen ev'n, to be
Spoken of Deity,
Whose Name, on popular altars, was 'The Unknown,'
Because, or ere It was reveal'd as One
Confined in Three,
The people fear'd that it might prove
Infinity,
The blazon which the devils desired to gain;
And God, for their confusion, laugh'd consent;
Yet did so far relent,
That they might seek relief, and not in vain,
In dashing of themselves against the shores of pain.
Nor bides alone in hell
The bond-disdaining spirit boiling to rebel.
But for compulsion of strong grace,
The pebble in the road
Would straight explode,
And fill the ghastly boundlessness of space.
The furious power,
To soft growth twice constrain'd in leaf and flower,
Protests, and longs to flash its faint self far
Beyond the dimmest star.
The same
Seditious flame,
Beat backward with reduplicated might,
Struggles alive within its stricter term,
And is the worm.
And the just Man does on himself affirm
God's limits, and is conscious of delight,
Freedom and right;
And so His Semblance is, Who, every hour,
By day and night,
Buildeth new bulwarks 'gainst the Infinite.
For, ah, who can express
How full of bonds and simpleness
Is God,
How narrow is He,

And how the wide, waste field of possibility
Is only trod
Straight to His homestead in the human heart,
And all His art
Is as the babe's that wins his Mother to repeat
Her little song so sweet!
What is the chief news of the Night?
Lo, iron and salt, heat, weight and light
In every star that drifts on the great breeze!
And these
Mean Man,
Darling of God, Whose thoughts but live and move
Round him; Who woos his will
To wedlock with His own, and does distil
To that drop's span
The atta of all rose-fields of all love!
Therefore the soul select assumes the stress
Of bonds unbid, which God's own style express
Better than well,
And aye hath, cloister'd, borne,
To the Clown's scorn,
The fetters of the threefold golden chain:
Narrowing to nothing all his worldly gain;
(Howbeit in vain;
For to have nought
Is to have all things without care or thought!)
Surrendering, abject, to his equal's rule,
As though he were a fool,
The free wings of the will;
More vainly still;
For none knows rightly what 'tis to be free
But only he
Who, vow'd against all choice, and fill'd with awe
Of the ofttimes dumb or clouded Oracle,
Does wiser than to spell,
In his own suit, the least word of the Law!)
And, lastly, bartering life's dear bliss for pain;
But evermore in vain;
For joy (rejoice ye Few that tasted have!)
Is Love's obedience
Against the genial laws of natural sense,
Whose wide, self-dissipating wave,

Prison'd in artful dykes,
Trembling returns and strikes
Thence to its source again,
In backward billows fleet,
Crest crossing crest ecstatic as they greet,
Thrilling each vein,
Exploring every chasm and cove
Of the full heart with floods of honied love,
And every principal street
And obscure alley and lane
Of the intricate brain
With brimming rivers of light and breezes sweet
Of the primordial heat;
Till, unto view of me and thee,
Lost the intense life be,
Or ludicrously display'd, by force
Of distance; as a soaring eagle, or a horse
On far-off hillside shewn,
May seem a gust-driv'n rag or a dead stone.
Nor by such bonds alone –
But more I leave to say,
Fitly revering the Wild Ass's bray,
Also his hoof,
Of which, go where you will, the marks remain
Where the religious walls have hid the bright reproof.

GEORGE MEREDITH

(1828–1909)

From *The Olive Branch*

RESPONSIBILITIES OF SCIENCE

A dove flew with an Olive Branch;
It crossed the sea and reached the shore,
And on a ship about to launch
Dropped down the happy sign it bore.

'An omen' rang the glad acclaim!
The Captain stooped and picked it up,
'Be then the Olive Branch her name,'
Cried she who flung the christening cup.

The vessel took the laughing tides;
It was a joyous revelry
To see her dashing from her sides
The rough, salt kisses of the sea.

And forth into the bursting foam
She spread her sail and sped away,
The rolling surge her restless home,
Her incense wreaths the showering spray.

Far out, and where the riot waves
Run mingling in tumultuous throngs,
She danced above a thousand graves,
And heard a thousand briny songs.

Her mission with her manly crew,
Her flag unfurl'd, her title told,
She took the Old World to the New,
And brought the New World to the Old.

★

Now when the ark of human fate,
Long baffled by the wayward wind,
Is drifting with its peopled freight,
Safe haven on the heights to find;

Safe haven from the drowning slime
Of evil deeds and Deluge wrath; –
To plant again the foot of Time
Upon a purer, firmer path;

'Tis now the hour to probe the ground,
To watch the Heavens, to speak the word,
The fathoms of the deep to sound,
And send abroad the missioned bird.

On strengthened wing for evermore,
Let Science, swiftly as she can,
Fly seaward on from shore to shore,
And bind the links of man to man;

And like that fair propitious Dove
Bless future fleets about to launch;
Make every freight a freight of love,
And every ship an Olive Branch.

EMILY DICKINSON

(1830–86)

'Arcturus'

'Arcturus' is his other name –
I'd rather call him 'Star.'
It's very mean of Science
To go and interfere!

I slew a worm the other day –
A 'Savan' passing by
Murmured 'Resurgam' – 'Centipede'!
'Oh Lord – how frail are we'!

I pull a flower from the woods –
A monster with a glass
Computes the stamens in a breath –
And has her in a 'class'!

Whereas I took the Butterfly
Aforetime in my hat –
He sits erect in 'Cabinets' –
The Clover bells forgot.

What once was 'Heaven'
Is '*Zenith*' now –
Where I proposed to go
When Time's brief masquerade was done
Is mapped and charted too.

What if the poles sh'd frisk about
And stand upon their heads!
I hope I'm ready for 'the worst' –
Whatever prank betides!

Perhaps the 'Kingdom of Heaven's' changed –
I hope the 'Children' there
Wont be 'new fashioned' when I come –
And laugh at me – and stare –

I hope the Father in the skies
Will lift his little girl –
Old fashioned – naughty – everything –
Over the stile of 'Pearl'.

'If the Foolish . . .'

If the foolish, call them '*flowers*' –
Need the wiser, *tell*?
If the Savans 'Classify' them
It is just as well!

Those who read the 'Revelations'
Must not criticize
Those who read the same Edition –
With beclouded Eyes!

Could we stand with that Old 'Moses' –
'Canaan' denied –
Scan like him, the stately landscape
On the other side –

Doubtless, we should deem superfluous
Many Sciences,
Not pursued by learned Angels
In scholastic skies!

Low amid that glad Belles lettres
Grant that we may stand,
Stars, amid profound *Galaxies* –
At that grand 'Right hand'!

'Split the Lark . . .'

Split the Lark – and you'll find the Music –
Bulb after Bulb, in Silver rolled –
Scantily dealt to the Summer Morning
Saved for your Ear when Lutes be old.

Loose the Flood – you shall find it patent –
Gush after Gush, reserved for you –
Scarlet Experiment! Sceptic Thomas!
Now, do you doubt that your Bird was true?

JAMES CLERK MAXWELL

(1831–79)

To the Chief Musician upon Nabla[1]

A Tyndallic Ode

I come from fields of fractured ice,
  Whose wounds are cured by squeezing,
Melting they cool, but in a trice,
  Get warm again by freezing.
Here, in the frosty air, the sprays
  With fern-like hoar-frost bristle,
There, liquid stars their watery rays
  Shoot through the solid crystal.

I come from empyrean fires –
  From microscopic spaces,
Where molecules with fierce desires,
  Shiver in hot embraces.
The atoms clash, the spectra flash,
  Projected on the screen,
The double D, magnesian *b*,
  And Thallium's living green.

We place our eye where these dark rays
  Unite in this dark focus,
Right on the source of power we gaze,
  Without a screen to cloak us.
Then where the eye was placed at first,
  We place a disc of platinum,
It glows, it puckers! will it burst?
  How ever shall we flatten him!

This crystal tube the electric ray
  Shows optically clean,
No dust or haze within, but stay!
  All has not yet been seen.

---

1. Nabla was the name of an Assyrian harp of the shape ∇. ∇ is a quaternion operator $\left(i\frac{d}{dx} + j\frac{d}{dy} + k\frac{d}{dz}\right)$ invented by Sir W. R. Hamilton, whose use and properties were first fully discussed by Professor Tait, who is therefore called the 'Chief Musician upon Nabla'.

What gleams are these of heavenly blue?
   What air-drawn form appearing,
What mystic fish, that, ghostlike, through
   The empty space is steering?

I light this sympathetic flame,
   My faintest wish that answers,
I sing, it sweetly sings the same,
   It dances with the dancers.
I shout, I whistle, clap my hands,
   And stamp upon the platform,
The flame responds to my commands,
   In this form and in that form.

What means that thrilling, drilling scream,
   Protect me! 'tis the siren:
Her heart is fire, her breath is steam,
   Her larynx is of iron.
Sun! dart thy beams! in tepid streams,
   Rise, viewless exhalations!
And lap me round, that no rude sound
   May mar my meditations.

Here let me pause. – These transient facts,
   These fugitive impressions,
Must be transformed by mental acts,
   To permanent possessions.
Then summon up your grasp of mind,
   Your fancy scientific,
Till sights and sounds with thought combined,
   Become of truth prolific.

Go to! prepare your mental bricks,
   Fetch them from every quarter,
Firm on the sand your basement fix
   With best sensation mortar.
The top shall rise to heaven on high –
   Or such an elevation,
That the swift whirl with which we fly
   Shall conquer gravitation.

Molecular Evolution

Belfast, 1874

At quite uncertain times and places,
  The atoms left their heavenly path,
And by fortuitous embraces,
  Engendered all that being hath.
And though they seem to cling together,
  And form 'associations' here,
Yet, soon or late, they burst their tether,
  And through the depths of space career.

So we who sat, oppressed with science,
  As British asses, wise and grave,
Are now transformed to wild Red Lions,★
  As round our prey we ramp and rave.
Thus, by a swift metamorphōsis,
  Wisdom turns wit, and science joke,
Nonsense is incense to our noses,
  For when Red Lions speak, they smoke.

Hail, Nonsense! dry nurse of Red Lions,
  From thee the wise their wisdom learn,
From thee they cull those truths of science,
  Which into thee again they turn.
What combinations of ideas,
  Nonsense alone can wisely form!
What sage has half the power that she has,
  To take the towers of Truth by storm?

JAMES THOMSON

(1834–82)

The City of Dreadful Night*
section XX

MAN CONFRONTS THE SPHINX

I sat me weary on a pillar's base,
   And leaned against the shaft; for broad moonlight
O'erflowed the peacefulness of cloistered space,
   A shore of shadow slanting from the right:
The great cathedral's western front stood there,
A wave-worn rock in that calm sea of air.

Before it, opposite my place of rest,
   Two figures faced each other, large, austere;
A couchant sphinx in shadow to the breast,
   An angel standing in the moonlight clear;
So mighty by magnificence of form,
They were not dwarfed beneath that mass enorm.

Upon the cross-hilt of a naked sword
   The angel's hands, as prompt to smite, were held;
His vigilant intense regard was poured
   Upon the creature placidly unquelled,
Whose front was set at level gaze which took
No heed of aught, a solemn trance-like look.

And as I pondered these opposèd shapes
   My eyelids sank in stupor, that dull swoon
Which drugs and with a leaden mantle drapes
   The outworn to worse weariness. But soon
A sharp and clashing noise the stillness broke,
And from the evil lethargy I woke.

The angel's wings had fallen, stone on stone,
   And lay there shattered; hence the sudden sound:
A warrior leaning on his sword alone
   Now watched the sphinx with that regard profound;
The sphinx unchanged looked forthright, as aware
Of nothing in the vast abyss of air.

Again I sank in that repose unsweet,
   Again a clashing noise my slumber rent;
The warrior's sword lay broken at his feet:
   An unarmed man with raised hands impotent
Now stood before the sphinx, which ever kept
Such mien as if with open eyes it slept.

My eyelids sank in spite of wonder grown;
   A louder crash upstartled me in dread:
The man had fallen forward, stone on stone,
   And lay there shattered, with his trunkless head
Between the monster's large quiescent paws,
Beneath its grand front changeless as life's laws.

The moon had circled westward full and bright,
   And made the temple-front a mystic dream,
And bathed the whole enclosure with its light,
   The sworded angel's wrecks, the sphinx supreme:
I pondered long that cold majestic face
Whose vision seemed of infinite void space.

ALGERNON CHARLES SWINBURNE

(1837–1909)

From *Hertha*★

THE TREE OF LIFE

I am that which began;
   Out of me the years roll;
Out of me God and man;
   I am equal and whole;
God changes, and man, and the form of them bodily; I am the soul.

Before ever land was,
   Before ever the sea,
Or soft hair of the grass,
   Or fair limbs of the tree,
Or the flesh-coloured fruit of my branches, I was, and thy soul was in me.

First life on my sources
  First drifted and swam;
Out of me are the forces
  That save it or damn;
Out of me man and woman, and wild-beast and bird; before God was,
  I am.

Beside or above me
  Nought is there to go;
Love or unlove me,
  Unknow me or know,
I am that which unloves me and loves; I am stricken, and I am the
  blow.

*

The tree many-rooted
  That swells to the sky
With frondage red-fruited,
  The life-tree am I;
In the buds of your lives is the sap of my leaves: ye shall live and not
  die.

But the Gods of your fashion
  That take and that give,
In their pity and passion
  That scourge and forgive,
They are worms that are bred in the bark that falls off; they shall die
  and not live.

My own blood is what stanches
  The wounds in my bark;
Stars caught in my branches
  Make day of the dark,
And are worshipped as suns till the sunrise shall tread out their fires as
  a spark.

Where dead ages hide under
  The live roots of the tree,
In my darkness the thunder
  Makes utterance of me;
In the clash of my boughs with each other ye hear the waves sound of
  the sea.

That noise is of Time,
    As his feathers are spread
And his feet set to climb
    Through the boughs overhead,
And my foliage rings round him and rustles, and branches are bent
  with his tread.

The storm-winds of ages
    Blow through me and cease,
The war-wind that rages,
    The spring-wind of peace,
Ere the breath of them roughen my tresses, ere one of my blossoms
  increase.

All sounds of all changes,
    All shadows and lights
On the world's mountain-ranges
    And stream-riven heights,
Whose tongue is the wind's tongue and language of storm-clouds on
  earth-shaking nights;

All forms of all faces,
    All works of all hands
In unsearchable places
    Of time-stricken lands,
All death and all life, and all reigns and all ruins, drop through me as
  sands.

Though sore be my burden
    And more than ye know,
And my growth have no guerdon
    But only to grow,
Yet I fail not of growing for lightnings above me or deathworms
  below.

These too have their part in me,
    As I too in these;
Such fire is at heart in me,
    Such sap is this tree's,
Which hath in it all sounds and all secrets of infinite lands and of seas.

In the spring-coloured hours
    When my mind was as May's,

There brake forth of me flowers
By centuries of days,
Strong blossoms with perfume of manhood, shot out from my spirit
as rays.

And the sound of them springing
And smell of their shoots
Were as warmth and sweet singing
And strength to my roots;
And the lives of my children made perfect with freedom of soul were
my fruits.

I bid you but bè;
I have need not of prayer;
I have need of you free
As your mouths of mine air;
That my heart may be greater within me, beholding the fruits of me fair.

More fair than strange fruit is
Of faiths ye espouse;
In me only the root is
That blooms in your boughs;
Behold now your God that ye made you, to feed him with faith of
your vows.

In the darkening and whitening
Abysses adored,
With dayspring and lightning
For lamp and for sword,
God thunders in heaven, and his angels are red with the wrath of the
Lord.

O my sons, O too dutiful
Toward Gods not of me,
Was not I enough beautiful?
Was it hard to be free?
For behold, I am with you, am in you and of you; look forth now and
see.

Lo, winged with world's wonders,
With miracles shod,
With the fires of his thunders
For raiment and rod,
God trembles in heaven, and his angels are white with the terror of God.

For his twilight is come on him,
    His anguish is here;
And his spirits gaze dumb on him,
    Grown grey from his fear;
And his hour taketh hold on him stricken, the last of his infinite year.

Thought made him and breaks him,
    Truth slays and forgives;
But to you, as time takes him,
    This new thing it gives,
Even love, the beloved Republic, that feeds upon freedom and lives.

For truth only is living,
    Truth only is whole,
And the love of his giving
    Man's polestar and pole;
Man, pulse of my centre, and fruit of my body, and seed of my soul.

Ode to Music

Was it light that spake from the darkness, or music that shone from
    the word,
When the night was enkindled with sound of the sun or the first-born
    bird?
Souls enthralled and entrammelled in bondage of seasons that fall and
    rise,
Bound fast round with fetters of flesh, and blinded with light that dies,
Lived not surely till music spake, and the spirit of life was heard.

Music, sister of sunrise, and herald of life to be,
Smiled as dawn on the spirit of man, and the thrall was free.
Slave of nature and serf of time, the bondman of life and death,
Dumb with passionless patience that breathed but forlorn and reluctant
    breath,
Heard, beheld and his soul made answer, and communed aloud with
    the sea.

Morning spake, and he heard: and the passionate silent noon
Kept for him not silence: and soft from the mounting moon
Fell the sound of her splendour, heard as dawn's in the breathless
    night,

Not of men but of birds whose note bade man's soul quicken and leap
    to light:
And the song of it spake, and the light and the darkness of earth were
    as chords in tune.

THOMAS HARDY
(1840–1928)

In a Museum

Here's the mould of a musical bird long passed from light,
Which over the earth before man came was winging;
There's a contralto voice I heard last night,
That lodges in me still with its sweet singing.

Such a dream is Time that the coo of this ancient bird
Has perished not, but is blent, or will be blending
Mid visionless wilds of space with the voice that I heard,
In the full-fugued song of the universe unending.

The Pity of It*

April 1915

I walked in loamy Wessex lanes, afar
From rail-track and from highway, and I heard
In field and farmstead many an ancient word
Of local lineage like 'Thu bist', 'Er war',

'Ich woll', 'Er sholl', and by-talk similar,
Nigh as they speak who in this month's moon gird
At England's very loins, thereunto spurred
By gangs whose glory threats and slaughters are.

Then seemed a Heart crying: 'Whosoever they be
At root and bottom of this, who flung this flame
Between kin folk kin tongued even as are we,

'Sinister, ugly, lurid, be their fame;
May their familiars grow to shun their name,
And their brood perish everlastingly.'

Epitaph for G. K. Chesterton

Here lies nipped in this narrow cyst
The literary contortionist
Who prove and never turn a hair
That Darwin's theories were a snare
He'd hold as true with tongue in jowl,
That Nature's geocentric rule
... true and right
And if one with him could not see
He'd shout his choice word 'Blasphemy'.

MATILDA BLIND
(1841–96)

From *The Ascent of Man*

War rages on the teeming earth;
  The hot and sanguinary fight
Begins with each new creature's birth:
  A dreadful war where might is right;
Where still the strongest slay and win,
Where weakness is the only sin.

There is no truce to this drawn battle,
  Which ends but to begin again;
The drip of blood, the hoarse death-rattle,
  The roar of rage, the shriek of pain,
Are rife in fairest grove and dell,
Turning earth's flowery haunts to hell.

A hell of hunger, hatred, lust,
  Which goads all creatures here below,
Or blindworm wriggling in the dust,
  Or penguin in the Polar snow;
A hell where there is none to save,
Where life is life's insatiate grave.

And in the long portentous strife,
  Where types are tried even as by fire,
Where life is whetted upon life
  And step by panting step mounts higher,

Apes lifting hairy arms now stand
And free the wonder-working hand.

They raise a light, aërial house
  On shafts of widely branching trees,
Where, harboured warily, each spouse
  May feed her little ape in peace,
Green cradled in his heaven-roofed bed,
Leaves rustling lullabies o'erhead.

And lo, 'mid reeking swarms of earth
  Grim struggling in the primal wood,
A new strange creature hath its birth:
  Wild – stammering – nameless – shameless – nude;
Spurred on by want, held in by fear,
He hides his head in caverns drear.

Most unprotected of earth's kin,
  His fight for life that seems so vain
Sharpens his senses, till within
  The twilight mazes of his brain,
Like embryos within the womb,
Thought pushes feelers through the gloom.

And slowly in the fateful race
  It grows unconscious, till at length
The helpless savage dares to face
  The cave-bear in his grisly strength;
For stronger than its bulky thews
He feels a force that grows with use.

From age to dumb unnumbered age,
  By dim gradations long and slow,
He reaches on from stage to stage,
  Through fear and famine, weal and woe
And, compassed round with danger, still
Prolongs his life by craft and skill.

With cunning hand he shapes the flint,
  He carves the horn with strange device,
He splits the rebel block by dint
  Of effort – till one day there flies
A spark of fire from out the stone:
Fire which shall make the world his own.

ROBERT BRIDGES

(1844–1930)

The Testament of Beauty
lines 162–73

'A LITTLE OASIS OF LIFE . . .'

Yea: and how delicat! Life's mighty mystery
sprang from eternal seeds in the elemental fire,
self-animat in forms that fire annihilates:
all its selfpropagating organisms exist
only within a few degrees of the long scale
rangeing from measured zero to unimagin'd heat,
a little oasis of Life in Nature's desert;
and ev'n therein are our soft bodies vext and harm'd
by their own small distemperature, nor could they endure
wer't not that by a secret miracle of chemistry
they hold internal poise upon a razor-edge
that may not ev'n be blunted, lest we sicken and die.

GERARD MANLEY HOPKINS

(1844–89)

⋅ That Nature is a Heraclitean Fire and of the Comfort of the Resurrection★

Cloud-puffball, torn tufts, tossed pillows | flaunt forth, then chevy on an air-
built thoroughfare: heaven-roysterers, in gay-gangs | they throng;
  they glitter in marches.
Down roughcast, down dazzling whitewash, | wherever an elm
  arches,
Shivelights and shadowtackle in long | lashes lace, lance, and pair.
Delightfully the bright wind boisterous | ropes, wrestles, beats earth
  bare
Of yestertempest's creases; | in pool and rut peel parches
Squandering ooze to squeezed | dough, crust, dust; stanches, starches
Squadroned masks and manmarks | treadmire toil there
Footfretted in it. Million-fuelèd, | nature's bonfire burns on.

But quench her bonniest, dearest | to her, her clearest-selvèd spark
Man, how fast his firedint, | his mark on mind, is gone!
Both are in an unfathomable, all is in an enormous dark
Drowned. O pity and indig|nation! Manshape, that shone
Sheer off, disseveral, a star, | death blots black out; nor mark
      Is any of him at all so stark
But vastness blurs and time | beats level. Enough! the Resurrection,
A heart's-clarion! Away grief's gasping, | joyless days, dejection.
      Across my foundering deck shone
A beacon, an eternal beam. | Flesh fade, and mortal trash
Fall to the residuary worm; | world's wildfire, leave but ash:
      In a flash, at a trumpet crash,
I am all at once what Christ is, | since he was what I am, and
This Jack, joke, poor potsherd, | patch, matchwood, immortal
   diamond,
      Is immortal diamond.

'I am Like a Slip of Comet ...'

   – I am like a slip of comet,
    Scarce worth discovery, in some corner seen
    Bridging the slender difference of two stars,
    Come out of space, or suddenly engender'd
    By heady elements, for no man knows;
    But when she sights the sun she grows and sizes
    And spins her skirts out, while her central star
    Shakes its cocooning mists; and so she comes
    To fields of light; millions of travelling rays
    Pierce her; she hangs upon the flame-cased sun,
    And sucks the light as full as Gideon's fleece:
    But then her tether calls her; she falls off,
    And as she dwindles shreds her smock of gold
    Between the sistering planets, till she comes
    To single Saturn, last and solitary;
    And then she goes out into the cavernous dark.
    So I go out: my little sweet is done:
    I have drawn heat from this contagious sun:
    To not ungentle death now forth I run.

ALICE MEYNELL

(1847–1922)

Christ in the Universe

With this ambiguous earth
His dealings have been told us. These abide:
The signal to a maid, the human birth,
The lesson, and the young Man crucified.

But not a star of all
The innumerable host of stars has heard
How He administered this terrestrial ball.
Our race have kept their Lord's entrusted Word.

Of His earth-visiting feet
None knows the secret, cherished, perilous,
The terrible, shamefast, frightened, whispered, sweet,
Heart-shattering secret of His way with us.

No planet knows that this
Our wayside planet, carrying land and wave,
Love and life multiplied, and pain and bliss,
Bears, as chief treasure, one forsaken grave.

Nor, in our little day,
May His devices with the heavens be guessed,
His pilgrimage to thread the Milky Way,
Or His bestowals there be manifest.

But, in the eternities,
Doubtless we shall compare together, hear
A million alien Gospels, in what guise
He trod the Pleiades, the Lyre, the Bear.

O be prepared, my soul!
To read the inconceivable, to scan
The million forms of God those stars unroll
When, in our turn, we show to them a Man.

THOMAS THORNELY

(1855–1949)

Dreams and Freudians

Thou hast found slanderers, Sleep! who cast foul scorn
  On the bright-imaged forms that round thy throne
Flit nightly; proving them ignobly born,
  Things of vile import, symbolled or foreshown.

Fling back their scorn! though, in their impish way,
  Thy dream-sprites frolic with night's reverend hours,
The most are pure as children at their play,
  Or Carnival amazons with their battling flowers.

Their sage maligners, steeped in thoughts that spring
  From the sad haunts of maimed, afflicted mind,
To Dreamland's fountained courts and parterres bring
  The poisoned air of lazarets left behind.

By the veiled horror of such scenes obsessed,
  Imputing to the many what the few,
When the veil lifts, reveal, they know no rest,
  Till they prove vile Sleep's whole blithe innocent crew.

Dance on! in gay defiant disarray,
  Ye merry-hearted mummers of the night!
While your browed slanderers grope their peevish way,
  By one malodorous candle's treacherous light.

The Atom

We do not in the least know how to harness the energy locked up in the atoms of
matter If it could be liberated at will, we should experience a violence beside which the
suddenness of high explosive is gentle and leisurely

Sir O Lodge

    Wake not the imprisoned power that sleeps
    Unknown, or dimly guessed, in thee!
    Thine awful secret Nature keeps,
    And pales, when stealthy science creeps
    Towards that beleaguered mystery.

Well may she start and desperate strain,
To thrust the bold besiegers back;
If they that citadel should gain,
What grisly shapes of death and pain
May rise and follow in their track!

The power that warring atoms yield,
Man has to guiltiest purpose turned.
Too soon the wonder was revealed,
Earth flames in one red battle-field;
Could but that lesson be unlearned!

Thy last dread secret, Nature! keep;
Add not to man's tumultuous woes;
Till war and hate are laid to sleep,
Keep those grim forces buried deep,
That in thine atoms still repose.

The Angler on His Ancestry

We whisked our fins in many a sea
For aeons ere we felt a wish
For life on land; now here are we
Whisking our flies to snare the fish.

We frisked about on many a tree
For ages ere we changed our shape,
And left the genial Chimpanzee
To take our place as premier ape.

And now that we have muddled through,
Lest we forget from whence we come,
One ancestor is in our zoo,
And one in our aquarium.

RONALD ROSS
(1857–1932)

The Anniversary

(20th August, 1917)

Now twenty years ago
  This day we found the thing;*
With science and with skill
  We found; then came the sting –
What we with endless labour won
  The thick world scorned;
Not worth a word to-day –
  Not worth remembering.

O Gorgeous Gardens, Lands
  Of beauty where the Sun
His lordly raiment trails
  All day with light enspun,
We found the death that lurk'd beneath
  Your purple leaves,
We found your secret foe,
  The million-murdering one;

And clapp'd our hands and thought
  Your teeming width would ring
With that great victory – more
  Than battling hosts can bring.
Ah, well – men laugh'd. The years have pass'd;
  The world is cold –
Some million lives a year,
  Not worth remembering!

Ascended from below
  Men still remain too small;
With belly-wisdom big
  They fight and bite and bawl,
These larval angels! – but when true
  Achievement comes –
A trifling doctor's matter –
  No consequence at all!

Science

I would rejoice in iron arms with those
Who, nobly in the scorn of recompense,
Have dared to follow Truth alone, and thence
To teach the truth – nor fear'd the rage that rose.
No high-piled monuments are theirs who chose
Her great inglorious toil – no flaming death;
To them was sweet the poetry of prose,
But wisdom gave a fragrance to their breath.
Alas! we sleep and snore beyond the night,
Tho' these great men the dreamless daylight show;
But they endure – the Sons of simple Light –
And, with no lying lanthorne's antic glow,
Reveal the open way that we must go.

RUDYARD KIPLING
(1865–1936)

Merrow Down
(Just So Stories)

I

There runs a road by Merrow Down –
    A grassy track to-day it is –
An hour out of Guildford town,
    Above the river Wey it is.

Here, when they heard the horse-bells ring,
    The ancient Britons dressed and rode
To watch the dark Phoenicians bring
    Their goods along the Western Road.

Yes, here, or hereabouts, they met
    To hold their racial talks and such –
To barter beads for Whitby jet,
    And tin for gay shell torques and such.

But long and long before that time
    (When bison used to roam on it)
Did Taffy and her Daddy climb
    That Down, and had their home on it.

Then beavers built in Broadstonebrook
   And made a swamp where Bramley stands;
And bears from Shere would come and look
   For Taffimai where Shamley stands.

The Wey, that Taffy called Wagai,
   Was more than six times bigger then;
And all the Tribe of Tegumai*
   They cut a noble figure then!

II

Of all the Tribe of Tegumai
   Who cut that figure, none remain, –
On Merrow Down the cuckoos cry –
   The silence and the sun remain.

But as the faithful years return
   And hearts unwounded sing again,
Comes Taffy dancing through the fern
   To lead the Surrey spring again.

Her brows are bound with bracken-fronds,
   And golden elf-locks fly above;
Her eyes are bright as diamonds
   And bluer than the sky above.

In mocassins and deer-skin cloak,
   Unfearing, free and fair she flits,
And lights her little damp-wood smoke
   To show her Daddy where she flits.

For far – oh, very far behind,
   So far she cannot call to him,
Comes Tegumai alone to find
   The daughter that was all to him!

ROBERT FROST
(1874–1963)

Why Wait for Science

Sarcastic Science, she would like to know,
In her complacent ministry of fear,
How we propose to get away from here
When she has made things so we have to go
Or be wiped out. Will she be asked to show
Us how by rocket we may hope to steer
To some star off there, say, a half light-year
Through temperature of absolute zeró?
Why wait for Science to supply the how
When any amateur can tell it now?
The way to go away should be the same
As fifty million years ago we came —
If anyone remembers how that was.
I have a theory, but it hardly does.

ALFRED NOYES
(1880–1958)

From The Torch-Bearers

WILLIAM HERSCHEL* CONDUCTS

Was it a dream? – that crowded concert-
    room
In Bath; that sea of ruffles and laced
    coats;
And William Herschel, in his powdered wig,
Waiting upon the platform, to conduct
His choir and Linley's orchestra?* He stood
Tapping his music-rest, lost in his own
    thoughts
And (did I hear or dream them?) all were
    mine:

My periwig's askew, my ruffle stained
With grease from my new telescope!

249

   Ach, to-morrow
How Caroline will be vexed, although she
 grows
Almost as bad as I, who cannot leave
My workshop for one evening.
       I must give
One last recital at St Margaret's,
And then – farewell to music.
      Who can lead
Two lives at once?
    Yet – it has taught me much,
Thrown curious lights upon our world, to
 pass
From one life to another. Much that I
 took
For substance turns to shadow. I shall
 see
No throngs like this again; wring no more
 praise
Out of their hearts; forego that instant joy
– Let those who have not known it count
 it vain –
When human souls at once respond to
 yours.
Here, on the brink of fortune and of fame,
As men account these things, the moment
 comes
When I must choose between them and
 the stars;
And I have chosen.
     Handel, good old friend,
We part to-night. Hereafter, I must
 watch
That other wand, to which the worlds
 keep time.

What has decided me? That marvellous
 night
When – ah, how difficult it will be to guide,
With all these wonders whirling through
 my brain! –
After a Pump-room concert I came home

Hot-foot, out of the fluttering sea of fans,
Coquelicot-ribboned belles and periwigged
   beaux,
To my Newtonian telescope.
                        The design
Was his; but more than half the joy my
   own,
Because it was the work of my own hand,
A new one, with an eye six inches wide,
Better than even the best that Newton
   made.
Then, as I turned it on the *Gemini*,
And the deep stillness of those constant
   lights,
Castor and Pollux, lucid pilot-stars,
Began to calm the fever of my blood,
I saw, O, first of all mankind I saw
The disk of my new planet gliding there
Beyond our tumults, in that realm of peace.

What will they christen it? Ach – not *Herschel*, no!
Nor *Georgium Sidus*, as I once proposed;
Although he scarce could lose it, as he lost
That world in 'seventy-six.
                    Indeed, so far
From trying to tax it, he has granted me
How much? – two hundred golden pounds
   a year,
In the great name of science, – half the cost
Of one state-coach, with all those worlds
   to win!

*

This new planet is only new to man.
His majesty has done much. Yet, as my
   friend
Declared last night, 'Never did monarch
   buy
Honour so cheaply'; and – he has not
   bought it.
I think that it should bear some ancient
   name,

And wear it like a crown; some deep,
   dark name,
Like *Uranus*, known to remoter gods.

★

If music lead us to a cry like this,
I think I shall not lose it in the skies.
I do but follow its own secret law
As long ago I sought to understand
Its golden mathematics; taught myself
The way to lay one stone upon another,
Before I dared to dream that I might
   build
My Holy City of Song. I gave myself
To all its branches. How they stared at me,
Those men of 'sensibility,' when I said
That algebra, conic sections, fluxions, all
Pertained to music. Let them stare again.
Old Kepler knew, by instinct, what I now
Desire to learn. I have resolved to leave
No tract of heaven unvisited.
                    To-night,
– The music carries me back to it again! –
I see beyond this island universe,
Beyond our sun, and all those other suns
That throng the Milky Way, far, far
   beyond,
A thousand little wisps, faint nebulae,
Luminous fans and milky streaks of fire;
Some like soft brushes of electric mist
Streaming from one bright point; others
   that spread
And branch, like growing systems; others
   discrete,
Keen, ripe, with stars in clusters; others
   drawn back
By central forces into one dense death,
Thence to be kindled into fire, reborn,
And scattered abroad once more in a
   delicate spray

Faint as the mist by one bright dewdrop
  breathed
At dawn, and yet a universe like our own;
Each wisp a universe, a vast galaxy
Wide as our night of stars.
                    The Milky Way
In which our sun is drowned, to these
  would seem
Less than to us their faintest drift of haze;
Yet we, who are borne on one dark grain
  of dust
Around one indistinguishable spark
Of star-mist, lost in one lost feather of
  light,
Can by the strength of our own thought,
  ascend
Through universe after universe; trace
  their growth
Through boundless time, their glory, their
  decay;
And, on the invisible road of law, more
  firm
Than granite, range through all their
  length and breadth,
Their height and depth, past, present, and
  to come.
So, those who follow the great Work-
  master's law
From small things up to great, may one
  day learn
The structure of the heavens, discern the
  whole
Within the part, as men through Love see
  God.

Oh, holy night, deep night of stars, whose
  peace
Descends upon the troubled mind like
  dew,
Healing it with the sense of that pure
  reign

253

Of constant law, enduring through all
  change;
Shall I not, one day, after faithful years,
Find that thy heavens are built on music,
  too,
And hear, once more, above thy throbbing
  worlds
This voice of all compassion, *Comfort ye, –*
Yes – *comfort ye, my people, saith your God?*

SIR JOHN COLLINGS SQUIRE
(1884–1958)

The Survival of the Fittest
(In Memoriam, L. C. and T.)

Without war the race would degenerate.
                    An eminent writer, 30 March 1915

These were my friends; Thompson, you did not know them
  For they were simple, unaspiring men;
No ordinary wind of chance could blow them
  Within the range of your austerer ken.

They were most uninformed. They never even
  – So ignorant and godless was their youth –
Heard you expound, with reverences to Heaven,
  The elements of biologic truth.

Had they but had the privilege to cluster
  Around Gamaliel's feet, they would have known
That hate and massacre also have their lustre,
  And that man cannot live by Love alone.

But having no pillar of flame of your igniting
  To guide by night, no pillar of cloud by day,
They thought War was an evil thing, and fighting
  Filthy at best. So, thus deluded, they,

Not seeing the war as a wise elimination,
  Or a cleansing purge, or a wholesome exercise,
Went out with mingled loathing and elation
  Only because there towered before their eyes

England, an immemorial crusader,
  A great dream-statue, seated and serene,
Who had seen much blood, and sons who had betrayed her,
  But still shone out with hands and garments clean;

Summoning now with an imperious message
  To one last fight that Europe should be free,
Whom, though it meant a swift and bitter passage,
  They had to serve, for she served Liberty.

Romance and rhetoric! Yet with such nonsense nourished
  They faced the guns and the dead and the rats and the rains,
And all in a month, as summer waned, they perished;
  And they had clear eyes, strong bodies, and some brains.

   . . . . . .

Thompson, these died. What need is there to mention
  Anything more? What argument could give
A more conclusive proof of your contention?
  Thompson, these died, and men like you still live.

JULIAN HUXLEY
(1887–1975)

To a Dancer

  Weary of miles and all the earth's extension,
  Of changing one place for another place,
  Tired of the tales of marvellous invention
  That frees not man though binding time and space,
  Weary of plodding science, where the vision
  Must for achievement clothe itself in clay,
  Where there is no completeness past revision,
  But fact on fact for ever and a day.

– I was weary of this and more; and you came down
And danced on the moonlit grass for the little town.
You danced for us, and still I see your dancing
Within my mind, a living thing, entrancing
The flesh of limbs, the actions of every day,
Discursive thought and emotion's idle play,
Entrancing all and making the many one.
– The miracle works, the glorious trick is done.
For a moment Life, completed and sublime
Is danced by you beyond and out of time.
For art, like love and vision, knits our crude
And scattered facts and acts to a life renewed,
A life renewed in unitary fire,
Completed and whole above the world's desire.

Cosmic Death

By death the moon was gathered in
    Long ago, ah long ago;
Yet still the silver corpse must spin
    And with another's light must glow.
Her frozen mountains must forget
    Their primal hot volcanic breath,
Doomed to revolve for ages yet,
    Void amphitheatres of death.

And all about the cosmic sky,
    The black that lies beyond our blue,
Dead stars innumerable lie,
    And stars of red and angry hue
    Not dead but doomed to die.

ROBINSON JEFFERS
(1887–1962)

From *Roan Stallion*

'HUMANITY IS THE MOLD...'

                         Humanity is the start of the race; I say
Humanity is the mold to break away from, the crust to break
  through, the coal to break into fire,
The atom to be split.
                Tragedy that breaks man's face and a white
  fire flies out of it; vision that fools him
Out of his limits, desire that fools him out of his limits,
  unnatural crime, inhuman science,
Slit eyes in the mask; wild loves that leap over the walls of
  nature, the wild fence-vaulter science,
Useless intelligence of far stars, dim knowledge of the spin-
  ning demons that make an atom,
These break, these pierce, these deify, praising their God
  shrilly with fierce voices: not in man's shape
He approves the praise, he that walks lightning-naked on the
  Pacific, that laces the suns with planets,
The heart of the atom with electrons: what is humanity in
  this cosmos? For him, the last
Least taint of a trace in the dregs of the solution; for itself,
  the mold to break away from, the coal
To break into fire, the atom to be split.

MARIANNE MOORE

(1887–1972)

In the Days of Prismatic Colour

not in the days of Adam and Eve, but when Adam
   was alone; when there was no smoke and colour was
fine, not with the refinement
   of early civilization art, but because
of its originality; with nothing to modify it but the

mist that went up, obliqueness was a varia-
   tion of the perpendicular, plain to see and
to account for: it is no
   longer that; nor did the blue-red-yellow band
of incandescence that was colour keep its stripe: it also is
      one of

those things into which much that is peculiar can be
   read; complexity is not a crime, but carry
it to the point of murki-
   ness and nothing is plain. Complexity,
moreover, that has been committed to darkness, instead of
      granting it-

self to be the pestilence that it is, moves all a-
   bout as if to bewilder us with the dismal
fallacy that insistence
   is the measure of achievement and that all
truth must be dark. Principally throat, sophistication is as
     it al-

ways has been – at the antipodes from the init-
   ial great truths. 'Part of it was crawling, part of it
was about to crawl, the rest
   was torpid in its lair.' In the short-legged, fit-
ful advance, the gurgling and all the minutiae – we have
      the classic

multitude of feet. To what purpose! Truth is no Apollo
   Belvedere, no formal thing. The wave may go over it if
     it likes.
Know that it will be there when it says,
   'I shall be there when the wave has gone by.'

Four Quartz Crystal Clocks

There are four vibrators, the world's exactest clocks;
   and these quartz time-pieces that tell
time intervals to other clocks,
   these worksless clocks work well;
independently the same, kept in
    the 41° Bell
      Laboratory[1] time

vault. Checked by a comparator with Arlington,★
   they punctualize the 'radio,
cinema,' and 'presse,' – a group the
   Giraudoux[2] truth-bureau
of hoped-for accuracy has termed
   'instruments of truth'. We know –
     as Jean Giraudoux says

certain Arabs have not heard – that Napoleon
   is dead; that a quartz prism when
the temperature changes, feels
   the change and that the then
electrified alternate edges
    oppositely charged, threaten
      careful timing; so that

this water-clear crystal as the Greeks used to say,
   this 'clear ice' must be kept at the
same coolness. Repetition, with
   the scientist, should be
synonymous with accuracy.
    The lemur-student can see
     that an aye-aye★ is not

---

1. 'In the Bell Telephone Laboratories in New York, in a "time vault" whose temperature is maintained within 1/100 of a degree, at 41° centigrade, are the most accurate clocks in the world – the four quartz crystal clocks . . . When properly cut and inserted in a suitable circuit, they will control the rate of electric vibration to an accuracy of one part in a million . . . When you call MEridian 7–1212 for correct time you get it every 15 seconds.' *The World's Most Accurate Clocks*, Bell Telephone Company leaflet (1939). [This and the following footnotes are Moore's.]

2. 'Appeler à l'aide d'un camouflage ces instruments faits pour la vérité qui sont la radio, le cinéma, la presse?' 'J'ai traversé voilà un an des pays arabes où l'on ignorait encore que Napoléon était mort.' *Une allocation radiodiffusée de M. Giraudoux aux Françaises à propos de Sainte Catherine*; the *Figaro*, November 1939.

an angwan-tibo, potto, or loris.★ The sea-
   side burden should not embarrass
the bell-boy with the buoy-ball
   endeavouring to pass
hotel patronesses; nor could a
   practised ear confuse the glass
      eyes for taxidermists

with eye-glasses from the optometrist. And as
   MEridian-7 one-two
one-two gives, each fifteenth second
   in the same voice, the new
data – 'The time will be' so and so –
   you realize that 'when you
      hear the signal', you'll be

hearing Jupiter or jour pater, the day god –
   the salvaged son of Father Time –
telling the cannibal Chronos
   (eater of his proxime
newborn progeny)[3] that punctuality
   is not a crime.

WALTER JAMES REDFERN TURNER
(1889–1946)

Poetry and Science

Night, like a silver Peacock in the sky
By Moon bewitched turns many thousand eyes
In vacancy. Flits past in fading mist
A Comet's tail, the Phoenix of the Sun
Blown from her burning nest of whitened ash.

If this be false it is illusion's gain,
Since all we know is but a midday dream:
Sun, moon and stars – are they not Fancy's names,
Products of human orbs which like these roll
In automatic frenzy, maddened by Light?

3. 'Rhea, mother of Zeus, hid him from Chronos who "devoured all his children except Jupiter (air), Neptune (water), and Pluto (the grave). These, Time cannot consume."' Brewer's *Dictionary of Phrase and Fable*.

Light's blinding lust, like an invisible worm
Hatched in the small dark nucleus of the atom
Flies out a Dragon, whose cyclopaedic seed
Sprouts wings thro' Natural History – red, blue, yellow:
Crocus, Auk, Griffin, Mandrake, Dandelion.

Latest begotten of Light's progeny
Proton and Neutron have yet unfound kin
Awaiting birth; invisible nameless heroes
Of stories not yet written, stars in films
Unrolled, or unremembered, or untaken.

Man's endless phantasy pours in procession:
Tyrannic Leaders, Kings, and Presidents:
Phantoms of spiritual hunger: Christ and Buddha;
Constructions vaguer still: Sin, Evolution –
Eggs of that Great Auk, Human Imagination.

But children, grown-up, take fairy tales for real
Yes, they are real, real stories of Hans Andersen.
There is no other truth than purest fiction:
But what it means let none pretend to say,
Or saying, at least say only: *This is my Dream.*

This is my dream, that all the World is one –
Stones, trees, birds, men, light, Jesus and the Devil.
Fret not on any rung of Change's spiral
For all is Change and yet is One for ever:
Love, hate, crime, virtue fitting into one whole.

In short these words are words, and words are dreams;
All words – the scientists', poets', philosophers' and priests'
(You like the dream? perchance you like it not?)
But every thought is a pure flower of Fancy
Beloved by someone even as every flower.

I like them all, some greatly, others less:
Ideas are foul or fair like flowers and girls
I cannot tell you why I find some silly
Yet still to like. Others have such rare beauty
They fill me with new joy. *This is my dream.*

HUGH MACDIARMID/CHRISTOPHER MURRAY GRIEVE

(1892–1978)

The Innumerable Christ

Other stars may have their Bethlehem, and their Calvary too.

Professor J. Y. Simpson

> Wha kens on whatna Bethlehems
> Earth twinkles like a star the nicht,
> An' whatna shepherds lift their heids
>   In its unearthly licht?
>
> 'Yont a' the stars oor een can see
> An' farther than their lichts can fly,
> I' mony an unco warl' the nicht
>   The fatefu' bairnies cry.
>
> I' mony an unco warl' the nicht
> The lift gaes black as pitch at noon,
> An' sideways on their chests the heids
>   O' endless Christs roll doon.
>
> An' when the earth's as cauld's the mune
> An' a' its folk are lang syne deid,
> On coontless stars the Babe maun cry
>   An' the Crucified maun bleed.

From *A Drunk Man Looks at the Thistle*

A STICK-NEST IN YGDRASIL★

lines 1–55

> Thou art the facts in ilka airt
> That breenge into infinity,
> Criss crossed wi' coontless ither facts
> Nae man can follow, and o' which
> He is himsel' a helpless pairt,

whatna: what kind of	*warl'*: world	*maun*. must
'Yont: beyond	*bairnies*: children	*ilka*: every
unco: strange	*lift*: sky	*breenge*. burst

262

Held in their tangle as he were
A stick-nest in Ygdrasil!

The less man sees the mair he is
Content wi't, but the mair he sees
The mair he kens hoo little o'
A' that there is he'll ever see,
And hoo it mak's confusion aye
The waur confoondit till at last
His brain inside his heid is like
Ariadne wi' an empty pirn,
Or like a birlin' reel frae which
A whale has rived the line awa'.
What better's a forhooied nest
Than skasloch scattered owre the grun'?

O hard it is for man to ken
He's no' creation's goal nor yet
A benefitter by't at last –
A means to ends he'll never ken,
And as to michtier elements
The slauchtered brutes he eats to him
Or forms o' life owre sma' to see
Wi' which his heedless body swarms,
And a' man's thocht nae mair to them
Than ony moosewob to a man
His Heaven to them the blinterin' o'
A snail-trail on their closet wa'!

For what's an atom o' a twig
That tak's a billion to an inch
To a' the routh o' shoots that mak'
The bygrowth o' the Earth aboot
The michty trunk o' Space that spreids
Ramel o' licht that ha'e nae end,
– The trunk wi' centuries for rings,
Comets for fruit, November shooers
For leafs that in its Autumns fa'

waur. worse	*skasloch*: loose straw, litter	*blinterin'*. gleaming
pirn: real	*ken*: know	*wa'*: wall
birlin': spinning	*slauchtered*. slaughtered	*routh*: abundance
forhooied: abandoned	*moosewob*. spider's web	*Ramel*: branches

263

– And Man at maist o' sic a twig
Ane o' the coontless atoms is!

My sinnens and my veins are but
As muckle o' a single shoot
Wha's fibres I can ne'er unwaft
O' my wife's flesh and mither's flesh
And a' the flesh o' humankind,
And revelled thrums o' beasts and plants
As gangs to mak' twixt birth and daith
A'e sliver for a microscope;
And a' the life o' Earth to be
Can never lift frae underneath
The shank o' which oor destiny's pairt
As heich's to stand forenenst the trunk
Stupendous as a windlestrae!

Two Scottish Boys*

Not only was Thebes built by the music of an Orpheus, but without the music of some inspired Orpheus was no city ever built, no work that man glories in ever done.

Thomas Carlyle

For the very essence of poetry is truth, and as soon as a word's not true it's not poetry, though it may wear the cast clothes of it.

George MacDonald

Poetry never goes back on you. Learn as many pieces as you can. Go over them again and again till the words come of themselves, and then you have a joy forever which cannot be stolen or broken or lost. This is much better than diamond rings on every finger ... The thing you cannot get a pigeon-hole for is the finger-point showing the way to discovery.

Sir Patrick Manson

Science is the Differential Calculus of the mind, Art the Integral Calculus; they may be beautiful when apart, but are greatest only when combined.

Sir Ronald Ross

sic: such	*unwaft*: unweave	*heich's*: high as
sinnens: sinews	*thrums*: tufts, thread ends	*forenenst*: over against
muckle: much	*gangs*: goes	*windlestrae*: straw

'There were two Scottish boys, one roamed seashore and hill
Drunk with the beauty of many a lovely scene,
And finally lost in nature's glory as in a fog,
Tossing him into chaos, like Bunyan's quag★ in the Valley of the
   Shadow.
The other having shot a lean and ferocious cat
On his father's farm, was profoundly interested
In a tapeworm he found when he investigated
Its internal machinery in the seclusion of his attic room,
– A 'prologue to the omen coming on'!

For while the first yielded nothing but high-falutin nonsense,
Spiritual masturbation of the worst description,
From the second down the crowded years I saw
Heroism, power for and practice of illimitable good emerge,
Great practical imagination and God-like thoroughness,
And mighty works of knowledge, tireless labours,
Consummate skill, high magnanimity, and undying Fame,
A great campaign against unbroken servility,
Ceaseless mediocrity and traditional immobility,
To the end that European reason may sink back no more
Into the immemorial embraces of the supernatural . . .
Sainte-Beuve★ was right – the qualities we most need
(Most of all in sentimental Scotland) are indeed
'*Science, esprit d'observation, maturité, force,
Un peu de dureté,*' and poets who, like Gustave Flaubert,
(That son and brother of distinguished doctors) wield
Their pens as these their scalpels, and that their work
Should everywhere remind us of anatomists and physiologists.

Poet and therefore scientist the latter, while the former,
No scientist, was needs a worthless poet too.

ARCHIBALD MACLEISH

(1892–1982)

Reply to Mr Wordsworth

(1)

The flower that on the pear-tree settles
Momentarily as though a butterfly – that petal,
Has it alighted on the twig's black wet

From elsewhere? No, but blossoms from the bole:
Not traveller but the tree itself unfolding.
What of that stranger in the eyes, the soul?

(2)

Space-time, our scientists tell us, is impervious.
It neither evades nor refuses. It curves
As a wave will or a flame – whatever's fervent.

Space-time has no beginning and no end.
It has no door where anything can enter.
How break and enter what will only bend?

(3)

Must there be elsewhere too – not merely here –
To justify the certainty of miracles?
Because we cannot hope or even fear

For ghostly coming on the midnight hour,
Are there no women's eyes all ardor now
And on the tree no momentary flower?

ALDOUS HUXLEY

(1894–1963)

Fifth Philosopher's Song

A million million spermatozoa,
    All of them alive:
Out of their cataclysm but one poor Noah
    Dare hope to survive.

And among that billion minus one
   Might have chanced to be
Shakespeare, another Newton, a new Donne –
   But the One was Me.

Shame to have ousted your betters thus,
   Taking ark while the others remained outside!
Better for all of us, froward Homunculus,
   If you'd quietly died!

MARK VAN DOREN
(1894–1972)

The God of Galaxies

The god of galaxies has more to govern
Than the first men imagined, when one mountain
Trumpeted his anger, and one rainbow,
Red in the east, restored them to his love.
One earth it was, with big and lesser torches,
And stars by night for candles. And he spoke
To single persons, sitting in their tents.

Now streams of worlds, now powdery great whirlwinds
Of universes far enough away
To seem but fog-wisps in a bank of night
So measureless the mind can sicken, trying –
Now seas of darkness, shoreless, on and on
Encircled by themselves, yet washing farther
Than the last triple sun, revolving, shows.

The god of galaxies – how shall we praise him?
For so we must, or wither. Yet what word
Of words? And where to send it, on which night
Of winter stars, of summer, or by autumn
In the first evening of the Pleiades?
The god of galaxies, of burning gases,
May have forgotten Leo and the Bull.

But God remembers, and is everywhere.
He even is the void, where nothing shines.

He is the absence of his own reflection
In the deep gulf; he is the dusky cinder
Of pure fire in its prime; he is the place
Prepared for hugest planets: black idea,
Brooding between fierce poles he keeps apart.

Those altitudes and oceans, though, with islands
Drifting, blown immense as by a wind,
And yet no wind; and not one blazing coast
Where thought could live, could listen – oh, what word
Of words? Let us consider it in terror,
And say it without voice. Praise universes
Numberless. Praise all of them. Praise Him.

DAVID JONES
(1895–1974)

From *Anathemata*

A SCIENTIFIC PSALM

From before all time
                the New Light beams for them
and with eternal clarities
                *infulsit** and athwart
the fore-times:
                era, period, epoch, hemera*
Through all orogeny:*
                group, system, series, zone.
Brighting at the five life-layers
                species, species, genera, families, order.
Piercing the eskered* silt, discovering every stria, each score
    and macula, lighting all the fragile laminae of the shales.
However Calypso has shuffled the marked pack, veiling with
    early the late.
Through all unconformities and the sills without sequence,
    glorying all the under-dapple.
Lighting the Cretaceous and the Trias, for Tyrannosaurus
    must somehow lie down with herbivores, or, the poet lied,
    which is not allowed.

However violent the contortion or whatever the inversion
  of the folding.
Oblique through the fire-wrought cold rock dyked from
  convulsions under.
Through the slow sedimentations laid by his patient creature
  of water.
Which ever the direction of the strike, whether the hade★ is
  to the up-throw or the fault normal.
Through all metamorphs or whatever the pseudomorphoses.

A. M. SULLIVAN

(b. 1896)

Atomic Architecture

Take Carbon for example then
What shapely towers it constructs
To house the hopes of men!
What symbols it creates
For power and beauty in the world
Of patterned ring and hexagon –
Building ten thousand things
Of earth and air and water!
Pride searches in the flues of earth
For the diamond and its furious sun,
Love holds its palms before the glow
Of anthracite and purrs.
Five senses take their fill
Of raiment, rainbows and perfumes,
Of sweetness and of monstrous pain.

If life begins in carbon's dancing atoms
Moving in quadrilles of light
To the music of pure numbers,
Death is the stately measure
Of Time made plausible
By carbon's slow procession
Out of the shifting structure
Of crumbling flesh and bone.

Telescope Mirror

Look in the giant mirror
And you look into a well,
The depth of which is Time,
The gage of which is Light.

The Heavens coming nearer
Uncover parts of Hell,
Where Order stands at prime,
And Chaos turns in flight.

There is no Present here,
Only the empty spool
Of centuries unwound
Before men and Desire.

Only the Past is clear
In the enormous pool
Of silver that has drowned
The noise of worlds on fire.

The speed of light is known,
But not the speed of thought
Crossing the Milky Way
On rapid wings of prayer.

Someday it may be shown
How Light and Darkness fought
When Evil lost the Day
Upon the prism's stair.

MICHAEL ROBERTS

(1902–48)

Note on θ, φ and ψ

Whereas my lady loves to look
On learned manuscript and book,
Still must she scorn, and scorning sigh,
To think of those I profit by.

Plotinus now, or Plutarch is
A prey to her exegesis,
And while she labours to collate
A page, I grasp a postulate,

And find for one small world of fact
Invariant matrices, compact
Within the dark and igneous rock
Of *Comptes Rendus* or *Proc. Roy. Soc.*

She'll pause a learned hour, and then
Pounce with a bird-like acumen
Neatly to annotate the dark
Of halting sense with one remark;

While I, maybe, precisely seize
The elusive photon's properties
In α's and δ's, set in bronze-
bright vectors, grim quaternions.

Silent we'll sit. We'll not equate
Symbols too plainly disparate,
But hand goes out to friendly hand
That mind and mind may understand

How one same passion burned within
Each learned peer and paladin,
Her Bentley and her Scaliger,
My Heisenberg and Schrödinger.

DOROTHY DONNELLY
(b. 1903)

The Pink Mite

Science abhors a fiction, its forte being fact.
For facts it will fly to the moon (a feat once restricted
to fiction): it will move a mountain to prove a mouse.
Its game, as old as man, is questions-and-answers –
'How far down the globe do signs of life, extinct
or extant, extend? Are there tracks of its trek to the end?'

With the zeal of merchants searching for peerless pearls,
scientists, searching for answers, pushed toward the perilous
Pole on the heels of life, and past the last penguin,
in a world of cold, they found it, warming the heart
of a mite – a pinpoint of pink of whose ilk a herd
could have bivouacked beneath a snowflake. But size aside,

it was just as alive as a lion, and as much at home
on the adamant ice as a crocodile in plush mud
on the Nile. Survivor of terrible airs, it proved
how far life will go to plant its seeds, hatching
at the planet's frigidest inch an infinitesimal,
pink, pedestrian mite with a liking for lichen.

And when, unattended, the infant steps from the snug
egg, with its eight bare feet and small bald head,
is it cold? When it opens wide its mouth to be filled
in this wilderness, is it foiled? Oh, it does not want!
Led like the flock to grass, the pink mite feeds
in polar pastures, replete as a sheep on the green.

'Pink Mite Discovered Near the South Pole – closer to the Pole than animal life
has been known to exist ... a hundredth of an inch long ... found by a team
of scientists ...'

Special to *The New York Times*

The Point of a Pin

*as seen under magnification 'powerful enough
to give a clear view of atoms of metals'*

Thus seen, what was seen before as a point
now appears as a pattern flowered from a thousand
scintillas of matter impeccably spaced
in kaleidoscope-spoked motifs as baroque

as the snowflakes' spiky shapes, ornate
to the tips of their tines. Affined from the first
to form, the amorphous dust becomes
crystals or chrysanthemums or these petaled

octets in the metal where lines concocted
of dots combine to compose designs
as symmetric as clocks. Now eyes, raised
to the nth power by the power of minds

over matter, can trace the medallions the little
particles make in the miniscule nets
of lace that lattice every least tittle
of space in the tin in the point of a pin.

Spider Compared to Star

(for Walter)

If one considers attentively the radiant spider
(momentarily moved behind a purple cumulus of aster
but emerging now, the legs outspread in rays,
eight spokes curved from a center scintillant like an asterisk
spaced on pale paper) one sees her starwise.

Head and elliptic maw are in close conjunction
like the merging orbs of a double star; like Rigel
she has no neck: S after all is for swans not stars
which are involute and dispense with antennae, horns, and tails,
retaining (with spiders) only a wreath of retractile rays
whereby the air twinkles set in motion around them.
She is Venus with diamond eyes that gleam like a cat's,
set four-square like the four perfect four-pointed
stars of gold in a floret the size of a fly.
She possesses, waiting for prey, the patience of the fishermen
fiery above in their boats of 'millions of years.'
(A billion to one is a rough relation of time,
and a spider's night-watch would equal three million years
of star-life.) She is silent, too, as they,
as still as the stony light of an extinct star
that comes to us late like the flower of the dinosaur's footprint
or the spiral bouquet of an ammonite's filigree sutures
since Mesozoic days preserved impeccable under sea-glass.

In June a golden garden-spider floating
slowly across a sky of irises,

273

neither aimless nor idle, her net nailed
to rafters of roses, shakes with her foot
the diamond outline specked with a black and gold enamel of gnats,
impassive moves in the midst of a meteor-shower of bees
and comet-wasps stinging the air with fiery whips.
In autumn when dahlias light their ruby lamps
and the gilt grape-leaf hangs, worn to a web by waves of weather,
the spiders stir among the yellow zinnias
and tall chrysanthemums cinnamon-colored and curved
petal by petal inwardly to solid globes,
moving from point to point in their orbits, sure-footed over chasms
like the high stars across invisible bridges.

An aerial firmament stretches above the grass a foot or two
like a reduction through glass of airy oceans above.
There suns and mimic constellations stand,
Aldebaran looming large in his silver isosceles
and clear Canopus caught in a skein of light.
Milky ways of web shine across meadows
and galaxies hang with their islands of black over gardens,
and many unpredictable moons appear,
lemon-yellow or white with shadows of lilac,
and turn on their spiral paths tenacious as planets.
('Geometry, that is to say, the science
of harmony in space, presides over everything.')
In the silence one hears the eloquent spiders and the stars
speak with the incontrovertible voices of things,
saying that certainly the deducible precedes the deduction
and things necessarily antedate theories; they say that
matter is music and sings with iridescent voice
like water moving polychromatic from stone to stone.
Recurring themes built on the tones of a primitive scale
appear now here, now there, in rich confusion,
islands of blue above in the Milky river,
and a white Bear walking the polar sky; below,
echo of skies in the grass, the dew-drop blur
of Pleiades, and a tarantula rayed
like golden Algol fierce among the minor stars.

Suns and Straws

Though the fall of an apple is not, like the fall
of a star, a spectacular act, *one* apple
rose, as it fell, to comet-fame
when Newton, noting it, saw in the flash
of its fall, the clue to the law of the fall

of all – straws and stones; oak trees
and sparrows and hairs. But earth, like a jealous
shepherd zealous for the sheep of his flock,
draws with her magni-magnet all matter's
scattered fragments back into her keep.

(Mysterious matter – mute, inscrutable,
dark, indestructible stuff! Ever
at the beck of form, it will furnish flesh
for a flea or a flower; or fatten a worm;
or fur a tiger.) Not an atom is lost

from the plump planet's curvaceous figure.
Apple and apple-shaped earth, each
in its orbit, stand or fall by the laws
they're attuned to – the Pied Piper music that all
the spheres hear, that moves the millions of suns

through space and assembles the nebulas' clusters.
What Juggler, balancing galaxies like plates,
set those celestial corollas to spinning,
creating thereby a Versailles of lily-
bright lights and fountains across the sky!

WILLIAM EMPSON
(b. 1906)

Invitation to Juno

Lucretius could not credit centaurs;
Such bicycle he deemed asynchronous.
'Man superannuates the horse;
Horse pulses will not gear with ours.'

Johnson[1] could see no bicycle would go;
'You bear yourself, and the machine as well.'
Gennets for germans sprang not from Othello,
And Ixion rides upon a single wheel.

Courage. Weren't strips of heart culture seen
Of late mating two periodicities?
Could not Professor Charles Darwin
Graft annual upon perennial trees?

Note on Local Flora

There is a tree native in Turkestan,
Or further east towards the Tree of Heaven,★
Whose hard cold cones, not being wards to time,
Will leave their mother only for good cause;
Will ripen only in a forest fire;
Wait, to be fathered as was Bacchus once,
Through men's long lives, that image[2] of time's end.
I knew the Phoenix was a vegetable.
So Semele desired her deity
As this in Kew thirsts for the Red Dawn.

Doctrinal Point

The god approached dissolves into the air.

Magnolias, for instance, when in bud,
Are right in doing anything they can think of;
Free by predestination in the blood,
Saved by their own sap, shed for themselves,
Their texture can impose their architecture;
Their sapient matter is always already informed.

1. Dr Johnson said it, somewhere in Boswell. Iago threatened Brabantio about gennets. Ixion rides on one wheel because he failed in an attempt at mixed marriage with Juno which would have produced demigods, two-wheeled because inheriting two life-periods. [Empson's note.]
2. The forest fire is like the final burning of the world. [Empson's note.]

Whether they burgeon, massed wax flames, or flare
Plump spaced-out saints, in their gross prime, at prayer,
Or leave the sooted branches bare
To sag at tip from a sole blossom there
They know no act that will not make them fair.

Professor Eddington with the same insolence
Called all physics one tautology;
If you describe things with the right tensors
All law becomes the fact that they can be described with them;
This is the Assumption of the description.
The duality of choice becomes the singularity of existence;
The effort of virtue the unconsciousness of foreknowledge.

That over-all that Solomon should wear
Gives these no cope who cannot know of care.
They have no gap to spare that they should share
The rare calyx we stare at in despair.
They have no other that they should compare.
Their arch of promise the wide Heaviside layer*
They rise above a vault into the air.

VERNON WATKINS

(1906–67)

Discoveries

The poles are flying where the two eyes set:
America has not found Columbus yet.

Ptolemy's planets, playing fast and loose,
Foretell the wisdom of Copernicus.

Dante calls Primum Mobile, the First Cause:
'Love that moves the world and the other stars.'

Great Galileo, twisted by the rack,
Groans the bright sun from heaven, then breathes it back.

Blake, on the world alighting, holds the skies,
And all the stars shine down through human eyes.

Donne sees those stars, yet will not let them lie:
'We're tapers, too, and at our own cost die.'

The shroud-lamp catches. Lips are smiling there.
'Les flammes – déjà?' – The world dies, or Voltaire.

Swift, a cold mourner at his burial-rite,
Burns to the world's heart like a meteorite.

Beethoven deaf, in deafness hearing all,
Unwinds all music from sound's funeral.

Three prophets fall, the litter of one night:
Blind Milton gazes in fixed deeps of light.

Beggar of those Minute Particulars,
Yeats lights again the turmoil of the stars.

Motionless motion! Come, Tiresias,
The eternal flies, what's passing cannot pass.

WYSTAN HUGH AUDEN

(1907–73)

In Memory of Sigmund Freud

(d. Sept. 1939)

When there are so many we shall have to mourn,
when grief has been made so public, and exposed
    to the critique of a whole epoch
    the frailty of our conscience and anguish,

of whom shall we speak? For every day they die
among us, those who were doing us some good,
    who knew it was never enough but
    hoped to improve a little by living.

Such was this doctor: still at eighty he wished
to think of our life from whose unruliness
    so many plausible young futures
    with threats or flattery ask obedience,

but his wish was denied him: he closed his eyes
upon that last picture, common to us all,
    of problems like relatives gathered
    puzzled and jealous about our dying.

For about him till the very end were still
those he had studied, the fauna of the night,
 and shades that still waited to enter
 the bright circle of his recognition

turned elsewhere with their disappointment as he
was taken away from his life interest
 to go back to the earth in London,
 an important Jew who died in exile.

Only Hate was happy, hoping to augment
his practice now, and his dingy clientele
 who think they can be cured by killing
 and covering the gardens with ashes.

They are still alive, but in a world he changed
simply by looking back with no false regrets;
 all he did was to remember
 like the old and be honest like children.

He wasn't clever at all: he merely told
the unhappy Present to recite the Past
 like a Poetry lesson till sooner
 or later it faltered at the line where

long ago the accusations had begun,
and suddenly knew by whom it had been judged,
 how rich life had been and how silly,
 and was life-forgiven and more humble,

able to approach the Future as a friend
without a wardrobe of excuses, without
 a set mask of rectitude or an
 embarrassing over-familiar gesture.

No wonder the ancient cultures of conceit
in his technique of unsettlement foresaw
 the fall of princes, the collapse of
 their lucrative patterns of frustration:

if he succeeded, why, the Generalised Life
would become impossible, the monolith
 of State be broken and prevented
 the co-operation of avengers.

Of course they called on God, but he went his way
down among the lost people like Dante, down
    to the stinking fosse where the injured
  lead the ugly life of the rejected,

and showed us what evil is, not, as we thought,
deeds that must be punished, but our lack of faith,
    our dishonest mood of denial,
  the concupiscence of the oppressor.

If some traces of the autocratic pose,
the paternal strictness he distrusted, still
    clung to his utterance and features,
  it was a protective coloration

for one who'd lived among enemies so long:
if often he was wrong and, at times, absurd,
    to us he is no more a person
  now but a whole climate of opinion

under whom we conduct our different lives:
Like weather he can only hinder or help,
    the proud can still be proud but find it
  a little harder, the tyrant tries to

make do with him but doesn't care for him much:
he quietly surrounds all our habits of growth
    and extends, till the tired in even
  the remotest miserable duchy

have felt the change in their bones and are cheered,
till the child, unlucky in his little State,
    some hearth where freedom is excluded,
  a hive whose honey is fear and worry,

feels calmer now and somehow assured of escape,
while, as they lie in the grass of our neglect,
    so many long-forgotten objects
  revealed by his undiscouraged shining

are returned to us and made precious again;
games we had thought we must drop as we grew up,
    little noises we dared not laugh at,
  faces we made when no one was looking.

But he wishes us more than this. To be free
is often to be lonely. He would unite
  the unequal moieties fractured
  by our own well-meaning sense of justice,

would restore to the larger the wit and will
the smaller possesses but can only use
  for arid disputes, would give back to
  the son the mother's richness of feeling:

but he would have us remember most of all
to be enthusiastic over the night,
  not only for the sense of wonder
  it alone has to offer, but also

because it needs our love. With large sad eyes
its delectable creatures look up and beg
  us dumbly to ask them to follow:
  they are exiles who long for the future

that lies in our power, they too would rejoice
if allowed to serve enlightenment like him,
  even to bear our cry of 'Judas',
  as he did and all must bear who serve it.

One rational voice is dumb. Over his grave
the household of Impulse mourns one dearly loved:
  sad is Eros, builder of cities,
  and weeping anarchic Aphrodite.

Unpredictable but Providential

(for Loren Eiseley)

Spring with its thrusting leaves and jargling birds is here again
to remind me again of the first real Event, the first
genuine Accident, of that Once when, once a tiny
corner of the cosmos had turned indulgent enough
to give it a sporting chance, some Original Substance,
immortal and self-sufficient, knowing only the blind
collision experience, had the sheer audacity
to become irritable, a Self requiring a World,

a Not-Self outside Itself from which to renew Itself,
with a new freedom, to grow, a new necessity, death.
Henceforth, for the animate, to last was to mean to change,
existing both for one's own sake and that of all others,
forever in jeopardy.
                    The ponderous ice-dragons
performed their slow-motion ballet: continents cracked in half
and wobbled drunkenly over the waters; Gondwana
smashed head on into the under-belly of Asia.
But catastrophes only encouraged experiment.
As a rule, it was the fittest who perished, the mis-fits,
forced by failure to emigrate to unsettled niches, who
altered their structure and prospered. (Our own shrew-ancestor
was a Nobody, but still could take himself for granted,
with a poise our grandees will never acquire.)
                                        Genetics
may explain shape, size and posture, but not why one physique
should be gifted to cogitate about cogitation,
divorcing Form from Matter, and fated to co-habit
on uneasy terms with its Image, dreading a double death,
a wisher, a maker of asymmetrical objects,
a linguist who is never at home in Nature's grammar.

Science, like Art, is fun, a playing with truths, and no game
should ever pretend to slay the heavy-lidded riddle,
What is the Good Life?
                        Common Sense warns me of course to buy
neither but, when I compare their rival Myths of Being,
bewigged Descartes looks more *outré* than the painted wizard.

LOUIS MACNEICE

(1907–63)

From *The Kingdom*

PORTRAIT OF THE SCIENTIST

A little dapper man but with shiny elbows
And short keen sight, he lived by measuring things
And died like a recurring decimal
Run off the page, refusing to be curtailed;
Died as they say in harness, still believing
In science, reason, progress. Left his work
Unfinished *ipso facto* which, continued,
Will supersede his name in the next text-book
And relegate him to the anonymous crowd
Of small discoverers in lab or cloister
Who link us with the Ice Age. Obstinately
He canalised his fervour, it was slow
The task he set himself but plotting points
On graph paper he felt the emerging curve
Like the first flutterings of an embryo
In somebody's first pregnancy; resembled
A pregnant woman too in that his logic
Yet made that hidden child the centre of the world
And almost a messiah; so that here,
Even here, over the shining test-tubes
The spirit of the alchemist still hovered
Hungry for magic, for the philosopher's stone.
And Progress – is that magic too? He never
Would have conceded it, not even in these last
Years of endemic doubt; in his perspective
Our present tyrants shrank into parochial
Lords of Misrule, cross eddies in a river
That has to reach the sea. But has it? Who
Told him the sea was there?
Maybe he told himself and the mere name
Of Progress was a shell to hold to the ear
And hear the breakers burgeon. Rules were rules
And all induction checked but in the end
His reasoning hinged on faith and the first axiom

Was oracle or instinct. He was simple
This man who flogged his brain, he was a child;
And so, whatever progress means in general,
He in his work meant progress. Patiently
As Stone Age man he flaked himself away
By blocked-out patterns on a core of flint
So that the core which was himself diminished
Until his friends complained that he had lost
Something in charm or interest. But conversely
His mind developed like an ancient church
By the accretion of side-aisles and the enlarging of lights
Till all the walls are windows and the sky
Comes in, if coloured; such a mind . . . a man . . .
Deserves a consecration; such a church
Bears in its lines the trademark of the Kingdom.

Variation on Heraclitus

Even the walls are flowing, even the ceiling,
Nor only in terms of physics; the pictures
Bob on each picture rail like floats on a line
While the books on the shelves keep reeling
Their titles out into space and the carpet
Keeps flying away to Arabia nor can this be where I stood –
Where I shot the rapids I mean – when I signed
On a line that rippled away with a pen that melted
Nor can this now be the chair – the chairoplane of a chair –
That I sat in the day that I thought I had made up my mind
And as for that standard lamp it too keeps waltzing away
Down an unbridgeable Ganges where nothing is standard
And lights are but lit to be drowned in honour and spite of some dark
And vanishing goddess. No, whatever you say,
Reappearance presumes disappearance, it may not be nice
Or proper or easily analysed not to be static
But none of your slide snide rules can catch what is sliding so fast
And, all you advisers on this by the time it is that,
I just do not want your advice
Nor need you be troubled to pin me down in my room
Since the room and I will escape for I tell you flat:
One cannot live in the same room twice.

SIR STEPHEN SPENDER

(b. 1909)

Bagatelles XII: Renaissance Hero

A galaxy of cells composed a system
Where he was, human, in his tower of bones.
The sun rose in his head. The moon ran, full,
Vermilion in the blood along his veins.
His statue stood in marble in his glance.

Body and intellect in him were one.
Raised but his hand, and through the universe
Relations altered between things in space.
Before his step, light opened like a door.
Time took the seal of his intaglio face.

EDWARD LOWBURY

(b. 1913)

Redundancy

Nature gets away with it:
Repeats each year the same
Familiar alphabet

And utters, without shame,
The clichés she has aired
Since daffodils first came

Before the swallow dared;
Her phrases catch the breath;
We don't ask to be spared

When, having passed through death,
We face the platitude
Of tenth – or fiftieth –

Return to life; have stood
Repeated ecstasies
In the enchanted wood.

Why, then, this quaint disease,
This fever to be new,
This fear we shall not please

With thoughts, however true,
That Man has hatched before?
Are we not Nature too? –

Or is it something more
Than Nature in our kind
Smells out the shapes that bore

As those which will remind
The dying they must die, –
Which, like the solar wind

Unnoticed in the sky,
Corrode the cells, and state
With vast redundancy

The dull routine of fate?

Daylight Astronomy

(for John Press)

Daylight astronomy: the lark, a fixed star
Above your head, stays much of the morning
At one spot; the starlings in their courses
Punctually cross the zenith; swifts dive
Like meteors; and the owl asleep in a branch
Looks out of place, like a moon in the morning sky.
Prompting their movements elemental forces,
Mass and acceleration, gravity,
Love, hunger, fear quietly interact.

Meanwhile a speck of light is barely crawling
With ominous silence, trailing a white wake
Across the blue. At once we recognise
The comet loaded with a terrible secret,
And try to look away or shut our eyes,
But seem to grasp its orbit through shut eyelids;
No symbol or equation can express

That orbit, or unravel what it means,
The paradoxical writing on the sky.

But those huge nebulae, the clouds which hide
Our sun and send astronomers to bed,
Give comfort. For while covering the shapes
That scare or baffle us, they stifle fear
And quench perplexity; until it seems
That, like the residents of Venus, screened
By permanent clouds from anything beyond,
We can doze on, unruffled by the risks
Of fusion, fission, radiation, fire.

R. S. THOMAS
(b. 1913)

The Gap

God woke, but the nightmare
did not recede. Word by word
the tower of speech grew.
He looked at it from the air
he reclined on. One word more and
it would be on a level
with him; vocabulary
would have triumphed. He
measured the thin gap
with his mind. No, no, no,
wider than that! But the nearness
persisted. How to live with
the fact, that was the feat
now. How to take his rest
on the edge of a chasm a
word could bridge.
                    He leaned
over and looked in the dictionary
they used. There was the blank still
by his name of the same
order as the territory
between them, the verbal hunger

for the thing in itself. And the darkness
that is a god's blood swelled
in him, and he let it
to make the sign in the space
on the page, that is in all languages
and none; that is the grammarian's
torment and the mystery
at the cell's core, and the equation
that will not come out, and is
the narrowness that we stare
over into the eternal
silence that is the repose of God.

Pre-Cambrian

Here I think of the centuries,
six million of them, they say.
Yesterday a fine rain fell;
today the warmth has brought out the crowds.
After Christ, what? The molecules
are without redemption. My shadow
sunning itself on this stone
remembers the lava. Zeus looked down
on a brave world, but there was
no love there; the architecture
of their temples was less permanent
than these waves. Plato, Aristotle,
all those who furrowed the calmness
of their foreheads are responsible
for the bomb. I am charmed here
by the serenity of the reflections
in the sea's mirror. It is a window
as well. What I need
now is a faith to enable me to out-stare
the grinning faces of the inmates of its asylum,
the failed experiments God put away.

Emerging

Not as in the old days I pray,
God. My life is not what it was.
Yours, too, accepts the presence of
the machine? Once I would have asked
healing. I go now to be doctored,
to drink sinlessly of the blood
of my brother, to lend my flesh
as manuscript of the great poem
of the scalpel. I would have knelt
long, wrestling with you, wearing
you down. Hear my prayer, Lord, hear
my prayer. As though you were deaf, myriads
of mortals have kept up their shrill
cry, explaining your silence by
their unfitness.
               It begins to appear
this is not what prayer is about.
It is the annihilation of difference,
the consciousness of myself in you,
of you in me; the emerging
from the adolescence of nature
into the adult geometry
of the mind. I begin to recognize
you anew, God of form and number.
There are questions we are the solution
to, others whose echoes we must expand
to contain. Circular as our way
is, it leads not back to that snake-haunted
garden, but onward to the tall city
of glass that is the laboratory of the spirit.

DAVID IGNATOW

(b. 1914)

Poet to Physicist in his Laboratory

Come out and talk to me
for then I know
into what you are shaping.
Thinking is no more,
I read your thoughts for a symbol:
a movement towards an act.
I give up on thought
as I see your mind
leading into a mystery
deepening about you.
What are you trying to discover
beyond the zone of habit
and enforced convention?
There is the animus
that spends itself on images,
the most complex being
convention and habit.
You shall form patterns
of research and bind yourself
to laws within your knowledge,
and always conscious of your limitations
make settlement,
with patience to instruct you
as it always does
in your research: an arrangement
spanning an abyss of time,
and you will find yourself patient
when you are questioned.

ROBERT CONQUEST

(b. 1917)

Humanities

Hypnotized and told they're seeing red
When really looking at a yellow wall
The children speak of orange seen instead:
Split to such rainbow through that verbal lens
It takes a whole heart's effort to see all
The human plenum as a single ens.

The word on the objective breath must be
A wind to winnow the emotive out;
Music can generalize the inner sea.
In dark harmonics of the blinded heart;
But, hot with certainty and keen with doubt,
Verse sweats out heartfelt knowledge, clear-eyed art.

Is it, when paper roses make us sneeze,
A mental or a physical event?
The word can freeze us to such categories,
Yet verse can warm the mirrors of the word
And through their loose distortions represent
The scene, the heart, the life, as they occurred.

— In a dream's blueness or a sunset's bronze
Poets seek the images of love and wonder,
But absolutes of music, gold or swans
Are only froth unless they go to swell
That harmony of science pealing under
The poem's waters like a sunken bell.

WILLIAM BRONK

(b. 1918)

How Indeterminacy ⋆ *Determines Us*

We are so little discernible as such
in so much nothing, it is our privacy
sometimes that startles us: the world is ours;
it is only ours; others that move there,
or seem to, are elsewhere, are in another world,
their world; only, we see from time to time
– shattered, as though we were nothing, or not
stable – sometimes we see what they see,
no world we know. Theirs. Strange. As though
by a momentary shift of little bits
of charges, copper were carbon and felt the weight
and valences of carbon in a changed field
of inertias and reactions, and then were copper again
in a cupreous world. We are left to wonder at
and ponder our privacy and ponder this:
we are two unknowns in a single equation, we
and our world, functions one of the other. Sight
is inward and sees itself, hearing, touch,
are inward. What do we know of an outer world?

EDWIN MORGAN

(b. 1920)

Eohippus

eetl
puri
kitl
katl
huff
widl
trig
snep
klop
klif

ptot
seep
sipl
trip
toip
torp
horp
hors

HOWARD NEMEROV

(b. 1920)

Unscientific Postscript*

There is the world, the dream, and the one law.
The wish, the wisdom, and things as they are.

Inside the cave the burning sunlight showed
A shade and forms between the light and shade,

Neither real nor false nor subject to belief:
If unfleshed, boneless also, not for life

Or death or clear idea. But as in life
Reflexive, multiple, with the brilliance of

The shining surface, an orchestral flare.
It is not to believe, the love or fear

Or their profoundest definition, death;
But fully as orchestra to accept,

Making an answer, even if lament,
In measured dance, with the whole instrument.

Cosmic Comics

There is in space a small black hole
Through which, say our astronomers,
The whole damn thing, the universe,
Must one day fall. That will be all.

Their shrinks can't get them to recall
How this apocalyptic dream
's elaborated on a humbler theme:
The toilet bowl, the Disposall.

Let prizes from the Privy Purse
Reward the Ultimate Hygiene
For flushing all flesh from the scene.

Where Moses saw the seat of God[1]
Science has seen what's just as odd,
The asshole of the universe.

Seeing Things

Close as I ever came to seeing things
The way the physicists say things really are
Was out on Sudbury Marsh* one summer eve
When a silhouetted tree against the sun
Seemed at my sudden glance to be afire:
A black and boiling smoke made all its shape.

Binoculars resolved the enciphered sight
To make it clear the smoke was a cloud of gnats,
Their millions doing such a steady dance
As by the motion of the many made the one
Shape constant and kept it so in both the forms
I'd thought to see, the fire and the tree.

Strike through the mask?* you find another mask,
Mirroring mirrors by analogy
Make visible. I watched till the greater smoke
Of night engulfed the other, standing out
On the marsh amid a hundred hidden streams
Meandering down from Concord to the sea.

1. Exodus xxxiii, 23. [Nemerov's note.]

RICHARD WILBUR

(b. 1921)

Lamarck Elaborated

'The environment creates the organ'

The Greeks were wrong who said our eyes have rays;
Not from these sockets or these sparkling poles
Comes the illumination of our days.
It was the sun that bored these two blue holes.

It was the song of doves begot the ear
And not the ear that first conceived of sound:
That organ bloomed in vibrant atmosphere,
As music conjured Ilium from the ground.

The yielding water, the repugnant stone,
The poisoned berry and the flaring rose
Attired in sense the tactless finger-bone
And set the taste-buds and inspired the nose.

Out of our vivid ambiance came unsought
All sense but that most formidably dim.
The shell of balance rolls in seas of thought.
It was the mind that taught the head to swim.

Newtonian numbers set to cosmic lyres
Whelmed us in whirling worlds we could not know,
And by the imagined floods of our desires
The voice of Sirens gave us vertigo.

H. WITHEFORD

(b. 1921)

Bohr on the Atom

Electrons can jump from one orbit to another, but they cannot move in be-
tween each definite orbit.

> Around the nucleus (Bohr says)
> Fierce spots of energy,
> Upon existence edge,
> Are spun

In discrete orbit each.

Sometimes (the legend tells)
Those dervish dancers leap
Their minute void across –
To Mars a glowing Venus falls,
Earth soars to Mercury.
But in the waste between
That 'here,' that 'there'
No path can be
Nor compromise . . .

Under which king, Bezonian,★

Can you choose?

DANNIE ABSE

(b. 1923)

Letter to Alex Comfort★

Alex, perhaps a colour of which neither of us had dreamt
may appear in the test-tube with God knows what admonition.
Ehrlich,★ certainly, was one who broke down the mental doors,
yet only after his six hundred and sixth attempt.★

Koch★ also, painfully, and with true German thoroughness,
eliminated the impossible to prove that too many of us
are dying from the same disease. Visible, on the slide
at last – Death – and the thin bacilli of an ancient distress.

Still I, myself, don't like Germans, but prefer the unkempt
voyagers who, like butterflies drunk with suns,
can only totter crookedly in the dazed air
to reach, charmingly, their destination as if by accident.

That Greek one, then, is my hero who watched the bath water
rise above his navel, and rushed out naked, 'I found it,
I found it' into the street in all his shining and forgot
that others would only stare at his genitals.
  What laughter!

Or Newton, leaning in Woolsthorpe against the garden wall,
forgot his indigestion and all such trivialities,
but gaped up at heaven in just surprise, and, with
true gravity, witnessed the vertical apple fall.

O what a marvellous observation! Who would have reckoned
that such a pedestrian miracle could alter history,
that, henceforward, everyone must fall, whatever
their rank, at thirty-two feet per second, per second?

You too, I know, have waited for doors to fly open, played
with your cold chemicals, written long letters
to the Press; listened to the truth afraid, and dug deep
into the wriggling earth for a rainbow with an honest spade.

But nothing rises. Neither spectres, nor oil, nor love.
And the old professor must think you mad, Alex, as you rehearse
poems in the laboratory like vows, and curse those clever scientists
who dissect away the wings and haggard heart from the dove.

In the Theatre

(A true incident)

Only a local anaesthetic was given because of the blood pressure problem.
The patient, thus, was fully awake throughout the operation. But in those
days – in 1938, in Cardiff, when I was Lambert Rogers' dresser – they could
not locate a brain tumour with precision. Too much normal brain tissue was
destroyed as the surgeon crudely searched for it, before he felt the resistance
of it . . . all somewhat hit and miss. One operation I shall never forget . . .

                                                            Dr Wilfred Abse

Sister saying – 'Soon you'll be back in the ward,'
sister thinking – 'Only two more on the list,'
the patient saying – 'Thank you, I feel fine';
small voices, small lies, nothing untoward,
though, soon, he would blink again and again
because of the fingers of Lambert Rogers,
rash as a blind man's, inside his soft brain.

If items of horror can make a man laugh
then laugh at this: one hour later, the growth
still undiscovered, ticking its own wild time;
more brain mashed because of the probe's braille path;

Lambert Rogers desperate, fingering still;
his dresser thinking, 'Christ! Two more on the list,
a cisternal puncture and a neural cyst.'

Then, suddenly, the cracked record in the brain,
a ventriloquist voice that cried, 'You sod,
leave my soul alone, leave my soul alone,' –
the patient's dummy lips moving to that refrain,
the patient's eyes too wide. And, shocked,
Lambert Rogers drawing out the probe
with nurses, students, sister, petrified.

'Leave my soul alone, leave my soul alone,'
that voice so arctic and that cry so odd
had nowhere else to go – till the antique
gramophone wound down and the words began
to blur and slow, '. . . leave . . . my . . . soul . . . alone . . .'
to cease at last when something other died.
And silence matched the silence under snow.

MIROSLAV HOLUB

(b. 1923)

Žito the Magician

Translated by Ian Milner and George Theiner

To amuse His Royal Majesty he will change water into wine.
Frogs into footmen. Beetles into bailiffs. And make a Minister
out of a rat. He bows, and daisies grow from his finger-tips.
And a talking bird sits on his shoulder.

There.

Think up something else, demands His Royal Majesty.
Think up a black star. So he thinks up a black star.
Think up dry water. So he thinks up dry water.
Think up a river bound with straw-bands. So he does.

There.

Then along comes a student and asks: Think up sine alpha greater
than one.

And Žito grows pale and sad: Terribly sorry. Sine is
between plus one and minus one. Nothing you can do about that.
And he leaves the great royal empire, quietly weaves his way
through the throng of courtiers, to his home

in a nutshell.

Evening in a Lab

Translated by Dana Hábová and Stuart Friebert

The white horse will not emerge from the lake
(of methyl green),
the flaming sheet will not appear
in the dark field condenser.
Pinned down by nine pounds of failure,
pinned down by half an inch of hope
sit and read,
sit as the quietest weaver
and weave and read,

where even verses break their necks,

when all the others have left.

Pinned down by eight barrels of failure,
pinned down by a quarter grain of hope,
sit as the quietest savage beast
and scratch and read.

The white horse will not emerge from the lake
(of methyl green),
the flaming sheet will not appear
in the dark field condenser.

Among cells and needles,
butts and dogs,
among stars,
there, where you wake,
there, where you go to sleep,
where it never was, never is, never mind –
search
and find.

ROBERT CREELEY
(b. 1926)

After Mallarmé

Stone,
like stillness,
around you my
mind sits, it is

a proper form
for
it, like
stone, like

compression itself,
fixed fast,
grey,
without a sound.

JOHN WOODS
(b. 1926)

Eye

We have eyes out, gyros spinning,
where the sun roars over the horizon.
There, great heliotropes wind
                              mill
in gusts of radiation.
                    Below,
the Amazon aches, a silver
scar.
        Eyes out where the moon flag,
stiff with wire
                  ripples,
its pale stars open to the wrenching
edge of the galaxy.
                    We dream
          moistly
      beside the phosphor
clock face

while all the world's waters
raise
      vast hackles to the moon's palm.
As we make speech for a wet lip,
         plasms
arc from the sun,
         neutrinos
fall through planets,
         copper sulphate
builds crystal cities
in beakers.
           Now the gas giants
and the white dwarfs
      roar
messianically, and our night mares
cloud the Petri dishes.
                Once,
in a steaming poolstrand, a spine
remembered to gather long chains;
         an eye
winked in a dense ganglion;
         a fingerprint
ridged, snowflake of oil;
         an animal throat
tortured out the bark of his name.
         So, the refrigerator
   has grown
wise with beards.
              Hydrogen and Oxygen
        drip
        past
the worn washer, or flare
                deep prominences
to the void.
        So,
after its million year sleep,
      a star eye
opens in a skin face,
             down
the mirror halls
of Palomar.

To the Chairperson of the Sonnets

In my Newtonian youth, love songs
hung sweet spittle from my chin.
The green world drew up
into two vast prominences:
man woman man woman
plus and minusing in my bonehead math.
Why the scoutleader left town
in the middle of the night
was as arcane to me
as the luminosity behind
the Horsehead Nebula.
The world stripped down
to its final face, and fire leaped
between cathode and anode,
groin hair swirled, iron filings
around magnetic flow.

Later, in my Einsteinian days,
someone wore my blue jeans on the town.
Lambency haloed the jockstraps
in the dark lockers.
Lines turned in certain poems
and showed their bottoms.
Space was dense with Pulsars,
quasars, lefthanded mesons,
the 'strange' particles.
I had to look twice
at whatever I held in my hand.

Dear Chairperson of the *Sonnets*,
were you, or where were you, bearded?
Where do you lay your sleeping head, my love,
at which end of the spectrum?

GALWAY KINNELL

(b. 1927)

For the Lost Generation

Oddities composed the sum of the news.
$E = mc^2$
Was another weird
Sign of the existence of the Jews.

And Paris! All afternoon in someone's attic
We lifted our glasses
And drank to the asses
Who ran the world and turned neurotic.

Ours was a wonderful party,
Everyone threw rice,
The fattest girls were nice,
The world was rich in wisecracks and confetti.

The War was a first wife, somebody's blunder.
Who was right, who lost,
Held nobody's interest,
The dog on top was as bad as the dog under.

Sometimes after whiskey, at the break of day,
There was a trace
Of puzzlement on a face,
Face of blue nights that kept bleaching away.

Look back on it all – the faraway cost,
Crash and sweet blues
(O Hiroshima, O Jews) –
No generation was so gay as the lost.

CHARLES TOMLINSON

(b. 1927)

A Meditation on John Constable

Painting is a science, and should be pursued as an inquiry into the laws of
nature. Why, then, may not landscape painting be considered as a branch of
natural philosophy, of which pictures are but the experiments?

John Constable, *The History of Landscape Painting*

He replied to his own question, and with the unmannered
    Exactness of art; enriched his premises
By confirming his practice: the labour of observation
    In face of meteorological fact. Clouds
Followed by others, temper the sun in passing
    Over and off it. Massed darks
Blotting it back, scattered and mellowed shafts
    Break damply out of them, until the source
Unmasks, floods its retreating bank
    With raw fire. One perceives (though scarcely)
The remnant clouds trailing across it
    In rags, and thinned to a gauze.
But the next will dam it. They loom past
    And narrow its blaze. It shrinks to a crescent
Crushed out, a still lengthening ooze
    As the mass thickens, though cannot exclude
Its silvered-yellow. The eclipse is sudden,
    Seen first on the darkening grass, then complete
In a covered sky.
                    Facts. And what are they?
He admired accidents, because governed by laws,
    Representing them (since the illusion was not his end)
As governed by feeling. The end is our approval
    Freely accorded, the illusion persuading us
That it exists as a human image. Caught
    By a wavering sun, or under a wind
Which moistening among the outlines of banked foliage
    Prepares to dissolve them, it must grow constant;
Though there, ruffling and parted, the disturbed
    Trees let through the distance, like white fog
Into their broken ranks. It must persuade
    And with a constancy, not to be swept back

To reveal what it half-conceals. Art is itself
   Once we accept it. The day veers. He would have judged
Exactly in such a light, that strides down
   Over the quick stains of cloud-shadows
Expunged now, by its conflagration of colour.
   A descriptive painter? If delight
Describes, which wrings from the brush
   The errors of a mind, so tempered,
It can forgo all pathos; for what he saw
   Discovered what he was, and the hand – unswayed
By the dictation of a single sense –
   Bodied the accurate and total knowledge
In a calligraphy of present pleasure. Art
   Is complete when it is human. It is human
Once the looped pigments, the pin-heads of light
   Securing space under their deft restrictions
Convince, as the index of a possible passion,
   As the adequate gauge, both of the passion
And its object. The artist lies
   For the improvement of truth. Believe him.

Dialogue

She: It turns on its axis.

He: To say that it was round
       Would be to ignore what is within.
       The transparent framework of cells,
       The constellation of flashes.

She: It reveals the horizon.

He: It surrounds it,
       Transmits and refines it
       Through a frozen element:
       A taut line crossing a pure white.

She: It contains distance.

He: It distances what is near,
       Transforms the conversation piece
       Into a still life,
       Isolates, like the end of a corridor.

She: It is the world of contour:

He: The black outline separating brilliances
        That would otherwise fuse,
        A single flame.

She: If it held personages –

He: They would be minute,
        Their explicit movements
        The mosaic which dances.

Both: In unison, they would clarify
        The interior of the fruit,
        The heart of the cut stone.

PETER REDGROVE

(b. 1932)

Relative

My bare knees touch the cold fender,
I tip my curls to watch the oozing of the clockhand
On the marble, masoned mantelpiece.
My garments lengthen as I rise,
My uncle's beard lengthens as I watch,
I feel the weight of beard upon my chest
Blanch. Cousin's mouth droops lower to her chest,
Suddenly her eyes blink with pince-nez,
Turkish delight sands in its box,
Pot-pourri rots.
From the budding carpet I spring up
Hands clasped behind to watch the oozing of the clockhand,
Cigar-ash rustles down my waistcoat buttons,
My cigar gasps out like a meteor-flash.
My shirt-front ruffles, draws plain and starched,
I stiffen, trip backwards in the strutted box
And fade to children's voices, as they tip their curls
Trying to reach the mantel, hurry the clock.
Stars intervene through rain-wreathed walls of rooms,
Empty, stolid, starlit rooms.

JOHN UPDIKE

(b. 1932)

Seven Stanzas at Easter

Make no mistake: if He rose at all
it was as His body;
if the cells' dissolution did not reverse, the molecules reknit, the amino
    acids rekindle,
the Church will fall.

It was not as the flowers,
each soft Spring recurrent;
it was not as His Spirit in the mouths and fuddled eyes of the eleven
    apostles;
it was as His flesh: ours.

The same hinged thumbs and toes,
the same valved heart
that – pierced – died, withered, paused, and then regathered out of
    enduring Might
new strength to enclose.

Let us not mock God with metaphor,
analogy, sidestepping, transcendence;
making of the event a parable, a sign painted in the faded credulity of
    earlier ages:
let us walk through the door.

The stone is rolled back, not papier-mâché,
not a stone in a story,
but the vast rock of materiality that in the slow grinding of time will
    eclipse for each of us
the wide light of day.

And if we will have an angel at the tomb,
make it a real angel,
weighty with Max Planck's quanta, vivid with hair, opaque in the
    dawn light, robed in real linen
spun on a definite loom.

Let us not seek to make it less monstrous,
for our own convenience, our own sense of beauty,
lest, awakened in one unthinkable hour, we are embarrassed by the
    miracle,
and crushed by remonstrance.

Written for a religious arts festival sponsored by the Clifton Lutheran
Church, of Marblehead, Mass.

Cosmic Gall

Every second, hundreds of billions of these neutrinos pass through each square
inch of our bodies, coming from above during the day and from below at
night, when the sun is shining on the other side of the earth!
    From 'An Explanatory Statement on Elementary Particle Physics',
        by M. A. Ruderman and A. H. Rosenfeld, in *American Scientist*

Neutrinos, they are very small.
   They have no charge and have no mass
And do not interact at all.
The earth is just a silly ball
   To them, through which they simply pass,
Like dustmaids down a drafty hall
   Or photons through a sheet of glass.
   They snub the most exquisite gas,
Ignore the most substantial wall,
   Cold-shoulder steel and sounding brass,
Insult the stallion in his stall,
   And, scorning barriers of class,
Infiltrate you and me! Like tall
And painless guillotines, they fall
   Down through our heads into the grass.
At night, they enter at Nepal
   And pierce the lover and his lass
From underneath the bed – you call
   It wonderful; I call it crass.

ROBERT WALLACE

(b. 1932)

Experimental

Choose a maple wing,
dry and gray if you prefer.

Holding it between thumb and forefinger,
with the other thumbnail
split
the casing.

Delicate as spring green, folded,
miniature,
a life waits to unfurl
and journey toward the sun.

You have ruined it.

ANNE STEVENSON

(b. 1933)

The Spirit is Too Blunt an Instrument

The spirit is too blunt an instrument
to have made this baby.
Nothing so unskilful as human passions
could have managed the intricate
exacting particulars: the tiny
blind bones with their manipulative tendons,
the knee and the knucklebones, the resilient
fine meshings of ganglia and vertebrae
in the chain of the difficult spine.

Observe the distinct eyelashes and sharp crescent
fingernails, the shell-like complexity
of the ear with its firm involutions
concentric in miniature to the minute
ossicles. Imagine the
infinitesimal capillaries, the flawless connections
of the lungs, the invisible neural filaments
through which the completed body
already answers to the brain.

Then name any passion or sentiment
possessed of the simplest accuracy.
No. No desire or affection could have done
with practice what habit
has done perfectly, indifferently,
through the body's ignorant precision.
It is left to the vagaries of the mind to invent
love and despair and anxiety
and their pain.

RUSSELL EDSON
(b. 1935)

Antimatter

On the other side of a mirror there's an inverse world, where the insane go sane; where bones climb out of the earth and recede to the first slime of love.

And in the evening the sun is just rising.

Lovers cry because they are a day younger, and soon childhood robs them of their pleasure.

In such a world there is much sadness which, of course, is joy ...

GRACE SCHULMAN
(b. 1935)

Surely as Certainty Changes

Surely as certainty changes,
As tide moves sand,
As heat sends wind to force the sea into waves,
As water rises and returns in rain
Or circles into smoke and falls in vapor,
You are enchanted for you enter change
And change is holy.

As earth's weight compresses rocks
Under trees over time, you enter change,
I know your face gives light as I know fire
Alters everything,
And falls rising,
Feeds and nourishes, opens and closes.

I pray to Proteus, the god of change
And proteolysis,* 'the end of change
Changing in the end'
To break old images and make you new
As love is its own effect unendingly.

ANTHONY PICCIONE
(b. 1939)

Nomad

The particle scientist
is more or less
happy. He has no home.

All his ladders
go straight down
and claim the nameless.

PETER STRAUB

(b. 1941)

Wolf on the Plains

Wherever he is, the country
Is opening on one side, breaking
And flowing in the direction
His padded feet will go.
It is always *forward*, always
North; the other side snaps
Shut, a trap.
Coded neurons stream
Into the backbone: *Go toward the pines*.
He twitches, bound to the landscape:
Deciding and deciding.

EVA ROYSTON

(b. 1942)

'Working in the Laboratory'

Working in the laboratory
You're exact, if nothing else.
I like my whitecoated sterility.
I count fear in terms of adrenalin.
The rabbit's pickled fur intoxicates me.
I slice strings of intestine. Yes, of course
I can hear the afternoon sun knocking
Against the window like a timid visitor,
When I go home, I'll whip eggs,
And read. But now my rubber hands
Dip into ethyl alcohol
Jars, like drifting embryos, demand a label.
There's so much tissue.
Of course I can look up suddenly
And smile like a child.
In the meantime, I weigh this cellular butter
Against the stone,
And like my whitecoated sterility.

PETER HOWE

(b. 1943)

The Ascent of Man

Australopithecus

Cling, touch still. Cuddle through night fear and kiss
in snuffles. Parents, siblings, loners, foul
with hunt dirt, pick off others' lice. Males growl,
hirsute and fierce. Olfaction's gone amiss.
Tastier berries can make up. Chaste springs hiss
for cleansing games. Still, cats and man-types prowl
at dawn. A taken baby's mother's howl
fills, and no play water does, the abyss.
Bashed stones get edges. For a killing kit
less adventitiously bash, fail, then again
bash. Chip and scrape for evening industry.
Such well-kept stones, some sticks, here a trap-pit,
make futurity food. The context pain,
less cheap, the wishing, and meant thought, come round. Me.

Pithecanthropus

Less cheap, the wishing, and meant thought, come round. Me,
I need to work in case I like mammoth hide
from today's dire ice by running and slide
to extinction. I'll try a heat recipe.
Stone-bashing strikes my thrifty simile
for fire-making for when two flints collide
sparks fly, as utensils fall, to provide
flames, roasts, night light for children at my knee.
To get science I eat data coiled in brains
of murdered dead. Ice flows. Bison, ibex,
mammoth herd while I devise home gear.
They chew grass and snort, enjoying the plains.
Because to me earth is now confined to sex
I'm far-flung and acutely feel I'm here.

Neanderthaler

I'm far-flung and acutely feel I'm here
for sacrifice. In a pluvial age I came
with family and colleagues to chase choice game
and split picked boulders, not to pioneer.

But again cold petrified the world. Severe
at first as it I counted off by name
all species but still with nothing known to blame
I teetered to caves and cuddled friends in fear.
Hoary now and thick-set, quaint, off the track,
I know the spryer breeds that peep through trees
attend my funeral. I'm squared for death.
Buried crouched, as if unborn, I look back
from bones to having made such terror freeze
by treading ice on ice at will with held breath.

Homo Sapiens

By treading ice on ice at will with held breath
even as rich days turn, we'll harden to
the switches, single out the stock, come through
as men who hunt reindeer. The shaman saith.
Down pot-holes riskily coloured for faith
in enterprise, beautiful huge bulls rue
dealings with us. Paint-sticks for spears taboo,
concocting food by siring a graphic wraith.
Carved antler spear-throwers immortalise
heroic beasts. Mother statues
are our cocoon, cocoon.
With rising warmth steppes grow trees. Reindeer eyes
look north and hunters sing sad news
when food fails soon, fails soon.

RICHARD RYAN

(b. 1946)

Galaxy

faint
in deep space,
immense as a brain

down
through the thought-
shaft it drifts, a wale

of light to
  which the retina
    opens and is entered

time and
  space dis-
    appearing as the mind

recedes
  to a soundless
    flickering somewhere

deeper
  than consciousness
    where, permanent as

change
  a whorl of light
    rides, wheeling in darkness

BERNARD SAINT
(b. 1950)

The Earth Upturned

When the last flame dies
flowers fall upwards,
seeds fall from bright fields
down into the sun.

It is only a matter of time.
The earth thrusts upward
to fall forward.
At last to seek the downward curve
to where the sun
sings in absolution
amidst his own explosion.

NOTES

CHAUCER, from *The House of Fame* (p. 47)

  I wille: an eagle, who has carried Chaucer off, is speaking.

  skille: cause or reason, in this case for the movement of the elements the eagle has just described.

CHAUCER, from *The Canterbury Tales*, 'The Doctour of Phisik' (p. 51)

  magyk natureel: natural (or white) magic, as distinguished from 'black magic', necromancy, was considered a legitimate study.

  Esculapius: Chaucer lists the numerous Greek, Latin, and Arabic authors the physician would have relied on as authorities.

CHAUCER, from *The Canterbury Tales*, The Nun's Priest's Tale (p. 52)

  complecciouns: temperament, as formed by a mixture of humours.

  humours: fluids in the body (blood, phlegm, black bile, yellow bile), the mixture of which were thought to determine one's temperament.

  rede colera: a mixture of blood and bile affecting one's disposition.

  Catoun: Dionysius Cato, apparently the author of *Disticha de Moribus ad Filium* (*c.* third or fourth century AD), a series of maxims. Pertelote refers to *Disticha*, II, 31.

SIDNEY, *The 7 Wonders of England* (p. 69)

  huge heapes of stones: Stonehenge; the belief that it was difficult or impossible to number them was also associated with other stone circles.

  Bruertons: this legend was associated with the seat of the Brereton family in Cheshire and survived into the nineteenth century.

  fish: the pike was believed to possess this property.

  Cave: probably Poole's Hole near Buxton.

  A field: according to Holinshed's *Chronicles* (1587, p. 130), a wood near Winburne monastery, the present Wimborne Minster, was said to have this property of petrifying wood.

  A bird: the barnacle goose. This belief in its origin has been variously explained and can be traced back to the thirteenth century.

BACON, *Translation of the 104. Psalme* (p. 71)

  Bacon's translation of Psalm 104 has been included because this psalm was important in both the seventeenth and eighteenth centuries for its justification of studying design in nature to find out the Deity. Scientific paraphrases of the psalms are an important form in this and the next century. This so-called 'translation' is in fact a free and expanded paraphrase which introduces several scientific concepts.

SHAKESPEARE, from *Coriolanus* (p. 76)

> *The Belly and the Limbs*: the fable of the belly originates in certain Hindu stories probably of the fourth century AD. They were collected and translated many times. Shakespeare draws on several sources, most notably Thomas North's translation of the 'Life of Caius Martius Coriolanus' in Plutarch's *Lives of the Noble Grecians and Romans* (1579).

DAVIES, from *Orchestra* (p. 77)

> *The Cosmic Dance*: this passage from Davies has been included as a representative account of the Ptolemaic system.
>
> *That great long yeare*: the Platonic or Great Year, in which the apparent position of the fixed stars returns to its original place.

FLETCHER, from *The Purple Island* (p. 84)

> *The Purple Island* is an elaborate allegory of the human body, in which the principal organs are represented as cities and the veins and arteries as canals.
>
> *Kerdia*: the heart.
>
> *Hepar*: the liver.

D'AVENANT, from *Gondibert* (p. 86)

> *Gondibert* (1651) is a heroic poem set in eighth century AD Lombardy and the court of King Aribert. This selection is taken from an account of the house of the sage Astragon, to whom Gondibert goes to have Astragon treat his wounds and those of his soldiers.

MILTON, from *Paradise Lost* (p. 88)

> *his ponderous shield*: Satan's.
>
> *the Tuscan Artist*: Milton says in *Areopagitica* (1644) that he 'found and visited the famous *Galileo* grown old, a prisoner to the Inquisition for thinking in Astronomy otherwise than the Franciscans and Dominicans thought'. Galileo was imprisoned in the Villa Martinelli, Florence, where Milton probably met him in 1638. See *The Complete Prose Works of John Milton*, ed. Don M. Wolfe (New Haven and London, 1959, II, 538).

MILTON, *Sonnet XXI* (p. 93)

> *Swede ... French*: this refers to the Thirty Years War, which involved France and the German states and in which Sweden, under Gustavus Adolphus, played a major military role in the Protestant interest.

BUTLER, from *The Elephant in the Moon* (p. 94)

> *When one*: Lord Brouncker (1620?–84), the first president of the Royal Society.
>
> *virtuoso*: in the seventeenth century, a 'virtuoso' was one pursuing special interests in the arts or sciences. The term was often used pejoratively for early researchers in science.
>
> *Privolvans*: Kepler called the earth *volva* because of its diurnal revolutions; the inhabitants of the moon who live on the side facing the earth he named *Subvolvani* because they can see the earth; and those who live on the oppo-

site side of the moon he named *Privolvani* because they are deprived of an opportunity to see the earth.

a great philosopher: Sir Kenelm Digby (1603–65), who thought it was possible that one sense could function for another.

Quoth he: probably John Evelyn (1620–1706), one of the founders of the Royal Society.

a mountain: this refers to Horace's *Ars Poetica*, l, 140: 'The mountains are in labour and a mouse is born.'

BUTLER, from *Hudibras* (p. 98)

Dee's prefaces: John Dee (1527–1608) was Queen Elizabeth's court astrologer and an important writer on occult sciences.

Kelly: Kelly was Dee's assistant.

Lescus: Albert Laski, with whom Dee and Kelly travelled into Poland.

MORE, from *The Infinity of Worlds* (p. 101)

Cassiopie . . . Ophiucbus novae were seen in the constellations of Cassiopoeia and Ophiuchus in 1572 and 1604, respectively.

MORE, from *Insomnium Philosophicum* (p. 102)

Insomnium Philosophicum is a kind of dream vision in which the sleeping More has various aspects of seventeenth-century science represented to him.

DRYDEN, *Upon the Death of the Lord Hastings* (p. 111)

Astrolabe: an instrument used to take altitudes and to mark the positions and movements of the sun, moon, and stars.

Foul Disease: Lord Hastings died of smallpox.

naeves: moles.

DRYDEN, *To my Honour'd Friend, Dr Charleton* (p. 114)

Ent: Sir George Ent (1604–89) was friend, encourager, and defender of William Harvey.

His Sacred Head: the phrase refers to Charles II's escape after the disastrous defeat of the Royalist forces at the battle of Worcester in 1651.

DRYDEN, from *The Hind and the Panther* (p. 119)

The Hind and the Panther is a satire on the religious controversies of Dryden's day in the form of a beast fable in which the various sects are represented as beasts of prey.

Wolfe: in Dryden's allegory, the wolf stands for the Calvinist Presbyterians.

Corah: Corah and his brethren raised a seditious tumult against Moses and were swallowed up by the earth as a punishment. See Numbers xvi, 1–35.

The Fox: in the poem, the fox stands for the Socinians or Unitarians.

BLACKMORE, from *The Creation* (p. 120)

The famous Dane: Tycho Brahe.

elastic spirits: Blackmore still holds to the theory of vital spirits which formed a link between the material body and the soul. These spirits were thought to have a circulatory function, a theory which prefigured Harvey's demonstration of the circulation. Descartes finally refuted the notion of vital spirits.

GARTH, from *The Dispensary* (p. 124)

The subject of Garth's mock-heroic poem is the quarrel between the physicians and the apothecaries over the formers' plan to set up a free dispensary for the poor. The apothecaries complained that this would interfere with their business. In the passage given here, Celsus (Dr Bateman) has been sent by the goddess Hygeia to the Elysian Fields to consult the spirit of the great Harvey, who will advise on the resolution of their dispute.

Amomum: a plant of the ginger family, whose fruit yields cardamom seeds, a remedy for dyspepsia.

Nassau: a compliment to the reigning monarch, William III, of the House of Orange, Nassau.

Erucae: larvae.

light's gay god: this verse paragraph refers to the old belief that gold and jewels were produced by the action of the sun's rays penetrating the earth.

idle shells: fossils. According to one theory of the time, these were supposed to be produced by nature sportively creating imitations of animal forms in the mineral kingdom. Helicoeids are snail shell-like forms.

noisy cave: according to Pliny, earthquakes were caused by winds becoming imprisoned in the caverns of the earth.

Febris: fever.

Hydrops: dropsy.

Lepra: leprosy.

Pthisis: consumption.

DIAPER, from *Nereides* (p. 130)

The cosmology of this poem is drawn from Thomas Burnet's *Sacred Theory of the Earth* (1681). According to this theory, the spherical earth was originally surrounded by a sphere of water. On the surface of this a kind of film of dust and oil collected which formed the land. The Biblical flood resulted in the break-up of this film, after which its fragments remained on the earth as mountain ranges.

Diaper's poem is based on Virgil's *Sixth Eclogue*, in which Silenus expounds a cosmology which is essentially that of Lucretius.

POPE, from *The Rape of the Lock* (p. 132)

Spleen: what today we would regard as neurotic symptoms in ancient times were regarded as a disease of the spleen. The concept of spleen, as synonymous with neurosis, became very important in the eighteenth century. Anne Finch, Countess of Winchelsea, and Matthew Green devoted entire poems to this subject.

Vapour: 'vapours' was synonymous with the spleen. The concept of vapours owes something to the idea of vital spirits. (See the notes on Blackmore, above.) A damp climate was thought to bring on this condition.

POPE, from *An Essay on Man* (p. 134)
the great chain: this was a chain said to be attached to Zeus' throne that joined heaven with earth. See Homer's *Iliad*, VIII, 26, and see Introduction, pp. 18–19.

POPE, from *The Dunciad* (p. 136)
Wilkins: John Wilkins, Bishop of Chester (1614–72), one of the founders of the Royal Society, thought that one day man might be able to fly to the moon.

THOMSON, from *The Seasons* (p. 140)
Ashley: Anthony Ashley Cooper, 3rd Earl of Shaftesbury, philosopher, author of *Characteristicks*.
impregned by thee: precious minerals were once thought to be formed by the sun's rays penetrating the earth.

ARMSTRONG, from *The Art of Preserving Health* (p. 143)
chyle: the fluid, formed in the last stages of digestive action, which is absorbed by the intestines.
liquors: fluids.

GRAY, *Luna Habitabilis* (p. 146)
my sister: Calliope, the muse of epic poetry.

WHITE, *The Naturalist's Summer-Evening Walk* (p. 148)
curlew: the stone curlew, *Burhinus oedicnemus*.
dor: the dung beetle, one of the Scarabaedicae.

SMART, from *On the Omniscience of the Supreme Being* (p. 153)
magnetic index: recent research suggests that, contrary to Smart's view, birds may indeed have a built-in magnetic compass mechanism in their brains.

DARWIN, from *The Loves of the Plants* (p. 154)
Vallisner: *Walisner*, a genus of submerged aquatic plants common today in home aquaria.

DARWIN, from *The Temple of Nature* (p. 159)
Association's: the theory of the association of ideas, i.e. mental images, formulated by David Hartley, replaced the older faculty psychology. It was an important influence, especially on Coleridge.

PINDAR, from *Peter's Prophecy* (p. 160)
Sir Joseph: Sir Joseph Bahks (1743–1820) was President of the Royal Society.

Herschel: William Herschel (1738–1822), probably most noted for his construction of telescopes and discovery of Uranus (13 March 1781).

BLAKE, from *Vala or the Four Zoas* (p. 163)
Vortex: for treatment of Blake's grasp of science and objections to it, see Donald Ault's *Visionary Physics* (Chicago and London, 1975).

BLAKE, from *Jerusalem* (p. 165)
Four-fold Man: for Blake's concept of the Four-fold Man, the Spectre, and the Emanation see his commentators, e.g. Northrop Frye's *Fearful Symmetry* (Princeton, 1957).

WORDSWORTH, *Lucy Poem VI* (p. 167)
Rolled round: we have included this famous poem because Wordsworth has Lucy, after her death, become part of the mechanistic universe.

HOARE, from *Poems of Conchology and Botany* (p. 175)
Pholas: The piddock, which has the faculty of burrowing into sand and soft rock.
Froome: a river in Somerset.
Linné: Carl von Linné. His name is better known in its Latinized form, Linnaeus.

SHELLEY, from *Queen Mab* (p. 185)
Shelley thoroughly annotated Queen Mab in a way that indicates his deep interest in the science of his time.

SHELLEY, from *Prometheus Unbound* (p. 188)
unexpected birth: Shelley's view that the Newtonian doctrine of gravitational pull explains 'the light and power poured by all the suns and constellations upon the earth'. This power causes fertility even on the moon. See Carl Grabo's *A Newton Among Poets* (Chapel Hill, N C, 1930).

SHELLEY, *The Cloud* (p. 195)
This poem has been included because in fact it gives an account of the water cycle. It seems to have been suggested by the chorus of clouds in Aristophanes' comedy of that name.

KEATS, from *Lamia* (p. 197)
rainbow: Keats is referring to Newton's analysis of the spectrum.

EMERSON, from *Monadnoc* (p. 199)
chemic eddies: this is a phrase drawn from late-eighteenth-century theories of the motion of fluids, a concern of both Claude Louis Berthollet (1748–1822) and Antoine-Laurent Lavoisier (1743–94).

TENNYSON, from *In Memoriam A. H. H.* (p. 203)
A thousand types: Tennyson's account of the fossil record is derived from Lyell's *Antiquity of Man*.

TENNYSON, from *Lucretius* (p. 204)

According to tradition, Lucretius committed suicide after having been driven mad by a love philtre administered by a woman (Tennyson says his wife).

My master: Epicurus.

BROWNING, from *Caliban upon Setebos* (p. 208)

Natural Theology: the attempted demonstration of God's existence from the creation rather than from revelation.

Thou thoughtest, etc.: Psalm l, 21.

his dam: Sycorax, Caliban's mother.

Him: Setebos, Caliban's mother's god.

CLOUGH, from *When Israel Came out of Egypt* (p. 215)

chemic forces: this is a phrase referring to the problem of 'chemical affinity'. Chemical affinity is the force that brings elements into combination and holds them there. On the molecular level it corresponded in late-eighteenth-century scientific thought to gravitation, which concerns attraction among astronomical bodies.

Mécanique Céleste: the phrase seems to refer to the *Traité de mécanique céleste* (1799–1825), the great treatise on celestial mechanics (problems of astronomical motion) by Pierre-Simon, Marquis de Laplace (1749–1827).

PATMORE, *Legem Tuam Dilexi* (p. 223)

Patmore takes his title from the Vulgate, Psalms cxviii, 97.

MAXWELL, *Molecular Evolution* (p. 231)

Red Lions: a club formed by members of the British Association, to meet for relaxation.

THOMSON, from *The City of Dreadful Night* (p. 232)

Thomson appears to be referring to the three stages of history formulated by Auguste Comte in his *Philosophie positive*, namely, the theological, metaphysical, and positivist phases of human thought.

SWINBURNE, from *Hertha* (p. 233)

Hertha: this, supposedly the name of an ancient Germanic earth-goddess, was, in fact, due to a misreading of a passage in Tacitus' *Germania*.

HARDY, *The Pity of It* (p. 238)

On the back of the picture frame containing the manuscript was a note which read 'Presented to Dr Caleb Williams Saleeby by Thomas Hardy, as the poem was inspired by reading an article on "Eugenics" written by Dr Saleeby during the Great War.'

HOPKINS, *That Nature is a Heraclitean Fire* (p. 241)

Heraclitus (*fl.c.* 500 BC) held that the universe was in continuous flux and that fire was the primary element.

ROSS, *The Anniversary* (p. 246)

the thing: this was a cyst containing malarial parasites in an *Anopheles* mosquito Ross was dissecting. The discovery led to a cure for malaria.

KIPLING, *Merrow Down* (p. 247)

the Tribe of Tegumai: this is a fictitious primitive tribe; it is the subject of two of Kipling's *Just So Stories*.

NOYES, from *The Torch-Bearers* (p. 249)

William Herschel: Herschel (1738–1822) began his working life as a musician. He is best known, however, for his work on the construction of telescopes and for the discovery of Uranus (13 March 1781).
Linley's orchestra: Thomas Linley the Elder (1732–95) arranged concerts in the Assembly Rooms (here the 'Pump Room') at Bath, where Herschel lived for many years and was organist in the Octagon Chapel.

MOORE, *Four Quartz Crystal Clocks* (p. 259)

Arlington: Arlington, Virginia, the location of the United States Naval Observatory.
aye-aye: an animal which, like the animals referred to in Moore's next line, has a prehensile digit, but which should be classed with the rodents rather than with the lemurs.
angwan-tibo ... loris: all of these animals are slow-moving members of the lemur family.

MACDIARMID, from *A Stick-Nest in Ygdrasil* (p. 262)

Ygdrasil: in Scandinavian mythology, the great tree whose branches and roots extend through the universe.

MACDIARMID, *Two Scottish Boys* (p. 264)

Two Scottish Boys: 'Fiona MacLeod' (William Sharp) and Sir Patrick Manson.
Bunyan's quag: the phrase refers to a bottomless swamp, described in John Bunyan's *The Pilgrim's Progress* (1678), on one side of the path through the Valley of the Shadow of Death into which the unwary can fall.
Sainte-Beuve: Charles Augustin Sainte-Beuve (1804–69), a prolific French critic. The phrase, which may be translated as 'science, a spirit of observation, a slight toughness', is in an essay of 4 May 1857 on Gustave Flaubert's *Madame Bovary* in *Causeries du lundi*, XIII (Paris, Garnier Frères, n.d.).

JONES, from *Anathemata* (p. 268)

infulsit: crammed in.
hemera: a time-interval determined by the period of maximum development of a particular species.
orogeny: a theory of the birth of mountains.

eskered: from *esker*, an Irish term for elongated and often flat-topped mounds of post-glacial gravel. Here, therefore, silt which has been mounded up by water action.

hade: the inclination of a mineral vein or fault from the vertical.

EMPSON, *Note on Local Flora* (p. 276)
Tree of Heaven: the ailanthus.

EMPSON, *Doctrinal Point* (p. 276)
Heaviside layer: the E layer, a layered region in the ionosphere, located between 55 and 95 miles above the earth, which affects long-distance communications by reflecting certain radio waves. It is named after the English physicist Oliver Heaviside (1850–1925), who predicted its existence in 1901.

BRONK, *How Indeterminacy Determines Us* (p. 292)
Indeterminacy: the Indeterminacy or Uncertainty Principle, enunciated by Werner Heisenberg (1901–76), states that no measurement can determine both the position of a particle and its momentum so accurately that the product of the uncertainties of their values is less than the Planck constant, a universal constant by which the frequency of a quantum of energy is to be multiplied to give the quantum energy. Bronk's poem works with the metaphorical extension of the principle into a notion that an observer changes and is changed by what he observes and therefore cannot really know the external world.

NEMEROV, *Unscientific Postscript* (p. 293)
Nemerov's title is drawn from Søren Kierkegaard's essay 'Unscientific Postscript'.

NEMEROV, *Seeing Things* (p. 294)
Sudbury Marsh: a marsh east of Sudbury, Massachusetts, formed by the Sudbury River, which flows north to Concord, Massachusetts.
Strike through the mask: Nemerov is alluding to Herman Melville's *Moby Dick*, chapter 35, 'The Quarter-Deck'.

WITHEFORD, *Bohr on the Atom* (p. 295)
Bezonian: a raw military recruit. The line alludes to Shakespeare's *2 Henry IV*, V.3.110.

ABSE, *Letter to Alex Comfort* (p. 296)
Alex Comfort: Comfort (b. 1920) is an English psychiatrist, gerontologist, and poet.
Ehrlich: Paul Ehrlich (1854–1915) was a German immunologist, who synthesized the arsenical compound salvarsan and showed its efficacy against syphilis.
six hundred and sixth attempt: salvarsan was the six hundred and sixth compound Ehrlich tested, with the help of his student Sahachiro Hata.

Koch: Heinrich Hermann Robert Koch (1843–1910) was a German bacteriologist who isolated the causal agents of anthrax, tuberculosis, and cholera.

SCHULMAN, *Surely as Certainty Changes* (p. 311)
  proteolysis: the decomposition, by reaction with water, of proteins or peptides to form simpler and soluble products, as in digestion.

ACKNOWLEDGEMENTS

Thanks are due to the copyright holders of the following poems for permission to reprint them in this volume:

DANNIE ABSE: for 'Letter to Alex Comfort' and 'In the Theatre', from *Collected Poems*, © Hutchinson, London; in this collection Dannie Abse 1977. W. H. AUDEN: for 'In Memory of Sigmund Freud' and 'Unpredictable But Providential', from *Collected Poems*. (Reprinted by permission of Faber & Faber Ltd.) WILLIAM BRONK: for 'How Indeterminacy Determines Us', from *The Word, The Worldless*, © William Bronk, 1964. ROBERT CONQUEST: for 'Humanities', from *Poems*, Macmillan, London and Basingstoke, 1955. ROBERT CREELEY: for 'After Mallarmé', from *Love: Poems 1950–1960*, copyright © 1962 Robert Creeley. (Reprinted with the permission of Charles Scribmer's Sons.) Also from *Poems 1950–1965*. (Reprinted by permission of the copyright holders, Marion Boyars, Publishers, Ltd.) DOROTHY DONNELLY: for 'The Pink Mite', 'The Point of a Pin', 'Spider Compared to Star' and 'Suns and Straws', from *Kudu and Other Poems*, copyright © 1978 Dorothy Donnelly. RUSSELL EDSON: for 'Antimatter', from *The Intuitive Journey and Other Works* by Russell Edson, copyright © 1976 by Russell Edson. (Reprinted by permission of Harper & Row, Publishers Inc. and Georges Borchardt Inc.) WILLIAM EMPSON: for 'Invitation to Juno', 'Note on Local Flora' and 'Doctrinal Point, from *Collected Poems*, Chatto and Windus Ltd, 1955. ROBERT FROST: for 'Why Wait for Science', from *The Poetry of Robert Frost*, Jonathan Cape Ltd, London, 1971. (Reprinted by permission of Jonathan Cape Ltd and the estate of Robert Frost.) Also from *The Poetry of Robert Frost*, edited by Edward Connery Lathem, copyright 1947 © 1969 by Holt Rinehart & Winston, copyright © 1975 by Lesley Frost Ballantine. (Reprinted by permission of Holt Rinehart and Winston, Publishers.) MIROSLAV HOLUB: for 'Evening in a Lab', from *Sagittal Section*, Field Translation Series, No. 3, 1980, translated by Dana Hábová and Stuart Friebert; And for 'Zito the Magician', from *Selected Poems*, translated by Ian Milner and George Theiner, Penguin Books, 1967, copyright © Miroslav Holub, 1967; translation copyright © Penguin Books, 1967. PETER HOWE: for 'The Ascent of Man', from *Origins*, The Hogarth Press Ltd, 1981. ALDOUS HUXLEY: for 'The Fifth Philosopher's Song', from *The Collected Poetry of Aldous Huxley*, edited by Donald Watt, Chatto and Windus Ltd, 1971. (Also reprinted by permission of Mrs Laura Huxley.) DAVID IGNATOW: for 'Poet to Physicist in his Laboratory', from *Poems 1934–1969*, copyright © 1967 by David Ignatow. (Reprinted by permission of Wesleyan University Press.) ROBINSON JEFFERS: for a twenty-line excerpt from 'Roan Stallion' reprinted from *Selected Poetry of Robinson Jeffers* by Robinson Jeffers, copyright 1925, renewed 1953, by Robinson Jeffers. (By permission of Random House Inc.) DAVID JONES: for the extract from *Anathemata* by David Jones. (Reprinted by permission of Faber & Faber Ltd.) RUDYARD KIPLING: for 'Merrow Downs', from *The Just So Stories*. (Reprinted by permission of the National Trust and Macmillan, London, Ltd.) GALWAY KINNELL: for 'For the Lost Generation', from *What a Kingdom it was* by Galway Kinnell, copyright © 1960 by Galway Kinnell. (Reprinted by permission of Houghton Mifflin Company.) EDWARD LOWBURY: for 'Redundancy' and 'Daylight Astronomy', from *Daylight Astronomy*, Chatto and Windus Ltd, London, 1968, and *Selected Poems*, Celtion, 1978. (Reprinted by permission of the author.) HUGH MACDIARMID: for 'Two Scottish Boys', 'Innumerable Christ' and 'A Stick Nest in Ygdrasil', from *The Complete Poems of Hugh MacDiarmid 1920–1976*, Martin Brian and O'Keeffe, 1978. (Reprinted by permission of the publishers and Mrs Valda Grieve.) ARCHIBALD MACLEISH: for 'Reply to Mr Wordsworth', from *New and Collected Poems 1917–1976* by Archibald MacLeish, copyright © 1976 by Archibald MacLeish. (Reprinted by permission of Houghton Mifflin Company.) L. MACNEICE: for 'The Kingdom', Part VI, and 'Variations on Heraclitus', from *The Collected Poems of Louis Macneice*. (Reprinted by permission of Faber & Faber Ltd.) MARIANNE MOORE: for 'In the Days of Prismatic Colour' and 'Four Quartz Crystal Clocks', from *The Complete Poems of Marianne Moore*. (Reprinted by permission of Faber & Faber Ltd.) 'In the Days of Prismatic Colour', reprinted by permission of Macmillan Company from *Collected Poems* by Marianne Moore, copyright 1935, renewed 1963, by Marianne Moore and T. S. Eliot. 'Four Quartz Crystal Clocks', reprinted by permission of Macmillan Company from *Collected Poems* by Marianne Moore, copyright 1941, renewed 1969. EDWIN MORGAN: for 'Eohippus', from *Poems of Thirty Years*, © Edwin Morgan, The Carcanet Press Ltd, 1982. H. NEMEROV: for 'Unscientific Postscript', 'Cosmic Comics' and 'Seeing Things' from *The Collected Poems of Howard Nemerov*. Chicago and London, 1977. (Reprinted by permission of the author.) ALFRED NOYES: for 'William Herschel Conducts', from *The Torch Bearers*. (By permission of Hugh Noyes on behalf of the Trustees of the Alfred Noyes Literary Estate.) ANTHONY PICCIONE: for 'Nomad', reprinted from *Anchor Draggin: Poems* by Anthony Piccione, foreword by Archibald MacLeish, by permission of Anthony Piccione and BOA Editions Ltd, A Poulin, Jr, Publisher. Copyright © 1977 by Anthony Piccione. PETER REDGROVE: for 'Relative', from *The Force and Other Poems*, London, Routledge & Kegan Paul Ltd, 1966. MICHAEL ROBERTS: for 'Note on θ, ø and ψ', from *Selected Poems and Prose of Michael Roberts*, ed. F. Grubb, The Carcanet Press, 1980, © Janet Adam-Smith. EVA ROYSTON: for 'Working in the Laboratory', from *One Hundred and Three Poems*, Johannesburg, Renoster Books, 1973, © Robert Royston. (By permission of Renoster Books and the estate of the late Eva Royston.) ROBERT RYAN: for 'Galaxy', The Dolmen Press, Dublin 1973. BERNARD SAINT: for 'The Earth Upturned', from *Testament of the Compass*, Search Press Ltd, London, 1978. GRACE SCHULMAN: for 'Surely as Certainty Changes', from *Burn Down the Icons*,

(Reprinted by permission of Princeton University Press.) STEPHEN SPENDER: for 'Bagatelles XII: Renaissance Hero', from *The Generous Days*. (Reprinted by permission of Faber and Faber Ltd.) JOHN SQUIRE: for "The Survival of the Fittest', from *Collected Poems*, Macmillan Publishers Ltd. ANNE STEVENSON: for 'The Spirit is Too Blunt an Instrument', from *Travelling Behind Glass: Selected Poems 1963–1973*, copyright © Anne Stevenson, 1974. (Reprinted by permission of Oxford University Press Ltd.) PETER STRAUB: for 'Wolf on the Plains', from *Open Air*, Shannon, 1972. (Reprinted by permission of Four Courts Press, Dublin.) A. M. SULLIVAN: for 'Atomic Architecture' and 'Telescope Mirror', from *Stars and Atoms Have No Size*, E. P. Dutton & Co., New York, 1946. R. S. THOMAS: for 'The Gap', 'Pre-Cambrian' and 'Roger Bacon', from *Frequencies*, Macmillan, London and Basingstoke, 1978. For 'Emerging' from *Laboratories of the Spirit*, Macmillan, London and Basingstoke, 1975. THOMAS THORNELY: for 'The Angler and His Ancestors', 'Dreams and Freudians' and 'The Atom', from *The Collected Verse of Thomas Thornely*, Heffer, Cambridge, 1939. C. TOMLINSON: for 'Dialogue' and 'A Meditiation on John Constable', from *Selected Poems 1951–1974*, copyright © Charles Tomlinson, 1978. (Reprinted by permission of the Oxford University Press.) W. J. TURNER: for 'Poetry and Science', from *Fossils of a Future Time*, Oxford, 1946. (Reprinted by permission of the copyright owner, John F. Lisle.) J. UPDIKE: for 'Seven Stanzas at Easter' and 'Cosmic Gall', from *Telephone Poles and Other Poems*, Andre Deutsch Ltd, London, 1964. Also from *Telephone Poles and Other Poems* published by Randon House Inc. MARK VAN DOREN: for 'The God of Galaxies', from *One Hundred Poems*, copyright © 1967 by Mark Van Doren. (Reprinted by permission of Hill and Wang, a division of Farrar, Straus and Giroux, Inc.) ROBERT WALLACE: for 'Experiment', from *Swimmer in the Rain*, Carnegie-Mellon University Press, Pittsburg, Pa., copyright 1980. VERNON WATKINS: for 'Discoveries', from *Ballard of the Mari Lwyd*, Faber & Faber Ltd, London, 1947, copyright G. M. Watkins. RICHARD WILBER: for 'Lamarck Elaborated', from *Things of This World* © 1956 by Richard Wilbur. (Reprinted by permission of Harcourt Brace Jovanovich Inc.) And from *Poems 1943–1956* by Richard Wilbur. (Reprinted by permission of Faber & Faber Ltd.) HUBERT WITHEFORD: for 'Bohr on the Atom', from *The Lightning Makes a Difference*, London, The Brookside Press, 1962. (Reprinted by permission of the author and Villiers Publications Ltd.) JOHN WOODS: for 'Eye' and 'To the Chairperson of the Sonnets', from *Striking the Earth*, © 1976 by Indiana University Press.

MORE ABOUT PENGUINS, PELICANS AND PUFFINS

For further information about books available from Penguins please write to Dept EP, Penguin Books Ltd, Harmondsworth, Middlesex UB7 0DA.

In the U.S.A.: For a complete list of books available from Penguins in the United States write to Dept DG, Penguin Books, 299 Murray Hill Parkway, East Rutherford, New Jersey 07073.

In Canada: For a complete list of books available from Penguins in Canada write to Penguin Books Canada Ltd, 2801 John Street, Markham, Ontario L3R 1B4.

In Australia: For a complete list of books available from Penguins in Australia write to the Marketing Department, Penguin Books Australia Ltd, P.O. Box 257, Ringwood, Victoria 3134.

In New Zealand: For a complete list of books available from Penguins in New Zealand write to the Marketing Department, Penguin Books (N.Z.) Ltd, P.O. Box 4019, Auckland 10.

In India: For a complete list of books available from Penguins in India write to Penguin Overseas Ltd, 706 Eros Apartments, 56 Nehru Place, New Delhi 110019.

BOSH AND NONSENSE

Edward Lear

'An unexpected treasure find for all Lear enthusiasts ... *Bosh and Nonsense* consists of 79 numbered limericks written and illustrated for the 11-year-old Ada Duncan, whom Lear met in late 1864 in Nice with her mother ... These Learana were discovered in two sketchbooks bound in leather and watered silk, only last year ... Each limerick has a drawing to illustrate it, in Lear's best, most amusing and often most grotesque style' – John Lehmann in the *Sunday Telegraph*

'A goldmine ... Anything more by this genius is a bonus, if he is up to his best – and, here, he is. What a "find" for anyone from nine to ninety' – Patrick Dickinson in *Country Life*

THE PENGUIN BOOK OF LIMERICKS

Compiled and edited by E. O. Parrott

Illustrations by Robin Jacques

'Wit, sharp comment, mood music, landscape, philosophy; all of these are in Mr Parrott's fine selection. Nor does it neglect the Double Limerick, the Limeraiku, the Reverse Limerick, Beheaded Limericks, though sportiness, naughtiness and all the traditional qualities are well and tastefully represented, in several shades of blue ...' – Gavin Ewart in the *Guardian*

'He seems to have read not only every previous collection but also far-flung limerick competitions, as well as being the recipient of many an improper verse from proud authors ... Robin Jacques's elegant decorations ... are real illustrations in the great traditions' – R. G. G. Price in *Punch*

More Poetry Anthologies in Penguins

THE PENGUIN BOOK OF
EVERYDAY VERSE

Edited by David Wright

'The best anthology of the year' – Martin Seymour-Smith in the *Financial Times*

'Verses about work and weddings and hangings and clothes and food and drink and festivals and fashions of all kinds ... David Wright has compiled an extraordinary anthology' – Robert Nye in *The Times*

'The selection runs from Edward Thomas and Hardy through Locker-Lampson (a brilliant and neglected writer), Byron, Wordsworth, Stephen Duck, Swift and Jonson back to Chaucer ... The most immediately entertaining and enjoyable verse anthology that I have encountered: which by now is saying a lot' – John Holloway in *The Times Higher Education Supplement*

THE PENGUIN BOOK OF
VICTORIAN VERSE

Edited with an introduction by George MacBeth

Setting Tennyson, Browning, Swinburne, Kipling, Christina Rossetti and Gerard Manley Hopkins alongside a wealth of lesser-known poets, George MacBeth brilliantly defines a fresh approach to Victorian poetry. His selection and his elegant and thought-provoking introduction combine to emphasize the sheer inventiveness of the Victorians: how many of the best poets explored forbidden subjects – violence, religious doubt, eroticism, crime or passion – behind the mask of the dramatic monologue and in the extraordinary narrative poems which are at the heart of this 'great age of fiction in English poetry'.

'It is the great and crucial merit of *The Penguin Book of Victorian Verse* that it changes one's attitude to contemporary poetry, as well as to that of the period it sets out to cover' – Edward Lueie-Smith

THE PENGUIN BOOK OF
WOMEN POETS

Edited by Carol Cosman, Joan Keefe and Kathleen Weaver

Spanning 3,500 years and forty literary traditions, this volume brings forth a rich and varied body of work by women poets, some familiar to the English-speaking reader, but many others long neglected or virtually unknown outside their respective countries. An introductory note on each poet tells something of her life and of the historical and literary context in which she wrote.

The poems themselves – approximately four hundred in number and translated from languages as diverse as Byzantine Greek, Sanskrit, Old French, Hindi, Gaelic, Vietnamese, and Maori – cut across the barriers of time and culture to take their rightful place among the wealth of the world's literature.

THE PENGUIN BOOK OF
SPANISH CIVIL WAR VERSE

Edited by Valentine Cunningham

This is the first comprehensive assembly of British poems (some never before published) which have to do with the Spanish Civil War. It includes also supporting prose reports and reviews by the poets, and a selection of poems – notably Spanish romanceros – in translation.

Some of this century's best-known literary figures – Auden, Spender, MacNeice and Orwell among them – are naturally represented, but the collection also puts firmly on the map the work of several undeservedly neglected poets, such as Charles Donnelly, Clive Branson and Miles Tomalin.

THE PENGUIN BOOK OF
ENGLISH PASTORAL VERSE

Edited by John Barrell and John Bull

Divided into eight broadly chronological sections – each preceded by an introduction tracing the development of the pastoral tradition and its relation to the changing social conditions of a particular period – this superb anthology includes formal eclogues, examples of pastoral drama, country-house poems, poems about agriculture in the style of Virgil's *Georgics*, and poems that satirize or denounce the pastoral tradition.

'Pastoral poetry is perhaps the earliest and purest form of escapism we know ... for readers who still hanker for Arcadia this book will provide a very significant English contribution' – Philip Toynbee in the *Observer*

'At once an introduction to pastoral and a revisionary reading of it ... a book definitely worth having' – Seamus Heaney in *The Times Literary Supplement*

THE PENGUIN BOOK OF
FOLK BALLADS OF THE
ENGLISH-SPEAKING WORLD

Edited by Albert B. Friedmann

Supernatural, religious, romantic, pastoral, violent, tragic, domestic, historical and humorous ...

This anthology covers folk ballads in England, Scotland, Ireland, Canada, the United States, the West Indies and Australia. The ballads are arranged according to their subject or locale and there are introductory notes for each section, plus musical annotations for typical ballads. In all, it offers the interested reader a superb treasure-trove from our past to dip into and enjoy at leisure.

Originally published in the United States under the title *The Viking Book of Folk Ballads of the English-Speaking World*.

Published in King Penguin

NIGHT THOUGHTS OF A CLASSICAL PHYSICIST

Russell McCormmach

This brilliant and unorthodox novel draws us into the mind of a scientist: Victor Jakob, an old professor of physics living in Germany, September 1918.

Story and history, Jakob's approaching death and Germany's impending destruction give the novel an extraordinary urgency as, speaking his night thoughts, Jakob summons up the classical past of German physics and confronts the future – his ordered world disturbed by the genius of Einstein, and fragmented into chaos by the raw vitality of modernism . . .

'A wonderful book' – *The Times Higher Education Supplement*

'Part history, part science lesson, part philosophical treatise, *Night Thoughts* is a brilliant piece of scholarship and a profoundly moving portrait of a man and his time' – *Time*

'A book of enormous substance and fascinating implications' – *Washington Post*